WITH HIM

ALL FOR YOU DUET
BOOK 2

KELLY FINLEY

With Him

Kelly Finley

© 2022 Kelly Finley Publishing, LLC

Visit the author's website at www.kellyfinley.com

ISBN: 978-1-7374516-9-3 (eBook)

ISBN: 979-8-9866222-1-7 (paperback)

This is a work of fiction. Names, characters, places, brands, media, and incidents are either the product of the author's imagination or have been used fictitiously. Any resemblance to actual persons, living or dead, events, or locales is entirely coincidental.

The author acknowledges the trademarked status and trademark owners of various products referenced in this work of fiction, which have been used without permission. The publication/use of these trademarks is not authorized, associated with, or sponsored by the trademark owners.

Edited by Kat Wyeth (Kat's Literary Services)

Proofread by Deborah Richmond (Kat's Literary Services)

Cover design by Caroline Johnson

Cover model - David Bodas Ventas

For my LGBTQIAA+ friends & family,
Thank you for teaching me how brave love can be

PREFACE

Content warning: Please be aware this story deals with characters discovering bisexuality and being outed against their will. Also, a character fighting cancer is in this story. Themes of sexual violence are also included. There is no on-the-page trauma, but rather memories of it. In the end, this is a story about celebrating life, survival, and ALL love.

With
Him

SPOTIFY PLAYLIST

With Him

∞

Love is a Bitch by Two Feet
exile by Taylor Swift feat. Bon Iver
Simple Things by Miguel
Good Stuff by Griff
Moth To A Flame by Swedish House Mafia feat. The Weeknd
Keeping A Secret by Bleachers
Forgive Me by Sofi Tukker, Mahmut Orhan
Don't Sleep (Freestyle) by SKYLR
Bad Things by Summer Kennedy

Nothing Compares by The Weeknd
Feel It by Michel Morrone
Lost on You by LP
Closer by Kings of Leon
My Enemy by CHVRCHES, Matt Berninger
Body Say by Demi Lovato
Silhouette by Active Child feat. Ellie Goulding
Infinity by Jaymes Young

Listen to the With Him Playlist on Spotify

1

Cade

Love Is a Bitch by Two Feet

Now

I'm going to hell anyway, so I might as well commit this sin. Because this one feels like heaven. Like pure bliss sliding through my veins, desire erasing every reason why I can't fight this anymore.

Because I want this.

And they need this.

Redix kisses the nape of my neck while he slowly unzips my dress. The teeth of the zipper open and so do I. Air rushes my exposed back where his fingertips linger down my spine before tracing back up to the straps of my crimson dress.

He hesitates with his body pressing against my back, with every part of him hard while his husky whisper asks, "Will you choose us, Cade?"

For the man in front of me, I have chosen him in so many ways.

Silas's kiss is different. Tickling his lips over mine, his tongue plays like he's going to spend forever in this moment and I don't want it to end either, not with where this is going.

"Yes," I answer through Silas's lips indulging my mouth, his hands skimming my hips while Redix gently bites down my neck making me moan at him dropping my dress to the floor.

I'm exposed in every way.

My darkest desires. My torn heart. My haunting secret.

I can't decide what I want except for *this* right now. Standing in a black lace bra and matching panties, I love two men and I won't choose.

Why should I?

I'm not the only force binding them together.

Redix slides my bra strap down, kissing my shoulder, sending tingles to the tips of my fingers.

There's as much passion and question in his kiss as I'm holding in my heart. His long strands tickle across my back while we share something taboo, something that may mend us, and with everything we've already shared, we *need* to do this.

We need to decide.

Do we hate each other for what I did?

Or do we love each other so much for it?

I don't know what to feel except his lips across my flesh,

his steel body pressing into mine, his warmth and smell are so familiar that I'm safe taking this risk.

Yes, I can let go for now and not know. I can choose *us* for two nights.

Because Silas is skimming the lace of my bra with the see-through fabric pulled taut over my pebbled nipples. He's touching my breasts like a sacred relic to treasure.

Like there are questions between us too.

Silas traces his fingertip over my nipple; the attraction between us slashes arousal to my belly down to a lush ooze between my thighs. Pinching his fingertips lightly over my sensitive nub, he twirls his touch knowing how to tease me because that's what we did for so long. Teasing each other to the point of such trust. To the point where the attraction between us isn't the question.

It's the love.

What does love look like between people when you don't see it the same way?

I try letting go of my questions, letting go of my need for answers, and I can... for now.

With Redix tugging down the lace cup of my bra, exposing my flesh for Silas, and saying, "Taste her," I lose my grip. With him palming my full breast and lifting my nipple to Silas's waiting mouth lowering to devour me; I'll keep falling. With sudden heat cascading down my body, one man sucks my nipple while another holds it for his taste and he gently pinches the other.

I'm going to drown in this pleasure with these two men and if I don't ever breathe again, maybe I shouldn't. Maybe this should be my end because I don't know my next day or answers.

Nothing in my life makes sense. Everything's out of control.

And that's what I always need; control.

But I lost it the minute I almost killed an evil man. A man who hurt Redix, who assaulted him because of me. A man who deserved it for hurting other women too, so hell yes, I had to do it.

But every day since has been a hell of the loneliest days, then the most passionate nights, followed by months of emotional chaos raging through my heart.

Redix hates me for what I did for him. And the reason I did it is why he'll never stop loving me either.

All while Silas anchored me in this storm, and I didn't know another man could be my best friend, but he is.

We've shared so much—the longest talks, the biggest laughs, the forbidden nights. I brought Silas's world back to him and he's been my accomplice while I wreak havoc on the world of evil men.

So that's my life now.

I go from a cover girl to a cop to a criminal to a cunt dripping for two perfect men.

The heartbreak and the healing of these two men lavishing my flesh—for what will surely be two days of them fucking me into my last shred of a self—is that they share so much.

More than me.

It's beautiful to me that they have each other too. That they found comfort in the other. But in a world like ours, with cameras hunting Redix for his fame, expectations burdening Silas because of his name, and laws restraining me in my job, can it last?

It's an assault on my senses; embarrassing if it didn't feel like fate that they look so much alike—with the same long hair, square jaws, lush lips, and eyes that claim your soul. And their bodies? Redix is taller, but Silas still has a few inches on my five-foot-ten frame. Muscles shred down both men's tan bodies and their hands hold expert talent at thrilling my flesh.

I'm so lucky... and I'm so *fucked*... in every sense of the word.

I'm standing between two beautiful mountains of masculine perfection and this valley's a paradise for most.

I fear it'll be my hell too.

Redix travels his hand down my belly making it flutter. His fingers sink under my panties while Silas won't stop sucking my nipples—my God what are we doing?

"Damn, you're so wet for us, Cade." Redix's voice; it's imprinted on my soul. I'd know it in a cacophony of a million because I've always and only wanted him.

Until he didn't want me.

Until he couldn't even look at me.

Through shouts and tears and excruciating silences, we destroyed each other and we've been trying to recover ever since. Can we?

He needed peace and I needed space and what if that's how we'll work?

Silas swept into my days and thrilled my nights and I could be another woman with him. Someone new. Someone free.

Then I'd see Redix again and I could never change. I could never stop loving him or wanting to sob at the ache of missing him and no matter how he smiled for others, I could see the question burdening his eyes.

Can he forgive me?

Because no matter how we fill each other with fury or hurt, the love is there and the passion is all-consuming.

"You're so fucking beautiful," Silas murmurs, sinking to

his knees before me while Redix's fingers tease through my soaking folds.

I look down into Silas's hazel eyes. Eyes that have brought me nothing but peace, the perfect man to start over with. He's been my joy even though my life has been a raging hell.

But we're so different.

I've never met anyone like Silas. Rules don't govern him; he won't let them. Freedom is all he demands and he wants it for me too.

But love comes with obligations. It makes us sacrifice. It makes us cry. It isn't always about what we want.

Love has seasons; hot summers, and sometimes it's winter and cold as hell.

At least, that's all I've known of love.

"Can I, Cade?" Silas's lips are so close to mine, the ones needing these men to fuck me so much it's insanity in my body, and who's he asking anyway?

Me or Redix?

Redix sinks his fingers inside my hungry pussy, the one he was the first to have, and I groan at the depths only he can touch. It's art, it's poetry, it's exactly how to touch me because he discovered my desire first.

But mine is *not* his to give away.

I gaze into Silas's eyes and he's asking *me*.

Because in our months together Silas has taught me so much. About sex, about love, about how big a heart can be, cherishing so many and breaking for a few.

This is what he's been teaching me: that I belong to no one.

That I can let go of one idea of love, and trust another will grow back.

"Yes."

It's my answer, it's my permission to give as Redix sinks his fingers in deeper and Silas drags my panties down my thighs.

They planned this. They orchestrated this night. They need this too, answering their questions. Surprises I've learned about Redix. Secrets I know about Silas.

The three of us need to do this together.

Redix spreads my folds for Silas's tender kiss and I'm chained to this wall for them to share me and I know...

This is the only way.

My world spreads open to them and this is how I've been torn for so long. Because this is about more than these two men.

This is about two others who are still out there.

Two evil men who've hurt so many they deserve to die too. They tried to hurt me first, but Redix protected me. He took their violence for me and our storm has raged ever since. Waves of revenge and justice for my plans for both evil men and I won't give up. I will find the women they took. I will get back the dreams they stole from me.

The question is...

Who will I share those dreams with?

Redix and I wanted that life together. We fought for those dreams. Are they gone? Is Silas the one I'm supposed to share them with? Because I could. I can see those dreams with either man.

The real question. The real secret I haven't shared... is that maybe I don't want either.

Maybe I want a life with both of them.

Or maybe I want a new life alone.

Redix turns my chin for his kiss, the one that reaches in and cradles my soul. I whimper at our truth, tears springing up to feel his passion swirling with hate. But we can still do this. Our love is stronger.

Silas kisses my lips, his tongue greeting my tender clit and I groan into Redix's mouth at Silas's lavish attention. Silas is everything good and I cherish him. I'll always be here for him.

The two men start claiming me, for the two nights they've promised, and it overwhelms my heart, my sex weeping to know...

How did we get here?

2

Redix

exile (feat. Bon Iver) by Taylor Swift

"Hello, my name is Redix and I'm an alcoholic."

"Hi, Redix," the group sitting in a circle of chairs replies.

My hands wrap around my paper cup of coffee as I lean forward to share.

"I... uh."

How the fuck do I say this?

I can memorize pages of lines. I can win a Golden

Globe acting like a rockstar in an orgy. Or a surfer staring down a monster wave. Hell, I even know every Taylor Swift lyric because she's hella talented and I did a music video for her.

But talk about my shit?

Nope.

It's been two months and the words are boulders in my throat. Stuck.

There are no secrets in this group.

Hell, it's secrets that got me here in the first place. I've been sober, my second time around, for seventeen months and ten days and brutal honesty is *the* reason why.

I stare at the white linoleum floor. The smell of the Christmas tree in the corner, my coffee, some guy's strong cologne, and the words I can't say—they all hang in the air.

Because if I share *this secret*, more lives get ruined.

And that's just what I need. To add another name to the list of—*How Redix Dean Fucked Up My Life*—people I've hurt.

"Redix," Mike, the guy who guides our meeting offers, "we're here to listen if you need to share."

Oh, I need to share.

I need to yell. I need to punch a wall, concrete preferably. I need to smash everything I own before I burn it all because I'm so fucking pissed at Cade.

I made her leave two months ago and I haven't seen her since.

She left me no choice. What she did made my life hell again. And when it's hell, it's hard staying sober. And I have to stay sober because the next time I put a bottle to my lips, I'm dead.

And just to mind fuck me on the daily.

Our fight keeps looping in my mind...

"YOU HAD NO RIGHT!"

It thundered from my soul. Tears fell from her eyes, and the home I bought for us... it fell around us too. Everything fell apart that day.

"This is my pain. My scar. My fucking hell I was finally over, peace I finally had, and you had no right to take it from me!"

She wouldn't answer me. She couldn't.

"Why would you do this to us, Cade? We were finally free." Every dream I lived for had her in it. But in one act, in one moral broken, *the highest moral*, she killed my dreams too. "I don't wanna believe it. But I do. I can see it in your eyes—it's true."

She just stood by the bed we shared, the one we wanted to make a baby in, and she couldn't admit a damn thing because then she'd admit to murder.

Cade Bryant will never be stupid enough to do that.

"You let them win!" I couldn't stop yelling. "You're one of them now. You're a criminal too. You hurt people too."

"There's always more than one victim in a crime." Her words were measured, careful not to indict herself or me if anyone gets called to testify. "The law isn't big enough to get justice for all."

"Justice?" I grabbed half a row of her clothes hanging in our closet and threw them on the bed. "That's not justice, Cade, that's vigilante murder. There was no trial, no jury, no sentence. You just fucking decided for yourself. You were judge, jury, and executioner."

"Don't do this," she muttered.

"I didn't do anything. I never got my say. You never talked to me about it. You sure as shit didn't ask me."

"You never asked me either."

She didn't flinch. Not while I piled her clothes on the bed because she needed to leave. I couldn't breathe next to her. I sure as hell couldn't sleep or even live with her. Not after what she did.

"You never asked what *I* needed to heal and I never judged your pain." She didn't yell. "Your addictions. All those other women. Every soul-crushing thing you did and I never hated you. I knew you were hurting, but I've been hurting too. They took from me too and from those other victims. So how dare you judge me?"

"All this time, I know I failed you and you never abandoned me." Fuck, I choked on the words. On pain. On love.

"Please don't do this," she murmured again.

I didn't listen. Even as tears wet her lips.

"You were the one I protected, Cade. You survived being the good one, while yes, I was the bad one for so long. And I got sober believing that. That the hell I went through was worth it because they didn't ruin you too." I broke. I gulped back tears; I couldn't help it. "That's all I believed. That if I could hang on and get strong again, we could be together. And now that's a lie because they *did* get to you. They ruined us both."

Her chin trembled. I'd never seen so many tears pour down her beautiful face. Her voice barely worked.

"I'm not ruined. Neither are you. They didn't win because our love survived." She glanced in dismay at her clothes on the bed. "Don't you believe in us?"

"I believed *in you*. But you killed that too."

"You can still believe in me. I'll always do the right thing, even if it's not the perfect ending."

I wanted to vomit. "So you killed TJ? What was his perfect ending? Did you shoot him or use your bare hands?"

Fuck, it made me sick imagining Cade going that far. I get the impulse. But to plan a murder? To actually do it?

What does that do to your soul?

That man, he's probably at the bottom of the ocean but he's still a ghost in our lives. TJ wanted Cade. He stalked her. He tried to attack her so I protected her and he ripped my soul into pieces for it.

Now he has hers too.

"What about Gentry and Derek?" I glared at her. "Are you gonna kill them too?"

Those two evil men were there too. They had the drugs, the power, and the intent to take Cade but I wouldn't let them.

So they went after me instead.

And I'd do it again.

But not for it to end like this.

Not for it to end us.

"There's a warrant out for Derek Baucom, and Senator Gentry Evans is a person of interest in a missing woman's case." She answered like a Sergeant, like a woman raised by two cops who knows exactly what *not* to say.

"And so if the law doesn't work this time either, you're gonna do it?" A suitcase in our closet, I dropped it at her feet. "You're gonna kill Gentry and Derek for what they did to me? To us?"

I stared into her purple eyes.

"Please don't do this," was all she kept saying.

I've loved Cade since we were nine years old. She was my best friend and I could read her every thought.

She was dying inside. Her heart, the one I cherish, I was killing it with my rage.

"You killing TJ left *us* with no room to live," I sneered.

She expected this all along... and she did it anyway. She knew I'd never condone this.

Would I? That she'd go rogue and kill the rapist who hurt us both?

No. She chose revenge over our love, so I chose no forgiveness.

"It's my job to protect people." Her lips quivered. "They looked like me, dammit, almost all the victims and I won't let another woman get hurt. I'll do whatever it takes to stop them."

"Including more murder?" I dropped her shoes by the suitcase.

That image of her killing TJ. It kept strobing in my mind, disturbing my soul.

Yes, Cade can fight. She can defend herself. I love that about her. But kill?

I couldn't love that. I survived too much violence to condone it. Ever.

"Murder will never free you." I confronted her. "It'll only kill you too."

Her stuff was piled on our bed. The suitcase lay open, ready, looking like an empty coffin and I was dying inside too.

I towered over her and usually, I'd pull her body to mine and hold her, and everything would be okay. *We* would be okay.

Not now.

"I'll never understand why." She stood silent and fuck, I hurt so bad but I kept going. "We were finally free of them.

We were starting over." It gripped my heart so hard. "Since we were eighteen, we had our dream together. To get married. To have kids. To have a house by the ocean. Remember? I lived for our dream when I was sweating and throwing up and shaking so bad my fucking teeth hurt. All I lived for was you."

That punched her chin. Turning toward the windows, she couldn't look at me.

But I invaded her space, trying to shove my pain into her heart too. "Now we're right back in that night again and that's not justice... that's hell."

It started dripping through my veins. A new pain, another reason for me to run.

Our hope and love—I stared at her beautiful profile—and I couldn't feel it anymore.

I only felt its absence.

"Go ahead, Cade. Do it," I seethed. "You've already killed our love. You might as well continue your killing spree."

I was vicious, furious.

I couldn't find reality in this horrible one that exploded into what had been our perfect week back together. It was supposed to become our perfect life because I was about to propose to her again.

I wanted our kids to play on the beach. I wanted to cook her dinners. I wanted to sit on a porch and hold her hand, staring at every sunset until my final one *with her*.

But Gentry Evans stormed into our lives just before I went down on one knee for her. Like everything else, he took that from us too, accusing Cade of killing TJ.

He loved destroying us all over again.

She fired back at Gentry that she knew his other crimes and that she'd end him too.

All while the ground opened beneath me and my finally happy world disappeared beneath my feet.

I didn't know her.

Did I? Did I *not* know she'd do this all along? Were there warning signs I should've seen?

Cade Bryant is a fighter. I always supported that. So tired of boys harassing her because she's so fucking stunning, she learned to protect herself when I couldn't. And she's wicked smart.

Fools think beautiful women have no intelligence. Bullshit. The beautiful need it to survive the threats that come their way.

Like hell I don't know that reality too.

This island, Hilton Head—she knows its every dark corner and luxury location. The water surrounding it, she grew up on it. Between her mother who was our Sheriff with an iron fist and her dad who spends his days on a boat, Cade is perfectly trained for this one act.

How to get away with murder.

"No matter how much you hate me, Redix, for whatever I have to do." Her hands shook while she started packing. "I'll never stop loving you."

When she cries, my heart has no restraint. I'll do anything to make her smile, to make her better.

But I watched tears pouring from her beautiful eyes that afternoon while she piled stuff into the suitcase.

And my pain dulled.

It was that wicked numb I'm addicted to. The one I sought for nine years. The one I find at the bottom of a bottle. The one that'll kill me if I ever touch another drop again.

After what she did?

That temptation dangled over my tongue.

Liquor never lets me down. It delivers freedom from this pain. Forever.

"Leave," I said to her and that terrifying urge to drink again. "Leave and never come back."

Who was that for?

Her. Me. Our past. My addiction. Her crime.

I turned my back on her and walked to the sliding glass door to the pool outside. Slamming it back so hard behind me, I cracked it and didn't give a shit.

I had to find my sanity, my sobriety.

It's all I have left.

We don't call or text. We avoid each other.

Cade's a ghost and our fight, our new secret... it haunts my soul.

"Redix?" Mike asks again as our circle gets impatient with my heavy silence. "Would you like to share or pass?"

"I pass."

I can't talk about it.

Not even if I need to.

I hate Cade.

I hate her for making me feel this way because I love her. I'd never hurt her, even by divulging to this group sworn to secrecy that she committed murder for me.

That truth is my new demon.

My eyes lift from staring at the floor and this place returns. In this sanctuary in a church with light streaming in through stained glass; I get lost in the dazzle of jeweled colors in the window before I look back at the crowd and the woman sharing now.

"Hi, my name is Karen, and I'm an alcoholic."

"Hi, Karen," we reply.

Her eyes find mine and she softly smiles.

Huh, I've never noticed her before. I don't notice many women.

And she's looking back at me... like that's exactly what she wants.

3

Simple Things by Miguel

I HAVE TWO CHOICES. I GRIN; AIN'T THAT THE STORY OF my life.

Do I go with the Tom Ford navy suit or the black Brioni? They're both tailored for me and I'd rather wear board shorts.

Hell, the expensive suits still hang in the garment bags my grandma gave me.

"Every southern gentleman starts with two suits," she said. "One for business and one for romance."

My grandma was the best.

That woman never left the house without looking like elegance defined. Then she'd hide behind her house and spit tobacco with me. She taught me how. My record is ten feet.

And Grandma was the only one who gave me a damn thing after I got caught. She took care of me until her final days, so I swear I'll make her proud tonight.

I need to pick the right suit because I won't let Cade down either.

She said her dress is crimson red and even if she bought it at a thrift store, tonight she'll look like the million-dollar model she almost was.

This is a big night for her.

For me too.

She's after an evil son-of-a-bitch and I'm about to confront my parents.

We haven't spoken in years and I know they'll be at this holiday party. It's the biggest one thrown every year in Savannah and every powerful player will be there.

I fucking hate it.

But for Cade, I'll do it.

Since Redix Dean broke her heart—again—we've been spending more time together. Mainly we fish. Sometimes we sail. Other times she looks so sad, I ask if I can hold her and she lets me. I pull her into my arms and we nap on the bed in my boat's cabin.

That's all.

But that's a lot to me.

We haven't kissed. We haven't done anything but be friends who are way too comfortable in each other's arms.

Because damn, when she's that close to me, I ain't gonna lie. I want her. Like there's only one other woman I've wanted this bad but I could never have her. And Cade's just as beautiful, so different in how she looks but stunning still the same.

Sometimes I can't stop staring at her.

She'll jump on my boat wearing cut-off jean shorts showing off her legs that go for miles. Then she'll yank her sweaty tank off revealing a bikini top barely covering her tits I'd die for. Then she'll cast a heart-slamming smile along with her fishing line.

Jesus, I can't help myself. I watch how her perfect breasts move with the arc of her arms, how her cleavage deepens then opens for my stare.

I can't tell you how many times I've popped wood at the sight of her.

Hell, who doesn't?

When I do, I know she sees it. I caught her glancing and it only twitched my desperate cock more, but that's as far as we go.

Wanting each other. Watching each other. I kinda like the long tease.

You can't tell me she doesn't want me too. I see it in the way she stares. How her lips part when I greet her with no shirt on. How she gets goosebumps when I brush against her (on purpose).

But she's in too much pain and I'm too stubborn to fall for another woman I can't have.

Because despite how Cade clams up about whatever happened between her and Redix, her heart belongs to him. It's as obvious as a goddamn lightning strike.

So why the hell put myself through this again? Why fall for another woman I can't have?

I fell for Charlie Ravenel and it's been hell. She was my babysitter, eight years my senior and my first love and time is an asshole because it didn't work in our favor.

Charlie went off to college, then she joined the Marines, then she married one, and I was so damn scared while she served in Afghanistan and I was right to be. She came home a widow and shot three times and I swore I'd take care of her.

She was twenty-eight and I was twenty and we could've made it work.

But Charlie didn't feel that way about me. Hell, she suffered so much she didn't feel anything. Then she took a job as a bodyguard in Europe and came back a few years later in love with Daniel Pierce.

How the fuck do you compete with *him*?

You can't.

He's a goddamn orgasm wrapped in a huge British celebrity bow and I don't blame her.

And when Daniel questioned me about planting all those flowers in Charlie's yard for her, she defended me to him saying, "Daniel Pierce, hush your fuss. Silas is like my little brother."

Yep, that'd be a boner-killer but mine was non-stop for her.

I never saw Charlie as my big sister.

No, I saw her as the most stunning badass I'd ever met and no one held a candle to her. Sure, I fucked around. I even fell in love, but still. If Charlie Ravenel called, I dropped everything for her.

But now she, Daniel, and their twins who I love so much too, they're away while he films *The Druid* in Spain and I felt hollow without her.

And him. I grew to care for Daniel too.

My life sucked. All the fucking around I did didn't help until Cade and I started hanging out more.

Hell yes, lightning can strike twice.

Because Cade Bryant looks nothing like Charlie, but damn if she ain't a hot badass too.

Where Charlie's petite, Cade's tall. Charlie's blonde and Cade is a brunette who wears her hair in this sexy short style that makes her look like she'll fuck you or fuck you up... and you'd drop to your knees for both.

So it's my motherfucking luck that I meet another incredible woman, and guess what?

She's in love with a celebrity too.

Redix Goddamn Dean.

Just drop the ball and call the game done if Redix Dean appears on the field of love because he wins any sex or heart thrown his way.

Game over.

So why put myself through this?

I don't know. That's a state of mind I'm a pig in shit for because I'm happy that way.

I'm not like most folks.

I trust my heart and wherever it takes me. I don't *need* to know. I've loved someone I can't have. I've loved someone who couldn't love me back.

Fuck it, I've learned the hard way that love doesn't kill me, so bring it.

I pick the navy Tom Ford because Redix will be there tonight and I know he'll wear black. He always does.

And I'm so damn tired of people asking me if I'm his brother.

If they only knew how we're VERY different.

But I can't hate the guy. Yeah, he keeps breaking Cade's heart like eggs dropped to the floor but the man is beautiful. It makes his sins easier to forgive.

And his sacrifice?

Cade told me what Redix did for her. How when they

were high school sweethearts Redix protected her from three men who tried to rape her, so they kidnapped Redix instead. She hasn't told me what happened to him. I respect that. It's not my pain to know... but I can imagine.

That sacrifice makes Redix more than beautiful.

It makes him a God to me because *that's love.*

Love like no one ever wants to know but can't deny.

So it's a humble compliment if people think we're spit from the same mouth.

But we're not.

While Redix and I look alike. While we both care for the same heart-stealing woman. I come from a world neither Redix nor Cade knows.

It's one I don't tell most about, because why?

I got kicked out of it, disowned for who I dared to fall in love with. But I never wanted that life in the first place.

You can't rob someone of something they didn't want.

But I miss my mom. And sure, I'd rather my dad be proud of me than disgraced, but I can't be the son he wants.

I'll die inside trying.

So here we go.

I'll slip this expensive suit on and yank a comb through the knots in my long hair and slide on these bespoke shoes custom-made for me. And I'll take Cade Bryant on a fancy date.

She'll hook her gorgeous arm in mine and together we'll enter the lion's den.

And nope.

I ain't fuckin' scared.

But maybe I should be.

4

I'M TRYING NOT TO MOAN, BUT THIS FEELS SO GOOD. My eyes close and this woman rubbing my feet is giving me the best pedicure of my life.

And I need it.

I need every ounce because nothing else feels good. And I mean... *not a damn thing.*

The man I love hates me.

The job I love; I'm a fraud now.

My parents? I looped them into my crime.

My friends can't know, so I have no one to talk to.

I could turn to Silas, but I'll never hurt him.

I made a deal with God to end three wicked men. I got

25

one, but two remain and my soul burns because I can't catch them. Yet.

And all of it is my fault.

If I let it, this pain would destroy me. It's the torture of missing Redix so much mixed with the ache of guilt and the irony that I did it all for him...

And I lost him.

The framed pictures I have of us? I put them in a drawer. I can't look at how he once loved me. Of us at eleven when my mom bought us matching red bikes. Of us at seventeen, the day after we first kissed and didn't want to stop. Of us a few months ago in his kitchen when he was teaching me how to chop onions and all I did was cry from the damn things and laugh.

We've fought before. We've fucked and made up.

We had more combustible passion between us than an oil tanker.

But it's gone. Not in a huge explosion.

No, in one crude wreck, we were over.

And I'm fighting like hell not to let it end me too.

With an exhale, I let one firm caress up the arch of my foot give me a quick break from this hell until I sense it; someone sitting down in the pedicure chair beside me.

It's what I bribed the shop manager to do.

Slowly coming back to my plan, I open my eyes.

I notice the short hem of her pink and palm tree Lilly Pulitzer dress first. Then her French-manicured tips. Then her three-carat diamond wedding ring. And then the curled ends of her long blonde hair.

But I don't speak. I let it fester. She recognizes me. I'm too tall with too many Redix Dean paparazzi pictures taken of me.

She clears her throat. "Excuse me?" There's nothing but kindness in her voice. "Haven't we met?"

Oh, yes. We've met.

She's Stacey Evans, the unfortunate wife to Senator Gentry Evans—the man I'm going to ruin—if not kill.

I turn her way with a genuine smile, "Why yes," reaching my hand out to gently shake hers.

Southern women don't shake hard, we merely touch to gauge the climate between us.

It's warm. Stacey's innocent. I know it like the sun will come up.

"But I can't place where we met," I say.

Bullshit. We met at Luca's golf resort months back when Redix and I were there for dinner. Stacey wet her panties at the sight of Redix even though she was standing right next to her husband, Gentry. He had to watch her public orgasm while I watched it too with delight.

Every chance I get, I'll stick a pin in Gentry Evans like a voodoo doll. But I can't take him out. He has my friend Pamela Ryan, the young woman who disappeared almost nine years ago and *I will find her.*

"We met at the golf resort," Stacey offers. "I could never forget. You're too pretty to miss." She's a rare society woman; one who dares to be sincere. "You're Cade Bryant, right?"

"Yes, and you're Stacey Evans, Gentry's wife."

A tight wince pulls her face but she turns it into a grin. "Yes, Gentry's wife." Then her smile lights up real. "You were with Redix Dean and my word, you two are a stunning couple."

I hide it; the flinch of my heart. "We *were* a couple. But we've been friends since we were kids so there's always that."

"Just friends with Redix Dean?" She leans back in her massage chair. "Girl, I don't know how you do it. No offense, but your *friend* is hotter than Georgia asphalt."

I like her too.

Why a funny woman like Stacey Evans is married to a piece of shit like Gentry Evans, maybe I'll find out. Because befriending her *is* part of my plan.

Stacey holds answers she doesn't know.

Think about it. If there's one person who can access files, accounts, and hidden places. If there's anyone who knows your habits like where you go and when; it's your partner.

And Stacey Evans is more than Gentry's wife. She's his political golden ticket. Her grace blinds everyone so they can't see the dark world Gentry hides.

She's a beautiful decoy.

Because that man is running a human trafficking ring, I know it. He started off small, trying to take me, then he took Redix, then he took almost a dozen women who looked like me. All those crimes were for the worst one night of our lives.

In that time, he's honed his crime.

He's gotten good, so fucking good that we can't catch him. We got close with Sarah Matthews; his last victim. He and TJ and Derek—his former foul trio—forgot the vials of their drug, the GHB that fuels their violence. They used it on the victims to get them to comply, to erase their memories and any evidence of their crime.

But I found those vials. One I submitted as evidence and it linked Derek's fingerprints to the crime. The other vial, well I used it for justice, for revenge against TJ.

I had to end his spree. TJ was the impulsive one. The

most dangerous in the short game because he was ramping up his attacks.

Gentry's the long game. He's woven his fabric of political power and family money into a wicked empire he's building.

Derek's the wild card. He's Gentry's cousin. He drove Gentry's car the night they took Redix. He held him down, laughing while TJ scarred Redix for life.

But why did Derek stick around? You'd think he'd run. But he came back until he had warrants out for him.

The search for Derek is on while I figure out how Gentry's getting away with this, and where he's hiding Pamela Ryan and Cam Le, the two missing women.

Being Stacey Evans's new friend? It may be a double win for me.

"No offense taken," I reply to her compliment about Redix. Shit, statues get horny when he walks by. "Redix Dean *is* hot."

"I can't imagine." The nail tech starts removing Stacey's old polish while she swoons. "I mean, I *can imagine*. Millions of women do."

"And men."

"Oh, don't get me started." She sighs and I'm onto something. *Redix*. That's how we'll bond. "Redix Dean is sweet too, isn't he? I just know it."

She's got a fantasy that's close to real.

Yes, Redix was sweet. The candy he loved eating off my body was evidence of it. *That* and every sentimental thing he did for me. Every time he held me or made me laugh. It makes my throat burn.

Because I have to let him go. Redix hates me. And after every emotion we've been through, hate was never one.

Ironically, TJ's death was our death. And I'll mourn losing Redix until the day I die but I had to stop TJ. Other women were getting hurt because of me and it was the least I could do.

No. It's the *only* thing I could do.

So why does life keep screwing me so wrong when all I did was try to make things right?

"Yes"—my voice softens—"Redix is a very sweet man."

"I knew it," she sighs. "Those are hard to come by."

That's odd words for a loyal wife. "Gentry's kind too?" Those words taste like shit in my mouth.

"Politicians don't get to be kind." Ice freezes her tone. "They're calculated. Everyone's a pawn for more power."

Am I any different than Gentry? Here I am trying to use his wife as a pawn to get to him.

Fuck, Redix was right. I'm gambling with my soul in this game.

"Tell me." She leans over. "Tell me one sweet thing Redix Dean does so I can believe in romance again."

Yeah, I really *do* like her.

We could be friends so I give her this. "We had our first kiss over a lemon sherbet ice cream cone so... let's just say ice cream became a *very* sweet way he'd enjoy me at night."

"Oh, sweet Jesus." She closes her eyes. What she's imagining? It's nothing compared to what my body will never forget. "I wish."

It's sad, the way she shakes her head. Like so much is missing from her life.

"There's got to be something sweet in your marriage?" Okay, that's a legit thing a friend would ask, not just a detective digging. "Just one thing?"

The roll of her blue eyes is subtle. "Gentry likes giving pearls. Lots of them." The triple strand she's wearing is evidence. "I mean... he *really* likes giving pearls if you know what I mean."

Gag. I have to fight it.

Redix giving me a pearl necklace? I've moaned for his hot jewelry several times.

Gentry? I'd rather be spewed with cabbage vomit.

"Maybe Gentry shows his love with romantic places? Or lavish trips?"

Okay, now I'm digging. But I need to know where "they play" as TJ admitted with my hands strangling his throat.

Where do those men take their victims? The ones who haven't come back?

"If Gentry's not on the golf course, he's on his yacht." The way she shifts, she's pissed. "And it's all business and I'm not invited."

Silence sits between us while she enjoys her foot massage and the polish dries on my toes.

What's next?

Gentry, golf, and his yacht.

That's what I'll investigate.

And this woman needs a friend. She deserves to know what evil she's married to. What if he's making her an accomplice and she doesn't even know?

"You got special plans for that fancy pedicure?" Her toenails are Christmas red.

"Yeah," she groans, "we have the Holiday Riverboat Party tonight in Savannah."

"Really? I'm going too."

Confession: I knew the Evanses would be going tonight. And I knew Stacey would be here this afternoon.

You don't even have to pay me to be a detective.

"You are?" She perks up. "Is Redix your date?"

No. Redix is my heart smashed into pieces.

Silas is my date and the man I really wish could put it back together. But the adult in me knows that's *my* damn job and no one else's.

"No, I'm going with a guy friend. A very hot one."

"Two hot men in a lifetime? What's your trick?"

There are no tricks.

Just fate who's a real fuckwad sometimes.

Still, I want to make Stacey laugh. "The trick is…" Her eyes widen. "You gotta be shameless and willing to try *all* tricks."

Bull's eye.

That strikes something in her that sparks a deep smile, one that lessens my guilt.

"So, I'll see you there?" She touches my arm like she needs this, someone to have fun with.

I do too.

"Yeah, I'll look for you and maybe afterward." How the hell am I gonna pull this off? "Let's grab coffee sometime. I'll tell you more of my tricks."

"It's a date," she replies like we just met on the playground and we'll be besties for life.

And maybe, even in this fucked up, scary world of some shitty men, that's how women survive it.

5

∞

IF THERE'S ONE WOMAN I'LL NEVER DOUBT, IT'S
Lorraine Morris.

She's got my back.

She's covered my ass.

And she writes hit shows and shares my love of greasy
burgers. It was my first week in LA. I was finding caloric
comfort in scarfing one down at Tommy's and...

"Young man"—Lorraine had no fear and I had grease
dripping down my wrists—"you belong on the screen."

We were ride or die instantly.

Lorraine gives me the best roles and too many chances.

So fuck yes, I move heaven and earth to help her too.

She's got to make an appearance at this swanky holiday party and I'll be another Lowcountry tourist attraction to help her ratings.

Lorraine hooks her arm in mine and declares, "Let's shovel some shit!" while our feet step aboard the Georgia Queen, Savannah's famous riverboat, for what's sure to be a cruise through southern politics.

The December night is warm enough to roam the decks of the three-level boat and ignore the big egos inside.

But that's why Lorraine's here. We head straight for the ballroom with its gold ceiling and I hear them; gasps and murmurs the minute we enter the large room.

Yeah, I'm used to it.

So is Lorraine. She's almost as famous. And you can't miss her signature braided locks, red eyeglasses, and "don't fuck with me" smile.

I side whisper, "Who do we schmooze first?"

"Everyone who gives me permission to shoot my shows in this state," she replies.

"*Shows?*"

I just wrapped my guest role for her pilot season of *The Tour* and I thought that was the only one she shot here. I'm on a break until production starts shooting season three of *The Band* this spring in LA.

"I want to move production here for your show too," she answers as we head to the bar. "We can shoot in Atlanta, use Tybee for beach scenes."

I order a seltzer for me and a bourbon for Lorraine while I don't buy it.

"So that's the only reason?" I eye her, handing her the drink before I sip mine.

She watches me over the rim of the tumbler before she admits, "You need to be here, don't you?"

Do I?

I've only stayed here in my almost empty house because my mom, little sister, and nephew are here. They come over a lot. Hell, I think my mom's trying to move in.

And I like my AA group here.

Malibu has my other sanctuary home but going back there will only remind me of what I'm missing.

Everywhere I go, it's Cade.

I'm a dumbass to think I can keep running from her. No, she's a part of my heart that's dying.

"You don't have to do that." I hug Lorraine. She's so tiny in my grasp. This woman; I'd give her my last kidney.

"Well, it's not a done deal." She squeezes me back. "The head of the Georgia Department of Revenue is here tonight and I gotta win her over."

"Shit," I huff. "You'll have 'em eating out of your hand."

She winks, "Maybe," and pulls us into the sea of people in fancy formal wear.

I'd prefer getting four cavities filled to the hour we spend working the room. My cheeks hurt from giving selfies. My bladder is full and my brain is empty from small talk.

Lorraine's stuck in a droning negotiation about tax incentives while my glazed eyes rise to a vision entering the ballroom.

It torpedoes my chest and I didn't know pain like this was possible. I see the most beautiful woman standing there, and all the times I broke her heart?

This is retaliation.

The elegant red dress she's wearing bombs through me. The sexy slope of her bare neck not wearing our infinity necklace scatters shrapnel into my lungs. Her stunning smile sends bullets flying.

And the man on Cade's arm?

The one who looks like my fucking twin?

This is war.

A cruel one like the one I waged on her fucking every woman who reminded me of her.

I was drunk as hell.

And that's no excuse.

But this guy? His navy suit says money. His hair knot says he doesn't give a shit about it. His full lips whisper into Cade's ear and the way she looks back at him; she's happy.

Fuck, this hurts.

And damn, I need to inhale.

Because... *I'm not happy.*

I made Cade leave and I didn't do it so I'd be happy. I did it so I'd stay sober. So I'd live.

But seeing her on the arm of another man? A man who I'd even turn my chin for?

This is a life I don't want to live.

Because he's hot and he hasn't fucked her yet because when he does, we'll have the same look in our eyes.

Cade will be our last fuck.

Lorraine's too close to me not to sense my destruction. She glances my way, clocks my gaze, and knows instantly.

"Excuse me, folks." She grabs my elbow. "This lady needs a little night air."

We go the opposite direction outside and I can't see. Lorraine tugs my arm while my logic is a maze.

Turn left, and I hate Cade and left again and I hate seeing her with another man. Turn right, and I can never forgive her, and back left because I want her to be happy.

I'm so lost. I miss her, but I can never touch her again.

Every fucking hour I think about Cade, us, and what she did. She didn't fix a thing. She made it worse. TJ still violates us and will until the day we die because we can't be together now.

That dark river or a bottle of Absolut? Gimme one to drown in.

"Talk to me." Lorraine pulls us to the deck railing where no ears are around. "You look like you saw a ghost but that's her, isn't it?"

"Yes." Light sparkles on the night current of the Savannah River. It's tempting, but the cool breeze gives me a needed breath while sending shivers down Lorraine's arms. I drape my jacket over her shoulders. "You need to quit saving me."

"You need to tell me what happened."

Though more than a foot shorter than me, Lorraine's like my big sister and won't back down.

"You know about what happened to me." My story, I'm starting to share it with no names, not even Cade's. But sharing about my secret scar and assault heals me and helps others.

But Lorraine knows it all, all but this last part and I trust her with my life.

"Cade, she"—every time I imagine it, disbelief floods me —"she got rid of the man who did it."

Lorraine's right eyebrow shoots up but she doesn't say a word.

"And I feel so guilty I want to drink."

"Guilt for what?"

"That a man—no matter that he deserved it—he died because of me. And I feel guilty because Cade did it because my relapse pushed her over the edge and now it's haunting her too, even if she'll never admit it. I want to forgive her, but I can't because it was wrong... for everyone."

"Sounds like 'wrong' is the wrong word."

She reads my confusion and explains, "Wrong implies there was ever going to be right in this situation. And there were too many people hurt—you, her, other victims. Nothing was ever going to make that right again."

"So what would you call it?"

"Desperate."

"Like she had no choice?"

"Did she?"

The black water captures my stare while I try to imagine another way. "I don't know."

"When you know that answer, you'll know what to do." She rubs my back. "I'd say let's leave, but we're kinda stuck in the middle of a damn river."

There are few others I'd rather be stuck in hell with. "I'll be alright."

"You sure?"

She, like everyone, even me, worries I'll relapse. "I promise." I rub her shivering shoulders. "Enough of my bullshit, let's get you back inside to yours."

Lorraine goes to the bar and I know it's to make sure my next drink is another seltzer. But my sobriety feels strong tonight. Though my heart doesn't. And I gotta piss like a racehorse so I weave through the crowd for relief.

Taking the stairs two at a time, I climb to the next level for the men's room. My eyes are down, steps turning for the next half flight when high heels fill my vision.

Black Louboutins.

They block my path and breath pops from my lungs.

It's her.

And I'm not ready for this. I glance up and the shock in her eyes; she's not either.

"Hey." She's the first to murmur.

"Hey." I'm supposed to step aside and let her pass. I

don't. What do I say next? "I like your hot date." Yep, I revert to an asshole when hurt. "Looks familiar."

"He's a nice guy."

"He's my twin. You have a type now?"

"Yeah"—pain and pissed-off swirl in her eyes—"it's called men who don't hate me."

"Low criteria."

"Matches how I feel."

Fuck, we're gonna make this brutal. "That's your fault."

"And he's my hot solution."

She tries to step past me but even three steps below her, I'm too big to pass.

What the hell do I want? Spin the wheel and tell me.

"Did you even think about what it'd do to us? Will you ever tell your parents what you did?"

The questions kill me.

Cold frosts her eyes. "Leave them out of this."

I try to imagine what her mom would say. As the former Sheriff, Mama G would be livid, but Cade's protecting her from the truth. And Cade's dad? Well, he'd probably load the gun.

Did she ever stand a chance of not being a lethal renegade?

I step aside and mutter, "Happy Birthday."

It's today, the seventeenth. And I mean it. And I hate like hell I'm not celebrating it with her because mine's the tenth. We're only a week apart. That, like most things, used to bind us.

Now... everything tears us apart.

"You too." Her tone, I don't know it.

She pushes past me and her perfume, it's not ours. It's not BOUND perfume. It's the new one from the same designer, the one we also did the ad for—FREE. And it seems she is.

Free to leave me in the wreck she made.

My next step, it's a blur until I hear, "Redix?"

I turn and the way she's staring up at me—vulnerable, loving. We're back on our beach for our prom and she's gazing up at me in the candlelight. That night I proposed to her, giving her an infinity necklace because she was the love of my life and I only wanted to spend it with her.

"Are you happy like this?" she asks.

No.

Because her neck is bare now.

"I'm healthy."

Tears fill her eyes as she nods.

All she ever did was take care of me. All we ever did was sacrifice for the other. Until there was nothing left of us.

She softly stammers, "Have a Happy New Year."

She's not being a smart-ass and she doesn't mean the eve. She means the rest of my life. She's letting me go...

Is that what I want? To be free of her too?

I swallow glass. "You too, Candy Cade."

No, it's what I need.

A tear escapes over her dark lashes before she turns away and I walk up the stairs and have no idea what kind of life I'm stepping into.

But it can't be with her.

Not if I want to stay sober. Not if I want to stay alive.

6

Cade

Good Stuff by Griff

I need to be bitter.

I need to seethe.

I need to move on and I can't because I'll never hate him.

All I remember is every reason I love him. The bike rides. The beach days. The ice cream kisses. The stupid onions. Our burnt pizzas and naps on the sofa. Our hot sex and his cute jokes and sweet gifts.

Redix was brutal. He kicked me out of the house he bought for us. I threw my suitcase in the car he bought me

41

too and I drove back to my place crying and didn't stop for days.

Sometimes, I still can't stop.

Because he almost died in my arms.

And I can't make myself feel anything but the good stuff.

That's why I did it. I had to free him even if I had to lose him to do it.

It's only fair.

He's healthy now. I gently push through the crowd, and that's all that matters. *Redix will live.* He won't slowly kill himself anymore. So it's okay if I'm dying inside. I swapped our places and I owed him that much.

"Hey." A hand gently pulls my arm. "Hey, you okay?"

My teary eyes lift to Silas. And I only fight back more tears.

Why can't I love him the way he deserves? Like I do Redix?

I do feel something for Silas. I cherish him. He's more than *hot* to me. He's everything new and safe and inviting me to live again.

What's that called?

"I just saw him."

It's all I need to say.

"Come on."

He takes my hand and leads me to the edge of the crowd. Long rows of dining tables draped in white table-cloths are pushed to the edge of the room, each centered in front of a tall window.

Finding an empty table, he guides me to the chairs by the window and pulls one out for me. I grab the linen napkin at an empty place setting and dab my eyes while I try to maintain my dignity and sit down.

Silas sits down beside me. He won't let go of my hand. "You need some water?" He picks up a crystal pitcher and pours me a glass.

"Thanks. I'm fine." The glass shakes in my hand while I take a sip. "I'm sorry. This was a mistake and now we're stuck here."

I see Gentry and Stacey in the crowd. Lorraine Morris and her gorgeous braided locks, I see them too.

"We're not stuck." He signals for a waiter. "Two Blantons please," he orders and still won't drop my hand. It rests on my thigh. "Nope, we're gonna turn your smile and this party out."

His wink lifts my lips and heart. He gives me a few moments to gain my composure and I'm being selfish. This night is about him too.

"Are your parents here?"

"Yep." His full lips pull thin before he sips the drinks just served to us. "They're by the stage. My mom's the blonde in emerald green."

I search the crowd and wow, you can't miss his mom. She stands like royalty. The man beside her, that's his dad smiling like he owns the room.

This doesn't add up.

All Silas has told me is he hasn't spoken to his parents in years, that they got in a fight.

Silas lives in a humble home by the river on Daufuskie Island. He said his grandmother left it to him. The free-spirited man rarely wears a shirt, always wears flip-flops, and has marine grease under his fingernails. But his parents look like cover models for *Southern Living* magazine.

"Silas, who are your parents?"

All I know about Silas Harper is that he's obsessed with

boats, owns his own repair service, and loves fishing with me.

That's feeling like half of the story.

"When I tell you"—he squeezes my hand—"I ain't guilty by association, promise me?"

"I promise."

Brace yourself.

"My parents are Earl and June Van de May."

Holy shit. Pick up a feather and break my bones with it.

"Van de May? Like the energy company? Like the university? Like the most powerful family in the South?"

He sucks bourbon across his teeth before confessing, "That's the one."

"You're not Silas *Harper*?" This is a distraction from my hell and it's welcome. "You're Silas Van de May?"

He glances my way. "And there's ten point three billion reasons why I don't use my real name."

"So why?" I stammer, seeing his resemblance to his parents, not the heir of a tycoon. "So why don't you live in Charleston with them?"

Because even I know that's where the Van de May fortune started.

A wisp of his hair has fallen from its knot. He brushes it back, not looking at his parents. Or me. His gaze is to the night outside.

"That's a long story for another night."

I've never seen Silas like this.

Usually, he smiles like nothing upsets him. Usually, he eats a bait worm to make me laugh before he steals one of my Lemonheads to chase the flavor down.

Now, the legacy of ten billion dollars drops on his shoulders.

"Wanna make a swim for it?" I joke because we need it.

"Nope."

Pulling another long sip, his eyes contemplate me. The lure in them suddenly cinches my sex. They're not backing down. Instead, it's like they're backing me onto a bed as he tempts me, "I'll tell you what I'd rather do."

"What?" And what the fuck? Who turned the heat up?

"I'd rather take a deep, wet swim *in you, Cade*."

My clit just joined the party. And my mind just left it because I was crying fifteen minutes ago.

But that's the power of Silas. He's a light switch to my emotions and I'm suddenly feeling very on.

He sets his glass down and asks, "You better now?"

"A little."

His heat leans closer. "I think we need to make you feel *a lot better*." His tone, his eyes on me; they're intoxicating and we've never gone this far.

"What's bringing this on?"

And why doesn't this feel wrong?

"This room is full of people with power and rules." He doesn't look at them. "They think they control us." I'm drawn like honey to his full lips and I need something sweet. "Show them they don't."

My eyes narrow. "But we haven't done anything together."

Not yet.

"Not *us*." Temptation dances in his eyes. "*You*." His thumb grazes my thigh covered by the tablecloth. "You're in control. You know how to make yourself feel better."

His hazel eyes, they're not suggesting retail therapy or a threesome with a pint of Ben and Jerry's.

Flames flush my thighs. "Right here?"

Why does this sound good to me too?

"Right now," he says. "I'll sit right here while you

remind yourself who you belong to. Not to him. Not to me. We don't belong to people, Cade. We belong to ourselves. And the rules weren't made for people like us, so fuck 'em."

He's speaking my gospel truth and I can see pain creasing his eyes. I want to ask him what's wrong, but right now he sounds so damn right.

No one can see me. And if they look my way they'll see a woman who deserves this. Who needs to feel like herself again. Or someone new. Anything but how I've been feeling for months.

"What about you?"

I don't want to be selfish.

"The thought of fucking you makes me leave *way* too much creamy evidence behind."

Fuck, I need CPR. Silas imagining fucking me? Of coming so hard for me? My heart just stopped and my pussy takes over. With him sitting beside me and no one else at this table, it's pulsing for this, begging me to do it.

My left hand holds his on my thigh while my right sneaks under the tablecloth and lifts the hem of my dress.

Silas sips his drink with his free hand. Watching me, he has the sexiest grin while I slide my hand under my lace panties and I'm wetting fast at this no-no.

Because yes-hell-yes.

I glide my middle finger into my lonely pussy and fuck, my clit sparks like an electrical fire while I start fucking my hand in a room full of people.

Oh my God, I can't believe I'm doing this.

"Does it feel good, Cade?" But Silas inspires me. "Does it make you feel better?"

"Yes," I sigh at the touch of my sex and this is all mine. Even if I get caught, I'm the only guilty one and hell yes, this world can go fuck itself while I fuck me.

His breath hovers over my shoulder. It looks like we're having a romantic chat. "Own your pussy like it belongs to you first. Touch yourself with no shame." We're not while his free hand holding mine caresses up my thigh. "Are you getting wet?"

"Yes." I stifle a moan.

Wet and swelling and glossing my fingers, the pump of my hand, it's subtle but knows how to do this. Like my best lover, it always delivers.

I'm staring at a room of the most traditional people in the South and I'm fingering myself under the table while a hot man holds my hand and says, "I bet your pussy's so tight and hot now it's throbbing to be filled," and *oh fuck.*

"Yes." My edge is minutes away and I could play here all night. From the crowd, uptight lips smile my way. They all do this behind closed doors but I'm doing it in front of them, my arousal glazing from my fingers to my palm.

It's not in me to follow the rules. I do what I have to. Usually, it's for others but this is for me. I need this pleasure. I need to be free.

Silas leans even closer, whispering in my ear. "I bet your pussy tastes like champagne. I bet you suck a cock like heaven until a man sees stars. I bet you fuck like dirty sin, begging for more, and I bet when you come, you moan like a naughty angel who can't be satisfied."

Who is this perfect devil and where has he been hiding this whole time?

I can't speak. My thighs go liquid and I can't be stopped. Silas won't let me. And when my sex-dazed eyes focus through the crowd, I see him.

Redix is staring my way. His eyes won't move because of the look in mine; *he knows what I'm doing.* He knows what I look like before I come. He taught me how.

There's no anger in his eyes. Or jealousy. I know his desire too. I was the first to touch it. To taste it. To feel it drip from me. We're captive to this lust. I'm the jailer and he and Silas are prisoners to my show and they're not looking away.

The fire in Redix's eyes. The steam in Silas's words. My pussy opens for both.

"Oh *fuck*," I whisper. Cum coats my hand and I'm looking straight at one man while another is beside me, touching me and I want more, but this is enough for now.

"That's it." Silas pulls my thigh wider. "It's your pussy. Take it." He unleashes me, making me pump harder. His lips ghost my ear. "You're making my cock hard as hell for you, Cade." His fingers are inches from my steaming sex. "I can hear you fucking your wet pussy like I want to. So I'm gonna go in the men's room, close my eyes and jerk my cock off imagining fucking you right here on this table for all to watch."

Redix's lips part. Silas's words unleash. "You'd like that, wouldn't you, Cade? For everyone to watch us?" He nips my earlobe. "For *him* to watch us."

"Yes." I come. "Oh." So hard. "Oh." Tiny noises leave my throat while I fight to hold my body still. Only my eyes reveal my quaking release while I come, clenching over my hand for these two men to witness. "Oh." I can't even slam my guilty eyes shut to that fantasy—*these two men*.

"Happy Birthday, Cade." Silas finishes his drink before staring back at me. "Who do you belong to?"

"Me." I huff.

"Damn right, sugar." He reaches for my messy hand. "Now put your cum on my palm so I can stroke it over my cock, so I can moan your name when I come to your sweet smell."

My God, he won't stop being dirty and free and I love it. I need it. I wipe my hand over his under the table while he charms, "Finish your drink and I'll be back with another."

I watch him leave. His navy jacket can almost hide the bulge in his pants but he's moving fast through the crowd, darting right past his parents. The sea of people moves and Redix disappears behind the waves of formal wear.

I'm still recovering my breath when a giggle escapes my lips. Did I just do that? Wiping my hand clean on a linen napkin, I grin, *yes I did*.

And damn, I feel hella good.

Maybe Silas is onto something.

My whole life, I've been the Sheriff's daughter. Or the disgraced cop's kid. Or Redix Dean's best friend turned girlfriend turned model woman. Then I became obsessed and three more men and revenge against them defined me.

And I don't know how to stop being that woman for everyone else. But I know where to start.

It's time I just do me.

7

Moth To A Flame by Swedish House Mafia & The Weeknd

THIS IS EASY.

I'm a pro at masking my desire in public. At holding an apathetic face while I want to pound my dick into flesh, mine or someone else's.

And damn.

Watching Cade come was like watching shooting stars. One after another and you can't believe the wonder.

Maybe I shouldn't be so stubborn. Maybe I *should* fall for her, all the way, even if she'll always love another man.

Because I care for her. Because I know what her favorite

fishing lure is. Because I know she hates "American Piss Beer" as she calls it. And because when she lets me hold her, I'm not an heir and I'm not a disgrace.

I'm just a guy who thinks she's funny as hell, so damn smart, and Jesus Christ, her eyes. They're so blue, they're purple. They're rare jewels like her and I'm lucky just to have a chance.

The DJ's playing "Santa Claus is Coming To Town" and I smile, gently dodging the crowd, because yes, *I'm coming real soon.*

Black marble thuds under my steps as I find the hallway to the men's room empty except for a large silhouette looming there.

I know him.

Millions do.

And I'm sucked into Redix's gravity with my steps closing in on him.

His eyes drop from my face, down to my hard-on, and back up to my eyes. That feeling of confrontation, I step right into it.

"Hey, man." I'll take the first word.

"She's not a toy." Redix has got three inches on me but damn, it's freaky. He's my mirror. "Don't play with her like she is."

"She ain't anyone's tragedy or a trophy either."

Redix Dean may beat the shit out of me, but I'll go down scoring pain too. I learned the hard way how to fight.

But his fists don't clench. His shoulders don't lift and his feet don't shuffle into a fighting stance.

Something else storms his eyes. And yes, they take your goddamn breath away.

He doesn't want to fight. "*Please* don't hurt her," he says, and I know it hurt him like hell to beg that.

"I won't hurt her."

"You say that, but you don't know"—his jaw clenches—"you don't know why she really cries."

And why he's fighting it back too, I see it and suddenly I want to hug him.

What is it between him and Cade? Whatever it is, it's a Mount Everest of magnificent love that can kill you if you take it on.

"Look, man." I like Redix. Hell, I more than like him. Like anyone, I'm two feet from him and under his spell. He makes my chest warm, my mouth wet and something sleeping inside me rouses awake. "I know a little about what happened between you two. And I'm sorry. It must be hell. But your love is obvious and it's breaking her heart not to have it anymore."

What the fuck am I doing?

I got no clue.

But you gotta feel this. It's overwhelming standing in front of him with thoughts of her in his eyes, of him fighting for her not to be hurt.

It's an opiate. It's love and my mind knows the logic but now my body and my heart feel it for the first time and it's potent.

"I don't have a choice." Every muscle in his perfect jaw clenches. Damn, even his anguish is beautiful. "It's about more than love."

I could pry. I could insult him. I could tell him how stupid he's being for letting her go.

He knows.

"Well"—and I'm not going anywhere—"I'll be there when she cries, I promise."

I should've just punched him.

His face turns to the side, flinching.

Fuck, that was the worst thing to say.

He can't bear the thought of me hugging Cade. So why won't he do it? What the hell can be so bad between them?

"Just take care of her please." Redix doesn't look at me. Some place else churns in his mind and it's not this riverboat. "Just promise me that, man. Promise me you won't hurt her and I won't get in your way."

Won't get in my way?

Redix Dean is Cade's air and maybe I'll get to be her water. One you can live a lot longer without.

"I promise." I put my palm out to shake his hand, and *oh fuck*, it's slick with Cade's cum on it and I forgot.

He's showing me his heart. He's dropping his ego for her and I'm not being a dick about it, but I can't pull my hand away now. It'll only offend him more.

When his big hand grabs mine, my pulse triples. My nerves turn into hot wires. And my heart is stunned...

Because he feels her cum on my hand and glances down at our palms, at our skin touching. Because his flesh is so warm, his grip so strong and it makes me sweat. Because when he doesn't let go and looks back at me, it's not anger or jealousy in his eyes.

It's a look I've seen before.

It's a question and a risk and a recognition and we don't say it aloud.

It's confusing us both so I say, "You can't stop someone from the love they feel for someone else." I loosen my grip. He does the same, eyes still on me. "At least... I'll never try to."

I push past him, his aroma marking my senses. He lets me go and I'm grateful because I'm a hurricane of forces raging through.

The men's room—there are four stalls in it and I take the farthest one.

Two men finish their business and wash their hands while I undo my pants and drop them to my ankles. My boxers only make it to my thighs because I'm getting so hard again, gripping my cock in a practiced pump.

What the hell?

Pressing my forehead to the cold metal stall wall, I can silence my breath but not my mind.

Cade fingering herself. Cade's eyes glazing over when she comes. Cade's tits in a bikini. Her fine ass in shorts. The V of her pussy in bikini bottoms, God, how does she taste? How good would it feel to fuck her? Damn good I know, pumping faster, my hips thrusting. Into where Redix's skin touched mine. His heat. His lips. His sexy eyes. They were on my hard dick.

"Fuck," I gasp as quietly as I can, cum hitting the wall and spilling over my fist. "Oh, fuck." I shudder with another rope of release.

And I'm fucked.

8

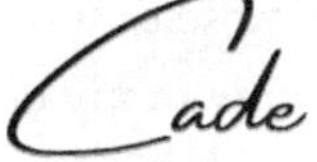

My Blanton's is finished and I'm parched for another.

How long does it take Silas to jerk off?

That tickles my stomach while I see Redix walk back into the ballroom. His eyes land on mine and I don't know that look.

Everything about that man. He loves root beer. He hates mustard. He likes to dance while he folds laundry. He loves it when I kiss his belly button. I can put him to sleep playing with his hair. I know everything about him but not *that look*.

It's not hate.

It's not love.

My heart flinches—he's been watching me with Silas. He's sad?

But this is what Redix wants. What he needs. For me to be out of his life for good.

I always believed we'd heal together but maybe I was wrong. Maybe the only way we survive what we've been through is to let each other go.

Maybe then, our nightmare will finally be over. I want that for him.

For me? I can't let go.

Besides, Redix has to beat women off with a stick, so I'm sure he'll move on soon if he hasn't already.

Damn, I'm a hypocrite. That hurt to imagine.

It makes me put my nose down to stop more damn tears.

Reaching for my phone in my clutch, I text Silas.

Missing you and my drink

I'd get it myself and I must look pathetic sitting at a table alone but I don't give a damn. I need to get my shit together. I still need to say hi to Stacey Evans and stick another pin in Gentry.

They're working the crowd but she keeps glancing my way. She's gorgeous in her white gown but she smiles too long.

She hates this too.

Finally, Silas appears with drinks in hand. I stand before accepting mine and without a word, we sip and he looks odd too. Like he just jerked off and that's hot, but it's something else.

"You okay?" It's my turn to ask.

"Yeah." He throws back the bourbon and sets the glass down. "Care to dance?"

I finish my drink too and take his hand.

A Michael Bublé holiday tune plays while Silas wraps his arm around my waist and he *can* dance. Like cotillion dance and now I know why.

Silas isn't just a free-spirited surfer dude. He's a prince to a southern fortune and trained to take over.

"Did I tell you how stunning you are tonight?" His words and steps are perfect.

"Five times."

"I'm going for twelve." He dips me. "For the twelve days of Christmas."

That makes me laugh and we're finally having fun like usual until I hear, "Son?"

His grip tightens and our dance stops. I turn and it's his mom and I step back for them to talk.

"Hey, Mom." It's sudden, how he softens and gives her a gentle kiss on the cheek. Like a man raised with manners, Silas introduces me, "Mom, please meet Sergeant Cade Bryant. Cade, this is my mother, June Van de May."

"Ms. Bryant." She smiles sincerely. "What a genuine delight."

"It's a pleasure to meet you."

"It's been a while since I've seen my son but if he's keeping your beautiful company, I understand why." Her eyes glimmer green. "Bryant? Like Sheriff Gloria Bryant? You're her daughter, right?"

"Yes, ma'am."

"Son."

A voice approaches over June Van de May's shoulder and Silas's father appears. Over introductions, Earl Van de

May hears my family name and his eyes shift from scrutiny to approval.

"Your mother built a strong legacy." His dad lifts his chin. "She's *lucky* to have a child who makes her parents proud."

Covertly, I grab Silas's hand. That was a low blow and it had to hurt. I'm right because he squeezes mine back.

"Well, you must come up." His mom sounds warm, desperate even. It's obvious she misses her son. "Silas, bring Ms. Bryant up for New Year's Day and our tradition. We're having black-eyed peas and collards for good luck."

Why a billionaire family practices that old southern tradition, I'm shocked. Then again, they define tradition now and that one's delicious.

But I don't accept. This is Silas's call.

"We'll see, Mom." He gives her another soft peck. "If our calendars are clear." His father says nothing.

"Thank you for the invitation." I try to ease the tension.

"Nonsense, dear." She leans in and pecks my cheek. "You're welcome in our home, anytime."

"Dad." Silas strains the word and that's how they say goodbye.

"Ms. Bryant, it's been a pleasure," his dad says before turning to continue his reign over the room.

"I'm sorry he said that," I tell Silas the second they walk away.

"Don't apologize for him. I'm used to it."

"I'd be honored to be your date to their party."

"You might prefer jumping into an alligator pit."

"With you? That'd be fun."

We start our next dance and halfway through another interruption sounds over my shoulder.

"Cade!" It's Stacey Evans. I know it before I turn around.

"Hey!" The quick hug I give her is legit. "You look amazing."

"You look like another magazine cover."

We fawn over each other while Gentry fumes over Stacey's shoulder. Oh, the questions that must trouble his pathetic mind. Let me give him some more.

"Let's grab that coffee," I suggest. "This Tuesday morning. Sound good?"

"Perfect," she says. "I finish yoga by ten. So ten thirty at C'est Bon?"

"Stacey, don't you have a prior engagement that morning?" Gentry's words pour hot tar over our plans. "You need to stay home for the painters."

Stacey rolls her eyes. "They're not scheduled to start until Wednesday."

"I moved them to Tuesday," Gentry lies, and now the games begin.

How can he block my access to his wife without betraying his guilt?

Stacey glances back at me. "Sorry, we're doing a quick house refresh before our New Year's Eve party." Her eyes light up. "You should come. You and…"

She looks up at Silas and I swear this woman's so lonely she's dropping her panties for him too.

"Stacey, this is Silas."

I don't know which last name to use for him so I don't say either.

"Silas?" Gentry steps closer like a cat over a koi pond. "Like 'Silas Van de May,' son of Earl and June? You were just speaking to them."

Fuck, that cat didn't stay in the bag long.

Then again, it's Gentry's corrupt prerogative to know the most powerful families and though Silas uses another last name, the public record of his lineage is crucial to those in the know.

"Yes." Silas doesn't offer more.

"Well"—Gentry licks his lips—"my lovely wife is always right. You two come to our New Year's Eve party and bring your parents if you like."

Gentry's shameless.

No, desperate.

He knows damn well that I'm after him, but he's too money hungry to avoid an opportunity to have the wealthiest donors in his home.

"We'll see." I wrap my arm around Silas's waist, feeling his abs tense to my first touch. "We may stay in and cuddle to New Year's Rockin' Eve and have a private celebration."

Stacey's eyebrows dance, Gentry smirks, and Silas kisses my cheek. "I'll toast to that."

He kissed my cheek.

The heat of his lips thrills my flesh even after they're gone. It heats my core, tingling my fingers but scaring my heart.

What am I doing?

I'm this close to Gentry, my enemy. I'm starting to adore his wife, Stacey. I'm making romantic plans with Silas. His billionaire parents just invited me to their home.

And all the while, like destiny wants to bake more fuckery into the layered shitcake of my life, the crowd parts and Redix is looking right at me.

At me holding Silas, a man I want to love.

At me smiling at Gentry, a man I want to kill.

Yes, Redix, this is me moving on.

He pushed me to do it. He knows I won't stop my plans for revenge and yes, I'm crazy to do it.

When he finally turns away and breaks my stare. I know it.

This is me... losing the love of my life.

9

∞

THERE'S A LIST OF THINGS THAT KEEP ME SOBER.

My steps. My meetings. My journals. My sponsor and counselor. I'll pick up a guitar or spin a new bowl on the potter's wheel I bought. I'll do a hundred bench presses or go for a run on the beach. That last part usually gets fucked because someone will recognize me and I can't run at night.

Not on that beach.

Not after what happened to me there.

My favorite thing that keeps me sober is this.

Playing with my nephew, Nicolas.

"Alright, little man." I look over the instructions for the LEGO Space Shuttle. "What's next?"

A pile of white LEGOs covers his bedroom floor and I'm six years old for this too.

"We gotta build the command module." His nose won't look up from his busy fingers and I love this.

Hanging out with him is simple. It's pure joy and I can forget this past weekend and seeing Cade with that guy.

Silas is his name.

I overheard someone whisper it like parlor gossip. Apparently, he's the heir to the Van de May fortune.

Fucking great.

He's hot, he's got Cade, and he's got billions.

And I don't know what I felt that night staring him down.

Too many emotions attacked me, and you'd think I'd want to punch the guy, but I have no right. That's just bullshit alpha male instincts telling me to, but those are fucking exhausting.

And for the insecure, small dicks who gotta prove with their fists what's not in their pants.

Sorry, that was alpha too.

I mean "they need to learn to love themselves" and all that shit.

That's what my counselor's been driving into my brain like an iron spike.

Slowly, it's sinking in.

But when I saw Silas up close, I felt something else. Fast.

Silas isn't me in a mirror.

No, he's the me I would've been before a few men tried to break me. I couldn't stop staring at Silas, wondering, *What would I be like if that night never happened?*

I'd be happy and whole and married to Cade. I'd have a simple life with her and love it.

That dream died with the old me.

The one Silas looks like.

I was talking about Cade, feeling her in my heart, and looking at him.

Anger left me and I felt warm and safe. I've never felt that around another man. Not after the ones I've survived.

And I knew Cade was safe with him too and that's all I want.

It was so fucking weird because I know what he got her to do under the table.

Wait. Nope, that's wrong.

Cade Bryant doesn't do a *damn* thing for any man if she doesn't want to.

No, she was doing that for herself. And my God, it was fucking hot.

My cock thickened and my throat choked while I couldn't tear my eyes away from it. How she was fingering herself and getting off in a room full of people. How Silas was whispering to her and making her come with everyone around and heat shot through my veins. Not furious heat, aroused heat like I wanted to sit across the table and watch them together.

What the fuck?

And then I felt it on his hand—her slippery cum and I swear I could smell her sweet musk on his skin and my brain didn't work. Only my body responded and that messed with my head and heart and I only made it worse by going home and jerking off about it late that night...twice... and the next morning.

See, it's bullshit.

I can't forget Cade. Or that she's with Silas.

But I can do this. Focus on someone else, not me and my drama.

I focus on my nephew.

Nicolas searches for the blue LEGOs that look like captain's chairs while I just watch. Usually, his mom, my little sister Renie's here too.

But for the first time, she asked me to babysit so she could go on a date.

I try not to be the protective big brother. I mean, Renie's twenty-four and an adult, but she's had it rough.

She got pregnant with Nicolas at eighteen. I was twenty-three at the time, living in LA, and my own drama case but I remember my mom calling me about it.

But who was I to judge Renie?

Teens have sex.

I told my mom to support her. I did. I sent her money. I bought her this beachfront condo and Renie's kicked ass.

As a single mom, she went to college for an accounting degree and now she works at a small firm. As far as I know, she doesn't date around.

She's too protective over Nicolas.

Just like me.

"Arghhh!" Nicolas throws the LEGOs down. "This is too hard! Uncle Red, it's too hard!" He flops down on the floor beside me, "I can't do it," and starts to cry.

Maybe the Space Shuttle was ambitious for six.

"Hey, it's okay." I smooth his hair. "Come here."

I lift him into a hug. He's also tired. It's ten o'clock and past his bedtime and I should've listened to Renie's strict eight o'clock rule.

This is why.

Nicolas melts into a heap of frustration in my arms and I love him. "It's okay, little man. We don't have to finish, and it's just a toy. We'll go putt-putt tomorrow and if you want me to help you again, I will. Okay?"

I wipe his cheeks and he nods with his teary blue eyes. "Let's get you ready for bed and I'll read you some more *Danny Do's*. Sound good?"

An hour later, I finally have him asleep. He's the cutest kid in Superman pajamas and I watch him for a while before plopping down on my sister's sofa, flipping on the flatscreen and scrolling.

The click of the front door turns my head to Renie entering and I can tell... she's crying.

"Hey, hey, hey." I jump up and rush to her. "What happened? Are you hurt?"

"No." She won't look at me.

"Renie, what's wrong?"

"Nothing." She lies and I pull her into a hug.

"Was it your date? Did he hurt you?"

Because I'll kill him.

That sudden impulse humbles me.

"No, I'm fine." She pulls away, tossing her blonde hair over her shoulder. "He's just an asshole, that's all."

"Renie, so help me God, if a man hurts you—"

"Redix, stop. It's fine. He didn't hurt me. He just disappointed me."

"Why?"

"Because I've been out with him before. A long time ago and I thought he'd change by now but he hasn't. He's a dick."

"Why the hell are you giving him another chance then?"

Fuck, tick another mark in my HYPOCRITE box.

Everyone gave my dickhead antics *dozens* of chances until I finally got my shit right.

Renie collapses in a chair, looking defeated. "Because he's Nicolas's dad, and I really wanted it to work."

Holy shit.

Me and mom never knew who Nicolas's dad was. Renie just said it was a one-night hook-up and the condom broke and wouldn't answer more. It was hard enough for her to be eighteen and pregnant.

"Look." I sit down on the sofa, trying to cram down every protective instinct I have. "I'll never judge you. I have no fucking room to, so if you wanna talk or need anything, I'm here."

She sighs, staring at the ceiling. "I always knew he was the dad. Don't freak out okay, but he was my first and then I got pregnant. Yes, I was drunk but I remembered him. And then, he disappeared for two years and showed back up and I told him about Nicolas."

"Has he met him?"

Because the only disappointing dick allowed around my family is me.

And I've changed.

"No." Renie snaps her eyes my way. "He's a fucking party animal with a mean streak and I won't let him meet Nicolas. Not until he gets his shit together."

Something. She's not telling me something.

"Renie, how drunk were you? Like could you even consent to sex?"

"Jesus, Redix, that's none of your business."

"But you said you were drunk. Like how drunk?"

"I don't know. It just happened okay. I was underage and at a bar and drinking when I shouldn't have been. He came up and flirted with me and I don't remember how it happened but I woke up in the backseat of his car, he was going so fast and it hurt like hell because it was my first time and there was never a condom. I remember that. When he was done, he dropped me off at home, and then he disappeared. What do you want me to say? I've been catching hell from Mom about it ever since."

"Do you know his name? Nicolas's dad?"

"Yes." She rolls her eyes again.

"Who is he?"

Because it sounds like he raped my little sister. And yes, I'll kill him.

"Derek Baucom," she grumbles.

And my world explodes.

10

It's been days since the riverboat party and Silas is acting weird.

Not like ghosting me, but he's lost in thought a lot.

He's helping me shop for a Christmas gift for Nina. She's the one-year-old daughter of my best friend Penny, and I'm scanning across too many choices.

"Should I get her a music bus or an activity block?" Standing in the aisle of the toy store, do I just buy everything? "She just took her first steps so maybe a walking toy?"

Quiet answers me.

Silas is staring at the ground. He asked to come, but he was just being nice.

"Hello?"

His eyes snap up. "What?"

"This is torture for you, isn't it?"

"No." A smile lifts his face. "It's fun. I want kids one day."

Why that flutters my heart, it's that same fear again. Are we getting too close? Are we going too fast?

I haven't even fucked him. Or kissed him. So why do I know fate is pulling me down that road?

"Then what's on your mind because it's not toys and kids?"

"Shit, I'm sorry." He grabs a box off the shelf. "Let's get the music bus and then a cup of coffee. I think we need to talk."

That sentence is a mouse trap ready to snap. "*Okay.*" But he's so good to me, I hold my tongue.

The amount of people in this toy store days before Christmas is a holiday hell. Weaving through the crowd, we make it to the long lines at the registers.

While we wait, my right cheek tingles so I glance that way.

Redix is two lines over. He's hiding under a baseball cap with a cart full of toys in front of him, but I'd spot him in a blinding blizzard.

He's looking at his phone but I know he saw me and my breakfast suddenly soars in my stomach. My feet want to bolt but I'm stuck. In a toy store. With another man. And why do I feel right and wrong at the same time?

"You alright?" Silas spots him too.

"Yeah."

Lying sucks ass.

We get through the line with our purchase, out the door, and into the parking lot before I hear the last thing I want to.

"Cade?"

Fuck you, fate. You're a piece of shit that won't stop stinking.

I turn around.

Redix is feet away with bags in his cart and eyes on me. "I need to talk to you."

Silas takes the bag from my hand. "I'll leave y'all to it," he says, jumping into the passenger seat of the Land Rover Redix bought me.

This is as awkward as Santa porn.

"Redix, this isn't a good time."

I don't have the heart for this. It's too vulnerable and feeling too torn between these men.

"It's not about us." His voice is low. "It's about Renie and Nicolas."

"What's wrong?"

That changes my mood instantly. They're like family to me too.

Redix steps closer, so close I can smell his BOUND cologne and my heart wants to scream at the torture, "I can't take this!"

"Renie told me last night who Nicolas's dad is."

Why does that put fury in his deep voice?

"And?"

"It's Derek Baucom."

That jabs my lungs, the logic punching through.

"What? Are you sure?"

"That's what she said. And she saw him last night. He's here somewhere on the island."

There's a warrant out for Derek Baucom. He's wanted

in the rape of Sarah Matthews and I suspect him in the disappearance of Cam Le.

I know he has her.

I know he's part of Gentry's crime ring.

Redix just stares at me while the dust settles from the bomb he just dropped.

"Does he know Renie is your sister?"

This can't be a coincidence.

Derek Baucom's one of the three men who attacked Redix when we were eighteen and now he's the father of Redix's nephew?

"I don't know but it's fucked up. Renie finally told me about him and I swear it sounds like he raped her. She was only eighteen and drunk for God's sake."

"Did you tell Renie he was one of the three?"

I don't need to say the three who...

But the flash of the horrific scar on Redix's buttock smacks my mind.

Derek, Gentry, and TJ assaulted Redix and left their mark on him in many ways.

They wanted me. Redix let them take him instead. And now he wears a scar that mocks our matching tattoos. It's forever carved into his skin and our souls.

"No." He's fuming, teetering on losing control. "I don't know what to do and I was gonna call you but I didn't know"—he glances at Silas in the car—"if I could."

"If Derek's back, you need to keep her and Nicolas safe. Keep them at your house, okay?"

He nods.

"Find out where they met up, what he drives, anything you can find out about him. And get me the contact number she uses for him. Can you do that for me?"

"I can try."

He looks sick and I want to wrap my hands around his chest and pull him in like I always do, but he hates me.

"Should I tell her?" he asks. "Tell her who Derek really is?"

"You don't have a choice. This is about their safety. He wants something if he's back here and risking getting arrested."

That terrifies me. Derek Baucom is a predator and not to be underestimated.

"You need them and your mom at your house with security there. Got it?"

"The cops?"

"No. A private detail that won't fuck around." It takes a second, then I remember. "HGR Security. The one Charlie Ravenel works for. Call them and get guards twenty-four-seven, okay?"

"Alright." He stands like he's ready to fight. "What else?"

"Let me talk to Penny and some of the other deputies. I'll tell them he's back and we'll come up with a plan. We'll have to come talk to Renie. Okay?"

He nods again. And what more is there to say?

Everything.

It's in his eyes and spilling from my heart. "It's not your fault." I know he's blaming himself.

"Yes, it is."

"You don't know that." I'm lying again.

"Don't blow sunshine up my scarred ass, Cade. It *is* my fucking fault." His voice raises and I can't debate him. "Derek targeted you, then me, then my little sister, and my nephew's dad is a rapist, and this is so fucked up and I'm so damn tired of it."

I can't help it.

My impulses always win.

I pull him into a hug because if he's hurting I'll kill again for him. He lets me hold him, for a painful second but he doesn't hold me back.

Pulling away, he says, "I'm fine."

The passenger door opens. "Everything alright?" Silas leans out and slices into the tension.

"We're fine," Redix says with eyes on him like a rifle scope.

But he doesn't hate Silas.

It's weird. Redix looks at Silas like he knows him. Like they share a secret.

Is it me?

"I'll follow up on those items." Redix steps back and this is business now. Serious business. "Thanks for the help."

And he does it.

He's not aware of the gesture but it's woven into my soul, the pain of it. He tucks a lock of his hair that's fallen from his hat behind his ear and he turns his back on me and... he leaves me... standing there.

It's what we do.

11

Keeping A Secret by Bleachers

There's a pink elephant riding in Cade's back seat while we circle through the Starbucks drive-thru.

I order an Americano and Cade gets whipped cream with coffee and a lemon pastry.

This woman and her sweet tooth.

She has the metabolism of a hummingbird to eat that way but look like a supermodel. Then again, her dad's the same way.

We're friends and when I hang out with Jeff Bryant,

he's a bottomless pit whose fifty-year-old body puts most twenty-year-olds to shame.

Yep, Cade struck the sexy DNA lotto.

We get our drinks and she pulls her car into a parking space and turns to me.

"You wanted to tell me something?"

I love this about her. Cade cuts straight to it. I can't stand it when folks hem and haw. Just fucking say what you feel.

"We got *two* things to talk about now." My coffee's too hot to sip. "Which one's first? Me or Redix?"

Her eyebrows shoot up like she's been caught. "You first. I talk about my shit too much as it is."

And damn, now I want to hem and haw. I could drag this out for days.

But fuck it.

"Cade, I'm bisexual and that's why my parents cut me off."

Nothing. Her face. Her eyes. She doesn't react while she finishes sucking sweet goop up her straw.

"It's bullshit they cut you off," she says. "That has to hurt you and I'm sorry."

"So *that's* what you get from that?" She keeps winning me over. "What about the bisexual part? It doesn't bother you?"

"Why should it?"

"It bothers most people. Everyone in my family. Most of my friends. Hell, most don't even know. And when I tell people I'm dating, it's usually a deal-breaker."

"Are we dating?"

"I have no fucking clue what we're doing but I like it."

She looks out her front windshield. "Silas, I don't know what we're doing either, but you being bisexual doesn't bother me at all. I'm totally fine with it because honestly, I'm too busy trying to figure out what *I* feel."

"It's obvious what you feel."

Her eyes cut my way. "*You're* gonna tell me how I feel?" Warning: never cross this woman. "You're a *brave man*."

Laughter bolts up from me because this is the first time I've kinda pissed her off... and it's funny.

"I ain't mansplaining. It's obvious; you love Redix Dean."

Now my coffee is cool enough. I take a sip before I add, "And you like me too and that's fucking with your head."

She flops it back on the seat and sighs. "I want to hear your story. I'm so tired of mine."

"My story?" I take another sip. "Well, my first love was a girl named Charlie Ravenel."

"Charlie Ravenel?" Her chin shocks my way. "You know her?"

"Yeah. She used to babysit me. You know her?"

"Yeah. We rode the bus to high school together."

"Well, then you know how beautiful she is, so of course, I fell in love with her but could never have her. At first, I was too young and then, Daniel Pierce came along, so I was fucked. Not by her, unfortunately, so I learned to move on."

"If Charlie was your first love, when did you realize you were bisexual? That you liked men too?"

"At The Citadel." Suddenly, this ain't an easy chat. My chest tightens. "My parents made me go, so I'd be a real southern man and all. I didn't want to, but I didn't wanna disappoint them. The fucking buzz cut alone felt wrong to me. But then I met Alec, and I didn't want to leave."

"So it was Alec?"

"Yeah, he was the college quarterback and in my barracks and company too."

"A bisexual man at a military college?" Cade's logic moves fast. "You had a target on your back."

"No shit. That's why no one knew. I wasn't weirded out by what I felt for Alec, I just knew like hell if I could show it."

"Did he know?"

"Yeah. At first, we were friends, cadets getting through the training. Then it was Thanksgiving and his family didn't have money to fly him home so he came home with me."

"Your parents didn't know?"

"Not at first. Hell, Alec and I didn't know until one night we got pretty wasted on my dad's bourbon and he told me how he felt. We, uh..."

Damn, I forgot how this hurts remembering him. How he had the best laugh in the world.

"We did everything together that weekend and I was in love. So was he, but we knew we had to hide it."

Cade reaches for my hand on the console. I didn't realize it; it was shaking.

"What happened?" Her voice is soft, so are her eyes and she isn't judging me.

"We hid it for a year. Everyone thought we were best friends. We were... and more. And I had all kinds of dreams that we'd be together forever. Like we could make it work once we graduated. But then..."

Bitter coffee churns in my stomach when I remember.

"We got caught together by his coach. It was just us in the barracks and we should've known better but we were young and dumb. And the fucking coach, that perv saw the whole thing. Alec was bottom that time and the coach clapped when I came. It was fucking sick what he did. That motherfucker watched us and waited and laughed, degrading us on purpose."

"Did everyone find out?"

"Hell no. The coach couldn't lose his star quarterback but I got burned. Because I was top, he said I 'defiled' Alec and it was my fault. They called my parents and kicked me out for dishonorable conduct and my dad hasn't looked me in the eye since."

"I'm so sorry." She squeezes my hand and I like her touch. "What happened to Alec? Do you keep in touch?"

"No. He's playing pro and I guess he stays closeted. Like he has a wife and all. I don't know. Maybe he's bi too."

"And your parents? They just kicked you out?"

"Yep. I don't give a shit about my family's money. Trust me. It comes with too many strings attached. Like if I want to inherit the Van de May fortune, I can't be with a man."

"Do you *want* to be with a man?"

"I want to love who I choose to love and be proud of it. No amount of money is gonna change that. My parents cut me off but my grandma stood by me. She understood. Deep down I wonder if she struggled with the same thing, but she never told me. She just gave me her family's old house on Daufuskie and a million to set up my business."

"She sounds badass."

"She was, but she passed away five years ago."

Cade's quiet and I finish my drink. It's a lot to dump on her but I feel better.

I've been wanting to tell her for a long time.

Now... I have to... because there's more to it.

"Why now?" She's reading my mind. The woman's a born detective. "Why did this come up now and not last year when we started hanging out?"

Fuck. Here we go.

I'm about to shoot my foot off when all I want to do is walk toward this woman.

"Because I met Redix at the party."

Her eyes get wide and my pulse jumps.

"Because I won't lie to you, Cade. I'm attracted to him. I haven't felt that way toward another man since Alec, but Redix confronted me about you at the party. And I felt like a dickhead because he was protecting you, and telling me not to hurt you, and I know he meant it. But the whole time I was like, *holy shit, I'm attracted to this man.* Like really hard."

She's gonna hate me.

She's gonna get jealous.

It's a betrayal of whatever we are and she's gonna tell me to get out of the car and never talk to me again.

I don't blame her.

"Everyone's attracted to Redix." She smiles. "I'm used to it. You're not feeling anything wrong."

"Thank, God." I huff.

Damn, that's been bothering me. And damn, she needs to stop being so fucking incredible.

"I don't want to be with him, Cade, I'm just attracted to him and I feel guilty about it."

"No need." She takes the last suck of her drink. "He doesn't want to be with me either so there's no guilt."

"He *does* want to be with you."

"He hates me."

Why won't she tell me what happened between them? Here's her chance but she turns to stone. Like nothing can crack her. Not even me sharing everything with her.

"He doesn't hate you and I'm not going to stand in y'all's way."

"Silas, Redix and I are done and I'm making peace with

it. But I've loved him for so long it won't happen overnight but it's for the best. I need to let him go."

Silence fills her car and it's heavier than the new smell of it.

This is a crossroads and we know we're at it.

But I'm not like most men.

"Look, whatever happens between us," I tell her, "you're free. You don't belong to me. Or to him. I don't believe in that shit. Acting like you own someone because you love them. Love is the opposite to me and I'm starting to love you."

Her chin drops with her eyes but I'm not afraid of this.

"You can be with me, Cade, and you can be with him. You can be whatever you want. Not like it's my permission to give. It's just what I believe. I don't know what's troubling you, but I feel it in my heart. You gotta be free to let it go."

She starts sobbing and I can't stand her pain. I reach across the car and pull her into my arms.

Her tears wet my T-shirt while she mutters into my chest, "I'm starting to love you too and I don't want to hurt you."

"You won't hurt me." Her hair smells like lavender. "Let me show you; the heart is big enough to love lots of people. Even if we can't be with them." I kiss her silky strands. "Trust me. I know."

I want to kiss her so much.

But she's still fighting this, I can tell. Like she's cheating on Redix to be with me. Or like she's cheating on me to still be in love with him.

And all I want to do is help her see love doesn't have to be that way.

It can be bigger if you let it.

12

Forgive Me by Sofi Tukker, Mahmut Orhan

SHE ALWAYS BRINGS MY FAVORITE DONUTS TO THE meetings—old-fashioned ones with no glaze.

Wonder if she noticed that about me?

"Hello, my name is Karen and I'm an alcoholic."

And now she's sharing again. This time I listen more closely.

"Hi Karen," we reply and she starts.

"It's been a rough week. I just get overwhelmed being a single mom. I love my son, don't get me wrong. I got sober when I found out I was pregnant but sometimes, I just need

82

a break. And that scares me because the only break I can get without a babysitter is in a wine bottle and I don't want to go back."

Karen's cute.

She can't help that she's a brunette with short brown hair just like Cade. But she wears hers in a bob, so it's different. And she's a single mom to a son and I'm a softie for that because of Renie and Nicolas.

I told Renie everything. I didn't want to ruin our Christmas but she had to know about Derek. It's for their safety.

Nicolas loves living at my house though. The pool is heated and he's always in it. But Renie's nervous now and I hate that.

I called HGR Security and have two guards on shifts. They shadow Renie and Nicolas wherever they go.

One of the guards is a woman—Scarlett. She covers the day shift and makes Renie feel less jumpy. The other guy, Keith. He covers nights and seems good too.

But I dread the meeting scheduled this afternoon. Cade and some deputies are coming over to talk to Renie.

Fuck, it's gonna be rough having Cade back in the house.

I bought it for us with hopes of a family there but after what she did—that dream's dead.

I don't hate her anymore. I just grieve the loss because I spent ten years dreaming of a life with Cade, and I held it in my hand for one perfect week before it was taken away.

It's so hard forgiving her for that.

She chose our past instead of our future. Why?

Our future felt like a castle I built in my mind. I escaped there in my darkest hours and it kept me alive. *Cade* kept me alive.

But now we're back in the haunted house of our past.

Or at least, I am.

When I saw her with Silas at the store, they looked happy. Guess he's her castle now.

He's good for her. I saw how she stands close to him and how he helps her with little things like taking the bags for her.

But I can't shake it.

I look at him and feel something and it's not weird. It intrigues me. It gives me hope. For what, I don't know. It lightens my chest and pulls me to him and that must be what Cade feels for him too.

Like I find myself thinking about her. That's not new. I do it every hour, if not every minute.

But now I think about Silas next and what does it mean? That I'm jealous? Shouldn't I feel like shit?

I do when it comes to missing Cade.

But the two of them together? I don't.

I just feel... what... *warm* when I think about them together. And then something else and I can't name it.

I can't really share what I need to say at these meetings, so I listen to Karen and then get lost in my head until it ends. Even if I don't talk, the group, the routine, it keeps me strong.

"Sorry, they're a little stale today." A voice speaks softly behind me while I go for my favorite donut. Karen appears at my side and grins. "I try to get them fresh, but I had to pick them up last night because today's been too hectic."

"My sister's a single mom, I get it. You're doing the best you can. And donuts are always good as hell."

Her smile is big and when she touches my arm, maybe I don't hate it.

"Thank you. I needed to hear that. All I do is feel like I'm failing."

Our chat continues into the parking lot and she tells me about her job; public relations for the tourist bureau. And about her family; they live in Beaufort. I get an earful by the time we reach my car.

"Would you like to get coffee sometime?" She's not shy but suddenly, I am. "And fresh donuts, I promise."

Would that be a date?

I've never done this with anyone but Cade because all the other women were easy pick-ups and fuck, when I'm drunk, I'm too easy.

But I'm stone cold sober now and what do I want?

"Redix, I know who you are," Karen says. "That sounds stupid to say the obvious but the whole group does and I'm just being honest. It's not fair because we all hide behind anonymity and you can't. We know all about you."

"Yeah"—I lean against my car—"it's a mindfuck some-times. I don't know who to trust."

"I get it."

She chews her lip, casting her eyes through her lashes.

Yep, that's flirting for sure.

"So full transparency." She wears red lipstick. It's kinda sexy. "I've seen the posts of you lately with some gorgeous woman. If that's your girlfriend, I don't mean any disrespect."

At least she's honest. And blunt.

"She's not my girlfriend anymore."

That sentence crushes my chest.

She grins. "Trust me. I didn't ask you on a date. It's just coffee and donuts." That's not true and she's hedging and it's kinda cute. "I have to be so perfect around my mom-friends, so it's nice just to hang out and really be me."

Why does this feel awkward?

Like it's wrong, but it's not. Cade's moved on. Hell, I made her. And if I can't be with her, I can't be alone forever.

"How about after our meeting next Monday?" My stomach twists but I make myself do this. "I got family stuff for the New Year but then I'm free."

"Sounds good." Her face lights up. "Have you got fun plans?"

"My mom, sister, and my nephew; we'll celebrate."

I'm about to be polite and ask about her plans but she blurts, "I'm surprised you don't have a hot date for New Year's."

"No."

"Still licking your wounds from that pretty ex-girlfriend? Is that why you don't share much?"

Shit, she's insightful. Or am I that obvious?

"Something like that."

"That's gotta be hard, I'm sorry." Her feet shuffle. I glance down. *She's wearing Louboutins.* Like I wouldn't know those black heels anywhere but it's an odd fashion choice for an AA meeting. "I mean, I recognize her to be honest. She's a local deputy, right?"

"Yeah."

It's weird talking about Cade to another woman. But this is what you do, right? You talk about your exes?

"How does that happen? A Hollywood actor meets a Hilton Head Sergeant? Did she arrest you or something?"

"We grew up together." Now my bare feet shuffle. "It's a long story."

"We've all got those." She steps back and I can breathe easier. "Well, see ya at the next meeting and for coffee next week."

"Yeah." Karen's also wearing a black leather jacket. It's

December but not that cool today. It just reminds me of Cade. "See ya."

The afternoon goes by too quickly and the doorbell rings promptly at four o'clock. I draw a deep breath while Scarlett answers the door and checks credentials.

"Hey stranger," Scarlett greets Cade.

They know each other?

Cade stands in my foyer in black slacks, and a white button up and she's here to work while her beauty still pummels my heart.

"Hey there," Scarlett greets another woman. She's dressed in a deputy's uniform along with another who enters behind her.

Cade makes the introductions. I shake hands and the other woman Scarlett seems to know too. I recognize her now. I've seen her at my sister's pool with Cade. Penny's her name and she's staring me down like I killed her family.

My mom takes Nicolas to his room and leaves us in the living room.

I'm an asshole because I don't have enough furniture yet for everyone to sit. So I stand with the others while Cade sits down with Renie on my one sofa.

"I need to ask you some questions about Derek Baucom." Cade touches Renie's hand. "Would you like some privacy for that?"

"No"—Renie lifts her chin—"I didn't do anything wrong so there's nothing to hide."

The smile that takes Cade's face, fuck, it's beautiful.

She's proud of Renie.

I am too.

While Cade asks questions about the last time Renie saw Derek, she jots notes on a little pad. When the questions get more personal, the care in Cade's questions, I've never seen her like this.

I've imagined what she must be like on the job. Smart, strong, a badass; like a fish born in police waters. Hell, she was. Mama G was pregnant with Cade when she was sworn in.

But this is a Cade I've never seen.

How she's so respectful to Renie. She doesn't push but she gets the information she needs to help her.

This must be what she's like with all the victims...

All the victims.

Ten women, Cade told me... and they all looked like her at eighteen.

The evil of it. The guilt of it.

I never appreciated how much it must haunt Cade. How she gets this desperate look in her eyes to catch the three men who did it.

Well, two men now.

That's what Lorraine said, it sounded like Cade was desperate, not wrong.

And I've been a morally righteous ass because I know the feeling now. I'm desperate to keep my sister and nephew safe from that man.

It sickens my soul that Derek Baucom went after my sister.

I still hear his laughter. I still see his mudflap girl tattoo. I still see the infinity necklace I gave Cade swinging from his neck while Derek held me down and TJ ripped into my flesh.

It hurt so much, *it burned...*

"Who's a pretty boy, now?" Derek hissed in my ear before he punched it.

"We're gonna make you real pretty for her." My ear was

ringing but I heard his snarl. Flames, a pain I've never known burned to my core while he laughed in my ear. "Even your blood is pretty, boy."

"Excuse me." I can't breathe. Knots choke my throat and I need air.

Standing outside by my pool, I stare at the calm horizon but my mind isn't. It feels frazzled like wires want to unravel but I need them to stay connected. To stay in control.

Derek went after Cade.

Then he went after me.

Then he went after my sister.

It's one thing if they hurt me. And I'd do it again for Cade. I'd do anything to protect my sister too.

But the damage is done and it won't stop wrecking us.

Something snaps and...

I need a drink.

Fuck. NO. Not this again.

It won't make me feel better. It won't stop this.

It'll only kill me.

Please. I pray. *Please help me.*

"It'll be okay." Her voice is like an angel because it saves me every time. A soft touch lands on my back. "We'll be okay."

I can't look at her. She'll see the tears I'm fighting. I'm supposed to be strong right now and I'm making this about me.

"Do you wanna talk?" Cade asks.

I close my eyes.

No, I want to run. Or I want to hold her and never let her go, but all she does is fill me with more guilt.

Cade killed a man for me. She violated every law and

every ethic she has to get revenge and it's my fault. I overdosed. I relapsed and I pushed her to the edge.

And now neither of us will ever be the same.

"Please tell me he can't hurt my sister anymore." It's all I can choke out.

"I swear to you. I'll protect her from Derek. I'm looking for him. She gave us some good leads so we catch him."

"I mean TJ too. Is he really gone?"

Ocean waves are all I hear.

Goddamnit, why won't she just admit it?

I spin around. "Swear it to my face that TJ is gone for good."

She stares up at me and her silent lips press so hard together I swear they turn white.

"You think you helped me, Cade?" The pain, the guilt; my heart snaps. "That you helped those victims too? You didn't. Until you admit it, it'll never be right."

"Taylor John hasn't been seen on this island in over sixteen months."

She's too cool about this. Too collected and too calculated like there was never any passion between us, so I fucking lose it.

"Tell me! Say it to my face!" Anger. It's ripping my seams. For my fault. For my sister. For Cade. "If it was so fucking right, then admit it! Is he dead?"

"Renie doesn't need to fear TJ."

Her control mocks my rage. She's telling me without saying it, and I feel sick.

"Go be happy with your new love. With Silas. Just know, after what you did, I'll never be happy again."

Tears spring over her lashes but she won't move.

Fuck, we've been here before. I've watched this horror film; our love murdered before our eyes. Over and over.

"You don't mean that," she murmurs.

"Don't tell me what I fucking feel! You have no idea what I fight inside! What I see when I close my eyes!"

The pain, it's worse now than it was the afternoon I found out. The one when Gentry ruined our lives again.

Because this time, she's moved on.

She gets to be happy.

She gets to be free.

"I'll suffer this the rest of my life, Cade, because you made it harder for me. Harder to stay sober. Harder to be happy. Harder to ever feel normal again. I can't even fucking tell anyone. I've got this goddamn cancer of a secret killing me inside and you put it there."

This hurts so much because I see it in her violet eyes.

How she finally gets it. How much I suffer. And how much I'm hurting her too.

I might as well kill her myself because there's nothing left. There's no air. No life is left between us and I want to fall to my knees and weep at the grave of our love.

"I can't tell you." She barely whispers, "It'll only hurt you more."

A glass door slides open and a voice pierces the air. "Cade, you okay?"

It's her friend Penny and her glare is aimed at me.

"I'm so sorry," Cade mumbles. "I never meant to hurt you."

I can't stop it; my tear that falls. "Well, you *did* hurt me. More than *they* ever could."

That turns her feet, running away, through my backyard before she disappears around the corner of my house while Penny storms my way.

"Listen here, you goddamn Hollywood motherfucker!" She's gonna pull her gun. Here it comes. "Quit breaking her heart! It's enough. You've done it too many times and there's almost nothing left of her. Don't you see that?"

By the time Penny's steps from me, she screeches to a halt at my tears too.

She can shoot me.

It'd probably hurt less than this.

And it'd be a lot faster than the life I have to live without Cade.

"Look." Penny grabs a breath. "I'll handle this case. I'll update you and your sister. Deal with me, not Cade. This is hurting you both."

"Okay."

Penny searches my eyes and I don't care. I'm a grown man who loved a woman so much the world can watch me weep over losing her.

"Give it time." Penny looks very pregnant and very compassionate. "Pain is a season that'll pass."

"Thank you."

It's all I can say to her kindness. She's Cade's best friend and I don't mind her chewing my ass out. But I'm not wrong. She has no idea what Cade did.

"Will you excuse me, please?"

I disappear through the door to my bedroom and pick up my guitar and pluck away at a song I need to learn to play. To stay sane.

Because I didn't mean what I said, that last part to Cade. *Fuck, I need to take it back.*

Those three men hurt me.

Cade didn't.

All she did was love me so I could survive it.

Everyone leaves and through my strums, starts, and stops, I hear silence fall over the house.

Finally, I can eat alone. I don't feel like talking to anyone.

Sneaking into the kitchen, I try to be quiet. I don't even turn the lights on. I'm searching for something in the walk-in pantry when the lights slam on and Scarlett's at the threshold with her gun drawn.

"Shit!" She groans. "It's you." I think I just pissed myself but I appreciate her stealth approach. "Sorry, thought you were in for the night."

"I was hungry."

"Didn't mean to scare you." She holsters her weapon. "I was getting ready to leave, then I heard a noise."

"I'll live." I set the soup can back. I'm not hungry now, but I'm curious. "How do you know Cade?"

Scarlett's eyebrows flick up like she doesn't want to answer. But she works for me and I should know these things.

"I dated her friend, Jameson, for a hot second before I moved to Atlanta. Then I helped her that day. The day she found you."

Holy fuck. I had no idea.

"How bad was it? I mean, for Cade?"

I almost died that day. That's the only thing I know. I was drunk as hell and Angie and some woman fed me pills like a Pez dispenser and I was breaths away from dying.

"Honestly?" Scarlett backs into the kitchen while I follow. "It was bad. I've seen some rough shit, but that was heartbreaking. She thought you were dead and you sure looked it, and she didn't care. She just held you in her arms until the medics pulled you away. And then your assistant wouldn't let her see you at the hospital. He said you wanted it that way and I've never seen someone so desperate."

"She was desperate?" *That word again.*

"Yeah, she *was*. If I hadn't been there, she would've shot up the hospital walls. Like she would've made Swiss cheese of that fucking place to get to you."

I can see her doing it.

"You know, Mr. Dean—"

"Please call me, Redix."

"Redix, I wish I had someone who loved me that much. Who'd fight for me like that. It's rare, and it's a shame to let it die."

13

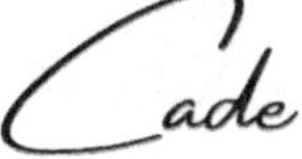

I wedge my foot into my Louboutins. "Thanks, Mama." I smile at her sitting on my bed, watching me dress for a New Year's Eve Party.

"You sure you want to go?"

Senator Gentry Evans's New Year's Eve Party to be exact.

"Yes." I shimmy into a silver sequined mini dress. "I'll have good company and his wife is a good person."

"Well, Stacey Evans may be good, but Gentry is heinous. He needs to be caught."

I start lotioning up my bare legs. "I'm working on it."

Mama's quiet for a bit. It's not like her and I worry.

"You look tired. Are you not sleeping well?"

"I'm fine." She rolls her pretty eyes. "And I gotta see this—Mr. Silas Van de May picking up my daughter for a date. Who would've known he's an heir to a fortune? Your dad's known him for years and had no clue."

"Because Silas doesn't want his family's money, and my family being here when he picks me up is weird as hell."

I dab on FREE perfume.

"Well, your dad wants to watch some damn fishing tournament and our satellite is out so deal with it."

Dad's out in my living room, making himself at home but I know it's also to give Silas his blessing.

I'm twenty-nine. I don't *need* their blessing, but my parents are former cops—they're gonna give it anyway.

And it's weird officially dating Dad's close friend. But they're almost thirty years apart, so is it really?

I loop on earrings and a bracelet next. In my jewelry box, the new infinity necklace Redix gave me... replacing the one stolen from us that night... my touch lingers over it.

How we left things? What he said?

I cried for a day over it. Like tears fell until I was empty. Until no more pain could bleed from my heart over him.

I know he didn't mean it. He's in pain. He feels guilt over Renie and Derek and it's got to be hell.

But I can't be battered by his storm anymore. I'm doing what I can. I always will. But if he wants to rage and rip his life apart again, I'm not going to stand by and get hurt too.

"You're thinking about him, aren't you?"

Mama's propped up on my bed and doesn't miss a thing.

"He really wants to know." I turn to her. "He wants me to admit it."

"Well tell him the truth then. Tell him me and your Dad took care of TJ."

"No." Steel firms my resolve. "If it ever gets out, and Redix knows the truth, he's an accessory, then you and Dad have one more person who'll have to testify against you."

"Darlin'." She sighs. "That makes as much sense as tits on a bull. By the time an investigation and trial get done and I get sentenced, I won't be alive. So tell him."

"Don't say that!" My mom jokes about her terminal diagnosis and it isn't funny. "Quit talking like that."

"Why?" She sits up. "You livin' forever?"

"No."

"Well me neither. Mine's just coming sooner so make peace with it."

We don't know how long Mama has and she and Dad are living like every day is a holiday and I do my best to help.

Mama's fearless. She jokes about it. Cries with smiles about it. Brings up memories and tells everyone she sees that she loves them.

She's riding her wave to shore with all the grace and grit you'd expect from her.

And I'm trying to be on board for her sake, but damn.

This is my Mama we're talking about.

"Listen to me." She pulls my hand to the bedside. "You go on with this man, Silas. Or you go on with Redix. Or you go on with some other person, I got no expectations. But either way, you GO ON. You hear me?"

"Yes, ma'am."

"You go feeling sorry for yourself or sorry about me and I swear I'll haunt your ass from the grave. I'll knock you so hard into tomorrow, and then I'll find you there and knock you into the next day too."

She's never laid a hand on me except for pulling me down into a big hug as she smiles.

"Life is lemon cake, Magnolia Cade. It's bitter and sweet until the last bite so you best enjoy it."

"Yes, ma'am."

I whisper in her ear and swallow down the burn in my throat at how much I love her and swear like hell I'll be strong for her too.

"Magnolia Cade!" Dad shouts from the living room and the whole damn building can hear him. "Where's the damn fishing channel?"

I pull away from mom and she laughs.

"You can take the man from the boat, but you can't take the boat from the man."

"Number one eighty-two!" I shout back, laughing.

My parents' love. It's had its ups and downs; it teaches me mine is gonna be the same. No matter who I'm with.

It's easy jokes and introductions when Silas comes to pick me up.

"I'll have her home by ten, Mr. and Mrs. Bryant." He makes fun of their hovering by the door. He knows my dad and wins my Mama over in a second.

Besides, the black suit he's wearing with his hair slicked back into a knot makes him look so sexy he'd win over a firing squad.

Minutes later, a valet parks his truck while Silas offers his hand and we step into Gentry and Stacey's palatial home and I have one plan.

Find Pamela Ryan and Cam Le.

My best friend disappeared from a bar in Hilton Head when we were twenty. All presumed she was dead until I got TJ to admit otherwise. Minutes from his death, evil smirked from his eyes along with the intel that both Pamela and Cam, the maid who went missing, are being held some-where by Gentry and Derek.

My gut tells me Derek has Cam.

And Pamela?

My God, it's been almost ten years but she's alive. Gentry has her. She was part of our trio growing up—me, Redix, and Pam—and Gentry witnessed it all.

So if he couldn't have me. And if he couldn't keep Redix. He took Pam.

And I'll draw my last breath finding her.

"Want some champagne?" Silas whispers in my ear over the band playing and it tickles my thighs.

"Just one for now"—I wink—"we got a job to do."

Silas knows Pamela's story. He knows why I'm here and he makes the sexiest accomplice.

A waiter passes with a tray of full flutes and Silas grabs us two. We're sipping and scanning the crowd and within minutes, Stacey Evans is by my side.

"I'm so glad you came." She wraps her arm around me and whispers in my ear. "I gotta tell you something."

Silas gets pulled into a conversation with a couple who knows his parents so I focus on Stacey.

"Are you okay?"

"More than okay." Delight dances in her eyes. "I'm dying to tell someone and my heart just knows you can keep a secret."

I chuckle. "Like a fucking vault."

Why I feel so connected to Stacey, I don't know.

Maybe it's because she's in danger and I want to protect her. Maybe it's because she's nothing but truly kind. Or maybe it's because she's another woman, so why wouldn't I?

"The painters that came over." Stacey pulls me into a

hushed chat. The music swirls around us while she confesses, "I learned a few tricks with a very skilled one."

This champagne is opium because I just went numb. In a good way. "One of the painters?" I'm proud of her. "Is that what you wanted?"

"Hell yes, I started it." She squeezes my hand. "I don't know what's gotten into me but Gentry's been so mean for so long, and I'm so lonely, so please don't judge."

"You deserve love too." I toast her glass. "Or at least a skilled trick."

"We gotta do coffee so I can tell you more," she gushes. "I'm just bursting and need to tell one of the few friends I trust."

"I got your back." I scan the crowd. "You sure Gentry doesn't know?"

"How could he? He was off on his yacht on one of his exclusive golf tours. I could have an orgy with a football team and he'd be none the wiser."

"Do you need me to call the Carolina Panthers?"

We both start laughing and that turns heads. Shit, we gotta be careful but this intel changes everything.

Stacey's ready to break free of Gentry's prison and I'm the jail-breaker who'll help.

"These golf tours?" I ask her. "What are they?"

She rolls her eyes. "They're through his rental company. Men book a golf tournament and they get a yacht trip and a condo here for a week too—all private, all elite, and all bullshit. I know they're fucking around the whole time."

Oh, I know it too.

I saw it myself between Gentry and TJ. But I didn't know Gentry's evolved it into a sophisticated business model.

One that screams criminal to me.

Another guest grabs Stacey's attention while I smile my way into getting Silas free of his chat. Pulling his hand through the crowd, I tell him, "Let's find someplace private."

"Well, Happy New Year to me." He's game.

Guests gather everywhere, outside and in. But the crowd thins down a hallway past a powder room leading to an impressive office.

It's empty and this is my chance.

"There's gotta be something in here," I tell Silas.

He scans Gentry's desk without touching anything. I start combing the rows of bookshelves—leather-bound classics I'm sure the dumbass Senator has never read. But there are lots of pictures of him on his yacht, fishing with groups of men.

I pause and scan the horizon of the photos for clues. *Where is he fishing?*

It's the Lowcountry islands but which one? There are dozens of islands, some public, some private. But I swear in a few I can barely see the Harbour Towne lighthouse on Hilton Head in the distance.

He's not going far.

And that's the only place Pamela could be. Maybe Cam, too. Hidden on one of those islands.

I'm about to ask Silas because he knows the terrain even better but heavy footsteps clip down the hall, headed this way.

Shit, we're gonna get caught.

"Come here." I yank Silas into my arms and plant a kiss on his lips.

It's a ruse at first, a desperate act so we won't get busted...

And then it's more.

It's the satin of his lips sliding over mine. It's the grab of his hands, pulling my neck and my body into his. And I match it, weaving my hands through his hair and yanking the lapel of his suit to where there's no space between us.

The moan that escapes our throats when our tongues touch. It's tentative at first, searching for more until we're both taking the other and giving into this desire and it flames to my sex. He groans into my mouth, tangling with my tongue and my desire puddles in my panties when I feel him grind his hard cock into me.

Oh fuck, he's so big and good at this.

Silas wraps around me like a silk rope and I crave the confinement. I want to wrap my legs around his waist and let him fuck me so hard and deep against these bookshelves; I've wondered about him for so long.

"Good God, Cade." He murmurs into our kiss and I forget everything but his mouth on mine, his body craving mine, his thick cock...

"Ahem." It startles us and I don't know why. "Making yourselves at home?"

Standing on the threshold, Gentry looks half pissed, half aroused. I can see his small pleasure tenting his pants at our show.

"Excuse us." Silas takes over. "We just wanted a little privacy and got carried away, New Year's Eve and all."

"Well, the ball doesn't drop for five minutes but be my guest," Gentry smirks. "Who am I to stop a Van de May man from what he wants?"

"Right now, we want another round of champagne," Silas answers, reaching for my hand and trying to get us out of this.

"By all means." Gentry doesn't move. "It's uncanny, Ms. Bryant, isn't it"—his eyes burn into mine—"how much Mr.

Van de May looks like Redix Dean? Must make this quite titillating for you."

Sweat slicks my palm along with my rage boiling up.

There's a letter opener on Gentry's desk that'll look really good stabbed into his neck... twenty times.

"Thank you. I get that compliment a lot." Silas saves me. "Mr. Dean and I do have some beautiful things in common. But in other ways, we're very different."

Silas uses his height, his status, and his fearless swagger to push our way past Gentry.

Finally, the evil fuck steps aside and lets us pass but not before Silas says, "Redix and I may look alike, Senator, but I assure you, we don't *fuck* alike."

Who that was meant for, I don't know, but I love hearing Silas own it. I'm tired of the comparison too.

Redix is a fire and Silas is a refreshing breeze. Both are needed, but I only want one right now.

Our kiss still tingles on my lips while I'm in a daze and the main living room is packed with society rubbing shoulders. The flatscreen above the fireplace is ticking down to New Year's and so is my heart.

I don't feel guilt. I don't feel shame. I don't belong to anyone, but I want to kiss Silas again.

We don't grab more champagne. Instead, Silas gently grabs my jaw in his hands while the crowd shouts down, "Five! Four!"

And his eyes search mine. "Three! Two!"

And I don't look away. "One!" I need this new year.

His lips land on mine again and the crowd cheers while my body rises to his. The tips of our tongues meet again and minutes don't exist. Painful years and sweet days melt away to his lush kiss swelling my heart even bigger.

Yes, I have a lot of love to give and he wants it. Skating

his hot lips to my ear, he asks, "You ready to go forward, Cade?"

My eyes are still closed and I see it clearly.

I hold Redix with one hand and Silas with another. And fuck you fate and this world with its rules because you've taken enough from me.

I don't have to let go of one man to love another.

"Yes," I answer under a shower of confetti.

14

Don't Sleep (Freestyle) by SKYLR

CADE'S QUIET WHILE I TURN MY TRUCK TOWARD THE mainland.

"Where are we going?"

Of course, she asks.

"I have a little place in Bluffton, a loft I rent from my friend Quincy."

"Damn, Silas. You're an onion with layers to discover."

She makes me laugh.

"It's nothing fancy. I need a place on the mainland and we fixed up the loft above his garage. It's simple but someplace new for *us*." I glance at her. "I figured there're lots of memories at your place."

Nodding her head, she looks out the window and I give her time.

If Cade changes her mind, that's fine. If we just hold each other, I need that too. But my God, if I finally get to touch her, to taste her, to fuck her, damn I'm gonna have to hold myself back.

It's been sweet torture watching Cade from afar but we needed the distance. Her for Redix and whatever's going on between them, and me because of Charlie and Alec.

Yeah, I've fucked other women, but you know it when you're with someone who's going to mean more. I live with my heart open and I felt it the minute I met Cade.

At first, she was about as interested in me as day-old bread. But everything's changing for her and it's pulling us together, no matter her past.

I love that she still loves Redix.

It's one of the things I respect about her. That she doesn't give up on someone. That she believes in the deepest love, one that won't die.

Too many walk away from love over one fight, one mistake, or one tragedy.

Maybe it's because I could never keep the loves I wanted. Even while I loved Alec, I loved Charlie too. To this day, I miss Alec. And if Charlie calls, I'm there. I don't have to fuck Charlie to love her. Though don't get me wrong... I'm dying to, but that'll never happen.

I don't need to claim Cade, or anyone, as "mine" to love them either.

People aren't possessions, they're gifts.

Lose one and you learn that real quick.

The porch light over the door above the garage lights

our way up the stairs. It's dark until I hit a switch and a couple of lamps turn on.

"Home, sweet second home," I pronounce while Cade looks around with a smile.

"Silas, this is nice."

"It's amazing what white paint can do."

The place is simple and what I can afford. A brand new studio apartment with all that's important: a big bed, a new bathroom, a small kitchen, and a chair. I don't need more than this.

I take Cade's hand and pull her to me. "You sure you're ready for this?"

"Yes." Her hands skim over my starched white shirt, teasing down my chest to my belt.

The strap of her dress is spaghetti thin while I play with it. "What do you want tonight?"

Her eyes sparkle. "Everything."

"That's a very long list with me."

"Then start at the top and work your way down."

"Like this?" I kiss her lips and I'm in awe again. They're so full, so soft and I've never kissed a woman with a mouth like hers. It pulls you in and you don't want to leave. I come up for air and kiss her ear next, "Like this," and find my way down her neck while she moans and grinds against me, driving me mad. I fear I gotta go slow with her, I gotta keep my animal instincts leashed.

But I've been staring at her neck for so long. With her short hair, it's exposed and long and all you want to do is sink your teeth into it; in the sexiest way.

"Silas." When she sighs my name, I give her shoulder a gentle bite because my cock is a dog on a chain for her. It wants to be set free. "Do you have condoms?"

"Yes."

I'm glad she asked now because once we start, I won't want to stop. It's short steps into my bathroom while I grab three from the drawer because this *will* be all night. When I turn back her way, she sees my supply in hand and grins.

"How many guests have you had up here?"

"Are you asking how many women I've fucked?"

"And men."

"No men. None other than Alec like I told you. And women? Maybe nine or ten."

She laughs. "That means eighteen or twenty."

Now I laugh with her. "You're telling me I'm the second man for you? What about women?"

"No women, though I'm not opposed." She kicks off her heels. "And men? Maybe fifteen Marines or so."

"Marines?" Fuck, that turns me on. "Nice choice."

"*Smart* choice." Her earrings and bracelet come off next.

"Why smart?" I put my jacket and the condoms on the chair.

"Because I only do..." Something drops her voice and her gaze to the floor like she's suddenly dropped into darkness.

"Cade, what is it?"

"I'm so tired of secrets."

"Then share them with me." I lift her chin and let her see what it meant to me. "Like I shared mine with you."

"Other than Redix and after that night." The pause she gives, it's like she's ashamed of this secret. "I only let men fuck me from behind and I close my eyes almost the whole time."

"Why?"

"Because I have to think about him to come."

"We don't have to do this."

"I want to."

"No. Let me be clear. I'm *not* doing this if you have to close your eyes to be with me." I search hers with mine. "*I'm not him.*"

She unbuttons my shirt while her body rubbing against mine awakens my heart and reminds my cock of how long I've wanted her.

"No, you're not and I need to be free of all that pain. So I want this with *you*, Silas, and I'll watch you the whole time."

Dropping my shirt to the floor, "I need to feel something new," she says, "and I need to feel it with you." My pants drop next while she follows to her knees and my body is a live wire begging for her touch. "And I'm going to start here."

Dragging my boxer briefs down, she stares at how much I want her. At how hungry my cock's been for her for so long. At how I'm fucking throbbing and swollen for her and the time she takes rubbing my thighs while her lips part studying my length, I'm already dripping for her.

She sees it, and with her hands still massaging my legs, her tongue darts out for my first drops. "Oh shit," I groan at the first feel of her mouth.

"What do *you* want, Silas?"

She's the one on her knees but I'm the one worshipping her. "Take your dress off. I wanna watch you naked while you suck my cock."

With a flick, her straps fall off her shoulders along with her sparkly dress to the floor. Underneath, she's only wearing black lace panties and I praise a sight that's teased me for so long. Her breasts. They're perfect. Full and natural and peaked for my eyes and I want to feast on them too.

But first, she teases my tip with wet kisses from those full lips. I'm holding back as she starts licking my shaft, dragging her tongue down to my base and back up to my sensitive crown, and goddamn, I could bang her throat but she beats me to it.

Cade goes from a tease to torture that's heaven while her cheeks hollow and she starts her attack. Sucking my cock like it's water in the desert, she feasts like she's the only one allowed to drink me.

No more holding back. No more past. We want to fuck the hell out of each other and, "Oh fuck, yes," I guide her. But she goes harder, and deeper, and, "Fuck yes, suck my cock," I can't get enough of her raiding mouth.

How spit drips from her plump lips. "Yes, that's it." How light gags hit her throat as she chokes down my cock, blowing my mind too. "You like it, don't you?" And her short hair in my grasp. And her eyes looking up at me. "You like watching me because it's *my* cock fucking your throat now." She's so damn sexy, moaning like she knows it too. "God, Cade, you're sucking my cock so good. So—fucking—dirty like I knew you would be."

I can come in her perfect mouth, but she stops.

Popping her lips off my cock, she offers her gorgeous tits up. "For you," she says. Her hands push them together into a tight cleavage that will be my death; please, and thank you. "You've been watching them and wanting them, haven't you?"

Bending my knees to indulge, "Hell yes, I have," I circle my tip over her nipples while I can't believe this is finally happening. "I've wanted to fuck you for so long."

My cock's slick from her mouth and when I start gliding between the soft skin of her breasts, *shit, this is hot.* "Gimme that cock, Silas." *She's hot.* Sucking my tip when it nears her lips, she's incredible and I'm so damn lucky. "You like fucking my tits, don't you?"

I can't stop worshipping the sight of it. The way she's looking up at me. I'm putty in her hands and so hard for her tits. "Damn, how this looks." My breath is leaving me and I need control. I groan it back before coming all over them. "I gotta stop."

I help her stand. With her heels off, her exquisite body is perfectly matched to mine, and I want to take my time with her.

Tracing over every inch, I discover her every slender curve and perfect pussy. How her legs are sculpted. Her abs are carved. Her arms are strong. She's a goddamn Amazon with full tits and a pussy ruling me.

Her eyes search mine while I memorize her. What she's looking for, staring back at me, I don't know, so I'll give her everything I have.

"Here." I walk us to a full-length mirror I propped against the wall. It's there to make the room look bigger. Now it reflects our sex and gives me a chance to give her this.

"Don't close your eyes." I fall to my knees with my back to the mirror while she's facing it. "Watch how *I'll* be the one making you come tonight."

Lifting her leg over my shoulder, I have to pace myself because I want to dive in. I want to fucking swim in her. Licking and nibbling up her thigh and as she starts shaking, I see how wet she already is, her sweet musk threatening my control. I look up and she's looking at our reflection, then down at me like she's desperate for this.

"Do you want me to watch me, Cade?"

"Yes."

"Then say my name."

Her fingers weave through my hair before she grabs it tight. "Eat my pussy, Silas."

Dipping my tongue in first, I taste what I've craved, what I wondered about for so long and she's more than I imagined.

"Oh God," she moans while I lick and lap through her folds. I'll memorize every part of her, everything that makes her moan because she starts grinding over my face and I'm hungry for more. "God, Silas, yes."

I groan while she leans forward, bracing herself against me because I swear I'll make her come all over my tongue.

My fingers explore where she opens for me and, "Yes, do it," cries from her voice and I drive them in while her clit demands my suck. Her gasps, her groans, her thighs shaking by my cheeks, this woman tastes so damn good. She's glossing my chin while her eyes pore over mine and her pussy fucks my face and fills my heart; *my God, I want her.*

"Yes, Silas, yes!" That's my name and the praise I need while she baptizes my mouth with her cum. I've never tasted a woman drip so sweet, her sex pulsing over my fingers while she does it again. Gripping my head so hard, all I can breathe is her and she's divine as she shakes over my face with another spasm.

After three quick breaths, she meets me on my knees. "Fuck me," she huffs. "Fuck me now," she insists before kissing me, and of all the things I've done, this is new. Tasting her tang on my tongue as it mixes with drops of my salt on hers; *damn, it's hot.*

And the list gets longer of all I want to do with her. Of all I can introduce her to.

She has no idea.

I grab a condom from the chair where I left them. I rip it

open as I tell her, "Get on your knees in front of the mirror. You're gonna watch us fuck."

Rolling the condom on, I relish the sight of her on all fours with a smile. She's two feet from the mirror and the most gorgeous pussy ever bent over for me.

"Fuck." I spread her open. "Let me see you." I can't get enough of the sight. Her ass. Her cunt. Her slick lips. Her wet thighs.

"Like what you see?" she asks with no shame.

"I'm gonna *fuck* all I see." I tongue her ass and she cries out and I'm so tempted to have it, but not now. Teasing her tightest hole with my fingertip instead, it makes her grind back on my hard tip toying with her entrance.

"Who's cock do you want, Cade?" I taunt her reflection, her violet eyes staring back at me barely nudging in.

"I want you to fuck my wet pussy so hard and make me come on *your* thick cock, Silas." Damn, she's getting dirtier and I'm all for it. "Twice," she demands.

"Woman"—I grab her shoulders—"you're gonna watch me fuck you so hard you'll forget *your* name," and I thrust in with a hard grunt. With talk like that, she wants it hard and her, "Oh fuck, yes" confirms it.

I can do this. I can pound her until we see stars and I start to and it feels so fucking good... but then I see her beautiful face in the mirror... at how her violet eyes start closing... and...

She's not just *any* woman and this isn't just *any* fuck.

I want her to forget *more* than her name. I want Cade to forget her pain, her broken heart, at least for a night.

Because she doesn't judge and she always loves and she always fights and she's so damn breathtaking doing it.

"Cade"—I pull her shoulders up—"watch us like this."

We lift up on our knees. We spread them wide so we

can watch while I slowly thrust into her and she slowly meets my ride.

My lips hum over her ear. "Do you see us?" We're stunning. We're captivating and my hand cups her breast while the other slides between her thighs and I feel my cock entering her again and again and "Silas" is all she sighs.

Her hand reaches up to pull my kiss to her neck. Her other reaches around, caressing my hip, telling me our tempo.

It's slow. It's long. I've never seen this and the way she's marveling at our bodies joined, I don't think she has either. "Watch, Cade. Watch me make you come." Her clit, her nipple, they're both in my grasp, and with a gentle pinch, I rattle and tug them until she bucks and trembles in my grasp.

"Oh, God." Her pleasure looks like pain because she lets it take her. She comes so hard, her body quakes but then she's grinding back on me and searching and not stopping.

"You want more?" I grab her hips. "You wanna forget your name?"

"Yes, I want to forget." She drops to all fours again. "Do it." Her eyes meet mine in the reflection. "Do it hard."

Oh, this permission. I'll lose my mind or sell it for free to fuck her like this. Thrusting hard into her, she cries out but I don't fear it. It's what she wants, groaning, arching her spine, and grinding back on me for more. With both hands grabbing her shoulders, I control each brutal plunge of my cock into her pussy, over and over, and *holy fuck*, I'm shaking.

She's watching me. She's watching us and this is it. This is what we need. "I knew you'd be so tight for me." I stare into her eyes. "So damn wet and hot and wanting it." Another slam. After slam. After slam. "I knew you'd need a hard fuck after you looked so damn dirty sucking my cock." Her eyes roll back with a moan.

"Watch," I demand and she opens them. "Don't close your eyes. Watch your pussy get fucked so hard." The gasps that leave her lips; she's loving this. The look in her eyes; I'm addicted. "Watch yourself come with my big cock fucking your hungry pussy."

Damn, her thighs are shaking. Mine are too. And my lips. My whole world is quaking at our fuck. I reach around for her clit, for her the release to see her set free. "Whose pussy is this?"

"Mine," she huffs.

"Is your tight, wet pussy gonna come because it loves getting fucked?" Her clit is so swollen, so ready.

"Yes," she huffs.

"*Yeah, you are.*" I rub it so hard, fucking her so hard that she breaks apart in the reflection. Her eyes fly wide open. Like she's letting go of something inside with her scream while I growl, "What's your name?" and she can't answer.

My cock, my need, my insanity, it's here and my breath can't be any thinner; I can't want any more than this. "What's my name?" With three more thrusts I grab her shoulders so hard and she sighs, "Silas," and I lose it all to her, everything rushing from me, all that I've held back for so long.

"Oh God, Cade." I can't help it. I close my eyes and toss my chin back while my body seizes. While I pray. While I can't believe we're together. Because she feels so damn good, and I'm so thankful, *finally*, for her.

We find our breath and our bodies on the rug. She turns around and I pull her into me.

"Happy New Year, Cade Bryant," I whisper into her hair.

"Happy New Life, Silas Van de May," she whispers into my chest and finds my heart.

I lift her chin. "It's your life, Cade, no one else's."

"I'm starting to believe that now." She pecks my lips before nuzzling into my neck and now... she's starting to get me.

15

"You like it black with no sugar, right?" Karen sets the coffee down in front of me.

How much is she watching me?

Then again, I've been watching her.

She sits right across from me in our AA circle and I notice how she always wears those heels, black leather, and lots of red lipstick. It's a hot look. It certainly dresses up a church.

"Yeah, thanks." I stand up and pull a chair out for her. Though it's a little cold—even I'm wearing a jean jacket—she wanted to sit on the patio of this coffee shop so I held the table for us.

It's fine by me. No one's out here so I won't get spotted. "How do you take your coffee?"

"Lots of cream and sugar." Her smile is permanent. "Coffee's optional."

I ask her about her New Year's, then she talks about her job and a project she's working on. When we get to mine, I tell her I'm waiting to hear if my show gets the green light to film in Georgia this spring. Lorraine should know any day.

I hope it's a yes, so I can stay with my family. If not, I might convince them to move to LA with me; anything to keep Renie and Nicolas safe.

"I gotta admit it's weird." Karen picks at her muffin. "Like you're Redix from my AA meetings but you're also *Redix Dean* and I can't stop staring, I'm sorry." She touches my knee. "I hope that doesn't weird you out."

"Not really." It does. And I don't want to insult her, but her hand on my knee makes it worse. "It's a surreal life, and if it starts feeling normal, you're in trouble. That means you're living in the lens and not in your life."

"What does that mean?"

"You either look at yourself the way you think others do, like through a camera lens, which is all I knew for so damn long, and it's toxic. Or you look at yourself as you really are, and that's what keeps me sober."

"Who are you really?"

It's lightning, the turn of my chin. That question strikes and Cade flashes in my mind. I sip my coffee and I can't answer.

Because I miss her.

And I fear I'll never stop.

"I'm sorry." Thank God, she takes her hand off my knee. "That's too intense for morning coffee."

I shrug. "It's my life."

"And it's been so public. All those videos of you. You were drunk in them weren't you?"

"Every day, for nine years, I was drinking."

"I can't judge. I did crazy shit too. One time, I danced topless on a bar."

That makes me laugh. "Sounds innocent compared to what I did."

It feels good finding the humor with someone who gets it. How when an alcoholic drinks, it owns your actions. We're serious about it in meetings. But if I can't laugh about it too, I'll go crazy.

"Yeah." Her smile is pretty. "You did some pretty fucked up shit, no offense. Like all those women? And those three going down on you with that Blow-Pop?"

"God, it's awful." It makes me wince and laugh at the same time. "It's so damn embarrassing."

"Embarrassing is the strip tease I did drunk in Walmart."

"Embarrassing is getting caught getting a blow job at the Golden Globes."

"Were there ever any men?"

I'm still laughing, "Maybe," she gets me. "I could've fucked the LA Rams and their cheerleaders and not remember a damn thing."

We're rolling. "Well, there's a few Clemson football players I went on my knees for," she admits, "so there you go."

We shoot the shit for another hour but this needs to go slow. I don't know what this is if anything.

"Sorry to cut this short." I stand up and offer her my hand. It's manners. "I got some work I gotta do."

She holds my hand to stand like Cinderella from her carriage and I know she's falling for me. But she's a single mom, and I gave up being an asshole for good, so I'm not taking advantage of her.

I walk her to her car. She twirls my way after she opens her door. "Dinner next time?"

I'm glad she asked because I never would and I need to try. This is the only way to move on from Cade.

"Sure, this Saturday?"

"Sounds good." She's leaning *way* too close to me.

It makes me flinch back and glance into her backseat. "Hey, where's your car seat?"

"Huh?" Her eyes dart that way then she laughs. "Oh." And pauses. "It's gross. My son had an accident so I had to hose it down. It's drying in my garage."

"That's not gross, that's the life of a parent." It's weird. She's never told me. "What's your son's name?"

She stammers, "Chandler."

"Chandler?" I laugh. "Like from *Friends*?"

"Don't make fun of me." She slaps my chest. "I'm a huge fan."

"Obviously." I grin as my phone buzzes in my back pocket and with all the shit that's going on. "Excuse me. I gotta check this."

BEAUFORT COUNTY SHERIFF

It lights up my screen and *oh shit*. "I need to answer this. See ya Saturday." It's polite. I peck her cheek and turn away, answering, "Hello?"

"Hey, Hollywood Motherfucker."

"Hey, Penny." She hates me and it cracks me up. "Everything okay?"

"Sorta," she says. "No new leads or anything, but we're looking. And I got a favor."

"For you, my favorite deputy—anything."

"Such a smooth talker." I know she's laughing. "Listen,

can you do a DNA swab of Nicolas's cheek? Like without upsetting him but if I bring you a kit, you think you can get one?"

"Yeah. Why?"

"Derek lived in New York. He was all over the place actually. Here, there, Virginia. But there are some unsolved cases that match his M.O., using the HGB and all. And his tattoo is described by the victims."

It flashes and I slam my eyes shut, trying to make it stop.

The mudflap girl tattoo on Derek's arm. I see it while he's laughing and punching my ears. Gentry's pinning down my ankles. TJ's yanking down my jeans.

"Redix? You there?"

"Yeah." My hands shake while I turn on my car.

"I'll bring a kit by this afternoon. Is that okay?"

"Yeah."

Razor blades. It's hot, the rip of my flesh. It burns to my ears as they fill with blood from Derek's punches.

"Hey." Penny soothes. "You okay?"

Dismissal was my response for nine years, but not anymore.

"No, I'm not. Talking about Derek brings it back for me too."

She's quiet for a second. "Thank you for sharing that with me. I didn't realize. I'll be more careful in the future."

"I don't need special treatment."

"No, but everyone deserves respect." Another pause. "I'll be by later today."

Our call ends and deep down, I wish it was Cade coming by.

Even if it's business, I want to apologize to her for being so cruel, for taking my anger out on her.

Cade's the safest place for me and when I'm in pain, I

guess deep down I know it. I lash out and she'll still love me. But that's not fair to her. It hurts her and that's the last thing I want.

It's like just when I healed from my own shit, I found out about Renie and I gotta dig so deep to find my peace.

Cade used to be my peace, even just the thought of her made it okay.

I guess I gotta find my own peace now.

It's hard because every time I drive, I feel like someone's following me. For weeks now and the feeling's making me paranoid. Everywhere I go, it's like I'm being watched. Not by media either. It's like I'm doing something wrong. And every time I sleep, I have nightmares. My best times awake are with my family or in my meetings.

I go home and the rest of the day I shop online for furniture. Me and Cade were supposed to do it together, but I need something for guests to sit on.

Nicolas and Renie come in the door and he's wide open when he gets home from school, running all over the house. I swear I'm signing that boy up for track team one day.

I love it. I chase him for hours. Then I make our dinner and Mom gets him a bath and Renie gets him ready for bed. The house is finally quiet again so I knock on Renie's bedroom door.

"Come in," she mutters.

"Got a few minutes?"

She puts her book down, "Maybe," and pats the bed beside her.

"What are you reading?"

"Hot smut."

I plop down beside her. "Save me the book."

I tell her about Derek and the DNA test Penny

dropped off. I ask if she's okay but she isn't fazed by it. She wants to catch his ass too.

"Why isn't Cade handling my case?" Renie drops her nose and the interrogation begins.

"Because we got in a big fight. Two actually and it's not professional if she does."

"Can't y'all work it out? You fussed when you were teenagers but always made up."

"We're not kids anymore."

"No shit. You're adults who should know better. You should work it out."

I play with the tassel on her throw pillow. "It's not that simple."

"Do you still love her?"

"I'll never stop loving her." The tassel tickles my fingers. "But I can't be with her anymore. I'm angry with her about something she did and it makes me want to drink. And I'll die doing that, so I have no choice."

When I put it like that, it sounds so simple. Sure as hell doesn't feel that way.

"You gonna tell me what she did?"

"I can't." That quiets her for not even a minute.

"Can I ask a question?" She settles into her pillow. "What do you love about her?"

My heart suddenly bursts. What *don't* I love about Cade?

Except for that one horrible thing.

"I could always see her big heart. Like how she was everything for everyone else. The tall, pretty girl. The one bullied about it. The Sheriff's daughter. The model. The cop. The one who has to protect victims. She's always taking care of people. But when she's with me and is just Candy Cade..."

Oh fuck. I choke on air. My eyes burn and this pain keeps sneaking up.

"When it was just us..." I stammer, remembering lemon kisses. I swallow down the rocks in my throat instead.

"When she was just my best friend..." I can't help it. I miss her. I miss us. I miss that dream I lived for. A tear falls to the velvet pillow and I don't care. "She was free and happy and fun and those guys took it away from her."

Renie reaches for my hand. "And you."

I can admit it now. "And me."

"Can I make an observation?"

Oh shit, when Renie says that. "Can I stop you?" I laugh and I needed it.

"Y'all are exactly alike."

"Thanks, Captain Obvious."

"I'm serious, Captain Asshole, you are. You're just like Cade. The son who took care of Mom. The brother who watched out for me. The guy who protected Cade. The good-looking man who smiles for every camera."

I wink. "You think I'm good-looking?"

"Shut up." She back-hands my arm. "Lemme finish." I get quiet. "You and Cade are just alike except for one thing."

"What's that?" I adore my sister.

"You ran," she says. "You had to leave to find yourself again and I get that. We all do. Mom missed you and so did I, but we got to talk to you and visit. Cade didn't. And then you dropped back into her life like a bomb. Twice. And she always took you back. She never stopped believing in you. None of us did."

Shit, she's right.

"Hey, look at me, you stubborn turd," she sorta jokes. I look up and we both have teary eyes. "Let Cade go. Let *her* leave this time and find herself. And let her fuck up like you did, a hundred damn times and forgive her and take her back."

"How'd you get so damn smart?"

"Quit joking." She smacks me again. "Did you hear me? Believe in Cade like she did in you and take her back."

"What if she doesn't want me back?"

"Did she ever stop fighting for you?"

"Cade Bryant doesn't stop fighting, period." I like talking about her like this. And all I can see now is her... *with him*. "But she's in love with some perfect man now."

"You're just saying that because you went on a date this morning."

"What?" My spine shoots up. "It wasn't a date. It was coffee with a friend and how the hell do you know about it?"

She rolls her eyes. It's constant around me.

"Because you're dumbass *Redix Dean* and there are pictures all over Instagram. Do you *not* check your hashtag?"

"No." I reach for my phone and type it in and *oh shit*.

Posts and reposts of me and Karen at the coffee shop are everywhere.

How the fuck did that happen?

16

Bad Things by Summer Kennedy

Twice I've spent the day with Silas's parents.

First, it was New Year's Day eating black-eyed peas and collards. Silas and I were still on a post-fuck high and nothing could burst our bubble.

It was supposed to be informal as we sat at his parents' kitchen island that's the size of a king's dining table. Three dozen other "close friends" were there too.

Everyone was kind to me, Silas's mom in particular.

"I donated to your mother's campaign for Sheriff every time," she said. "We need more women in power."

I see where Silas gets his feminism.

But not his dad. He beamed around me, but you could freeze lava with the way he treated Silas.

"I'm sorry he ignores you." I held Silas in bed that night. Sleeping at his loft feels like a new life and I love it. "Can I do anything to help?"

"I wanna see my mom, even if my dad's a dick, so if you'll keep being my eye-candy of a date, that helps."

Silas doesn't take it out on me, but I saw the hurt in his eyes. How they treat me like I'm perfect and redeem Silas from his supposed sin.

It's the opposite.

Silas is all good, all redemption, and all heart, and I'm the one who sinned in the worst way.

The second day we spent with them was the following weekend. We went up to Charleston for a regatta. Silas crewed for his dad but he told me the only thing he barked at him were orders.

I stood shoreside with his mom and she grabbed my hand saying, "Thank you for bringing our son back to us."

"He misses you," I told her. "I think he misses his dad too, but he's not going to be someone he's not."

"I love my son no matter what." Her eyes hid behind sunglasses, but tears were in her voice. "I'm working on my husband, but he needs time. You being here helps."

It pisses me off and hurts Silas. Like it's okay if he dates a woman. But not if he dates a man. Like only half of him is acceptable and that breaks my heart because all of Silas is perfect to me.

Women or men, I love that he's so free with his heart.

My whole life I've lived on guard. Maybe it's because I was always at risk. But every day, in subtle ways, and sometimes Silas outright says it—I'm free too.

I'm not exclusive to him. I belong to no one. I can love who I want, fuck who I want, and he celebrates it.

That helped when I saw those posts of Redix with some woman. I have no right to be jealous. Redix needs someone to help him through all this Renie stuff and if it's not me, then okay.

But *that* woman?

She's wrong for him. One damn picture on my phone shouts it in my ear.

Why can't I shake it? Maybe I *am* a jealous bitch and don't want to admit it.

But that instinct crawls under my skin along with the one I'm culling tonight.

This is my third event with Silas and his parents and it's a doozie. A huge fundraising gala at Festival Hall in Charleston and every power player is here—including Senator Gentry Evans and his lovely wife.

That same lovely wife is fast becoming my friend and I swear I'll do anything for her.

There was finally a light in her eyes as she confessed to me days ago, "I swear I'm a woman on a rampage and I love it. Fuck, Gentry. I know he fucks around so I'll fuck *whoever* I want too."

"Why do you stay with him?"

We were splitting a lemon square and huddled into a private corner of a cafe near her house.

"Because of my dad. He has Alzheimer's and needs full-time care I can't afford. It's thousands a month. My mom died when I was young so it was just me and we didn't have much. I married Gentry right after college and I was so naive I signed a prenup. I have no career experience. No money of my own. So if I divorce Gentry, what'll I do with my dad?"

"I can help you."

"Thank you but"—Stacey grabbed my hand—"your friendship's all I need."

"Speaking of." I had to tell her, not everything, not until I know the scope of it. "Stacey, Gentry's into some shady shit. Like, people are getting hurt. I can't prove it yet, but I worry about you."

She was quiet for a bit, chewing on her lip.

"I sense it. Something's been off with him for years. Like I don't know him anymore. At first, his arrogance was cute. Now, it's terrifying."

We spent an hour talking about all she knows about Gentry's businesses. The property he owns. Habits he has. My mental notes are long and I remember it all.

That's what finds me here. Silas and I stand in the middle of Festival Hall. He's looking delicious in a tux and I rented a white Valentino dress because I'm on the hunt.

Stacey doesn't know the names of the men who pay for Gentry's exclusive golf tours, but she knows a few faces. We suspect some will be here tonight.

And I know if I pull this thread—which men pay for Gentry's "golf tours"—I'll unravel the illegal ring he's running of women, sport, and violence.

"Promise me, Sergeant." Silas sways with me on the dance floor and every time I look into his hazel eyes the world disappears for a second. "Once you're done being a badass tonight, you'll let me show you some fun."

"This *is* fun." His hand rests on my ass cheek and my short dress thrills with the desire brushing between my bare thighs. "And you're a badass too, helping me and all."

"All I'm doing is faking it for my parents when what I really care about is you and helping those missing women."

He twirls me, making me promise him, "I'll do anything for you too," before pulling me back into his arms.

"I know." His nose nuzzles mine. "That's why I'm taking you someplace after this."

"Where?" I rub against him. "What is it? Is it close?"

"Damn, you make interrogations hot." He laughs. "Can you tie me down too?"

"Yes." I'm not kidding.

His lips tickle my ear. "It's a private club. It's a place we can really be free."

Lust rushes to my thong so fast. Of course, Silas knows such places, and damn, kill this cat, I don't care... I'm curious.

"Is it a deal?" He twirls me once more.

"Yes."

I'm beaming at him until my eyes land on Stacey who's trying to get my attention. Standing across the dance floor with Gentry, she's smiling beside a bald man who's toasting Gentry.

The look in her eyes?

That bald man is one of *them*—the exclusive golf tour men.

The rest of the night, I schmooze with Silas and his parents. They introduce us to couples who own everything you touch. All the while, I keep that man in my sights.

He's with his wife. They're working the room too. He hovers like he owns her and her face and French twist are pulled so tight, I swear she's gonna break.

I'm too good at this. I know it when I see a woman who's being hurt.

It takes too long for Baldy and his wife to move toward the exit. I give Silas a signal and we follow.

I need that man's name. If I can investigate him, hopefully, he'll reveal evidence leading to Gentry.

The valets hustle outside, pulling luxury cars up to the curb. All while I can tell Baldy and his wife are in a fight. He's hissing low and she's cowering away. He grabs her arm and yanks her into a threat he whispers in her ear.

That motherfucker.

I know what's next.

Our cars pull up at the same time and I tell Silas, "Call the police then block him in."

It's happening so fast. The couple disappears into their Rolls Royce. Silas jumps in the driver's seat of my car while I rush to the woman's passenger door to witness Baldy grabbing her neck in a painful choke while he's yelling something.

"Excuse me, Ma'am?" I tap on her window. "Ma'am, I'm sorry but I think you dropped something."

He lets go of her and her frightened eyes turn my way. There's nothing in my hand but a scheme to open her door.

"It looks like a diamond earring from your bag." My smile is innocent. My hand on the door handle isn't. All it takes is her one click and I swing it open.

"Come with me." I grab her hand and she's just as compliant with my orders. "It's okay. I got you."

"What the fuck?" The abusive shit shouts. "Eva, get back in here!" He opens his door so fast. "Stupid bitch! Get in the damn car!" He steps around the front of his car while I push her gently toward mine.

"That's my car. Go! Get in there. You'll be safe." She rushes for my passenger door. Silas is at the wheel and ready for the next move.

"You nosy bitch!" Now Baldy targets me. "Who the fuck do you think you are? Leave my wife alone."

"I'm Sergeant Cade Bryant and you assaulted your

wife." I position my feet. "Turn around and put your hands on the car and don't make a scene because they're all watching."

A dozen people stand on the granite steps of the hall's entrance, Silas's parents included. They're all witnesses to this.

He rushes to shove my shoulders with both hands, sneering, "Fuck you" and it's training. It's over ten years of men like this and I don't even think.

I step left while my right hand flies up, cupping his chin and slamming him back while my right foot kicks his ankle out from under him. He falls to the ground in my grasp while I use his shock to flip him on his stomach.

"Stay down," I command, grabbing his wrist and torquing it back. He yelps, he squirms, he tries to fight me but my knee's in his back and the pain in his hand is too much. "Fight me and you'll make it worse." I'm one snap away from breaking it.

And I can't help it. I think of his wife, of so many women.

"See asshole." I squeeze his bones about to break. He screams out while I hiss in his ear, "Fuck with women again and this is what you'll get."

Men in the crowd rush to help me. *That's cute.* I don't need them because this man looks up from the concrete in red-faced pain and he knows he's done for.

It's an hour while the Charleston police get my statement. The man is in cuffs in the back of a patrol car. His wife is safe with a sister who came to pick her up. Witnesses seal his fate and an officer gives me his name.

Claude Olan Turner III.

This bald, rich dick is the sledgehammer I need to knock Gentry's world down.

∞

TELL ME A BLOODY KNEECAP AIN'T SEXY AND I'LL POINT to Cade Bryant and prove you wrong.

She didn't even know she was bleeding until we jumped into her car and I told her.

"Do you still wanna play?" I ask her from the driver's seat, watching her dab her kneecap with a tissue.

"Hell yes." She grins up from her task. "It's only midnight and now I'm *really* in the mood."

"Sugar lips, *every* man got in the mood watching you kick ass tonight."

That amuses her. "Sugar lips?"

"That's what they taste like."

I shift her car into drive but she grabs my arm.

"Wait," she says and I press the brake. "Before we go anywhere, or do anything, I just wanna know." Her hand won't leave my arm. "What are we doing? You and me?"

Putting the car in park, I turn to her. "Do you really *need* to know?"

"Don't you?"

I sift through my mind, searching my heart and all I feel is sure.

"No, I'm kinda happy not knowing what we are."

"But your parents think we're serious. All of South Carolina society thinks we're an item. We've spent every night together for two weeks and you're my dad's close friend. But I don't know what we really are."

Desperation, sadness, insecurity; none of that appears in her violet eyes. It's just pure curiosity shining through and making me smile.

"You just listed what other people think or expect." Damn, she's hot. Like she-can-kick-your-ass-and-you'll-love-it hot. "What do *you* want?"

"I don't want to hurt you. And I want to help you with your family. And I don't want to lose my fishing buddy."

"And *fuck* buddy."

The look she cuts my way is serious. "Silas, you're more than my fuck buddy, I want you to know that."

I'm trying to lighten the mood after a helluva night for her, but she's right. What connects me and Cade is more than sex. Really hot sex. And everyone around us can see it.

But for every true answer I give her, there are many more my questions in my heart.

"I feel like one of those fish that can fly," I confess. "You ever seen 'em? Like they need to swim *and* fly and that's me. I don't want to hurt you either. You're much more than a friend or a fuck to me, but I can't tell you what that means."

"Doesn't that bother you?"

"No. I don't need to know what my next day will be, what the rules are, or what someone expects me to do."

Her eyes challenge me and I hear myself.

"Spoken like a rich white man, I know, but that's not it." I look out the window and try to find a way to say it. "I fell in love with a woman I couldn't have. Then fell in love with a man I couldn't be with and I just learned not to know."

"All I've ever known is knowing." She shrugs. "Knowing that I loved Redix. That I was going to marry him. That I was going to get the men who hurt us. I always had my life planned. And now—"

"And now you're free."

She doesn't reply. Her eyes cast down and she's looking for chains that aren't there anymore.

"Cade." Her eyes lift up. "Let's not know together."

"And then what?"

"And then we'll know it when we feel it." I lean over for her lips and pull her into a kiss. Damn, when I touch her, I'm vacationing in a paradise I know I'll have to leave. "Do you still want to go to that club?"

She sighs over my lips, "yes," and in twenty minutes we're there.

The brick building is nondescript. It's one of the dozens that used to be the Navy Yard by the river. Now businesses are popping up. But I was introduced to this place years ago and come back from time to time.

And of course, the detective asks, "How do you know about this club?"

I clear my throat because, unlike Charlie or Alec, this history isn't romantic.

"A friend of my mom's owns it. She's secretly a dominatrix and hosts private parties every Saturday night."

I drop that bomb and let Cade see through the dust.

"You know that sounds like *Fifty—*"

"I know." I stop her. "Maybe that's where she got the idea but it's not like that. Faye reached out to me after my parents disowned me. Guess she put one and one together, pun intended, and I come sometimes." I laugh. "Another pun intended."

"So you're into BDSM?"

I park the car outside the building. There are a couple dozen parked here. Some I recognize.

"Nah. That's not my kink. A little bondage, yeah. But pain doesn't get me off."

I give her a lot to ponder while I take her hand and lead her to the door where two guards stand.

"You don't have to do anything," I explain before we go in. The guys know me and only ask for our phones. "We can just watch. But get ready. You'll see a lot."

"Silas, I'm not a virgin college reporter." She doesn't need to roll her eyes. Her tone lays me flat. "I did BDSM modeling campaigns, I've been a cop for seven years and I fucked Marines for fun, sometimes two at a time. I'm fine."

And she's not fazed.

The man bound to a St. Andrew's cross, the woman bent over a paddling bench, the two men fucking on a sofa; none of it makes her bat a lash. Not even when Faye comes up to greet us in black latex with nipple clamps on her bare breasts does Cade's hand twitch in mine.

"Long time no see." Faye pecks my cheek and offers her hand to Cade. "Mistress Faye at your service, if you like."

"I'm Cade." She shakes her hand like it's a bridal shower. "Thanks for having us."

"Oh, Ms. Cade, I haven't had you... yet." Faye winks. "But the night's just starting." She sashays away and I guide Cade to the bar.

"There's no alcohol served. But they're known for their virgin lemon juleps."

"I'm never leaving," Cade announces, accepting her drink with a smile.

Truth is, I can't tell you why I thought this was good for us. I just felt it. I know Cade doesn't believe me about not knowing. That she won't hurt me and I expect nothing from her.

I just like being with her. And I *really* like fucking her.

I know it'll drop my heart like an atom bomb. If Cade's the right one for me, it's gonna hit me in a moment that will define the rest of my life.

For now, I want her to have this.

She's everything for everyone else.

What'll she look like if she only thinks about herself? In a huge room with people seeking what they desire with no shame too?

"Let's sit down." I lead her to my favorite sofa. It's purple velvet and gives us a great view of the room.

"What do you like doing here?"

Her question is for me but her eyes scan the room. There's a group on the stage to our left, and couples, and triples with singles mingling about.

"I like watching." I gesture to the two men. "I like fucking." The couple by the bar also demonstrates. "I like being watched."

We sit, sipping our drinks and holding hands while the sounds of sex and music fill our ears. I kiss her cheek. "Do you see anything you like?"

"I don't know what I like yet," she says as she stands up. "But right now I feel overdressed."

She slips her dress off and drapes it neatly over the sofa behind us. The surge in my cock is instant. She stands before me and the room in stiletto heels, a white lace thong, and a matching strapless bra and she's a lighthouse. A beacon of statuesque sex that quickly summons a man and a woman over.

"Care for some company?" The nude woman, a gorgeous redhead with long curls that look aflame doesn't offer introductions. Other than with Mistress Faye, names aren't used here.

Cade glances back at me like she's testing my freedom dictate.

"Please do," I invite the hot couple to join us.

He's wearing a dark beard, a shredded body, and nothing else except a hard-on for Cade. Or me. Or both.

I have to be careful until I know.

The man takes the leather chair beside me and the woman sits on the sofa on the other side of Cade. When her hand reaches out to caress Cade's thigh, Cade turns to my lips for a kiss.

I give her the strongest one I have, my lips and tongue blessing her mouth and whatever she wants. This night is for her. For her to ask questions and not know the answers.

She only needs to know pleasure.

Her lips ghost over mine like she's asking me, like she has to be sure. "You're free," I tell her and she spreads her thighs.

Moaning into my mouth, kissing me with a tongue that's got my cock like granite, I catch glimpses. *I want to see this.*

How the woman unclasps Cade's bra in the front. How she takes Cade's nipple into her mouth and that makes

Cade gasp into mine. Her tongue dances in my mouth, matching the woman's circling her perfect pink peaks arched for all to suck.

I pull my lips away for a second to glance to my right. The man is watching them and his cock is equally enraptured. Then he looks at me and I'm getting more confident.

I could do so much tonight. I've watched men here. I've fucked women here. My kink is the men watching me fuck their women. Not because I want to own, degrade, or shame them.

No, I want to fuck them until they feel such pleasure they scream for more. Until they both know how good it should be and that they're lucky to have it, to have each other.

Because I want it.

I want to find that *one* who's free to love me forever.

"Silas," Cade calls my lips back to hers and I give them, I give it all to her. She mews into my mouth when the woman's hand slides under Cade's thong and I feel drops of cum wet my boxers for the way Cade writhes over the woman's hand.

It's not long.

Not with the woman working Cade's pussy into a smacking lust. Not with Cade glancing away from my kiss to see the man and others watching us. Not with her leg draped over my thigh. She's spread open for all to see and her back arches as she groans into my mouth with her first orgasm.

"Oh God," she cries... and we're just getting started.

18

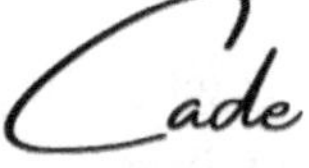

I'M GONE AND I WANT TO DISAPPEAR.

This riptide of lust pulls me under and all I am is wave after wave of demand and desire and only wanting more.

The plush sofa barely creaks to this gorgeous woman moving to kneel between my legs. Like it's a waltz, like they know their next steps, Silas leaves my side and moves to stand behind her.

Stripping off his black jacket, his black tie before his starched white shirt, and then his perfectly tailored pants, his boxer briefs drop last and he's a sight.

The woman turns to watch the spectacle too because holy hell, you *have to.* Look at how his body is pure muscle

140

with deep lines guiding you to the next. Look at how his hair dusts pasts his shoulders. Look at how his cock is full and proud and aimed at me like his eyes.

I look at the man to my right who's enjoying the sight too. A moan grabs my throat at the man jerking off to Silas's hard beauty. From a table by the sofa, Silas grabs a condom and with one knowing look, he asks the woman who smiles and answers yes to his question.

She pulls my thong off while my belly flips and heat burns to my edges while I shift my hips and spread my legs wider for her. Silas watches us as he rolls a condom on and kneels behind the woman.

There is no permission required, only verbal consent and I'm not jealous. I'm not anything but a woman who wants to be sucked and fucked until hell could break loose and I don't give a damn.

For the first time, I'm no one.

I'm not a saint or a sinner or a savior. Her tongue flicks fire through my clit and all I am is moans of "Yes," with my body demanding even more. Lacing my fingers through her silky tresses, I tilt my hips, spreading my thighs wider with my eyes watching Silas sink into her pussy with a grunt.

I love his primal grunts.

Blood thumps through every part of me. The pulse of it matches the drum of Silas's cock into this woman while he grabs her hips and makes her mouth thrust into my pussy with each luscious pound of his hips.

Oh fuck, this is heaven.

This isn't wrong and it's everything right and I don't need to know a damn thing but that I'm going to come. Her expert fingers dip inside me and I'm dripping for more. With a hard flutter of her tongue over my nub and Silas's jaw dropped at the sight of me and this woman, I'm flying.

My back bows while my arms flail like wings and I cry out over the music. The lights twinkling on the dark ceiling blur my vision and my breath wants to climb up the walls but I grab it down with a loud groan.

She doesn't stop. And Silas leans over her, his chest to her back. He's tall enough to reach my wet pussy too and take his own taste while his hips still thrust into the woman's backside.

"She tastes so sweet, doesn't she?" he asks her between the licks they alternate, and they grin, and why haven't I done this before?

Drips of my awe wet my ass cheeks and the sofa beneath me.

Another couple has gathered to watch and let them. Let them see how Silas sucks my clit, and pulls away for the woman to curl into my taste and back and forth and my thighs start to shake.

"Do it." Silas rises up. "Come." He grabs her hips and starts thrusting because she's moaning into my pussy and right there with me. "Fucking come so hard," he growls and she does, gasping into my sex. I thrash against her mouth and we both ride this long wave to shore.

Silas helps her up to the sofa beside me. She flops back to watch because he's standing up. *Because he's not done.* Ripping that condom off, he discards it and grabs another and the man in the chair is still jerking off.

The gaze in his eyes at Silas is like he's craving a masterpiece. A work of art that you come back to see time and again and I will too. I need to come again.

I've never been with a woman and having my pussy expertly eaten is a welcome gift but I need cock. *Now.* And having that thought. Having that one shameless demand and satisfying it.

Hell yes, I'm free.

The white leather ottoman behind Silas is big enough for him to lie on. Taking my hand, he pulls me to him. I playfully push him down while I straddle him. He secures a fresh condom on and I don't hesitate once he's done. I need sex like water. Sliding down his length, he grabs my hips and we go.

Watching only me, his eyes won't leave mine staring down at him. My hands brace on his steel pecs and we're aware of the new couple watching us. Of the woman going down on her knees to our new voyeur. Of our previous companion touching herself to our show. Of her companion who's sitting beside her now, his eyes rapt and seeking his pumping finish to ours.

But it's nothing to the trust I feel. To the praise I want to give Silas. To the pleasure I feel as he shares this with me.

We don't know what we are together, and we don't need to.

All I see are his eyes watching mine. All I know is his warm hand reaching for my breast, palming its weight and teasing my nipple. All I feel is that pleasure and his cock filling me, his base hitting my clit, and his hips matching my ride.

All I want is the freedom he delivers.

His other hand grips my hip hard and he wants this; my hard grind and roll over his shaft as he groans loud for all to hear.

"Fuck yes," and I know he wants to say my name. "Show them how you fucking ride my cock." I want to cry his name too but I can't so it's just me. "Fucking take me," he roars. "Take what you want and let them watch you do it."

It's what I ask myself. What I need to know. What I need to let go of now and trust I'll feel it again.

What do I want?

Only this storm in my body. It's raging in my heart. It needs to break across the rocks of so many painful years and be gone forever. I throw my body into this, desperately needing to let it all go.

"You love this, don't you?" He's taunting me. The woman on the sofa fingering herself comes to our fuck. "You love them watching you get fucked." The man to my right comes in the mouth of a woman on her knees, both of them enjoying our show.

"Yes." I can do this. I need this and I won't stop until I have it.

Silas sees I'm suspended above him, above my cliff. "Who's pussy loves this cock?" Oh God, I know our audience wants me to say it's his. "Who's pussy is this?" The bearded man on the sofa who wants Silas comes to his taunts. He comes because he wants to be me, fucking Silas's hard, luscious cock. Silas sees the man come and groans because he's ready too. "Who's pussy is gonna come so hard?"

I jump. "Mine." I crash, my hands grabbing his shoulders, my chin dropping to the shudders breaking across my body. "Mine." It shakes my lips, quaking my thighs. "Mine." That truth pours from my depths along with my cum down his shaft.

"Fuck, yes!" He thrusts into me and my answer. "Yes!" He opens his throat, his ribs seizing with gasps while I feel him pulsing inside me with groans of "Oh God," as my name threatens to escape his lips.

The room, the audience, the world, and my heartbreak,

they disappear while I take Silas's kiss. His arms wrap around me, pulling me deeper into him, and I feel new.

I am.

And in this void of a place I've never known. I'm happy. I'm free...

And suddenly I think of him. *Redix.* And he's here with me. He'll always be and I hold back my cry into Silas's kiss because this isn't our end.

This is our beginning.

19

Nothing Compares by The Weeknd

My foot bounces when I'm nervous. It's a new habit for my sober body that doesn't know what to do.

My heart feels wrong. But my head says it's right. And for so long I did everything wrong.

So this. I can make myself do this.

I can sit across from Karen at this romantic Italian restaurant. I can order a seltzer while everyone else drinks wine. I can make polite conversation and order the veal piccata she wants. And I can smile while my armpits sweat.

Because I don't belong here.

"I'm sorry."

I've said it twice already but I can't let it go. It's been two weeks since some tourist took that picture of me and Karen at the coffee shop and the poor woman has been hounded.

"I'm fine." Her red nails bat my apology away. "It's not that bad. My friends are jealous and my neighbors gawk and I feel like JLo and Ben so I'm not complaining."

Ben fucking hates this shit too, especially when his kids are targeted, but I hold my tongue. I don't have it as bad as him, so one coffee chat posted ain't the end of the world.

"Besides," she says, "they all want to know if we're dating, so I guess we officially are."

We are?

That's news to me. I sip my seltzer and let it slide. If one coffee and one dinner make two a couple, then who am I to debate it?

There's a mountain of shit I don't know about dating like a normal person.

And there's a mountain of pain I feel because I don't want to.

I know what I want. I just don't know if I'm strong enough to have it again.

For the rest of my life, I see myself with Cade. Married to her. Our kids run around the house and jump into the pool. I strum a guitar on the sofa while she sits on the other end eating candy. She drops ice cream on her chin and I wipe it away with a napkin.

That's what I want.

But what if a year into that, I think about what she did and it taunts me and I pop open a beer without thinking? Or we get in another fight about it because she won't admit it and I flood this secret between us with Absolut instead?

"Ahem." I fold the napkin in my lap and try to clear the awkwardness from the air. "Who watches Chandler while you're away?"

"Um." She pushes salad around her plate. "My friend Jennifer. She's available all the time."

"My sister went through a phase with my nephew when he'd melt down anytime she left him. Nowadays, that boy is on me like a bur in fur. I think he likes having a man around too."

"Where's his dad?"

That question sets off fireworks, ones I can ignore as easily and I reach for a sip of soda.

You mean the man who attacked me and raped my sister? That dad?

Damn, I'm sitting on thumbtacks. I don't know how to talk to Karen.

Shouldn't this be easy? Shouldn't I be excited?

I'm not. I'm nervous as hell in this dimly lit restaurant that's full of couples in love when all I want to do is beg for my love back.

"His dad was never around." I force myself to answer. "That's for the best, trust me."

Don't think about it. Don't think about it.

"Same goes. Once my ex found out I was pregnant, it was SEE YA! Such a jerk. It was all perfect until I got pregnant."

"Weren't you drinking though? Couldn't have been that perfect."

"Oh, uh. Yeah. No. I was drinking and it was bad and then I found out I was pregnant and then he left."

"Getting sober while pregnant must've been hell."

Hell would've been a spa vacation compared to the detoxes I've known. I get so sick, it's inhuman. It's why I didn't want Cade around. No one wants an audience for that. And by the time I felt better, I felt shame.

"Yeah, it was," is all she offers.

Fair enough. I get not wanting to talk about it.

"Well butter my biscuit"—a voice I've heard for twenty years sounds over my shoulder—"*look who it is.*"

It's quick, my leap out of the booth. "Mama G." I pull her into a fast hug. "I've missed you."

When I pull back to see her smile... I swallow down my shock.

Her skin doesn't glow and she feels like delicate bones in my arms.

"You feelin' okay?"

"I'm fine," she lies.

I'm about to fall over myself with worry, but Cade's dad walks up and pulls me into a back-slapping hug.

"Hey, Son." His hug is tight and those words shred my heart. Jeff Bryant is the closest I have to a dad. And I miss him and Mama G. *And Cade.* "You're looking fit as an ox."

"Yes, sir." A cough takes the air and I remember. "Oh, uh. Excuse me. Gloria and Jeff Bryant, please meet Karen Brown. Karen, these are..."

So many years. So many memories. Cade and Christmas and our birthdays with her parents. They should be mine too.

"These are my second parents, so to speak."

"Ms. Brown." Mama G has the grace of a queen. "It's very nice to meet you."

A bit of polite small talk volleys between us before Mama G asks, "Will you please excuse us, Ms. Brown? I need to speak with Redix for a spell."

Cade's dad stays at our table, chatting with Karen while I get pulled toward an unoccupied corner.

Mama G doesn't ask. "We need to talk." She commands.

"It's not serious." Getting caught with Karen feels like a betrayal. It's not. But tell that to my guilty heart. "This is only our second date, I swear."

"Son, you're doing nothing wrong. I see what's going on." Her hand grabs mine and her grip is weak, her skin feels like cold silk. "That's why I need to talk with you."

"What's going on?"

"Life. That's what's a-wastin' and I got no time for it. So let me just say it plain—it was me."

"Ma'am?"

"All this"—she flits her hand toward my sad-ass attempt at dating—"because you think Cade did it. She didn't. *I did.*"

My heart bungee jumps from my chest before my logic jerks back, trying to understand what she just said.

"You hear me?" She's losing patience with my shock.

She's talking about TJ and making no sense. How could Mama G pull that off? Honestly? Not as sick as she's been.

"Gentry said it was her." I don't want to believe that piece of shit... but I do.

"Gentry Evans is so dumb, he could throw himself at the ground and miss." Mama G's still a badass, making me laugh. "But we're smart enough not to say anymore."

All I've ever known is a truth so hard from Mama G's mouth she'd make God confess to guilt.

But still. It doesn't add up.

"Did you hear me?"

"Yes, ma'am." I'm a cadet in the Mama G Army and I won't disobey orders.

"You do with that morsel what you wish. Just know this too. There were months I was so mad at Jeff, I couldn't stand to look at him. It took me too long to realize anger is the hot belly of love. It's when you feel nothing that love is gone."

"Yes, ma'am."

"Now... you go be a gentleman and tend to your date."

"Yes, ma'am."

I offer her my arm and escort her back to the man she loves. And I don't want them to leave but they do.

I can't even force myself. My date is over and my mind is spinning. I feel bad for Karen but she has no clue what I just learned.

If I believe it.

Because Mama G doesn't lie. But she does protect the ones she loves. To death, I know she would and Cade is no different.

So what's the truth? And does it matter?

"That was her parents, right?" Karen can't hide her disappointment as we stand closely between our cars in the parking lot. "That woman is the former Sheriff, I recognize her from the news."

"Yeah."

"What about her Dad?"

"He was a cop too but left the job early. Long story."

"Were y'all married? Is that why her dad called you 'son'?"

What Cade's dad means to me. How he saved me that night. And her mom, what she just told me? They're my family no matter who I'm with.

"We weren't married, but our families are close."

"That must make this hard."

Fucking excruciating.

She shuffles on her heels. "Look, if this isn't gonna work."

"I don't know what's gonna work."

I don't want to lie. Her heart looks broken and I don't want to hurt her.

"Then why are you here with me?" She closes the distance between us. "Why did you go out with me again?"

"Because I know I have to try. And you seem so familiar—"

"Then let's try." She moves fast, cutting off my words by putting her lips to mine and pulling my neck down.

It happens so fast. She's kissing me and shock keeps me from pushing her away until I just let her. I let her kiss me because I know how to act through a kiss while other thoughts storm my mind.

What if Cade didn't do it? Do I want her back? Will she even take me back? What about Silas? Why doesn't he fill me with rage? Why do I wonder about him too?

Karen's tongue searches for mine and I try hard and search too, but I feel nothing pressed to her lips. Not my heart. Not my body. Not even my dick responds.

"Karen." I pull away, trying not to hurt her. "I need to figure my shit out. It's only fair to tell you."

"I understand." Her cheeks are flushed but her words are controlled. "We do steps, right? I'm here and we'll do this in steps. As slow as you want. Just one more date."

And because I'm tired of letting people down and breaking their hearts and bombing their lives as my sister said.

"Okay," I agree.

Because this feels like a current pulling me down the river when all I want to do is sink into dreams of Cade.

20

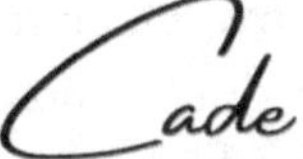

"Leave." I gently nudge Penny toward her minivan. "Go get a box of chocolates and five screaming orgasms."

"Five? Two would be a win for me, but rub it in Ms. I Went To A Sex Club And Had A Public Threesome."

I don't blush. That memory tingles my body and a not-guilty smile lifts my lips.

I share everything (almost) with Penny and she's been munching popcorn from the sidelines of my adventurous sex life with Silas lately.

"You'll have at least three tonight," I promise her, "with those toys I put in your gift. Happy Valentine's Day."

"Alright, fine." Penny drops into her driver's seat beside the red bag I left her. "I'll be back tomorrow by noon. Please don't let her get off her schedule."

I get to babysit my goddaughter, Nina, while Penny and her husband get a rare night off. More like getting off, I hope for her sake.

"I've got this." I hold Nina and munch her fat cheeks, making her giggle. "We're gonna have a blast. We're going for a walk, and some ice cream, and then it's a gourmet dinner of baby food, and then a late night watching *Bridget Jones*."

Seriously, spending Valentine's with a one-year-old is perfect.

Silas wanted to do something romantic, but I wanted to do something for Penny. Deep down, I've only known Valentine's alone. Not since I was eighteen—when Redix made us a picnic on the beach—did I spend it with someone.

"I'm just a phone call away." Penny lingers with her car window down.

"Leave." I flit her away.

"Text me if you can't get her down for bed."

"Leave." I blow her a kiss. "Or I'll shoot."

Finally, Penny drives away and I load Nina up in her stroller for a long walk.

Our stroll toward Coligny Park relaxes us. Nina's content to chew on a toy and watch cars cruise by. I need the time to clear my head.

Life has felt like a three-ring sex circus. Three Saturdays in a row I've asked Silas to take me back to the club. Each time, we fuck for all to watch. And I know we're a helluva show. Silas's allure attracts eager viewers. We always invite a woman to join us and I descend into an ocean of lust for a night of looking for something, but I can't find it.

Then our weeks are wonderfully mundane. Work. Sleep. We grocery shop together and I click away all night on my laptop searching satellite images and all property records for where the hell Gentry is hiding Pamela and Cam.

I have no proof for warrants. Not enough evidence to search private property, but I feel it. They're so close I can smell them on the breeze if the wind shifts right.

And I'm losing patience.

Not like I had much in the first place.

Everything's so unknown, so uncertain. I have no control. I feel like I'm free-falling.

"What can I get you?" The teenager behind the ice cream counter asks.

"One scoop of chocolate in a cup, please." A tub of lemon sherbet sits beneath my nose and I can't.

I can't taste it without Redix.

Besides, Nina loves chocolate and Penny said it's okay. I stroll us over to a bench and feed her little spoonfuls.

"Nicolas! Slow down!" A commotion races by in a little red jacket and pounding feet follow. "Nicolas! Wait!"

That voice. It's carved into my heart and makes it ache.

Redix runs past me. Scarlett's on his heels. They're chasing after a six-year-old and catch up with him at the front of the ice cream store.

I watch while my pulse whooshes in my ears. Scarlett stands guard while Redix picks Nicolas up and gently admonishes him before kissing his forehead and ordering him a scoop of bubble gum ice cream.

It floods my veins.

Redix looks so natural with the boy in his arms. So

loving and protective. And when they turn to find a place to sit, his eyes land on me and we both grab the breath punched from our lungs.

"Hey." He steps my way.

"Hey." I smile at them.

Scarlett's discreet. She keeps a watchful distance but I see her grin.

"Hey, Cade!" Nicolas bounces up to me with ice cream coating his cheeks. He reaches for Nina's chubby hand. "Who's this?"

"This is Nina. She's my goddaughter."

"May I?" Redix gestures to the end of my bench and I smile so he takes the seat, gazing at Nina. "She's cute like her mom." She does look like Penny.

Nina starts fussing with the audience like she wants out of her stroller.

"Can I feed her?" Nicolas eyes the spoon in my hand.

"Sure." I unbuckle Nina and lift her out but she's attracted to Redix, reaching his way. *Typical.* "She's got a crush."

He sees it too, reaching out to take the squirming toddler. In one fast grab, her sticky chocolate hand grabs a fistful of his hair and we laugh.

Can't blame her.

Nicolas is done with his cone and starts jumping up and down. "I want to feed her!"

"Here." I pass the bowl to Redix and give the spoon to Nicolas. "Use this and Uncle Red will help you."

The sight—a gorgeous man with a baby girl content on his knee while a little boy feeds her ice cream. Yep, my ovaries sing.

"Careful with her." Redix soothes when Nicolas gets too eager. "Take your time."

And that takes me.

To the time Redix was my best friend, making me laugh. To the time he was my boyfriend, sharing my every first. To the ten years he left me. To the months he came back and we were healed. And now to the time we're not together anymore.

I'm slipping farther from his shore when all I want to do is swim back to him.

It's not long till Nicolas gets bored and itches to run.

"I got him." Scarlett clocks it and follows him down the boardwalk where he starts splashing in the park's fountains.

Redix doesn't move. He hands me the spoon and I feed Nina the last bite.

I can't look him in the eye.

What if he knew?

Everything I've done. With Silas. With other women. At a club.

Part of me feels guilty.

More of me misses Redix and oddly wants to tell him. Not to hurt him, but we've shared so much. It doesn't feel right. He should know this part of me too, the one he helped me find first.

How last weekend I found a woman between my legs and Silas in my mouth and I was incoherent with desire.

The only thought I had after my mind blitzed out with a huge orgasm and I adored Silas's kisses was, "*I wish Redix was here too.*"

"I'm thinking of opening a gallery here." He fills the heavy silence. "I've got all these bowls and plates I make. I'm thinking I'll open a place and hire a staff to sell them and we'll donate the money we make to my crisis centers."

"That's a great idea." I can't help but smile and meet his eyes at that. "They'd sell like hotcakes."

"I thought about bringing artists in too." We start talking. Like we always could. "You know, Lowcountry and Gullah artists who sell their baskets and art. I even thought about funding artists' residencies. Paying them to live here and create and teach about the history and art from here."

It burns; my tears that want to fall at his inspiration. He's so happy talking about it. "People would love it." I believe in him. "You could even do art tours out to the islands."

"Yeah!" He takes the baby wipe I hand him and starts carefully cleaning Nina's sticky hands. "I didn't think about that, but that's awesome. We could offer art tours and do festivals and raise awareness about teen mental health at the same time."

This isn't the Redix I knew.

Yes, the wild boy in him wants to start a new business. But the man who's been through hell only wants to help others. And the one who loves himself now wants to do it in a way that celebrates art and life.

This is Redix Dean now.

And I love him even more.

"How you been?" He's watching my eyes. "You keeping Mama G out of trouble?"

That was a joke. And a verbal hug. And why that odd look in his eyes?

"She and Dad have an adventure scheduled every week. They left for Vegas yesterday for a week of shows and gambling. They're living their best life for as long as..."

I shrug, holding back a Hoover Dam of tears as to why and Redix sees my strain.

"Hey, Candy Cade." They're soft. His words. "I'm here if you need to talk. Or not talk and go for a walk instead."

"Thank you," is all I can push over my lips.

Redix loves my parents. You can't rip away a part of your heart and survive. He grew up with me. He's fused into every part I am, making my parents his too.

Nina squirms in his arms and reaches for me.

When Redix passes her back, his hands brush mine, and warmth cascades over my soul.

Is this us now? Just old friends?

His eyes lock on mine while a baby passes between us and, no. We're both in that moment, our last one together, when we made love and wanted to make our own baby.

Why does that feel like forever ago? And why does the wish in his eyes still call to me?

"I like him, Cade. A lot." Redix shocks me, not holding back on his words like he used to. "Silas is a good man, and he takes care of you and I'm happy for you both."

It's sincere. I know him too well and every crease on his beautiful face is telling the truth.

He used to get so jealous at even the thought of another man. Like the Marines I liked to pick up for one-night stands. Redix would fuck me like he wanted to erase them from my body.

But he's not acting like that about Silas.

There's no tension in his muscles. No narrowing of his eyes. They're wide and open and has he really let me go forever?

"Your girlfriend seems nice." But I'm lying. That hurt to say but I do it for him. "I want you to be happy too."

"We do AA together," he shares without a smile. "I guess we're dating but it's not serious. We're not—"

"You don't owe me details."

I can't bear to hear it.

I'm a hypocrite from hell but I don't want to imagine Redix with that woman. It feels wrong.

"Then why do I feel like I do?" he asks, searching my eyes and closing the distance.

Only a baby resting on my shoulder is between us and the heat of him wraps around me like a velvet blanket.

"Why do I feel wrong with her, but right about you and Silas? Why don't I want to punch him, and why do I have to make myself hold her hand, and why do I always hurt without you?"

It's raw. It's real. It's Redix like I've never known him.

His emotions used to overwhelm him. They tortured his big heart while he held his face in smiles or sexy smolders for everyone, acting like he was perfect. On the outside he was. On the inside, only I could see his pain.

Now, he sees it too. He's healthy enough, mature enough to say it with no shame.

"I don't know."

And it's a me I don't recognize either.

I don't have the answers anymore. All the smart-ass comments that usually fly from my mouth are gone.

We're just sitting together in a pile of questions and a love that time can't erase with a baby in my arms and this feels right beside him.

Nicolas's laughter from the fountains fills the air. The ocean in the distance roars deep. My heart thunders in my chest staring up at Redix and his phone is buzzing like a swarm of hornets in his back pocket.

He ignores it.

"Cade, I know." His gaze pierces my soul as only he can. "Mama G told me." God, his lips. I miss them and I want to kiss them... and *what did he just say?*

"What?"

"Mama G told me about TJ."

The buzzing. It's in my brain. It's in his back pocket. It's blowing up my world with what-the-hell-is-going-on?

"Dammit," Redix mutters, reaching for his phone. "Sorry."

"What's wrong?" The way he answers it; it's gotta be his sister or his mom. "What do you mean 'everywhere'?"

His eyebrows pinch. His huge shoulders thunder up and... *something is wrong.*

"Alright. Alright. I'll check." He grabs a breath. "We're on our way home."

"What's wrong?" He hangs up and starts tapping at his phone screen while I have to know. "Was that Renie? Is it Derek? Is she okay?"

"Hang on, Detective," Redix grouches to my questions. "Renie's fine."

Nina's resting on my shoulder while Redix has his nose down, his chest huffing while he reads whatever's on his phone screen.

"Redix, what is it?"

"Holy fuck," he mutters again. "Holy mother of fuck."

He's scaring me. *"What is it?"*

Silently, he offers me his phone while he gazes in shock at the horizon.

I read the screen. It's TMZ. It's a breaking story in black, white, and red with headline reading...

REDIX DEAN DOES IT AGAIN.
THIS TIME WITH HIS GAY LOVER.

My eyes scan fast. Over the grainy, dark image of Redix with another man who's on his knees before him in a club, clearly giving him a blowjob. Over the copy that reads "Exclusive", it goes on to say that an unnamed man reported his phone stolen, only to have these photos archived on it and leaked to unknown sources.

Why am I not surprised? Why am I not shocked that Redix has been with a man, or men also?

Because when he's drunk, it's all impulses and desires owning his actions. The problem has been he does it in public, where he's at risk.

"Hey." I touch his arm. "It's okay. It's nothing to hide."

What he said about TJ and my mom; I don't care. That's done.

It's the look on his face. This is his new hell.

"I won't hide it." He won't look at me. "I've done so much drunk, I'm not surprised. But that man just got outed and that's not okay."

"You can't see who it is." The detective in me thinks fast. "You can barely confirm it's you."

"It is and they'll figure it out. I'm not ashamed of being attracted to a few men before. I'm *ashamed* of how I behaved drunk. Trust me. They'll find out who he is and that's not fair. They can come after me, not him."

Redix being with a man is news to me, but it's the same story. It's what I love about him. How he worries for others, and always wants to protect them.

But he's right.

This is blood in the water to media sharks.

"Do you know who he is?"

"No. I..." He stammers, pausing to process. "I didn't remember it until I saw that picture. Now I sorta do. And one other time, I think. With the same guy at the same club."

"Why now?" My logic won't stop. "Why did this story leak now?"

"Probably because I took Ms. Ryan to the Golden

Globes last month. The press thought it was sweet that I took my childhood friend's mom, and it raised awareness about Pamela's missing person case." A wince hits his cheek. "But they're cynical fucks. I bet some thought Ms. Ryan was my beard or something. They were looking for an angle to fuck me."

"Maybe." It sounds plausible. But it feels off. Still, I assure him, "It'll be alright."

"I'm not worried about me. I've caused enough trouble for everyone." He lifts his chin. "Nicolas!" he shouts and heads turn his way. "We gotta go!"

Scarlett moves, wrapping her hand around the boy's shoulder and escorting him our way.

"I'm here if you need to talk," I say. "If you need anything."

I want to hug him. I want to help him. But he's pulling away too fast.

"Thanks." He grabs Nicolas's backpack. "I gotta get him home before I get spotted out here."

He's not focused on me. Or on being outed. All he cares about is getting his nephew home safe because we both know...

A hellstorm of press is coming his way.

I DON'T KNOW WHAT RICH DICKHEAD IS GONNA BUY this yacht but the owner, Mr. Nash, sure wants to sell this Sea Ray so he can upgrade to a new one.

It took me weeks to get it working again after his son and college buddies ran it aground on a sand bar and fucked the engines up.

That's my job.

Trying to get a lipstick stain off the ivory upholstery on the berth cushion in the cabin is not.

And don't get me started on the used condoms I found *not* thrown away.

The commission is high though. If I can sell this for Mr.

Nash who's too busy doing fuck-knows-what in Palm Springs, I get a big cut. He's sending a potential buyer over today and the payout better be big because it's only February but I'm sweating my balls off trying to get this cabin pristine.

"Hello?"

A deep voice calls from the dock and shit, I need more time, and damn, I left my shirt at the helm.

"Hop aboard," I shout out. *Fucking lipstick.* "I'll be right up."

I'm about to call Cade. She's gotta know the secret to this, but for now, I cover the stain with a pillow.

I catch a glimpse of myself in the cabin's mirror. Sweaty, bare chest. Hair in a messy knot. Marine grease smeared on my shorts. Boat shoes that've seen better days.

Fuck, not the look of a half-a-million-dollar salesman.

It's seven steps up the wooden ladder to the helm and I say, "She's a beauty, isn't she," going for the hard sell anyway before the sight punches my gut.

He's equally shocked.

"Yes." Redix stands on the deck of the stern. "She *is* a real beauty."

Have you ever zapped your finger in an electrical socket by accident?

That's the feeling you get at the first sight of Redix. Then, it's heat firing through your nerves while logic takes a quick break and you get to look like a stunned dumbass in his presence.

How long can we stare at each other while my hands start sweating and I map his eyes combing down my naked chest?

Long enough for me to kiss my commission goodbye.

"You want me to show you around?" Fuck it. I'm

fucking the hell out of his ex-girlfriend and I love her in a way, and I don't hate him so what the hell? "Or do you wanna chop me into chum?"

No, I don't hate Redix.

I feel him burn like a long fuse down my body.

How he's wearing his hair down, faded jeans, flip-flops, a white T-shirt that barely exists, silver rings on his tan fingers, and I'm feeling anything but hate.

"Show me where they keep the knives," he answers and his grin raises a white flag.

For now.

"You're standing on one of the best parts of the boat. That stern has a helluva deck. Lift that lid. There's a grill and a gourmet station under it."

When in doubt, I jump into my job, and honestly, this boat can sell itself.

Redix starts nosing around. I give him a wide berth. Sitting on the bench in the cockpit, I stay out of his way while he starts studying the helm.

"She's got inboard propulsion. A VesselView link system. Automatic engine trim..." and I spew a list of the features while he nods, taking it in.

And damn, his shoulders are wide. The silhouette of the muscles across his back as he studies the helm makes words rattle off my tongue while I have to stop my eyes from studying his perfect ass.

What the fuck? No. What about Cade? No fucking way. He's off-limits.

He follows me down the steps into the cabin without a word. He just uses his eyes, listening as I show him the forward berth, the aft berth, and the flatscreen with a gaming system there. The head, its shower, and teak floors. The sound system and the...

Am I insulting him or boring him?

"You know much about boats?"

"Some." He clicks open a storage cabinet. "Jeff's raised me around them and—" he stops.

He just mentioned Cade's dad.

And his shoulders drop like he stabbed himself in the heart.

I know pain on another man when I see it. He won't even turn around and look at me.

I've met Redix three times now; each one overwhelmed me with a sensation I don't want to admit.

Yeah, I've seen him on screens for a decade, and me like millions am stunned by the sight.

But you don't know a person from a screen.

You know them when they're feet away and in so much pain you can feel it seeping from their pores. The energy around them is heavy with sadness and whatever plagues their soul and you're a total dickface not to want to help.

"What do you want to use a boat for? Fishing?"

Fuck, I don't know how to dig us out of this awkward hole we're sinking into.

It's powerful... but I'm trying.

He turns around. Desperation tenses his eyes. "I want it for my family. To teach my nephew to waterski. To take my mom out looking for dolphins." He plops down on the ivory sofa. "We're kinda prisoners in my house right now."

And I know why.

Anyone who has a device with media does.

A week ago, a story about Redix and some man he was with years ago exploded in the press and I can't imagine his life since.

It's twisting his face. Not with shame. Not anger either.

He looks like he's gone fifty rounds and had the hell

beat out of him, and he's two more punches from falling. Like he's strong as hell and has a lot of pride but he's human.

He can't take anymore.

"Look, man. This boat is perfect for that. I fixed it up myself. You can run like hell in this vessel or you can troll nearby." I won't look away from him. "I made sure it works for both."

Because I know his history with Cade. I know what he did for her. How he sacrificed himself and took the violence from those men who wanted her first.

And I damn well know the guilt she feels about it and I don't know all the details but the agony on his face is heartbreaking. Like he doesn't want to run. Or stay nearby. He wants to drown.

A hard swallow moves down his throat and he stares out of the galley window.

"Thanks. You've done a great job taking care of it. It's a beautiful boat."

He just said much more. About him. About Cade. About the blessing he just gave. You'd think he'd be happy but his eyes are searching for which way to go.

I know the look.

When your heart tells you to do something for someone else, but your soul is dying as you do it. When you love someone and they aren't in your arms. When it hurts to be near them but you'd rather have that pain than nothing at all.

I felt that way about Charlie. She was my everything. I felt that way about Alec. He was my dream.

And I tried and couldn't find a way to be with either of them.

I can't do this. I can't watch him suffer.

"It happened to me."

Who gives a damn that we love the same woman? Doesn't that make us more alike than some dumbass dude I shoot the shit with at a bar?

"I got outed too," I tell him.

He tilts his head and studies me and I don't know what he's thinking. My mind is confused but my body is sure, sweating at his intensity.

Either way, I swear looking at Redix Dean is like gazing at the aurora borealis. Your jaw just drops and you keep talking.

"I was a cadet at The Citadel and got busted with my boyfriend and humiliated by a football coach." I drop onto the sofa across from him. "I got kicked out of college, my parents found out and kicked me out too. I walked out of their big house with what I could throw in a duffel bag in five minutes. That was over six years ago and I don't regret it."

"I'm sorry that happened to you."

"I'm not. They raised me to be an entitled asshole and all I wound up being was entitled to be myself. I love who I love with no apologies."

His elbows rest on his knees and he clasps his hands, his eyes peering up through his dark eyebrows. "Do you love her?"

I mirror him and lean forward too. "Yes, I do. And so do you."

"It's no disrespect, man. I'll never stop loving her."

"I hope that's true." I'm about to leap off a cliff saying this, "Because she misses you too. She doesn't say it, but I see it in her eyes."

The confession. The intimacy. My vulnerable admission that Cade's not "mine"—he deserves it.

With what he survived for her; he's earned it.

And it silences him. Like he's opening the gift I gave him and appreciating the magnitude before he asks, "Does she know what happened to you?"

"Yes. She knows everything about me. I'm an open book. I'm a bisexual man who has a billionaire's last name and all I want is a simple life and true love." His foot is bouncing. "But Cade isn't so open. She's holding back with me and whatever is it, it's killing her inside and I suspect it has to do with you."

"She's done everything for me. Too much actually. And I can't decide how I feel about it."

"You did everything for her too. I got a lot of respect for you, man. It only makes me like you and want to see y'all together."

That shocks him. "You giving her up that easily?" Like it pisses him off too.

"Hell no. She's not mine to give."

"No." He chuckles and I swear it quakes my heart. "She's not anyone's to own. That's what I love about her. You might as well try trapping water in your fist."

Why can't more people do this?

Share what they love about someone instead of feeling like they have to keep the person for themselves. There are too many incredible things about Cade to want to keep them from the world.

I need to see his smile again. "You ever get her started on the right way to hang toilet paper?"

His face lights up and we both say, "Over!"

His big laughter fills the tiny cabin and it moves through us and our eyes keep finding each other.

"Thanks," he says. "I needed that." He throws himself

back on the sofa and gazes up at the skylight. "I'm sorry man, but I'm about to lose my fucking mind. I don't care about that damn story. I've done so much shit drunk, all I worry about is that I never hurt someone. But that guy got outed and apparently, he's a football player, an LA Ram and it's gonna fuck up his career. I got money saved. I don't give a shit about my career. I'm just so damn tired of messing everyone's life up."

"I get it with not outing someone." I kick his foot like we're buddies on the playground. Why? I don't know. "But he was the one sucking your cock in a public club, so he's gotta own that too."

The moment those words slide off my tongue, the vision fills my mind, and my cock responds.

Redix and his cock and me sucking him off.

Shit. Stop it.

He drags his hand over his face and huffs. "I never thought of it that way."

I'm thinking of it that way. And I shouldn't be.

I'm staring at his thighs in a way I shouldn't be. I'm noticing the buttons on his fly and the generous bulge under them in a way I shouldn't be. I'm roaming my eyes across his abs in a way I know I can't. And I wonder about his lips and his tongue when I need to stop.

Not because he's a man.

It's because he's Cade's.

Silence sloshes around us for too long. It lifts his head off the back of the sofa and I catch it.

How I'm not wearing a shirt and he's taking mental pictures. How I'm still leaning his way and suddenly, it's hot as fuck in here. How when he leans forward to mirror me again, he's moving into me, into my space, into my heart and body and he knows it.

I always have to be careful. I can never assume a man is into me.

This world tolerates, hell it encourages men to take women without permission. And the only ones who suffer the consequence are the women who didn't consent.

But even when you just *ask* some men, when they act interested, violence, deadly violence, can be the outcome. That fear keeps so many hidden.

I can't read this wrong and mainly it's only my wish which is so wrong, but something pulls Redix and me together. It's more than attraction. It's more than the perfect woman. It's more than two bodies in a confined space.

I care about him. I *see* him. Fuck, people say we look alike and yes, we do to an eerie degree but it's on the inside. We recognize each other in a way that gives me faith.

"So what do we do next?"

He's asking about it too. It heats my blood with certainty.

And my answer is dangerous. And it would betray Cade, so I draw a breath and say, "You buy a boat today."

He grins. "I've got an appointment to check out a pontoon tomorrow."

"A pontoon? What are you? Seventy?"

He still grins. "I could make it look good."

Desire answers from my veins, "Yes, you would."

It's in his eyes too. "Sold."

"And you're gonna stop blaming yourself because *that doesn't look good on you*. It's bullshit."

"Sold." It's relaxing his face, his wide shoulders too.

"And everything else?" I stand up because I can't breathe. This cabin is getting smaller and this is getting much bigger than I can handle.

"Yeah?" He stands up too.

The rise and fall of his chest is a foot from mine and I swear he's looking at me like I just pulled him from the ocean and put that breath there. Like I saved him and he wants to thank me.

"I don't have the answers, man, but—"

I barely finish before his lips are on mine and his kiss is a supernova. It's a million fucking lights ripping breath from my lungs while his lips are so perfect, aggressive and soft and grabbing at mine. The stubble on his chin scratches against mine and I dare to search for his tongue, and he groans into my mouth when I find it.

What are we doing? What are we doing?

I couldn't fight this current pulling me under if I wanted to because I can feel the hard planes of his body push into mine. His lips moving with mine.

And I don't want to fight it.

"Fuck," he mutters into my mouth and that's what I feel, and what I want to do. And I'm terrified and so damn ready. His hand grabs the back of my head and I match him too. "Fuck," he keeps sighing, coming up for air and we both grab for breath before our lips dive in again, our tongues swimming together and wanting much more *and what the hell are we going to do?*

It's tentative. My hand reaches for his waist, where his jeans meet his cotton shirt and the flex of his body into mine, of his cock urging hard against mine. And everything I want to do with him. Taste from him. Feel from him. My naked chest feels home brushing against his and I moan from forgotten depths and I can't find any reason but one.

"Fuck." He rips his lips from mine and huffs, "We have to stop."

Our foreheads press together because we know why.

We love her... and this is the hottest fucking mess.

We don't say anything. We don't pull away and we don't move forward. The heat of his lips still sears across mine. My hands still touch him and his grip is still in my hair.

"I have to tell her," he says.

"*We* have to tell her." I can never lie to her.

"How?"

"I don't know."

His deep voice pours the question over my heart. "What do you want?"

I lift my forehead to find his eyes. They look as deep as the ocean floor and I drop my heart like an anchor to them. "I want you both."

God, I can see it. Lust demands I imagine it and my heart says it's right, but my mind fears I'm wanting too much.

He shakes his head, stepping back. "I'm not going to hurt her."

"I don't think it will."

"She's going through enough." He rakes through his hair. "I won't risk it."

"I won't risk lying to her. Nobody wins when we keep secrets."

He looks at me like I just spoke a gospel truth he wants to kneel to. It's two long breaths from his lungs before he says, "We do it together."

"Agreed."

"Just give me a little time. There's so much shit with this man after my sister, this fucking story and the damn press and then there's Mama G." The pain hits his face. "We just can't bomb her life. Okay?"

"Okay" because I need the time too.

It wasn't supposed to go this far. It wasn't supposed to

feel this strong.

Yes, I told Cade I was attracted to Redix. She's got to be used to that from women and men because he's the goddamn sun of gravity pulling people to him.

But all I want is Redix *and* to pull Cade into my arms and give her answers I don't have yet.

And what does Redix want?

I see a man with a big heart who's searching, who deserves something real and safe, that won't hurt him anymore because he's fought so hard to survive.

I can't answer that question for him. But I'm willing, no, I *want* to ask it with him, with Cade too. I've always been a rebel heart and this is the hill I'll die on I guess.

It's mindless; my steps up the ladder. We both need air. We both need time. I just kissed Redix Dean and I want much more than that with him and I love Cade Bryant.

I gotta find my steps and my goddamn mind as I grab a fresh breath of air and emerge from the cabin.

Redix is waiting at the bottom of the ladder. I glance back at him and smile before turning my head to glance across the marina's dock.

"Oh shit." I duck down.

"What?" Redix is too loud.

"Quiet." I peek back up over the edge of the helm's window to be sure.

Bald head. Chest like a barrel. Eyes like a shark. I've seen his picture on Cade's laptop. In her police files. I know those eyes and they're searching our way.

"What the fuck, man?" Redix whispers.

"The guy. The one who went after you and your sister. He's got a mudflap girl tattoo, right?"

His nostrils flare. "Yeah."

"He's fifty feet away at the top of the ramp and looking

this way." I jump back down the ladder and secure the hatch closed.

Redix rushes to the cabin window and pulls a curtain aside. "I'm gonna fucking kill him."

"Not if he kills you first." Redix glances back my way as I warn, "He followed you here, dude. Gotta be. I bet he's been following you the whole fucking time."

22

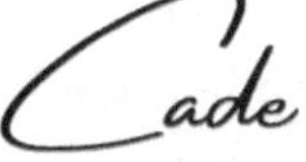

THE LEMON CURD CAKE IS FAMILIAR COMFORT TO ME. But you can stun me with a wet noodle at the dish Stacey Evans is serving from her mouth.

"So he's got a sexy friend. He's on the same painting crew and he's got these tattoo sleeves and I've never been with a man with tattoos and it's so hot."

"So both of them?" I'm opening an investigation into Stacey's XXX-rated sex life. What's gotten into this woman? A hot painter and his best friend apparently. "You slept with both of them? Together?"

Who am I to judge?

"There's no sleeping," she whispers. "No bed either.

We use the formal living room where Gentry entertains his asshole friends." A chunk of blueberry muffin pops into her smiling mouth. "That's what makes it even hotter."

If the world could harness the wrath of a woman pissed off, all its problems would be solved. There's enough of us getting so damn pissed, watch out.

Until then, we deserve to fuck along the way given how the world has fucked so many of us so far.

And Stacey Evans is leading by example.

"Just don't get caught," I beg her. "I want you to be happy, but I worry what Gentry will do if he finds out."

Stacey shrugs. Like her heart's been lonely for so long. Like Gentry's so cruel, any kindness from others overwhelms her. It's obvious; she's so desperate for the touch of another person she's willing to risk all to get it.

"I'm serious." I touch her hand. "He'll kick your dad out of that facility for sure, but what will Gentry do to *you*? He's far more evil than you imagine."

I can't tell Stacey everything.

How I'm working with the FBI on this case. Arresting Claude Olan Turner III at that fundraising gala in Charleston for assaulting his wife was my lucky break.

Claude Turner's ownership of a fleet of tour buses was the thread I needed to pull. I found an FBI agent willing to dig into how they're connected to Gentry's exclusive tours. The open case on Cam Le's disappearance was enough for the agent to start her own cyber investigation.

Because if you can't catch a man red-handed, catch him with green in it. With the money he exchanges for his crimes.

It's not a blood-pumping action scene or a hostage scenario.

No, it takes tedious work and time digging through bank

transactions to find the guilty one that'll take someone down.

So I'm sitting on the point of a needle, hoping to bust Gentry the *right* way, the *long* way. And I'm sweating bullets at what his wife is doing in the meantime.

"I'll be fine." Stacey squeezes my hand back. "I'm going through his files for you. I'm looking for some proof because I'm smarter than you know."

"Oh, I *know*. What do they say about blondes? *You're* the dumbass if you believe it."

She laughs before sipping her tea. The corner where we sit in this cafe feels like a retreat from the madness lately. If my mind isn't on someone else's drama, it's on mine.

My mom told Redix about TJ.

That can ruin so many lives: his, his family's, my parents'. They'll all suffer if what I started ever gets out. And what Mama said about her time if it does? That's the worst.

Pamela and Cam are out there somewhere. And Gentry has them.

I can't let my mind dwell on what they have to endure. It'll fill me with such anguish, such rage that'll cloud my logic. I've got to stay focused and find them.

Derek Baucom is lurking on this island.

What is his vendetta against Redix? Is he obsessed with Renie? Does he want his son? Too much evil motivates a man who's hurt the ones I love.

Redix was outed.

Paparazzi are everywhere. He and his family are prisoners in his world. Yeah, it's a rich one, but no one wants to live trapped.

Silas has been so sweet through it all.

The man takes my laptop away after midnight and

makes me forget my troubles. Yes, he enjoys it too. The intensity of his moans is primal when he's inside me. There's no torment in the time we're connected.

And through it all, I feel so damn guilty.

I'm the center of this storm wrecking everyone's lives and I just want to collapse on the sand and beg for a fucking break.

"Hey, enough of my shit." Stacey's witnessing my mental descent. "I worry about you too."

"I'm fine."

"You're full of shit. I'm not holding back with you, missy. Don't start doing it with me."

If she can confess to threesomes she's been having while cheating on her shithead husband, I guess I'll share too.

"I feel so confused, so overwhelmed that I just want to drown, you know? I have no fucking clue what to do with my life but catch evil men. And that sounds all lofty and shit but it isn't. It's all my fault in the first place."

Stacey knows everything but what's not my right to tell. Redix's scar. Redix's maybe rape. That I almost committed pre-meditated murder for him but my parents did it instead.

Yeah, there's a lot of fucking drama swamping my life and I'm sinking.

"So it's *your fault* some men have fucked-up, violent ideas of the world?" She challenges me. "It's your fault they think if they want something, they're entitled to it? It's your fault they want all the power and no damn responsibility when they wield it? It's your fault when they make rules that only serve them?"

Damn, look at the brain on Stacey.

She's smart. As fuck. And pissed. As hell. I love her.

"You know better." She pats my hand. "You're just tired. You've been through a lot for so long and you need a break, and no bullshit, it doesn't look like it's coming yet, but it will."

"Fuck." I throw my chin up. "If I finally get a break, what the hell will that look like?"

"Look. Silas is as fine as a frog hair split four ways and maybe he's the one. Maybe he's the break for you." Her pause weighs a ton. "Or maybe you just need a break from *them*."

That grabs my chin down. "Them?"

"Yes, them. Silas *and* Redix. Girl, I ain't one to talk, but you got a lot of steamy pots on your stove. Maybe it's time you get out of the hot kitchen and give yourself a cool break."

Why she makes so much sense makes me feel dumber than a tree stump.

All I've ever known is loving Redix. Or missing him. Or fighting for him. Or escaping into Silas, hiding in his simple and seductive world because I didn't want to face my own.

Who am I if I don't let a man define me—a lover or an enemy?

I'm about to answer her. I'm about to go down the list of things I want to do alone. Find a porch and sit with a stack of books. Travel. Scuba dive. Do jigsaw puzzles and drink beer. I'm about to start finding some smutty books online like my mama reads when my phone vibrates.

It's Silas... and it's odd. He's busy showing a boat to some wealthy asshole.

"Hey," I answer while Stacey starts clearing our table. "What's up?"

"He's here." Silas sounds out of breath. "Derek Baucom is here at Shelter's Cove, wearing a black T-shirt and khaki cargos. Call it in now."

"Okay." I have a dozen questions, but there's only time for one. "You okay?"

"Yeah, we are. Hurry."

We?

I don't have time. "I'll be right there."

23

∞

"Is she on her way?"

Half of me wants to see her. That'll never stop. The other half of me knows this dread. One I fight to avoid; hurting Cade yet again.

I glare out of the cabin window, watching that fucker Derek plod down the metal ramp of the dock next to the one this yacht is moored in.

Silas stands behind me, watching too.

He's behind me and way too close and I like it.

"Yeah, she's coming. Should we just go out there and jump his ass?"

"No." I've been raised around cops too. "We don't know if he's armed and he'll be long gone by the time we get to him."

Derek's neck cranes, scanning this marina with over four dozen yachts and sailboats in slips. "Besides, if we interfere with Cade's job, she'll shoot us *after* she shoots him."

I'm fighting every instinct to rush that man, to tear Derek limb from limb. I could smash his skull open on a boat cleat and smile while I do it.

And if I didn't have this drama playing out before me, I could turn around and kiss Silas again. I could kiss him and touch him and, my God, he makes me feel better.

He didn't have to do that. He didn't have to be so kind and show me around the boat. He didn't have to be professional, and a gentleman trying to make me comfortable.

He does have to be good to Cade, or I'd fucking kill him but he doesn't have to be so warm about it.

It surprised me. What he told me about being outed at The Citadel? And how he was kicked out of his parents' house?

That had to have been rough as hell.

Men are supposed to be tough. We're supposed to "be a man" and show no emotion unless it's angry-as-fuck.

I'm supposed to be a possessive, insecure, immature dick and act like I own Cade and beat the shit out of any man who "takes what's mine."

And women are supposed to love men like that?

What fucking bullshit.

Damn, can't people see what a slippery slope that is? It ain't romantic. It's fucking violent and dangerous.

I know.

I barely survived it.

Many people don't.

Those three men thought Cade was theirs because she's so beautiful, because they wanted her, and men are raised "not to take no for an answer."

Cade screamed, "No." I remember barely being able to slur, "No." And those possessive men didn't stop until Cade's dad showed up with a gun.

So fuck you, World, for raising men to be its biggest problem. And thank you to other men who refuse to be.

Silas is one of them, one of the good ones.

His phone rings.

"Yeah," he answers, "it's the Sea Ray. White hard top. Thirty-five footer. Last slip off the third ramp."

That's Cade looking for us.

He ends the call and we say nothing. In the meantime, Derek walks back up the ramp toward the sidewalk in front of the building of condos. He's looking but he can't see me.

Goddamn, I thought my paranoia that someone was following me was from my guilty heart. But I was right. Derek's been following me this whole time.

What does he want?

"Shit, I hope she's careful." Silas watches over my shoulder. "What if you're right? What if he's carrying?"

"She is too." Derek starts walking toward the patio bar, scanning the crowd. "And I can guarantee you she's a better shot than him. That woman was raised with a baby rattle in one hand and 9mm in the other. Trust me."

I'm not worried about Cade. In situations like this, she's fine. It's everything else I worry about.

Derek and his stalk of my sister and nephew. Mama G and what she told me. That damn story getting leaked and an innocent guy whose life may be ruined.

And Silas.

I shouldn't have kissed him.

I could fucking lie and say, "I don't know what came over me," but I do.

I've never met a man like him. Not sober at least.

Yes, he looks like me and that could be weird as hell, but he's different in ways I wish was.

That's what I'm drawn to.

I've only met him a few times but you can smell the freedom he lives with like the salt in the air. He's intoxicating. *Invigorating.*

He makes me want it too.

Because I've never been free. I've been trapped my whole life. Taking care of my family since I was a kid. Smiling for every fucking camera. Being what I had to be for everyone else.

It's more than wanting freedom to be with a man. I've never been scared of those feelings in the past. LA is crawling with hot men and you have no pulse to not notice them.

Close-minded and insecure are not my flaws. With the violence I've survived, I'm all for more love in this world.

I didn't remember the man from the club until that picture triggered my memory. He was funny. He had nice eyes. I bought him drinks and he told me stories of growing up on a farm in Kansas. I remember... some story about a donkey had me rolling.

I don't remember how it happened, but I remember him kneeling before me. I was watching him, my cock almost not responding with all the vodka in my blood, but my heart wanted to. Because that man was hot and kind, and funny and I was damn lucky he was showing me his affection.

Because I needed it.

I went back the next week.

I remember the relief I felt to find him again, that sticks with me. One more night we told stories. One more night I gave him my affection, a sad excuse it must've been in my drunken stupor, but he returned my adoration and that must've been when the picture was taken.

Like a bullet of beauty, Cade charges around the corner of the condo building. There's a swarm of deputies around her. Her hand is on her weapon but she won't draw it in a public place. Deputies cover the marina while she looks across it and I swear she's looking straight into my guilty heart.

It's not guilt about attraction. It's guilt about destruction. Because that's what I've done... *again*.

I kissed Silas without thinking.

It was a feeling, one so strong toward his big heart, and damn, I wish he'd put a shirt on. It was a kiss I'll never forget but it's one that can destroy Cade's delicate world.

I've done that too many times.

She heads this way and Silas unlocks the hatch and pulls it open. He pokes his head out and I hear her say, "Stay down until we've cleared the area."

A police radio cracks. She talks on it while Silas looks back at me. I sit my guilty ass down on the sofa again and wait for this next injury.

It'll hurt me.

But it'll hurt Cade worse.

"They're clearing the condo building and the other vessels." Her voice nears and I prepare myself for when she sees me sitting here.

"Okay." Silas backs down the ladder and almost blocks me from her sight.

"Guess the dickhead buyer bailed on you?" she asks as she turns her back and descends into the cabin.

I can smell her perfume. BOUND. She's wearing our scent again and it wafts with memories I don't deserve.

"No," Silas answers.

"I'm the dickhead," I answer, and you could crack Cade open with a thumbtack at her shock.

"You?"

She looks so badass. Tight black jeans. White tank. Black tactical boots. The woman could do a strip tease in hospital scrubs and make a dead man come.

"Since when do you want a boat?"

"Since that evil shit, Derek and that story have turned my family into prisoners in my house."

That turns her attention whip fast back to where it would go anyway. "They're looking for him. Stand by."

Her radio cracks with updates of deputies clearing locations and finding nothing.

"He followed me here." I clear my mind too. "I think he's been following me for weeks. That means he knows my house. Where I go. Where Nicolas goes to school because I pick him up."

Fuck, that just occurred to me. "Who's covering Nicolas?"

"Scarlett and your sister." Cade watches through the cabin window, her eyes scanning. "They're picking him up from school."

"I want Scarlett in school with him."

"They'll never allow that," Cade answers. "It's disruptive and may scare the kids. Nicolas too." She turns back my way. "Y'all may want to pull him out until we catch Derek."

"Great," I mutter, "another life I get to ruin."

My pity party would sound way more legit if Cade knew how I just fucked up again.

Silas opens the cabin's refrigerator. "Here." He hands Cade and then me bottles of water. Seems this may take a while.

He sits on the edge of the berth cushion. I'm still on the sofa and Cade turns her back to us while she surveils the marina from the cabin window, volleying replies on her radio.

It happens three times. The guilty exchanges between me and Silas.

We needed time.

Fate's an asshole because we don't get it.

Because the cabin is so small Cade starts to smell it's not right. She turns my way and I swear the woman is a microscope. In ten seconds, she can count how many trimmed pubes I have and how many times I've jerked off this week thinking about her.

Eight times, not pubes.

And yes, there's more to confess while she gets the final "all clear" notice on her radio.

"Copy," she replies, turning to us. "Shit. He's gone. But I promise we'll catch him."

She can't hide the frustration in her voice while her eyes frisk my body.

Lifting her nose, her stare bounces. From me. To Silas. From Silas. To me.

My feet sweat at her glare and the NSA needs to hire her because she'd crack any code. I'm about to crack at the look from her violet eyes alone.

"What's going on?" she asks and of course, her eyes land on me because fuck-ups are my thing.

I hear it.

How Silas clears his throat to answer but the words fire from my mouth first because if anything, I owe her honesty.

"I kissed Silas less than an hour ago. I kissed him, and I want to do more with him, and I love you, and I want you back because I'm fucking miserable without you, and I'm a selfish asshole like usual for it all."

Her head jerks back.

"I'm sorry." I stand up and confess, "It's my fault. I shouldn't have done it. I shouldn't have fucked up your world again. Y'all got something good, and I'm the dumbass who made you leave, and I'll regret it until the day I die, but I swear I'm so sorry, and I only want you to be happy."

"Fuck." Her hands fly up. "Fuck, turn off the fire hose and let me breathe."

Shit, it all just shot from my mouth and I close my eyes.

I fucked up. Again.

"It's not his fault." Silas stands up beside me. The triangle we're standing in is so damn ironic. I almost laugh but this isn't funny.

"I want you and I want him too," he says. "And we all just need to talk about it."

I don't speak. Silas doesn't either. We just watch while Cade shakes her head and stares at the skylight.

She has the biggest heart. Will she forgive us?

She has the temper of a viper. Nope, she's gonna kill us.

"I can't believe it," she finally mutters. "Talk about a straw and a camel's back."

This can go so many ways when all I want to do is hold her because I feared this. It's too much for her right now.

Breath rises and falls from her gorgeous body. I watch it through her thin tank. I've kissed those ribs and her pebbled nipples. I've pressed my lips to her breasts so many times that my heart is buried beside hers.

I'm never wrong about her and I wince, preparing myself for what I regret is next.

"I need a break." Her eyes land on Silas first. "I just need to catch my breath after ten years and let everyone take care of themselves because I'm going to crack or kill someone."

She's not kidding, and it hits me harder than Silas will ever know because she's done both.

Wait? Does he know?

I glance at him... he doesn't.

This is about romance for him. About dates and new love and sex and fuck, I'm jealous for the first time.

I don't have that with Cade anymore. We have too much darkness that binds us too.

"You have my blessing," she says. "I mean it." Her eyes lock on mine and... *what's happening?*

"I love you, Redix. I always will and I'll never stop. And you know that." Tears well up behind her lashes and I swallow rocks. "You fought to live knowing that I'll always love you and please, never forget that. But now, you finally love yourself too, so you'll be okay." The certainty in her voice; I feel it. "If you want to be with Silas, please, be happy. You deserve it because being with me threatens that and it makes you wanna drink."

"Cade, I'm stronger now. No one can make me drink but myself."

"I believe you." Tears cling to her jaw, and I can't believe we're doing this in front of Silas but why not? He's part of this. "But for the first time, Redix, this isn't about you. My whole life has been about you and I don't regret a second of it."

She gulps back a sob and fuck me, I want to hug her but I know better. She needs to say this.

"I'm not mad about anything that's happened," she says. "I'm grateful because I've lived for it too. I lived for just the thought of you for so many years and every time you ran, I knew you'd come back.

"But what about me? What if I want to run? Because I do. I want to do it alone and figure out who I am without the ghost of you or the hope of you." She's never looked like this. "I need to let you go."

"Candy Cade, I—" but I stop.

Because the pain in her eyes; it's killing us but stopping her now would only make it worse.

"And I love you too." She turns to Silas. "You're right. I don't know how to name our love. And I cherish it because of that. Because you taught me that."

"I'll never hold you back." Silas sounds so sure with her. "It's your life."

"I know." She wipes her cheek, smiling at him. "You have my blessing. You two are the most incredible men I've been lucky to love and I want this for you.

"Just don't hide anymore, Silas. You say you're free, and you are in private clubs or a bedroom, but would you take Redix to your parents' house as your date? Are you ready to stand in that storm and face them? Because they roll out the red carpet for me; they want *me* to be with you. But *you* deserve that red carpet, that acceptance from them, not me."

I can't believe it as it happens.

As Cade steps toward me and kisses my cheek. *My cheek. Not my lips.* "You can ride bikes and burn pizzas with him too. It's okay." Her whisper ghosts my ear. "Just save the ice cream kisses for our memory."

It's a blur. It's a stun my heart bears witness to as she kisses Silas's cheek next. "Take him fishing and make him smile. He can be your best friend too."

We have no words, only stunned silence as we watch her climb the ladder and leave us standing side by side.

24

TWICE I'VE RUNG THE DOORBELL AND STILL NO answer. I know my parents have ears that work, and they have an entire house staff.

So they're ignoring me.

Should I ring it again? Hell, should I even be here?

I look down at the new brown boat shoes I bought for this... and I have to try.

Cade was right.

It's been two months since I've seen her. Two months since she gave me and Redix her blessing. We were so shocked we didn't know what to do with it.

At first, we sulked and grieved her in our own ways. He went back to his life; I went back to mine.

I miss waking up to her. I miss her empty candy boxes lying around. I miss my fishing buddy.

Then a couple of weeks ago, Redix called to apologize, talking like Cade ending us was his fault.

I don't see it that way.

Cade and I were on borrowed time.

And I know what she means about figuring out who you are when you're not loving someone else. I did it for so long with Charlie, maybe I don't know either. It's not to say that I didn't love Alec too. I did. I still do.

But I've never known an adult minute when I haven't been in love with someone else or searching for it.

Redix called to apologize and it turned into a meeting on the boat the next day. He did buy it, and I spent three hours showing him all its bells and whistles.

It was a long three hours because I wanted to say more, but I didn't. Neither did he. It's like talking about Cade hurt too much.

We ignored her blessing though she meant it. I knew it by the look in her eyes. It's like she wasn't hurt at all by us.

There was something else she needed to heal from.

What Redix and I needed in those hours was painfully obvious too, but we didn't act on it. Attraction cracked between us but we just laughed, especially when he came in too hot with the boat into the slip and about wrecked the damn thing.

That was funny.

And when he yanked his shirt off and jumped in the water because it was hot as hell for April, that was just *hot*. I caressed the throttle knob watching as he climbed aboard dripping wet and I had to turn my head.

I'd be proud to show up with a man like Redix on my arm at any gala. Not because he's Redix Dean and a celebrity folks drool over.

It's because I wish I could be more like him.

Yes, my love is big. I don't believe in limits or rules. But Redix loves deep. Deeper than I've ever known, and there's no doubt he loves Cade more than most people have ever had to prove.

I huff, staring at the haint blue ceiling of my parents' grand front porch.

Because Cade may be gone but her calling bullshit on me still rings in my ears.

I haven't been free.

I've been trapped, needing the one thing I'd really like— my parents' love.

How many minutes pass, I don't know. But I hear honey bees swarming by the edge of the porch. A lawn mower buzzes in the distance. My shoes shuffle over the porch rug with a pineapple on it and...

No one's answering.

At least I tried.

I turn to tread back down the stairs, out to my truck parked in the circular drive. It looks like a jalopy in front of this mansion. I grin; why the fuck not?

"Wait!" The voice turns me back as my mom swings the door open. "Sunshine, please wait." That's what she called me when I was a boy because I was "so happy and bright" she used to say.

It's almost Easter and she's dressed for it in a pink eyelet dress. It's her favorite holiday. Her egg hunts are epic.

"Son, please don't leave." She rushes down the stairs and throws her arms around my neck. "I wanted to answer but he told me not to, but I can't do this anymore, not even for him. I miss you and I just need to see you."

That's my dad she's talking about and for my mother to defy him, well she does it all the time but not about this. I know their marriage. This is a deal-breaker.

"It's okay, Mom," I whisper into her hair. "Y'all may have kicked me out of the house but you're always in my heart."

That makes her cry. Gentle sobs shake her shoulders and I keep her in the hug. I can feel the lithe yoga muscles and relief on her body as she holds me like it's my first day of kindergarten.

"I love you." She strains through her tears. "I love you and whoever you love."

"He's not welcome here. Not without proper company."

The voice booms from the porch and it takes a big inhale to steel my spine.

My dad.

He went from being my hero, my Titan of the sea, to my mentor, to my biggest disappointment.

For a man as wealthy, as powerful and strong as my father is, he sure will break to rules that divide his own family.

"This is my home too, Earl." My mom spins on her heels. "I'll invite the entire county jail here if I want."

"It's alright, Mom."

Shit, this is starting a war when all I wanted was peace.

"No, it's not alright." She stands taller than I've ever seen her. "Six years, Earl, you've kept me from my son with your backward ways. I thought you'd come around. That you'd miss him too. That maybe lightning would strike sense into your thick skull. Or time would. But no. You go on and close your heart and die that way, but I won't."

"June, we're not making a scene in front of the entire house."

My dad stands in pressed pants. Even his golf shirt is ironed. His blond part is perfect. His tan is flawless. His shoes have no marks. It's all about appearances with my dad. What everyone else sees. Some things never change.

"What about your wife?" I ask him. "What about your son?" Because I've had enough. "You always told me a man does for his family, but what are you doing, Dad? You're tearing ours apart and breaking Mom's heart."

Mom wraps her arm around my waist; it's clear she's made her choice.

"My marriage is none of your concern, boy." Damn, my dad can be a real dick. "Leave now or I'll call the authorities."

"For what, Earl?" My mom shouts. "Your mother put his name on this house too. This is his estate. His land."

My dad folds his arms. "Over my dead body."

"If that's how you want it!" My mom snaps back. "Fine. I'll step over any dead body who tries to keep me from my son anymore."

Holy fuck, where's mom been keeping this?

She's firing all shots like she's been holding back and now it's time to storm the beach.

"Mom, just drop it." I don't want this. I don't want to upset her. "You can visit with me anytime you want."

"In that piece of trash by the river your grandma left you?" Dad raises his nose. "No Van de May belongs there."

"Cut the shit, Dad. Grandma *made* you a billionaire. Grandpa died when you were five and she turned the company into an empire. Not you. She was a widow raising a young son and broke all the rules to do it. And maybe that's why you're so angry because you lost your dad and you don't how to be a good one."

I march toward him, across the driveway, and up the stairs. He doesn't flinch, not even when I'm inches above his height.

"And you know what, you stubborn old man?" I want to poke his chest, but I don't. "No matter how you treat me like shit. No matter if you wanna disown me, you can't."

"No man *like you* can run this family."

"A man *like me*? Like I'm an insult? Fuck you, Dad. You're lucky to have me as a son. I can love a man. I can love a woman. I can love whoever the hell I want... because at least I LOVE. And that's more than you're capable of right now. You have an incredible wife, a good son and you're too damn stubborn to fight for us. But hear me out..."

I stare down eyes that match mine. His jaw and brows are mine too. And somewhere deep down, he's still the man who showed me how to tie a rolling hitch knot. He's the one who made the best grilled cheese sandwiches after a rainy day on the water.

"I still love you, Dad." With the clench of my throat, I swallow it down. "*That's* how you can't disown me. *That's* how I'm *THE* Van de May. I'll love you until the day I die. And deep down"—I poke his chest this time—"you still love me too. Maybe one day, you'll be man enough to act like it."

I trod back down the steps.

That's not the talk I wanted to have, but that's the fight we needed. It should've happened years ago.

But I was a kid then. I was too shocked and scared and hurt and mad.

Not anymore.

I know who I am. I don't know who I'll love next, but at least I know *I will.*

"Bye, Mom." I pull her into a hug. She's dried her tears and grabs me back. "Come see me next weekend. Will you?"

"Nothing but death will keep me from it." She throws down that old Southern phrase and it's not hyperbole with her.

When I jump in my truck and turn on the ignition, I want to punch the air triumphantly.

Because Cade's right. I didn't need her by my side to confront my dad or to see my mom again.

There are some things we gotta do on our own.

25

I'M NOT USED TO AIR LIKE THIS. IT'S CRISP AND THIN and feels like tiny icicles awakening my lungs instead of the heavy, steamy air I live in.

Spring in the Appalachian Mountains is nothing like the season on the Lowcountry coast. The six-hour drive cleared my mind too. With each week alone, I'm getting better at it.

Crashing my parents' vacation here helps. But they asked me to. They're renting a mountain chalet for the week, clicking down a list of places to go. They begged me to come this week, so I took it off.

"You need another blanket?" I ask my mama who's

sharing the sofa with me. We have the doors open to the panoramic view and the morning breeze is refreshing but cool.

"Nope." Mama tugs at the afghan covering her legs and mine. "This smutty book is keeping me plenty warm."

My mama and her books. I read them when she's done but I can't handle steamy pages right now. It only turns up my sex drive that's been in fifth gear with thoughts of Redix and Silas. And since I'm on a self-imposed celibate hiatus, I'm not torturing myself.

Mama "hmphs" and that lifts my eyes from the thriller I'm reading.

"I don't get it," she says.

"Get what?"

"When women authors write this about men."

"Write what?"

"Jeff!" Mama shouts out to my dad frying bacon in the kitchen. "Come here, hun."

He pops his head around the corner. "Need more coffee?"

"No," she replies. "Answer me this." Her book falls to her lap and she shimmies her thin body up to start her interrogation. "Do your balls tighten up when you come?"

I spew my coffee. Like legit. It splatters my pages, the afghan, the microsuede sofa, and a bit of Mama.

My dad laughs.

"Mama!" I admonish her. "Ewww!"

But she holds her line of questioning because that's Sheriff Gloria Bryant.

"I'm reading a fuck scene," she explains, "and this author wrote that the man's balls tighten when he comes, but I've never heard of that. Is it true?"

Her tone sounds like she's asking my dad about the migratory patterns of bottlenose dolphins. But no.

"Mama, I don't want to know about Dad's balls."

"Why?" She fires at me, equally unfazed. "You think I don't fuck your dad?" Her grin is too thrilled to say it, "Well let me tell you, *I do*. As much as I can."

"I can't keep up with her." Dad sips his coffee, grinning, after he says, "I'm a lucky man."

"Both y'all need to stop." The vision in my head needs to stop too. "I know y'all fuck, I just don't need a blow-by-blow about it."

Bad choice of words and yep, my Dad picks up the ball (another pun unintended).

"Speaking of blows." Dad dances his eyebrows at my mama. "*It is a Saturday*."

"Ewww! Stop it!" That's a fact I'll never be able to burn from my brain—oral sex Saturday for my parents.

"Oh, lighten up." Mama gently kicks my leg under the blanket. "Like you don't fuck. All those times I caught you and Redix. He ain't quiet, you know. And don't tell me you didn't get a piece of that Silas hunk, cuz if you didn't, let me whomp you upside the head for being a dumbass to miss out on that fine man too."

"You're my mom. You can know about my sex life. But no offense"—I yank at our blanket—"it's not a topic of conversation with my Dad."

"Why?" My dad looks too amused. "I saw how Silas was hot for you the minute y'all met. And do you know how many used tissues you and Redix used to leave behind on my boat? I know all about your sex life. I just don't ask you about it."

Kill me now.

The book in my hand makes the perfect cover for my

flaming red cheeks because all the times Redix turned me into a fucking dessert buffet are firing through my mind. And after those XXX visions, here come the sex club adventures with Silas too.

This sofa needs to be ten feet deeper so I can sink and die in it of embarrassment.

"Well, I need an answer." Mama chimes up. "Do your balls tighten before you come?"

"Can't say that's what I feel," my dad answers, and please no, I can't think of testicles right now. "But ask around. I'm curious too."

I drop my book. "Do NOT start a text poll about balls." Because I know my mama.

"Too late." She's already tapping into a group text on her phone. "My guys will tell me."

All the men who worked for Mama, hold your morning coffee because you ain't gonna believe what she's texting you.

For the next thirty minutes, Mama's phone pings, and she won't stop giggling at the answers and her replies.

I could roll my eyes and leave the room. But never. She's too funny like this. She's too cute and too happy and I just want to weld this memory into my heart.

My dad comes over and laughs at the text messages too before refilling her coffee and giving her a soft kiss on the head. "You need to eat so you can take your pills."

His reminder is gentle. His care is unrelenting.

"I ain't hungry." Mama makes a mule look willing.

"I ain't asking if you're hungry." But Dad can pull her rope anywhere. "I'm telling you to eat some breakfast."

This is the love I've seen and I know I'm lucky to witness it. It pushes tears to my eyes but I blink them away.

I want this kind of love too one day. I want to fuss about

breakfast and talk about balls and embarrass the hell out of my kids.

When we were teens, I was this open with Redix. For a few fleeting months when we were back together as adults, it was this natural too.

I did the same with Silas. I shared everything with him except for the darkest secrets I couldn't reveal.

But I don't have either man now.

And honestly, that's okay.

My soul needed to stop the marathon I'd been running for over ten years. I need this time. My mind needs a break. My body is tired. And my heart can only take so much.

The old me would feel guilty for leaving Redix and Silas like that. Years ago, I would've stayed and taken care of them. I would've loved them, fucked them, and fought for them.

But they're grown men. They can take care of themselves and if they can't, they need to learn how.

And so do I.

This is me taking care of myself. For two months I've been alone and I love it. And maybe that's not long for some, but for me, it's forever.

All I remember is every day waking up either excited to see Redix or missing him. He was my first thought. And when he pushed me away, I fell into Silas's strong arms so fast it wasn't fair to either of us. Yes, he'd been waiting on me... but what do I want?

I come home to my empty condo and there's no void. There's peace. I don't have weekend plans and I love the freedom. I don't check my phone for missed texts or posts on social media because I don't care.

I focus on my job and my cases and I make sure I get a daily run on the beach too.

My world revolves around me for a change. Not forever. Just for now.

Speaking of phones, somewhere in the frenzy of pings from my mama's, I missed one from mine until another gets my attention.

It's Penny and I excuse myself to the deck to answer her call.

"Hey. Everything alright?"

"My water just broke."

"What? Are you okay? Do you need an ambulance?"

"Relax. I'm at the office and it looks like I peed the floor. No biggie."

Penny refused days off before she was due. She said she could be bored waiting at home or at work, so she'd rather have the distraction.

"Well, get your ass to the hospital." I have no patience. I'm six hours away and helpless.

"I am. Hank's on his way. My mom's watching Nina. Bitch, this ain't my first rodeo. Chill out. I gotta update you."

"Okay." I know what about. Derek and Renie's case. Everyone's working on it and Penny's in charge. "What's up?"

"The DNA sample Redix got from Nicolas matches three open rape cases out of New York." Her voice sounds strained. "So when we catch Derek, he's going in for good."

"But we gotta catch him."

That's the problem. Derek Baucom is a slippery eel. I know he's hiding on the water somewhere and slithers onto the island for his stalk. There's just a lot of damn water to search.

"We will." Penny groans. "But you gotta take lead because I'm taking the three months off I've earned."

"Yeah, you are." I wish she could get more maternity leave.

"Just tell me you can handle this without another shouting match with Redix. I know y'all run hot, but someone needs to work with Renie."

"We'll be fine." That's true. I'm not mad at Redix. In fact, I want him to be happy. "Renie and I go way back. I got this."

"*Goooodddd.*" She groans even louder.

"Bitch. Get to the hospital." She's gonna have that baby in the office, I swear.

"I am," she says before she gasps. "Oh, that was a good one." Contraction, she must mean. "By the time you get home, your godson will be here."

"I'm looking forward to it. Love you. Now go!"

I end our call and stare at the misty mountains. I need to get back to work. The thought of leading Renie's case again fires me up. She's like a little sister to me.

And I can handle being around Redix again.

Maybe.

What if he and Silas are a thing now? It's not odd to imagine, just new. All I've known is Redix fucking lots of women when he was drunk, and only me when he was sober.

Thoughts of him with Silas warm my heart, and flame through my sex.

But what if Redix is still with that woman from his AA meetings too? Imagining him with her? I want to shoot something.

I'm such a hypocrite.

Because what if Silas has been going to the sex club alone? As fine as he is, there'd be a long line of fucks waiting for him. That kinda makes me jealous.

No, it makes me sad.

I know he's free about sex and God knows I've enjoyed how he's taught me to be too, but I can just sense it.

Silas wants more. He needs more. He has the biggest heart and it's casting a wide net, hoping to pull love into his life.

Is it me? Is it Redix?

I don't know.

Because no matter if I ever love another man, they'll have to share my heart with Redix.

Maybe that's an asshole admission, but it's true and I'm making peace with it.

"What's rattling in that skull of yours?" Dad appears by my side.

"Everything."

"Me too." He huffs the fresh mountain air. "I can't figure it. What the hell made them open up my case again?"

Dad asks what we have no clue about.

He's been retired for almost twenty years as a former cop. You'd think the reason why—that he got investigated for excessive use of force—would be water under the bridge. Yes, my dad beat the hell out of a man who was sexually abusing his five-year-old daughter. There's no excuse for what my dad did, but I understand it.

That's why he took early retirement. That's why he and Mama divorced. She was disgraced by his outburst and it almost took down her job as Sheriff too.

But now, some reporter's investigating it again, asking around, saying she wants to do a feature on police brutality and corruption.

It's an important issue but why focus on my dad, we don't know.

"Was that the office?" Dad asks.

"Yeah, Penny's in labor so I gotta head back today. We just confirmed DNA matches on Derek Baucom in other cases so when we nail his ass, we got him for good."

Dad nods. "What about Gentry?"

How my dad hates that man too. What he must've seen the night Gentry, TJ, and Derek attacked Redix, I can't imagine.

Actually, I can and I don't know how my dad didn't kill those guys then.

"The FBI is pursuing the cybercrime route with him. His golf tours are a cover for a larger ring, I know it. We just need the proof."

"That can take some time."

"Yeah. But at least the attacks on women stopped, so we have some."

Those attacks stopped because of what me, my dad, and Mama won't say aloud—*we* stopped them by putting TJ at the bottom of the ocean.

Dad's quiet. And I don't need to peep a single word to know exactly where his mind goes next.

"Y'all ever gonna work this out?"

My history is too short, too easy with Silas. I know he's asking about Redix.

"He can't forgive me. The whole TJ thing ripped open a wound he fought to heal. Even though Mama told him it was her, he still blames me. He hasn't said it, but I can see it in his eyes."

"Give him time. He's got a long list of people to forgive, starting with himself."

I shrug. That's true. But I'm not even leading that horse to water anymore. Redix has to drink on his own.

"How does he feel about you and Silas?"

"He likes him." *A lot.* I don't say it.

"I don't blame him. Silas is a helluva man too."

Dad tousles my hair like I'm in the middle of a school-yard conundrum and not almost thirty and in love with two hot men.

"I don't envy you," he says. "But I also don't worry about you anymore." I eye him back. "Since you were a baby, folks went on about how beautiful my daughter was, and that scared the hell out of me, but not anymore."

"Why? Because I'll kill a man now?"

It's a joke. And it's not.

"That, and"—Dad wraps his arm around my shoulder—"love doesn't kill ya, Magnolia Cade. It just makes you feel a lot. All the good and all the bad. And that's a gift to cherish because it's a lot better than feeling nothing at all."

I bury my face in his chest, smelling my childhood in Dad's cologne. He's talking about me. He's talking about him and Mama too.

They spent too many years apart, feeling angry and hurt, and now they're cherishing every day they can get because we all only get so many before they're all gone.

THE SIX-HOUR DRIVE home passes quickly. Thoughts and miles fly by.

I'm going home to an empty place, and I like it. I don't know what will happen, and that makes me happy. I don't know who I'll fuck next and that's fine by me. My shoulders feel ten pounds lighter.

Yep. Zero fucks can cure many things.

It's late afternoon as I pull into the QuickTrip gas station before crossing the bridge back to Hilton Head Island.

I need to fill up on gas and candy.

And my favorite store owner is here too. "Afternoon, Ms. Dubois," I call out as I make a beeline for the candy aisle. "You doing alright?"

"It's spring break." She smacks her gum while I set my goodies down on the counter. "I'm busier than a cat covering crap on a marble floor."

Damn, she's like my mom.

"Glad to hear it." I lay a ten down and don't want the change. "Have a good one," I wish her as I turn toward the glass doors...

And stop dead in my tracks.

The parking lot is full of tourist cars fueling up, but I'd spot him in a hurricane.

Senator Gentry Evans stands by his parked BMW on the edge of the parking lot. His back is toward me but I'd know those damn madras pants anywhere. He's talking to someone and I can't see who but I know if it's in a gas station parking lot, it's criminal for him.

He does official business on the golf course.

It's a few minutes while I stand, munching Lemonheads, waiting to see. I hope it's not Stacey. I hope they're not in a fight because I'm not in the mood to kill him today. I'd rather have pizza tonight.

When he finally steps his pancake ass aside, my ribs yank a breath in so fast.

It's that woman.

The one Redix is "dating" from his AA meeting. She's standing in the parking lot, wearing a leather jacket on April Fool's Day and this ain't a joke.

She's working for Gentry Evans. It's obvious by her nods and cocky smile.

I'd say, "this bitch" but I won't waste my fourth favorite curse word on her.

"Fuck, shit, and damn" go first before an "I knew it" hisses from my soul.

The question is, *what am I gonna do about it?*

Feel It by Michele Morrone

Lorraine went all out on this trailer.

She's gotta be forking over almost ten thousand a week renting this thing for me. It's got a double-length white leather sofa. Ebony wood cabinets. A huge flatscreen on one end. A plush queen-size bed in a room on the other.

All this for moving our production to Georgia.

It's like she owes me something, but I'm the one who's thankful. Shooting closer to home makes my life a lot easier.

This week we're shooting beach exteriors on Tybee

Island, so it's real damn convenient. It's only an hour and a half to drive home.

I flip through my pages for tomorrow while my foot bounces. All this luxury and I'm still nervous.

Lorraine's on her way to meet with me about "an opportunity" she said. Of course, I'll hear her out but I don't want an opportunity that takes me far away. Not now. Not with this shit with Derek and keeping my family safe.

And with Cade gone.

And with Silas here.

I'm nervous as fuck because he's coming by too. He finally found the spare key to the boat I bought, and instead of sending it to me like a normal business transaction, I invited him to come to set.

Because this ain't business.

Every day I think about him. And Cade.

Since I can't have her, why don't I feel guilty about wanting to be with him too?

If there wasn't so much history, this would've been done weeks ago. I've never had these feelings for another man, not like this, and I couldn't have resisted him this long.

But there is Cade.

And I don't feel guilty. I'm waiting on her. I respect her. I love her and miss her.

There are photos on my phone of her that I scroll through every day. There's a framed picture of her on my dresser. I took it when she was last lying beside me in bed. She was giggling because I know her ticklish spot (her right thigh) and damn, she'd stop a war with her laugh.

I get that she needs time. I had my chance, so she deserves hers. And I don't know what that means for our future—if we even have one.

But right now she gave me and Silas her blessing.

And with the way I'm feeling, I have to do this.

It's starting to drive me crazy. Not to drink. But damn I need to fuck. I can do it all day to my fist. Thoughts of Cade will get me there in minutes. But now thoughts of Silas float into my mind too and desire crawls beneath my skin, clawing to get out.

I can imagine how damn good it would feel if I ever get to satisfy this urge.

I don't know if Silas still feels the same way. But I need that boat key. And I need to find out.

Tap. Tap, tap, tap. Tap. The distinct knock on my trailer door isn't the P.A. calling me to set. I'm done for the day. That's Lorraine's knock.

"Come in!" I shout and look up to see her whoosh in with a grin from ear to ear.

"You like the digs?" she asks, admiring her lavish gesture.

"I'm fine in a pop-up tent."

"No, you're not. You're the first on the call sheet and too damn famous and sexy to be sitting out where all the tourists are looking for you."

Our show, *The Band*, shooting here in Georgia has whipped up my fans and it's a constant battle keeping them from trying to sneak on set.

"Want a drink?" I get up and grab her a bottle from my refrigerator. A Cheerwine soda. It's her favorite.

"Thanks." She takes it and a seat.

"You're killing me with the suspense." I drop back onto the sofa. "What's this opportunity? And please tell me it ain't filming in London or Madrid."

"Nope." Three long sips she takes, milking the tension and her next ask. "It's something that might film here. Interested now?"

"Is it your show too?"

"Of course."

I lean back. "Pitch."

"I can't say much. It's too new, but before I waste time with the studio, I want to know if you'll consider it."

I just cock my head. Two shows I've done with Lorraine. Why the hell would I say no to another?

"Daniel Pierce pitched me a series," she says. "Like a *True Detective* but way sexier. He wants to co-star as the straight-laced detective led astray and we need an undercover narc with a heart of gold." She pauses for effect. "We need *you*."

"Sounds intriguing."

"Enough to consider it? We've got his screenplay in the writers' room now. I can get it to you in a month."

"Yeah." This really does interest me. Playing life on the other side of drugs? That could be a fun challenge. "Send it when it's ready."

Tap. Tap.

That's the P.A. knocking.

"Excuse me." I get up to open my door.

"Mr. Dean. We have your guest, Mr. Harper, here to see you."

Who's Mr. Harper?

I look over the P.A.'s shoulder and see Silas standing there like a cat-that-ate-the-canary. I forget he doesn't use his family's name. "Yes, thank you."

I step back, holding the door for Silas. The P.A. hustles away while he climbs up the stairs.

"Hey." His voice is low. His eyes stare deep. They answer my question. *Yes, he still feels it too.*

"Hey," I answer, but I gotta hold back. This is work after all. "Silas Harper meet Lorraine Morris."

I turn to introduce them but they laugh and rush to hug each other like long-lost friends.

"Well, damn this world is small." Lorraine pulls him in close. "And that's fine by me with your fine ass in it."

What the hell?

"Hey, gorgeous." Silas squeezes her back.

"Y'all know each other?"

"Yeah!" Lorraine laughs. "Every time I visit Daniel Pierce and his gorgeous wife Charlie Ravenel on Daufuskie, this hot young man is my personal ferry service."

Silas looks comfortable beside her while Lorraine's eyes bounce from him to me. "Anyone ever tell you y'all look like—"

"Yes," we answer, and all laugh.

"Seems we have mutual friends everywhere." I could explain more to Lorraine but this story could get long and I really want to be alone with him.

His eyes have hooked on mine and my body is a mile ahead of my brain. It's like we last left each other with so much tension, ice is crashing around us to the heat.

"Well, I'll leave y'all to it." And it's like Lorraine can read a room like a menu because she knows my history— good and bad. "Think about my offer," she says before a goodbye peck on my cheek. "And you"—she turns to Silas— "still owe me a night out in Savannah."

"Yes ma'am," he replies, leaning against the long row of kitchen cabinets.

Lorraine leaves and lots of questions remain.

"You know Charlie Ravenel too?" he asks.

"Yeah. She went to high school with me and Cade. Long story. And she worked security detail on Lorraine's show I just did."

Silas's eyebrow shoots up like there's a big story behind what I just said about Charlie.

"How do you know her and Daniel Pierce?" I ask.

"When I was visiting my grandma on Daufuskie for the summers, Charlie would babysit. She was my first love and broken heart."

"So you went from loving Charlie to loving Cade?"

"I'll never stop loving Charlie," he answers. "Don't think I'll stop loving Cade either. Hell, I even love Daniel Pierce." His steps narrow the distance between us and heat scorches to the tips of my ears. "What can I say? I care for a lot of people." My body gnaws with a tension that almost hurts when he's this close. "And I care for you too."

That didn't take any time.

I thought this would be a long talk and a lot of guilt but he came here with the same question in his heart. The same need in his body brushing against mine.

"Here's your key." He drags it from his pocket before setting it on the counter beside me.

"Thanks," I mutter.

We aren't kissing. We aren't talking. He just pulls me by my waist into his body and no words are needed. I get a very hard impression of what he wants next.

He's so close I can feel his breath on my lips while I ask, "Can we do this?"

"She gave us her blessing."

"Do you *want* this?" I'm so sober, but he's flooding my senses to drunk levels.

"You can feel how much I want you."

Yes, I can. His cock is hard, urging against mine under jeans. He's wearing jeans too and there's too much denim between us. The impulse to grab, the urge to be touched seizes my mind.

"Have you been thinking about this?" I lift the hem of his black T-shirt, just enough to skim the flesh above his waistband.

His skin is hard satin and I'm mesmerized by the ridges, by his abs undulating beneath my fingertips.

His lips open to my touch, to my tease across his flesh while he answers, "I think about you all day." The pad of his thumb drags over my bottom lip. "I can't get you out of my mind."

The tip of my tongue licks his thumb and I want more of his flesh in my mouth. I crane my neck and start sucking his thumb, just so I can know the flavor of his skin.

"You've been thinking about me too." He still hasn't kissed me and his thick appendage tastes good in my mouth and I want more while he reaches for my cock, dragging hard down my length. "Haven't you?"

Oh, fuck. I think I moan it too. I pull back from his thumb and go for his lips. Damn, how I've been thinking about him. About how his shadow scrapes against my chin. How his soft lips cushion his hard teeth when his warm tongue calls mine to play.

He tastes like cinnamon and sex. He smells like coconut and fucking on the beach. I press him back against the countertop and we have no space but this. But his mouth taking mine and his hand stroking my cock over my jeans and fuck I want him.

My hands wander under his soft shirt, up his iron stomach, over his rock pecs. It's so different than Cade. She's all firm curves with a velvet cushion over her flesh to devour.

But he's everything steel. Everything rigid and smooth and like me.

"Can I take this off?" I tug at his shirt. I'll never assume with anyone. Woman or man.

"You can take whatever you want," he replies, ripping it off and throwing it to the floor faster than I could.

"Damn." I press my palms down his body and I want to take him. I want to feel him. I don't know this journey across another man's flesh, not that I remember, and I can't believe I'm doing this. Not out of shame. But because I've wanted Silas for months.

Our lips are still meshed. Our tongues are still greedy. Lust makes me want to have him so fast, but I don't know how or if I can.

When I reach for his cock tenting his jeans, he growls back into my kiss and cups my hand and I know I can do *this*. I can stroke him and sense drops of my own pre-cum at the feeling of his hard cock filling my hand.

He answers me, unbuttoning his jeans before dropping his zipper and pushing them down. I break our kiss and gaze down because I have to see him. I've been wondering for so long.

His jeans hang from his thighs. His light grey boxer briefs can't contain his surging cock and the light drops of his cum darkening them. Shit, he's hot. Dragging the thick, white band of his boxers down, I've never touched another man's underwear, pulling it down with both hands to reveal what I never thought I'd crave.

The anticipation. The slow reveal. The deep line of his tan obliques and the line where the sun doesn't see his skin all beckon my search. When I see the top of his trimmed dark blond patch and the base of his wide cock appear, my fucking mouth waters.

I almost hesitate. I know what will spring before me, what will demand my mouth to taste, to lick and I want to revel in this wonder but my desire is too impatient.

Pulling his boxers down his thighs, his cock aims at me,

leaking and swollen, and I let out a primal groan as I wrap my fist around his shaft and greet this new pleasure.

"Oh fuck, yes." He moans and helps me. Wrapping his hand over mine, we pump his cock, his lips reaching for mine again and we're both moaning. We're both seeking this. Wanting this. How I know how to stroke him. How to twist and pump and thrill him until his thighs shake for me is the biggest turn-on. He's hard putty in my hands and I'm going to milk every drop from him. And lick it up too.

"I want to taste you," he says, pulling away from my kiss, and pressing his forehead to mine while stroking my length. "I want to suck your cock and you can take all the pictures you want. It's no secret or shame. I want you, Redix Dean."

"You want my cum in your mouth?" He's swelling in my tight grip; a feeling I never want to let go of. "You want to wrap those scruffy lips around my hard cock and let me fuck your deep throat?"

"Yes." He's pumping our fists faster, his shameless hips meeting our tempo. "I want you to watch me. Watch me suck your cock while you love every fucking minute of it."

His lips are trembling. His thick vein is growing more rigid against my palm and he's going and I'm vicious with my grip because I *will* fucking take him there.

"Show me, Silas." He gasps. "Show me how you want me. How you come thinking about my cock in your mouth. Of my cum shooting down your throat and spilling over your chin." He groans. His eyes drop and watch too, panting and thrusting into my pounding fist. "Let me see your cum," I demand. "I think about it too. I want to watch it shoot from your cock into my fist."

"Oh fuck." He cries out and I get my wish. "Oh fuck." It coats my hand. It splatters across my jeans, his creamy ropes landing on my blue shirt and I squeeze him harder for more. "*Daaaammmn,*" he heaves with another rush, ribbons of his cum decorating my jeans and my cock surging desperate for him underneath.

"Fuck," he huffs and pulls me into another kiss. A deep one. A long one while he recovers his breath and I'm aching for more. More of him. More of his sex. More of his big heart. I want to keep being free with him. I want to *be* like him.

It's more than attraction to his body. It's like pieces of me heal with him, they get stronger with him. Only one other person does this to me.

I lift my hand to my mouth and lick his cum off for him to watch and I've never seen a man look back at me this way. Helpless. Hungry. Humble. And I love the salty taste of him like a new favorite dessert.

"Your turn," he says, reaching up to cup my jaw and start another round of this intimate dance.

He starts unbuttoning my jeans. I want to remember this, gazing down to watch him.

"Is this okay?" he asks.

Like he knows more about me than most. About what I've survived. Why I stayed drunk for so long and why I still have nightmares. His touch is tentative. *He does know.* Cade must've told him.

"Do you think about her too?" I ask while his palm keeps friction against my shaft.

"Yes, I do."

"Do you miss her too?"

"Every day. I think about you both. Is that wrong?"

"It doesn't feel wrong." I reach for my zipper, our hands shuffling to make room for each other. "I think about her, I think about you and I swear I moan and come to you both."

"We'll get her back," he swears before taking me in another kiss and his lips are starting to feel like another home for me. Like another place I'm safe and free and I don't have to fear what he will see when I drop my pants.

I'm about to tell him. To prepare him. The scar on my buttock, it's horrific and he'll at least feel it, if not see it when I do. And I don't know how I feel about that, but I trust him.

"I need to tell—"

Shit, the phone in my back pocket starts buzzing. I ignore it. I start to tell him again but it buzzes more and I worry that's someone outside my trailer door.

"I have to check."

He grins and understands.

But it's not a number from the crew. Or my family.

It's Karen from AA texting me.

Please help me.
I'm staring at a bottle of wine,
a glass I just poured
and I need help. Please

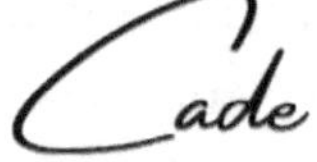

27

Lost on You by LP

IT DOESN'T TASTE THE SAME. THE LONG LICKS I TAKE OF the lemon sherbet ice cream coat my tongue but it's not right.

I made myself come back to this ice cream shop by the park. The one where I had my first kiss. The one where I had my worst night. My dreams were taken here... and I want them back.

But the ice cream tastes too bitter. Without Redix standing in front of me with his devil grin licking the cone too, there's no going back.

I used to want that—the impossible dream of changing that night. Of swapping my place for Redix's and letting those men take me like they wanted to instead of him.

I would've survived it. And I would've killed them the next chance I could.

Yes, it would've changed me and hurt me in ways I *can* imagine.

But this is where Redix and I are different.

He wanted peace afterward. I wanted war.

Now, I don't even want that.

Don't get me wrong. This tiger ain't changing her stripes. No, I'll sink my fangs into any evil man. I'll just take them down a different way this time.

I'll admit I regret how it went down with TJ. Not that he's dead. He had to be stopped. But I hate that I let it possess me. I let him stalk my mind as much as he stalked me. I was equally obsessed, equally out of control for revenge.

But when it comes to Gentry, I got all the time in the world. Because one hasty move on my part and Pamela and Cam can disappear for good. So I'm weaving the perfect rope to wrap around Gentry's skinny neck.

And Derek?

I got one ready for him too. He's wanted in so many cases all he needs to do is stick his neck out and he's done.

But now I got a new itch to scratch.

That woman Redix is dating from his AA meetings. Fuck patience from heaven. I'm pissed as hell. I know what she's up to. I know what she did. Twice.

Redix's heart is too big. He's too kind to see it. He has his AA meetings on Monday mornings but I won't violate that sanctuary for him. I know it helps to keep him alive.

Tossing my half-eaten cone away, I gotta do this. I have

to tell him about her. And I need to update Renie anyway on Derek's case so I can walk my flip-flops into Redix's house and not lose my shit.

I promise.

It's a Wednesday and almost four o'clock. I drive to his home and ring the doorbell. I'm not on duty or in uniform. Nope. I'm calm and smiling and they should be home because school gets out at two o'clock.

Scarlett lets me in. "Well hello, hot stuff." She's incredible. I wish she had more time to hang out but she's working all day guarding Redix's family and sleeping all night for the next one.

"Backatcha." I wink. And no, I'm not wearing this white mini sundress to get Redix's attention.

And I'm lying. A bit.

"Who's home?"

"They're out by the pool." She points to the wall of windows and Renie and Nicolas on the other side.

"Where's he?"

Scarlett shrugs. Keeping tabs on Redix isn't her job. And disclosing her client's personal life could make her lose it.

I walk across the living room and notice the furniture Redix has bought. That *hurts*. We were supposed to pick it out together. We were supposed to do a lot of things together.

"Hey," I call out to Renie when I open the sliding glass door and step onto the pool deck.

"Well, hey yourself." She sits up taller on her lounge chair.

"Hey, Cade!" Nicolas shouts from the diving board.

"Hey, buddy!" I shout back.

He jumps in and swims to the side while I sit beside

Renie and quietly update her on Derek and the other cases in New York.

"I guess when I'm honest with myself," Renie tells me with her eyes glued to Nicolas, "he did it to me too. I never did say 'no' but I never said 'yes' either and he sure didn't ask. I was too drunk and later too devastated to admit it."

"You're not alone, unfortunately," I reply. "It sadly happens like that a lot. You're not to blame. It's the criminal who didn't ask for consent who is."

"I know that now," she says. "Nicolas!" She shouts. "Stop running!"

He's throwing a beach ball in the heated pool and running around the wet edge to the diving board to jump on it.

"But at least I got him." Renie can't help but smile.

Nicolas is a cute boy. He's got her DNA and laughing eyes. He doesn't look a bit like his evil father. No, he looks a lot like Redix did at that age and it melts my heart.

I want to ask her where Redix is. Maybe he's on set, but I don't.

"He didn't come home last night." She reads my mind. "He's never done that before and it scares me. Makes me worry he's drinking again."

"I'm sure he's fine."

Did I want to know that? That Redix stayed out last night. He's not drinking again. I can sense that. But who was he with? Silas, I hope. Not with that woman.

"Nicolas!" He's running again. "That's the last straw, young man. You're in time out."

Renie jumps up like the good mother she is. "You've got five minutes," she tells him. "Sit right there on that chair." She turns back to me. "I gotta get him a dry towel. I'll be right back."

She disappears inside while I smile at Nicolas. His knees are bouncing and goosebumps rise across his skinny shoulders in the cool spring breeze.

"Watcha doing here, Cade?" he asks. "How come you don't come over no more?"

Because I love your uncle so much I sacrificed our future together so he could have one.

"I'm just catching up with your mom," I say. "Sorry, buddy. Sometimes work keeps me busy too."

"Let me show you my new trick!" He jumps up like he already forgot he's in trouble and he's fast.

Running around the edge of the pool again, I shout this time at his wet feed padding across wet pavement, "Nicolas! Stop running, please!"

And it happens so fast. Like we feared it would.

He slips. Falling over the edge as he turns its corner, he smacks into the water after knocking his skull against the concrete edge of the pool.

"Nicolas!" I jump up. Without a thought, I dive in. He's knocked out cold and blood smokes in the water around his tiny head.

I get to him fast and flip him on his back so he can breathe.

"Nicolas!" Renie shouts, running back outside.

"Call nine one one," I tell her, swimming with his tiny body to the pool steps. "He's breathing but call them."

Scarlett is standing behind Renie and already on it.

Damn, if we haven't been here before.

"Is he okay?" Renie rushes to the steps and moves to take him from my arms.

"Careful," I warn her. "Lay the towel down. We need to keep him still in case he broke something."

I heard the smack to his skull and it makes me sick. The blood staining his blond hair is scary too.

"Oh my, God, Nicolas." Renie carefully starts dabbing at the contusion with the edge of the towel.

"He'll be okay." I hope I'm right.

The medic arrives quickly. It's minutes and he's loaded up onto the gurney and into the ambulance.

All the while I can't shake the memory of seeing Redix like that. Of watching his almost lifeless body rushed away in an ambulance.

Renie rides with him. Scarlett and I follow in her car and I try calling Redix. I'm wet and shivering as my call rolls to voicemail. I hate texting this but he leaves me no choice.

> Meet me at the hospital.
> It's Nicolas. He'll be okay.
> But get there ASAP

By the time we arrive and park too, they have Nicolas rushed in for scans while Renie stays by his side in case he wakes up.

It's another hour before he's done. And another hour after that when they find him a room to keep him for observation overnight.

They think he'll be fine and he seems it. Nicolas wakes up and starts talking like nothing happened. He thinks getting his head shaved for stitches is fascinating. He asks for a mirror to see it.

That makes me and Scarlett chuckle from our chairs in the hospital room while his mom looks so relieved by his bedside.

Minutes later, a commotion approaches from the hallway. The smell of him arrives along with the sound of high heels clicking in after him.

"Hey." Redix rushes into the room with his eyes on Nicolas. His shitty girlfriend clicks in behind him. "Hey, buddy. You okay?" Redix gently brushes over Nicolas's shorn head.

"I got stitches! See!" Nicolas turns his head so we can all see them. It's a hard sight on Redix but he forces his smile.

"I see," he says. "You okay?" He reaches for Renie next.

"Yeah," she squeezes him back. "Just scared the mess out of me, but we're fine. They want to keep him overnight just in case."

Redix finally turns his head and clocks me and Scarlett sitting in the corner.

Did he just wince?

"Cade saved him," Renie announces, and I swear she does it to spite his girlfriend.

"It's no biggie," I mutter because if I open my mouth too much, that girlfriend of his is in the perfect place and will look really good with *all* the stitches I wanna give her.

"Thanks," he says to me, and like he just woke up, he remembers who he came in with. And who he spent last night with, it doesn't take a genius to figure that out.

"Um..." Redix makes the introductions and saves me for last. Because how do you introduce me?

"This is the first woman I loved, kissed, lost my virginity to, proposed to, sacrificed myself for, left for ten years, came back and fought to get her back, and almost proposed to again, but then kicked her out and now I told her I want her back and I'm attracted to her sorta ex-boyfriend."

Nope. That takes too long.

"Karen, this is Cade," is all he says.

"Hi," she says. That guilty smile needs to be smacked off her face. "Nice to meet you."

"You sure about that?" I ask her.

Fuck. That just slipped out, I swear.

Scarlett coughs, Renie grins and Nicolas is oblivious while Redix cuts me a look that wants *my* blood.

The interesting thing?

Karen's not even nervous around me. That either makes her a sociopath or a stupid shit. Or both.

It's a long hour while they visit with Nicolas and I get to watch her squirm. Scarlett keeps stifling her smile beside me because she knows the impulse I'm holding back.

I don't have to tell her Karen's on my shit list. Scarlett knows guilt when she smells it too.

"Well, we should let you get some sleep." Redix is wrapping it up. "I'll make sure we have your favorite popsicles when you get home tomorrow, okay?"

It thrills my ovaries how sweet he is with his nephew when he kisses his cheek goodbye. And when he hugs his sister.

I stand up. "I'll walk y'all out."

He looks at me like that's as good of an idea as playing with live electrical wires. In the rain.

But fuck this. I may not make a scene in front of Nicolas but cue the camera for when the three of us are alone.

We don't say anything on the walk down the hall. Or down the elevator. Or out the doors into the parking lot. But Redix looks as comfortable as getting an enema, and Karen holds his hand like that's gonna save her.

It's almost midnight and I ask, "Where'd y'all park?"

Redix hits his car fob and he's parked at the very edge of the lot under a canopy of palmetto trees. He looks at me nervously while I follow them there.

I know he thinks I'm jealous or that he's doing something wrong. I can't watch him suffer anymore because of her.

"Karen"—I step into her cloud of perfume—"you have one minute to tell him the truth or I swear I'll strangle you so hard *it* and your eyes will pop out."

"Cade, stop it!" Redix is sweet to be defending her lack of honor.

"Tell him." I keep my eyes on her.

"I don't know what you're talking about." She shakes her head like a shocked virgin watching porn.

"You're so full of shit, your eyes are brown."

"That's enough." Redix wedges between us. "What the hell is going on with you?"

I glare at her and tell him, "She wants your gorgeous cock so bad she's afraid to tell you that she works for Gentry Evans." I watch her reaction.

It's stone. It's cold.

"What?" He steps back.

"She's lying," Karen seethes. "She's just jealous."

"I'm as jealous of you as your tits are real." Enough of her bullshit, I turn to Redix. "She works for Gentry Evans and he planted her in your AA meeting. She leaked the story about that man you were with at the club and she's got some reporter looking into why my dad retired from the sheriff's office so long ago."

The smirk on her face says it all but Redix doesn't see it. He's looking at me like I just kneed his nuts.

"That can't be." Betrayal twists his handsome face as he turns to Karen. "You wouldn't do that, would you? You're in AA. You're in recovery like me. You wouldn't lie about that?"

I hate this for him. I hate she did this to him. He needs those meetings and she just violated them.

"What was last night, then?" Redix asks her frozen face. "Was it real?"

Please don't tell me he made love to her thinking they shared a grueling journey to sobriety. Damn, that'd be so wrong of her.

"She's lying," is all Karen can repeat. She doesn't even answer his questions or validate his pain.

That hurts him and that's all it takes.

"Answer him, now!" I grab her by the throat and slam her against his passenger window. "Or I'm gonna make you *real* fucking sober with pain."

Redix doesn't stop me this time. He's stunned silent.

"Tell him!" I'll do it again for him. It's taking me over and I swore I'd have more control but he's hurting and my thumb starts pressing down on that critical artery in her throat.

Her eyes shock wide open. Her body stiffens like a board. Her lips lock up while her neck tries to thrash in my grasp but I'm too strong.

She didn't think I had this in me.

Wrong.

I squeeze harder. And smile.

"It's true." She coughs. "It's true." She grabs her throat when I suddenly let go and take two steps back before I snap her neck next.

"Gentry can't even hire a good fucking liar." I sneer. "Tell him how you caved and pissed your pants." I can smell it. "And watch your back because I know where you live."

"Get out of here." I wanted to say it next, but the words seethe from Redix's throat. "Now."

She runs for the entrance of the hospital, her Louboutin heels clicking fast over the black pavement.

"I'm sorry," I tell him while I watch her stop in the breezeway and grab her phone. "I'm so sorry she did that to you."

"Are you?" He looks at me, equally hurt. "Because you looked a little too thrilled to almost strangle her to death."

"Damn, right," I tell him. "She tried to hurt you. She tried to hurt my parents. What do you expect me to do? Get a mani/pedi with her?"

"You didn't have to do it this way."

"I didn't have a choice."

Yes, I did. And that felt good. And he knows when I feel good. He can see it in my eyes.

"Can you even stop yourself sometimes?" He's dismayed. "Or does it just take over and you gotta hurt someone too and make it worse?"

"Listen here, Hollywood. We don't all get happy endings and justice when the fucking credits roll. I know you've been through some real pain, but don't you dare judge me on how I handle mine and the world I live in. Or how I do my job. All day long, you earn millions while you're surrounded by people who love you, who want to fuck you. But me? I sacrifice my life and people either hate me or they want to kill me. So don't come at me because you're mad about her."

"I'm not just mad about her. I'm mad about a lot of fucking things."

"Is that so? Well then bring it. Make me your emotional bitch you gotta take it out on because I'm used to it by now."

Damn, we're so close, we go right at it.

My mouth knows no edit with him and he's not holding back either.

"I wouldn't take it out on you if you told me the fucking truth." Yep, he's not backing down either. "You could've told me you had a plan to get TJ because I know that's how it went down. That it had something to do with us fixing Ms. Ryans's dock and your dad's old boat." His eyebrow arches up. "See. I'm right."

How the fuck did he just read that on my face?

Dammit, he knows me too well and when did he get so smart about covert crime?

"I know you were helping those victims too," he says, towering over me while his BOUND cologne wafts down. "But I'm mad as hell because you never told me. We never talked about it and you owed me that. I finally told you everything, showed you everything. You know my soul, Cade, so why didn't you talk with me first? That's what hurts."

"If I had told you, it would've risked you and my parents."

"Fine. Then fucking let it. Haven't we been through enough? Don't we love each other enough to survive that together? But no. You won't admit it to me and I can't live with secrets. They'll fucking kill me because they pressure me to drink thinking about how you risked our love for him, for the man who hurt me most. So yes, I'm fucking mad as hell." He grabs a breath and grabs my heart like it's the last thing he'll hold. "Because I love you so much and I lost you and I can live without you, Cade, but I'll never be happy doing it."

My world, my head, they're spinning so fast. There's no dark, empty parking lot around, it's just us. It's just this question.

"Then what will make you happy now?"

"This," he says before crashing his mouth into mine. His

hand grabs the back of my neck and his other pulls my body into him while his tongue claims our kiss.

It's a rush. It's a surge over us and this is where we belong, it doesn't matter the pain.

We have this love too and I grab him, pulling him back into my body, back into my heart with his long hair in my tight grasp. Our breath and lips and tongues and bodies tumble together as we can't get at each other fast enough.

"Now." He lifts my thigh, wedging me against his car. "I'm not waiting anymore for you." The smocked top of my dress tears down in his grip, exposing my breasts while he swears, "I want you back now, Cade."

"Then take me." My hand finds his jeans and makes quick work of opening them enough to grab his swollen cock. "Fuck me right here and show me how you want me back."

I don't care who sees us, let them watch. I know Karen can. Our bodies are half covered by shadows as Redix frees his cock to answer my demand.

Hell yes. Let her watch *who* he really loves. *How* he really loves. That we'll do *anything* for each other.

He lifts me up, his hands wrapping around my ribs, bringing my nipple to his mouth for his hard suck. "Yes," I cry out at the return of his mouth to my flesh. His full lips, his soft tongue with his toying circles, it rushes arousal to my sex while he moves to the other one, leaving them dripping with his spit like they're his.

"Fuck, Redix, now." I pull my panties to the side. He's squeezing my thigh so hard in his grasp, lifting it to wrap around him while our bodies know how to align. They know this by instinct, by the urge and primal routine. It's more than muscle memory. It's our souls forever bound together. His cock drives in and buries inside me, stretching and burning and I groan at his massive return.

"Oh God, Cade." His voice, his breath, they're so deep against my ear while he drives in again, making me gasp. "Fuck, you feel so good," he swears and I don't even feel the steel of the car behind me; I just feel his steel. He's everywhere I need him inside and he never left. He's always here.

I could get lost, I could let go and not care but I see over his shoulder and Karen's silhouette looms in the distance of the hospital entrance watching us. And it makes me recall, it makes me fear...

"Redix," I huff. "You don't have a condom on."

"I don't need one." He wedges his forehead against mine. "I've only been with you. I only want you." He thrusts into my pussy again, proving it.

"And him," I say. "What about Silas?"

"And him." His lips dust over mine. "I want him too but we haven't—"

"But you can." I pull his shirt up and grab his back even harder, feeling his muscles flex under my grip. "And I want you to."

"We all want to. All three of us." He nips my bottom lip. "But I want *you* right now. I want to fuck you right now because you feel so damn good. Because you're the only woman, Cade. The only one I want."

His cock is seated in me while he grinds hard, those fucking hips of his working magic across my nerves and rubbing the base of his shaft against my clit like he knows how. He's the goddamn maestro of fucking me.

He pulls back, his eyes searching mine because he knows he's getting me there and he loves watching it. Glancing over his left shoulder he sees it too—Karen's watching us from the distance. She knows better than to record this if she wants to live, but let her memory never forget.

He turns back and grins. "She didn't stand a chance," he says pulling his cock out of me and leaving me huffing.

"What are you—"

But I see too quickly what he's doing and fuck yes, he drops to his knees before me. Draping my leg over his shoulder, he lifts my dress higher and starts his feast of my pussy and she *better* be watching. This is love. This is lust. This is Redix Dean eating me out like I'm his last meal.

She could never have him.

Grinding my pussy over his outstretched tongue, I ride his face, over his nose, and back down to his chin; I have no shame and he has no hesitation. Wedged against his car, I lace my hands in his hair and let him devour me, his lips sucking my clit. My eyelids start dropping. I'm watching Karen in the distance and he's groaning into my drenched pussy and fuck her, I come on his mouth so hard and loud, *he's mine.*

And he's not done.

Surging up so fast, he wraps my legs around his waist and he's a hard piston in my pussy again with his brutal thrusts and "Yes, fuck me, Redix," I love it.

"Is that what you want, Cade?" He asks me between kisses with my cum on his lips. "You want me to fuck you and him?"

Oh God, that vision is taking me to heights I've never known. "Yes," I sigh. "Fuck us both. Is that what you want?"

"I want to taste you both in my mouth." His chin still glistens with my arousal and my clit is a firecracker about to explode. "I want him to watch us. I want to watch you with him. I want everything together."

He's close too. His thrusts pin me to the car and I'm

about to jump. "I want both of you," I confess over his quivering lips. Mine are too. "I want you both to fuck me at the same time."

I leap. I confess it and I send myself falling into his eyes and he falls with me, releasing his deep groan with my gasps. I come so hard on his cock, spasms quake my core and it hurts so good because this is us; pain and pleasure and love and passion and our lives together, we must find a way.

"As long as you stay with me," he sighs as we find our breath. "As long as I don't lose you." He nuzzles his nose to mine. "You're always my first, Candy Cade."

28

THE PILE OF LAUNDRY IN MY HAMPER IS OBSCENE. I throw my wet bath towel on top of it and I swear I'll do it tomorrow and just air dry for now.

I've been busy. Everyone is back on the water and I've got a waitlist of repairs to do. I love it though. Nothing makes me happier than fixing something with my bare hands.

Well... a couple of things do, but I don't have either one of them to make me happy right now.

The way I left things with Redix the other night bothers me.

It was so intense. It felt so right what we were finally doing and damn, I wanted him too.

But then he got a text from that woman in his AA group and I guess I have to admire him. He dropped me to help her. Like it was part of his sobriety code of ethics and I get it.

But something felt wrong.

He kept apologizing, rushing us out the door of his trailer so he could go bail her out of whatever crisis she was in.

I sat in my truck a few minutes afterward, trying not to feel used.

It sorta worked.

Redix wouldn't do that, would he?

He wouldn't use me to get his bi-curious rocks off and then ghost me. He's not that kind of man, is he?

Yeah, he has a wild past. I've seen the videos online. I don't know everything, but I know he was drunk during them. And I know whatever broke him and Cade up, it has to do with his sobriety now.

He's changed, I guess.

I'm just getting to know him and he comes with lots of baggage, so I can't explain why my heart feels open to him. Just like it does to Cade.

But I don't doubt her and I know why. She reminds me of another woman who I trust with my soul.

But Redix?

It's different with him than it was with Alec. I was barely an adult with Alec. Now I'm a grown man and I know what I want. I want Redix and his passionate heart. I want Cade and her fire. They're so different than me and that pulls me to them.

And I meant it. I want Cade *back*.

That's not the right word.

I don't want to go back to just me and her. I want the three of us in the future. Not just because it's my wildest fantasy.

My heart wants to feel it.

I want to feel a drop of the love Cade and Redix share. I want that in my life. I want it in my heart.

It's like they swim in the deep end of life and maybe I've been too shallow.

I slide on a pair of grey boxers and flop on my bed. My friend Quincy's outside in his yard and I can smell his cigarette smoke from up here in his garage loft.

That reminds me of someone I miss, who I haven't talked to in months. I check my phone. It's midnight here. Six a.m. where she is. With baby twins and Daniel filming, I bet she's up.

"Hey, you little shit." Her beautiful face appears on my screen... and she smiles. "Long time, no see."

"Hey, Charlie Girl." Damn, my first love still rips my breath away. "How y'all doing over there?"

"We're great. Look at who wants to say hi." She turns her phone on video chat towards the cutest little boy on my screen. "Say hi, Duke. Say hi to Silas." He lifts his chubby hand toward the screen.

"Hey, little one." God, he's getting big. "Where's Caroline?"

Charlie turns the screen back to her. "Daniel has her outside. They're picking strawberries for breakfast."

As much as I love this woman, and always will, "happy for her" doesn't describe it. Every time I see her stunning face, the bullet scar across her cheek reminds me of how she deserves every happy day she has now.

"What's going on with you?" she asks. "I know it's something. I can see it on your face."

"Nothing." I lie and she laughs.

"Either tell me or put some clothes on because one of those needs to happen."

I wander my hand down my abs, holding my screen high so she can watch. "I thought we could sex cam." It's too fun teasing her.

"You couldn't handle it."

"That's true."

"Quit procrasta-flirting and tell me what's going on."

"I think I'm falling in love. Again."

"About time."

Charlie knows I love her. I never made that a secret. That I wanted to fuck her more than breathe? She learned about that recently.

And she knows about Alec. She was serving in Afghanistan when I wrote to her about him. I told her what happened with my parents and she called me as soon as she got the letter. I could hear the loud aircraft from the base she was stationed at in the background but she didn't care. I had her undivided attention because she was worried about me. The feeling's always mutual.

"I'm falling for two people, actually."

She smiles at the screen and it's like she's sitting next to me in bed. *I wish.*

"That sounds like you," she says.

"What do you mean 'sounds like me'?"

"You have a big heart." She grins. "I raised you that way."

"You did not *raise* me. I had too many wet dreams about you for you to be talking about raising me."

"I'm so flattered and splattered."

She goes for the joke and damn, I'm next if her husband Daniel Pierce ever fucks up again.

"Don't tempt me," I reply. "Tell me what to do. I have all the feels for another woman and man. They're a couple with a heartbreaking past and I worry I'll get my heart broken too if something happens."

"You just might. But if you feel so strongly for them, it's worth the try."

"Easy for you to say. You have the perfect marriage."

"Oh kiss my go-to-hell, I do not. You of all people know that."

"I'm not saying y'all are perfect. I'm saying your love is. Like it's real and tested and I want that too."

"You wanted it so much that you told Daniel you'd do a threesome with us."

"Still do. I'll rearrange my dance card for you any day, Charlie Girl."

She blows a kiss at the screen. "I'm in Spain."

I wink back. "And I'm right here waiting for ya."

We always do this. We flirt and it's no disrespect to Daniel. I think he likes it actually. Jealousy gets him off. *Lucky man.*

"Seriously, though." She props her phone up on something while she sips coffee. I can see she's wearing an old USMC midriff T-shirt that gives me a peek at her abs. Shit, she's hot. "Why are you so afraid of getting hurt? That's not like you."

"Maybe these two are different."

"Maybe," she says. "Or maybe it's something else."

"Like what?"

"Like you don't want to be hurt again, like how your parents hurt you, so you don't let yourself love hard enough to really be vulnerable."

That's a truth bomb and it drops close to my heart. "Maybe you're right."

"Look, I buried my parents. I buried my first husband and I've been through some shit. Life can hurt like hell but you survive it because love makes it worth it. And you find it again. In the craziest ways, trust me."

"I trust you more than anyone."

"Besides, you're so hot. Who's to say you won't break *their* hearts?"

"You think I'm hot?" That stirs my cock, I can't help it.

"And I think you're smart, and sweet and sexy too, and we're all lucky to have you."

"Quit flirting or I'll tell Daniel."

"Please do," she laughs. "Then I'll get fucked hard tonight. He's treating me like a porcelain doll lately and it's driving me nuts."

"Why?" And why does she put that image in my head? Charlie getting fucked hard by Daniel Pierce. I want tickets to that show. And to join in. "Wait a minute." It hits me. "You're pregnant again, aren't you?"

"It's really early so don't tell anyone, okay."

"I won't and congratulations. Y'all are gonna have a mess of kids."

"No, we can have a few kids and a million fucks. That's what I signed up for."

A cry storms the background and she turns her head and signs something. "Are you hungry?" she asks her son. "Hey"—she turns back to me—"I gotta go."

"Thanks for the chat."

"Thanks for your big heart. Someone will cherish it one day, I promise. I know I do."

"Love you, Charlie Girl."

"Love you too, little shit. Call again soon." Her fingertip ends our chat and I sit back up, taking it all in.

Charlie's pregnant and life is great with Daniel. That's good.

Cade wants to be alone and Redix has his hands full with another woman. That's not.

And there's shit-all I can do about any of it.

The tennis ball on my nightstand calls my hand to toss it. I do this every night. It drives Quincy batshit hearing the ball bounce off the wall and pissing him off is fun.

But this isn't. Because the dust settles in my heart about what Charlie said—*I don't love hard because I'm afraid of getting hurt again.*

Why does God keep making women so damn right?

I MUST'VE FALLEN asleep because my lamp's still on and the tennis ball's in my hand when a gentle knock raps on my door.

That's not Quincy's bang.

Rubbing the sleep off my face, I hope it's her. It *sounds* like her. Or maybe this is just an amazing dream.

When I pull the door open, it's not. I'm wide awake and Cade's standing on my porch in a tiny white dress. My eyes swear her legs go for miles and her tits are the perfect stopping point.

Her eyes drop to my body in only boxer briefs and whatever she was gonna say fails her because her jaw drops too.

"Wanna come in?" It's obvious.

"Can we?" Her smile is tentative.

We?

Redix steps up behind her and I didn't see this coming. A dozen assumptions drop through my logic but it doesn't matter. Even on *my* porch, they belong together.

"Sure." I step back and don't know what to think. I just feel. Worried. Excited. Confused. My life isn't mine anymore as the two of them enter, their beauty together sucking all the oxygen from the humble room.

This is why they're on that iconic BOUND perfume ad together. *This* is why no one can set eyes on them and not be dazed at how it's even possible such human perfection can exist together, let alone love each other.

They're goddamn radioactive sex standing side by side.

I drop into my one chair and just take it in. Because whatever's coming my way, I'm gonna need the strength.

"We owe you some answers." Cade sits on the edge of my bed because she's comfortable here.

Redix leans against the door because he's not. Like he knows he hurt me last time and he's not sure how pissed I am.

"It's a long story," she says, "but to cut it short—I had to catch my breath for a second. I had to make sure I remembered who I was before I let my life get taken again by men."

"I never wanted to take you," I defend myself. "I only wanted you to be free."

"I know. You've been my dearest friend, my accomplice, and my sexy, soft place to fall and I can't find a label for how I love you, but I do. And that'll never change. But I had to make peace with it. Part of me *is* my past. And I can't fight it, kill it, or run from it. I'd just be grateful if you could love me and everything that comes with it."

I glance at Redix and *he comes with it.* Pain storms his eyes because *he's* her past.

Jesus Christ, what happened?

"I've told you everything about me"—I look back at her —"and you're still hiding from me. Both of you."

A lump swallows down her elegant neck while she turns to Redix and he nods. He's ready for me to know too.

"I was eighteen when those guys—the ones I told you about—when they tried to take me one night, to hurt me," she explains. "Redix protected me and let them take him instead. And he doesn't remember what they—"

"I do." Redix's voice breaks in. "I remember some. How they drugged me. Beat me up. Cut me. Maybe they did more to me and that haunts me because I'll never know but at least I'm strong enough to talk about it now. I wasn't for nine years. I lost my mind and Cade to booze and pills and I fought to get it back. To get *her* back. And we were almost whole again, but then I saw those guys again and I relapsed and almost died. And..."

He stops and looks at Cade.

This is their dividing line. I can feel it.

This is what broke them.

"And I almost killed the man who hurt Redix the most," she finishes. "I had to because he was hurting other women too. And I couldn't catch the man using the law so I trapped him." There's a clench to her jaw before she confesses, "But my parents stopped me and they ended him instead. And I tried hiding that from Redix because if it got out, everyone I loved would be at risk." She turns her chin toward Redix, swearing it to him. "But I'd do it again because I had no choice."

"And she knew I needed the truth and peace to stay sober." His eyes burn back into hers. "That the fight needed to end, and what she did only started another one. And I'm trying to make peace with that because I love her. She's my best friend and my life is empty without her."

The storm between them calms and part of me is honored they told me; the other part has questions.

I turn to Cade. "This is what you've been hiding?"

"Yeah. You knew about Gentry and Derek. TJ's the one who's... gone. So if I told you too, you'd be an accessory. But my mom confessed to Redix because she doesn't give a damn if she gets caught."

"I ain't judging you about ending an evil man," I admit because I helped do it for Charlie.

I can't say that either, but I suspect Cade would understand.

"But where do I fit in with y'all? This is a helluva story and there's no room for me in it so why are you here?"

Her face goes soft. She gets up and steps to my chair and takes my hand. There are so many questions inside me but her touch is a powerful answer that makes me stand.

"Because you *made* the room. You opened my heart and helped me see I'm free to move on. That my life can belong to me again, not the men who attacked me and Redix." She tucks a lock of my hair behind my ear. "Silas, you're the beautiful soul who cooled my painful fire."

My lips grab for those words from hers. I've never felt this adored, this amazed to know a woman like her. And to be able to kiss her? To pull her into my arms and sink into every part of her?

This passion has always been just out of my reach like Charlie is. But Cade isn't. She's in my hands, she's pressed to my body, and I can have her.

She moans into our breath reunited and I hear the shuffle of feet and pull back for this answer too.

"What about you?" I ask Redix with my hands cradling Cade's face. "Why are you here?"

Cade steps back and clears his path to me.

"I'm here for you." Redix steps my way. "Cade's *always* with me. No one stops my love for her. But you remind me of the man I would've been if not for that night. You help me see I can be him again. You're fucking incredible. You love and live with no fear and you make me feel like I can again too."

But I *am* afraid. And when he cups my jaw, the power of his touch, I'm scared of how I feel for them, but I can't resist it.

"I'm sorry about the other night," he says. "Nothing happened with her. Karen was playing me and Cade helped me figure it out. I hate that I left you like that. I never want to hurt you, but sometimes I don't always know what to do."

"Kiss me," I demand. "That's what you can do."

And he does. Cade's kiss still warms my lips and when Redix's meets mine it's a fire, a heat I didn't know possible. He's tangling with more than my mouth, my lips, and my tongue. He's marveling at my heart and I'm equally in awe of his. Of how brave he is, how strong he is and he doesn't even know it.

"What do we do?" I break this kiss and have to know this final answer. Each of us is asking it. "How do we do this together?"

29

Closer by Kings of Leon

"WE JUST RUSHED YOUR WORLD," CADE ANSWERS. "WE came in here like a hurricane, so you tell us. What do you want, Silas?"

The floor beneath my feet is solid wood planks but I swear it wobbles, it quakes to her question. Not in my wildest dreams did I ever think I'd get this chance.

"I want both of you." I try to look them in the eye. Her. Then him. And it's almost too much. *It is too much.* His dominating beauty and her stunning appearance. I'm in a maze of lust and don't know which way to turn.

"You tell me," I say to Redix, remembering what they just told me. "You've been through hell. I don't want to upset you or anything."

Is it possible for desire and wonder to blow through a man's eyes with gale force?

Yes. He looks back at me with a grin barely pulling his lips and answers, "Take her and take me too; however you want me." He glances at Cade. "If that's what you want?"

"Yes." She pushes her dress down, exposing the tits I lust for before her dress falls to the floor and she's standing before us in only a white lace thong.

"However you want," she tells me, and God, this can go so many ways. It's overwhelming all the choices, all the consent, all the desires I can fulfill with the two of them. Because I've never felt this permission. This power to be wholly me and wholly fucking the hell out of who I want. Both of them.

But something tells me where to begin. With who and how this all started.

"Let him watch how I fuck you," I tell Cade. "How you don't close your eyes when I make you come too."

I look at Redix and half expect him to protest. To act possessive over Cade. But he doesn't. There's a thrill, a desire in his stare and it runs deep for this.

"And you," I tell him. "Stand right beside me and let me taste how much you like watching me fuck her."

Cade crawls down to all fours on the carpet in front of my mirror wearing nothing but a smile and a thong. I step into my bathroom, leaving my boxers there, and pulling condoms from the drawer.

When I come back into the room, my heart jumps to see Redix stripping down too. His gaze goes from her ass in the air for me, to my hard cock while he pulls his T-shirt overhead.

I have to drag a breath over my lips to make sure this is real.

"I have a scar." He warns me. "She's the only one so far who's seen it." While he unbuttons his jeans, a soft cry escapes Cade's lips and we both look at her.

This is very real.

"Hey." Redix rushes to her side. He kneels on the floor beside her and lifts her eyes to his. "I'm okay," he assures her. "I promise."

She kneels up and it's this poignant kiss between them. Like their mouths and bodies are grabbing for years and so much shared and not even time can capture what they have together.

That's the power, the love I want just a taste of tonight.

"I'm so proud of you," she whispers over his lips. "I love you."

"I love you too." He grazes his thumb across her cheek. "This isn't pain anymore. This is love." When he looks up at me, I'm humbled to be included in his question. In their answer. "Right? This is love."

"Yes." I'm beginning to feel it. A new sense of it because God knows I'm witnessing it.

"Alright then." Cade drops back to her hands and knees and looks at me in the reflection. "Fuck the hell out of me, Silas, and make sure Redix enjoys it."

Holy hell, this woman takes charge even on all fours, lifting our smiles and cocks at the same time.

Redix stands back up. I swear he towers above me as I drop to my knees behind Cade. But I wait for him. She's ready. I'm ready, but I won't do this without him.

I see the slight tremble in his hands as he pushes his

jeans and then his boxers to his ankles and steps out of them. I hold my breath for what I'll see upon his rise back up and I'm not prepared when I do.

His tan ripped thighs. His deep belt of obliques. His groomed hair. A tattoo of two dorsal fins on his hip bone. It matches the one on Cade's. His soaring cock and holy shit, he's perfect and hung like mad. Saliva pools in my mouth but then a sharp breath leaves my lungs when he moves to show me his scar.

Cade watches in the reflection while he turns to his right, letting me see his left buttock. He's not afraid and willing to share this, so I confront it too.

It's horrific and harrowing. It's two shapes, dorsal fins I know because I've kissed the tattoo on Cade's hip bone and she flinched. It was an odd reaction and she asked me not to do it again... and now I know why.

His scars run deep. They're carved wide across his sculpted glute muscles and there's no denying it. They marked him because of her. They wanted to do this violence to her, but he protected her and he endured it instead.

Oh my God, this is what they've survived together.

"I'm not hiding anymore." His voice is strong, unwavering as he turns back to face me. "*We're* not hiding anymore."

He catches Cade's look in the mirror and all I can do is reach my lips out and kiss his thigh. To kiss any part of his flesh for what he did for her. To witness how much a man can love another person.

I want this. I want him. And her. I've almost lost my erection to the shock but then he starts stroking his in my face and says, "Show me how you free her too," and there's no pain in his eyes. He's staring into mine and claiming his desire and, fuck, mine surges back.

I see Cade watching me in the mirror. "Show him, Silas." She arches her back, opening for me. They need this. She needs this and I've never felt a demand in my body so powerful.

I pull her thong down to hug her thighs and slowly swipe my fingertip up her perfect pussy. It's already glistening for me while I roll a condom on.

I tease my tip through her lips while hers part in anticipation and Redix's cock hovers inches from my mouth.

"Tell him." I tease her with words, circling her entrance while a drop of cum leaks from Redix's cock. I want to taste it but I want this first. "Tell him how free you've been, Cade." I barely push into her pussy and she moans while I say, "Tell Redix how bad you've been for me."

She doesn't make a sound until I drive into her and she gasps while I stretch my tongue for his cock and lick his first drops.

"Oh fuck!"

I swear it cries from both of them. And me too. Because I taste his salt on my tongue. I sink into her tight wet heat and don't ever let this end.

"Tell me." Redix holds his girth up to my mouth. I lick around his crown and flick his sensitive ridge with my tongue while he groans before he demands, "Tell me, Cade. What did you do with him?"

I pull back and drive into her, again and again. Sliding my shaft and seating it deep inside her, I watch her in the mirror. She's enraptured by the sight of my mouth exploring Redix's proud cock and it's like she doesn't hear anything but his moans and my grunts.

I give her a playful smack on the ass and say, "Tell him or I'll stop fucking your wet pussy until you do."

"Oh shit," she groans at my taunt and I pull her up by the shoulders.

She's not getting out of this. She's not going to come until she stops hiding too.

Redix drops and we're all on our knees while he reaches between her legs and pulls her by the back of her neck to his lips.

"Tell me, Cade." He starts playing with her clit and I can feel his fingers on my cock while I'm thrusting into her. "Tell me how dirty you were for Silas."

She smiles back. Like she was only teasing to get us here and that drives my hips harder while I reach to pinch her nipple and fist his cock with my other hand and he groans at my grasp.

"Say it," he says. "This sweet pussy of yours isn't coming until you do."

His hand scissors her clit and the sides of my cock pumping into her and she needs to say it because fuck this feels so good. And it's so hot watching us in the mirror.

"Grind that hungry pussy back on his cock." He's taunting her to her edge. "Show me how you love fucking him and tell me how dirty you'll be for us now."

"Tell him." I tug her nipple and she gasps while he rattles her clit. "Tell him what you became."

"Silas fucked a woman while she ate me out." She teases the image over Redix's lips and his teeth nip her bottom lip to the confession. "And then he fucked me like a sweet slut in front of a room of people." She gasps again. "In a sex club. Three times."

"You're gonna be our sweet slut now, aren't you?" Redix taunts her, still holding her by her neck. "You'll be so fucking dirty you'll fuck us both for all to see, won't you?"

His mouth takes her kiss next while he smacks her clit and she bucks against me, coming so hard over my cock and his hand that he has to hold her up as it crashes through her. I've never heard her groan so loud. I grab her hips to stay inside her and it's only the beginning.

"Are you gonna be a sweet slut for me too?" He smiles while she gasps for breath. "I want to see it, Cade. See you be so free."

"Yes," she swears back to him and after one more kiss from her, he stands back up.

"Did you do this in that club?" Redix asks me while he holds his cock back to my mouth.

"No," I answer while I can't hold back much more. "Only you."

My hips slam into Cade's back side, bouncing off her perfect ass and fucking her sweet pussy that's starting to wet my thighs.

Redix puts his fat tip to my lips. "Then wrap your mouth around my cock if you want to taste me while you fuck her. And know that I just fucked her an hour ago. Her cum's still on my dick and she's loving this, both our cocks railing her pussy in one night."

The groan from Cade at his confession, at his taunt, it's primitive. It's guttural and it sways her back to take me too. Like her body, her nature demands both of us. Like she can't get enough of us.

And to be inside her, where he was too, his cum probably still dripping from her. This is what I wanted the other night in his trailer. His flavor. His pleasure too. To let go and have this together, all three of us. My lips open for his cock again and this time, it's no tease.

I want it all.

I hollow my cheeks and slide down his shaft. Taking as much of him as I can, damn, I've wanted him and he tastes so good filling my throat until my soft gag.

"*Fucckkk*," he roars as I watch him from my knees. He's blissed out. His jaw drops watching my mouth full of him and he gets this vision, seeing my cock pounding into Cade's pussy too.

It's going to end us. I can see Cade out of the corner of my eye. She's watching in the mirror and she's coming soon. We're a euphoric sight. We're a reflection of three bodies and lust and love and trust shared and please don't let this just be one night.

Redix reaches his hand in my hair. He's not forcing me, he's telling me. His cock's swelling in my mouth, his pre-cum tingling my throat. He's close, but not sure, so I lock my eyes to his and moan so fucking hard with his cock in my mouth that he loses it.

Not even words fall from his lips. Just deep grunts while his thighs shake and I swallow what I can of his cum because he won't let me go. He shoots again down my throat and I pull back, letting it spill over my lips and chin and Cade's hips shake in my grasp. She comes at the sight of us, at me gazing up at him.

That takes me, yanking me down into an orgasm that blinds me as I feel her turn in my grasp, her lips searching for my Redix's-cum-covered kiss and he kneels for it too.

The three of us share this. This taste. This moment. And I don't know what more we'll share but it's starting to seep through my veins too.

This is how close we can be. This is how deep love can go.

30

∞

SHE SLEPT IN MY ARMS, LETTING ME SPOON HER WHILE she held Silas's hands. His bed is small for our three bodies, but I love it this way. It reminds me of sleeping on the sofa with Cade and how it traps us together.

Silas wanted it this way. He said he was the last one to sleep with her and we needed this reunion.

It has been too long since I've held Cade. She's home to my body and there's no warmth like hers. When she's beside me, I don't have nightmares.

I open my eyes to find him looking at me from his pillow. Sunlight streams in from the window and he's brighter.

"You snore," he says.

"No, I don't."

"Not you." He flits her nose. "You."

"Fuck you," Cade murmurs.

"Okay." He wedges into her.

"Careful, darlin'." I tickle my lips over her ear. "You say that now and you're gonna get a two-for-one deal."

"No one's getting anything until we shower." She rolls to her back and tortures us with tits begging for our suck.

"Alright." I circle her nipple. "All three of us. We rub-a-dub-dub in the shower together."

"No can do." Silas crawls out of bed and damn his ass is cut and fuck a shower. I want *him*. "That shower stall barely fits me."

He walks to the kitchenette at the corner of his loft. I glance at Cade and we both smile at his tan nudity. He's such a tease.

"Quit eye-fucking me," he says with his back turned. "I can't make coffee with a hard-on."

"Go shower." I nudge Cade out of bed. "Because once we're caffeinated, I'm fucking someone real soon."

"Me first." She pecks my cheek before crawling out of bed.

Silas glances over his shoulder and grins, watching her disappear into his bathroom. Then he glances back at me and I'm not shy. I lay naked with no covers and my arm above my head, just hoping I torment him half as much as he does me with that body.

"How do you take it?" he asks as he turns around and yes, you can start a pot of coffee with a hard-on.

"I have no idea but I'm willing to learn what I like with you."

He leans against the tiny countertop while the carafe

behind him fills and I don't know if it's his heart or his cock that's asking, "You really haven't done much with a man before?"

"Not that I remember." I sit up and grab another pillow to put behind me because we need to have this talk. "All I remember is what those pictures triggered. That man at the club. Twice I recall now, but that's it. I'm not trying to hide it or anything. It's just that not-remembering is exactly what I tried to do for so long until it almost killed me—twice."

Cade steps naked and dripping out of a cloud of steam.

"Got any towels?" she asks Silas, and he rolls his eyes.

"Shit. They're all dirty. Sorry." He opens a closet door. "I wasn't expecting a guest." A clean white T-shirt appears in his hand. "Or two." He tosses it her way. "Here, this is all I got."

I'm not complaining. Watching Cade dry her incredible body off, damn, I'm next. I jump up for the shower and swat her ass on my way there.

She giggles and swats mine back before going for her first cup of coffee.

When I'm done, I turn off the shower lever and Silas is standing in the doorway, watching me with a clean blue T-shirt in his hand.

"Need me to dry you off?" he asks.

I'm about to say, "Hell yes," but Cade calls out, "Y'all start without me and asses will be whipped."

"Promise?" I shout back, taking the T-shirt and a kiss from Silas while our naked bodies rub past each other in the doorway.

I pour a cup of coffee while Cade taps on her phone and Silas showers up. Cream swirls in my cup as I pour it. I usually take it black, but Silas has the flavored stuff and I'm ready to try everything.

I meant what I told him last night. It just rushed from my heart and it was true.

I look at Silas and he's everything I would've been. I was just like him. Wild. Free. Happy and fun. Yeah, I had responsibilities. Sounds like he did too. Can't be easy growing up under the rules of a billionaire who believes in southern tradition.

But all that spirit inside me was crushed. It's like Derek Baucom held me down while TJ and Gentry ripped me apart and bloody pieces of me were left in the sand that night.

Cade's dad saved my life.

Cade saved my heart.

And now I'm searching for my soul back.

And when I look at Silas, I hope I find a soul like his.

I stare out his window, looking out over the river and swirls of marsh grass until I hear Cade mutter, "Fuck yes."

"What?" I turn around, thinking it's gonna be something sexy with Silas, but her nose is down to her phone. "What's going on?"

"Stacey, Gentry's wife, she just texted me. She found some bank statements he tried to hide in an air-conditioning vent."

"Gentry's wife? Why are you texting her?"

"We're close now. She hates Gentry too, but she's stuck in their marriage, so she's trying to help me catch him."

"Catch him how?"

"His money. His businesses. That's how you take a man like him down." Her eyes lift up and find mine. "I promise. I'm using the law this time."

I'm trying to make it settle with my heart in ways that don't disturb me. What she almost did to TJ, that she *planned* it, but Mama G finished instead.

And no, I ain't weak and afraid to fight back. TJ deserved it. He needed to be stopped, I get that now.

But have you ever loved someone who almost committed pre-meditated murder? Try it. It carves questions into your soul you don't want there. And she did it because of me. That'll fuck with you too.

I trust Cade with my life, but I've seen her snap. I saw her last night with that Karen piece-of-shit. Cade's not like most women. She'll kill you with her bare hands.

I love those hands. But can I live with them?

"Your new boat." She yanks me back to the moment. "Can we go out on it today?"

"Yeah. Why?"

Silas appears in the doorway as naked as the two of us and it's hard to focus. Her tits and his cock, and mine wants a whole other conversation.

"There's a couple of islands I want to check out. Gentry doesn't know your new boat. But he knows Silas's by now."

"What are you looking for?" Silas asks, using the same blue T-shirt to dry himself off.

"Two missing women. That's where you can hide them," she answers. "I wanna invite my dad too. Between you," she nods to Silas, "and my dad and my research, maybe we'll find something."

Did she just hear herself?

"You want to go out on my new boat with me and Silas and your dad?" I let that sink in with her. "That man is gonna smell this threesome from a mile away and me and Silas will get our balls shot off."

She cocks her head, considering our new conundrum. I expect her to cringe and agree. But she shrugs and says, "He's gonna find out anyway."

"Pump the breaks, NASCAR," I warn. "We need to

think about this. Are we really gonna go public, the three of us, and just expect everyone to be happier than a pig in shit about it?"

"They won't be." Cade puts her phone down. "I'll be called a whore and slut for sure. You have your publicity and career to think about. And Silas, well. You've already lost your inheritance. What more can they do to you?"

"I don't give a fuck about my career." I humph, "Hell, it'll probably help. I've been cashing in on that wild-sex life myth for so long. I'm not the one I'm worried about."

"I don't care either," Cade echoes. "I've been bullied and judged my whole life. At least now, I'm having fun."

Silas doesn't speak. His shoulders drop and he turns his chin.

"What is it?" I ask him.

"I'm finally talking to my mom now. She's come by a few times and it's good having her back in my life. She likes Cade, says she'll like anyone I love, but you *and Cade?* That's pushing it. I could lose her again." He toes the floor. "And my Dad's been calling. Leaving messages that he wants to talk. That he's been thinking."

That quiets me. Cade too.

My mom worships the fucked-up ground I've walked on. And Cade's parents are so warm, I don't worry about them.

"Well, I don't know about your Dad but just have your mom meet Mama G, Cade's mom." I want to cheer him up. "She'll teach her to chill real quick."

That makes Cade chuckle, and me recall, "Like that time when we got caught fucking on her balcony, remember?"

Cade starts laughing and I tell Silas, "We got out of

school early for senior exams, and every chance I could get, I was fucking Cade, of course."

"And I was fucking *you*," she chimes in. "Don't make it sound like I was the virgin and you were the stud."

"Okay, Ms. Horny Pussy, yes. You pushed me back on the lounge chair, pulled my zipper down, and your dress up and we were fucking right there." Silas grins and we're getting amused. "So she's riding me and I'm about to come when her mom appears in the doorway, asking us why we're home so early."

Cade falls over laughing. "Oh my God, I was so embarrassed. My dress covered us, but I knew she could tell what we were doing."

"*Yeah*, she could because I had the big O on my face and you wouldn't stop twitching with that tight pussy on my cock and while you explained to your mom about exams, I came right inside you."

"My poor mom!"

"Your poor mom? Poor me." I laugh. "That woman wore a gun on her hip. I was coming inside the Sheriff's daughter and it could've been my last one." I tell Silas, "You think you and Cade's dad are friends, but just you wait. He'll hawk it real fast that we're fucking her. So will her mom."

"I'm not hiding it from them," she insists. "Look, we don't have to tell everyone. We can be discreet, but life is too short with my parents and I'm sharing everything with them. Trust me; we can trust them."

"I trust them." Silas aims for his bed. "And I want to hear more about you riding Redix."

The tug in my cock is sudden. Blood rushes through my veins and I set my coffee down and aim for the bed too because this is on.

Whatever this is, we *will* have it.

Silas is kissing Cade by the time I join them. I don't hesitate, spreading her thighs and taking my favorite kiss of her pussy that's still drying from the shower. She tastes like soap and sugar and wanton sex, and I moan into her folds.

That arches her back, my tongue teasing circles around her clit while Silas does the same around her nipples.

Goddamn, she starts writhing and moaning and it's so fucking hot. It's not going to take her long because this is all new to us. It's a body rush across our mountains of flesh twisting on the bed and I could do this all day.

Twisting two fingers inside her, I pull her clit into a suck between my lips while Silas does the same to her nipple. His fingertips tug at her other one and she snaps. Breaking across my tongue, she comes thrashing under our touch and that's just the intro.

When I glance up and see Silas's erection, how it's so hard for her pleasure, I want his too. I move over and grab his thighs and flip him to his back. Dragging my tongue up the thick vein of his cock, I've never done this to a man. Not that I remember. It was always me getting my cock sucked, but I want this so bad.

Grabbing his base, I lift his mass for my mouth and I'm moaning before it's even sliding between my lips. He tastes like soap too. Like salt and man and he mixes with Cade's cum still on my tongue and I'm starving.

I'm an animal feasting and Silas's back bows off the bed with his, "Fuck, yes." He grabs my hair. "Yes." He thrusts his hips. "Yes, suck my fucking cock." And I groan, feeling mine leaking.

Heat approaches my face and I open my eyes to find Cade's staring back at mine. There's lust in them. Delight too. She drags the tip of her tongue up one side of his cock while I do the other and I've never heard a man moan like that. Silas is coming apart to this and fuck, it's incredible.

"Give me your pussy," I hear him growl and Cade turns to straddle his face with her mouth still joining mine in this meal.

We take turns. I plunge down his length, as far as I can, loving his hard cock in my mouth while I knead his balls to see if he likes that too. His legs spread wider with his groan, telling me he does, and *all* I want to do between his thighs makes me take his fat tip as far as I can into my throat.

"Fuck!" It's muffled by his face in Cade's pussy while she goes next. I hold his base up, rubbing his dripping tip across her gorgeous lips before she locks her eyes to mine and fills her mouth with another man's cock.

Damn, that gets me off. Only him. Any other man and this wouldn't happen, but Silas is special. You can't walk into a room he's in and not feel it wave over you.

The man's his own breed. He's not a billionaire. He's not a mechanic. He's not a ladies' man or a toy for anyone. He's a warm ocean of care and charisma and so much sex appeal that you want to drink and drown in his salt, every drop of it.

We take him. Back and forth. I plunge down his shaft and then Cade does. Silas is a lucky man. I *think* I know what I'm doing. I know how I like my cock sucked by the one who does it best. She's doing it to him too, so no wonder his hips are thrusting for more of our mouths.

Cade starts gasping, getting that look in her eyes. Her violet ecstasy clings to my gaze as I get to watch this. He's making her come again. Silas is licking her pussy while we suck his cock and it has her shaking. She can't breathe. She doesn't want to.

So I do it. I sink my mouth down on his shaft and he's

right there with her. Swelling and firming even more against my lips and here they go. I squeeze his base hard and knead his balls and he rockets into my mouth. I hold my tongue out for more and Cade comes moaning at the sight of his cum spurting across my lips.

I'm about to as well. I kiss and caress his semi while she gets her breath and I'm hard as hell and desperate.

"Show him." I fall on the bed beside them, tugging at Cade's thighs. "He wants to see how you ride me, so show him, Cade."

She goes for it, swinging her leg over and I'm seated so fast inside her wet pussy that I gotta grab her hips and my sanity. "Goddamn, woman," I huff and hold on.

Once he's recovered his breath, Silas is kneeling beside her. His eyes are glued to where our bodies join, and I'm trapped by the sight too.

"Lean back and show him how you love riding my cock." This is my favorite position with her.

How she spreads her thighs wide and I can see my shaft slick with her cum while she pistons up and down my cock and her clit swells for more. Fuck, it's beautiful. The way she leans back and braces her hands behind her on my thighs, arching her breasts to the perfect peaks to watch their bounce.

She's a goddamn Amazon of sex like this. Totally in charge. Totally ruling this fuck and you want to be her subject. You want her taking you however she damn well pleases.

"She gets so wet fucking like this," I tell Silas. It's not a taunt. It's obvious. "See how her cum drips to my base. She's so fucking dirty and in control like this. She's gonna pour it down my cock."

That makes Cade moan because she loves breaking

rules and not being the good one all the time. No, she likes being the bad one too.

"I see," Silas sighs. "I'm gonna taste it too." His mouth lowers and I fight to hold it back. So does she. Because when his tongue licks where my cock is sliding into her pussy, we both groan like never before because we've never known this pleasure, this taboo, and why not? It's fucking incredible.

"*Oh fuuucccckkk,*" she cries out while he licks her clit and I fuck her pussy, feeling his tongue each time he darts it out for a taste of me too. "Fuck, don't stop." She cries out. "Fuck yes, you two." She's so gone. Her hips are shaking in my grasp and she's in ecstasy.

His long hair blocks the sight but I can feel him and he's taking me too. But not without her first.

And she is my first. And my last. My heart knows it while I'm enraptured by this sight of her pleasure as I've never seen.

"Oh fuck!" She screams out, falling over us with convulsions he's ready for. Lifting up from our fuck, Silas grabs her throat and takes her in a kiss while she keeps coming, milking my cock with her spasms while I twist beneath with my own release.

"Oh, God." I groan at the vision. At the two of them. At my new world. At all the pain. It's gone in the stars of pleasure that seize my mind while I come so deep inside Cade. "Oh, God." Because this is what I can be now.

I'm not afraid to live. To feel. To love. It won't hurt me anymore. These two make it all worth it.

31

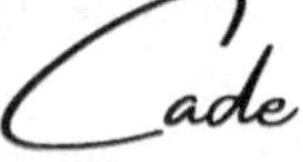

IF YOU COULD PAINT THE COLORS INTRIGUED, AMUSED and proud they would color a rainbow down my mama's face.

Though her skin doesn't glow and her face is thinner than I've ever seen, her eyes light up watching me, Redix, and Silas.

Redix has tucked her under a thick blanket on the outdoor lounge sofa in the cockpit of his new boat. Silas fetched her a bottle of water. I gave her a spare pair of sunglasses to wear while she sits there watching us.

Like she knows.

So does Dad.

We're going slow through the no-wake zone and there's no escaping her scrutiny.

"So how exactly do y'all work?" She finally asks and Redix tosses his chin up laughing.

I swear Silas blushes and I just answer, "However we want. It's not like there are rules for this."

"It's not like you follow them." Redix pecks me on the cheek.

My dad is studying the nautical maps I've marked up. All the islands I know can't be suspected have red Xs over them. I know he heard Mama and my answer. But he's not saying a word and suddenly I worry.

He's gonna shoot their balls off.

Redix senses it. He glances over at my dad and then cuts me a "I told you so" look. Silas grins at the top of my dad's head. Yeah, they're friends but fucking his daughter and her ex-fiancé is pushing that bond to the max.

But my mama? Nope.

She kicks the hornets' nest with pure glee.

"Jeff," she says, "has the cat and her two dogs got your tongue?"

Sitting beside her on the sofa with the map spread out on the table in front of him, Dad doesn't look up.

Redix steers the boat. Silas stands beside him and I'm between two men I love and my parents who are trained to kill and how to get away with it.

Yep, this was a great fucking idea.

Like turning your back on a tiger.

"I got one question." Dad finally sounds off. He doesn't look up, like the maps are way too interesting to him and my new threesome love is boring as hell but he asks to be polite, "Do either of you feel your balls tighten when you come?"

I've never heard my mama laugh so loud and I join her.

Silas and Redix exchange confused glances before laughing too. And finally, Dad looks up and says, "Either of y'all break her heart, don't worry about me. She'll kill you herself."

And that's his blessing.

I knew my parents would be okay with this. They have bigger fish to fry.

Mama tries hiding it with brightly colored tracksuits and cute hats, but she's losing weight fast. And her hair has no luster and her skin doesn't glow. All the life in her is in her big mouth, huge heart, and whip-smart mind.

We all know what's coming. We just don't know when.

"Well, y'all need to answer the damn question." Mama won't relent. "Because I'm as lost as last year's Easter egg and I need this riddle solved."

"You wanna know about my balls, Mama G?" Redix smiles back at her. He *is* the son they never had. "I keep 'em smooth and firm like a peach." He's loving this too. He and my mama can riff for days. "But no, they don't tighten up. They just deliver a big sloppy grin for your daughter."

She asked for that image and now my stomach hurts from laughing.

"What about you, Silas?" Mama has no patience. Yep, apple and tree right here. "You're family now, so tell us."

"You wanna know about my family jewels?" He's diving right in.

"They're worth ten billion." Dad's in on it too. "That's about what? At ten bucks a sperm times a hundred million. Hell, that's a billion bucks every time you blow a wad."

Redix yanks the throttle back because he can't steer and die from laughter at the same time. None of us can.

God, it's gonna be a perfect day, and damn, I'm so lucky.

"I did raise my daughter to have expensive taste." Mama toasts Silas with her bottle of water. "Pun intended."

"Mama!" Why I protest, I don't know. What won't we laugh about now?

"Me and my balls are very happy." Silas pulls me into a hug. "But no, they don't tighten when I come. They just stroke a big, creamy check."

And then it happens.

It's not like we forget ourselves, it's just that the moment is too pure. There's too much life and love and happiness on this one lavish vessel in the water.

Redix leans over and kisses Silas. Not a hot one. A sweet one. Then he does the same to me and we three look at my parents because what else is there left to say?

"You have our blessing," my dad says. "And you have her"—he wraps his arm around Mama's thin shoulders—"full of more questions so gird your loins, boys."

More banter travels between us while we head out into the sound. I put out a fruit platter with Mama's favorite cream cheese dip while Redix steers and Silas points the way to go.

As the water narrows into one of the many rivers that lead inland, the mood turns quiet. And serious.

"There's no telling what's on some of these islands," Dad tells me as we lean over the map. "Some are hundreds of acres with dense trees and brush. You sure as hell can't see nothing from the water."

"I'm working on a drone," I tell him. "But if he's smart, which unfortunately he is, he's got something well hidden."

"But no matter where he's going," Silas chimes in, considering the map of where the Atlantic meets the coast of the states of Georgia and South Carolina. "All these barrier islands, you gotta have a place to dock a boat."

"But wouldn't that make it obvious?" Redix pulls the throttle back to neutral while we slosh in front of one of the largest islands, Daufuskie. It's public with hundreds of residents, Silas included. It's not suspect, but there are islands around it that are private property.

"What if he knows you'll look for a dock and just to be the sneaky fuck he is," Redix says, "he times his approach with the tide and runs a small boat ashore? You don't need a dock for that, just rubber boots."

It sinks to the pit of my stomach.

All of them are right. And while I'll put a drone up in the air and scour over the top of every private island across the Lowcountry, the tree canopy is thick, even in the winter.

"Your best bet is the money trail with Gentry," Mama advises. "When you got as much as he does, it's gonna fall out along the way and lead a trail right to him. Just stay on it and don't give up."

"His wife found statements for a bank account she didn't know about," I update her.

"There you go," she says, "See—men and their money. They'll stick their dick out in the breeze for sex, but they sure will squirrel their money away to hide their own nut."

"What about Derek?" Redix asks while Dad's got binoculars out and so does Silas.

The tide is high. We waited for this hour so we could get as close as we can from the water to some of these islands right off Hilton Head.

"Derek's hiding somewhere out here too." Redix scans the horizon and seethes. "And I'm fucking sick of living scared with Renie and Nicolas, waiting for his next move. Scarlett guards all day. Keith guards all night. And they can't go anywhere without their shadow. It's taking a toll on us."

"Derek's hiding on a boat somewhere," I answer him. "I know it. But that means he's gotta come ashore for supplies, so we'll catch him. He'll get lazy and we got him, I promise."

Redix wraps his arms around my neck and buries his nose in my hair. He's exhausted with this. We all are. But Derek's lived his life on the run. We just have to wait him out.

"Well, at least y'all got each other."

Mama lifts our eyes and the smile on her face looking our way is serene. Redix has his arms around me and Silas is holding my hand.

No, we're not the picture of southern tradition. But we are the picture of love and lust in the Lowcountry, so fuck you, Rules. You were never fun to follow anyway.

We spend the rest of the afternoon searching. Marking off islands in the area we know can't be it. But once the tide starts rolling out we have to head back.

Silas docks Redix's boat in the slip at the marina because he jokes with Redix, "You're a little heavy-handed with that throttle. You gotta learn to ease it in."

My parents don't hear the joke because Dad's helping Mama wrap up in her jacket but I clock it loud and clear.

"Speaking of easing it in." I grab two handfuls of ass, one cheek from each. "Grab the marine grease because that's what we're doing tonight."

"You want a Marine too?" Redix winks.

"You two warm me up first." I tease back.

Silas helps Redix tie down and lock the boat up while I help Dad with Mama.

Years ago, she would've leapfrogged over the edge. Now she shakes. She doesn't have much energy for this.

I'm about to descend into a dark hole of worry about her when Mama grabs my hand as she stands up on the dock.

"Now, you and me," she says, "we're gonna sit a long spell while you answer all my questions, you hear?"

Mama's smut books have her mind racing about me and Redix and Silas. *If she only knew.*

"I just gotta know this for now." Her grin makes the Devil look like a choir boy.

"What?"

"Do they make *your* balls tighten when you come?"

She punches me again with laughter. "I don't have balls."

"Yes, you do." She barely backhands me. "I raised you to have the biggest pair."

"No, you raised me to have ovaries."

"You got me there." She winks. "They're even stronger."

∞

THE LAST PERSON I EXPECT TO SEE IS SITTING ON THE steps to my screened-in porch.

And I ain't got the patience for this.

I'm exhausted.

I spent the week on St. Simons Island, summoned by a priority client who should've rebuilt the engine of his fishing yacht years ago. He thought he was doing me a favor by letting me crash on it while I fixed it. The only favor I got was the handsome check I earned.

What pissed me off was leaving Cade and Redix behind. We never got the night Cade wanted. It was an hour after our boat ride with her parents before I was called to Georgia for a week.

Now, I'm back. I'm fucking soaked from the downpour I hit on the river on my way home, and I have to deal with *him*.

My dad.

I've been avoiding his calls, so in typical Van de May style—he won't be ignored.

I yank my hair out of its wet knot, and because his only offense is breathing so far, I'm already pissed.

I snap. "I thought a Van de May doesn't belong at this piece of trash by the river?"

It's not a piece of trash.

My house on Daufuskie is perfect. It's simple, humble, and hiding under a tree canopy covered in Spanish moss with the best views of the sunset. And my dock is upgraded to top of the line.

Dad must've taken the ferry over, or a private charter, because I don't see a boat moored here.

"I didn't come all this way to argue with you." He doesn't move from his spot blocking the path up to my house.

"Then why are you here?"

"Because your mother has spent the past month living at her sister's house and not ours where she belongs."

I shrug. "Not hearing my problem to fix."

"You're the reason I got a problem."

"I'm your son, so if you're gonna reduce me to a problem, get off my porch. I won't be insulted on my own property."

Dad throws his chin up to the sky. "I swear she spit you from her mouth."

"Who? Mom?"

"No, Grandma. *My mom.* You're just like her."

"That's high praise."

No one can insult my grandma, not even her son.

That woman meant the world to me. She was my partner in tobacco-spitting crime. She made the best pecan pie in the world. And she was the first to say I was wonderful as I was; no sense in changing.

"Yes, it *is* high praise." Dad rests his elbows on his knees and this is gonna be a long talk because his ass ain't moving. "So quit acting like I licked all the red off your candy and listen to me."

I huff. Taking it down a notch. "Go on then."

"Your mom's been gone and don't ever challenge a southern woman to a silent standoff. Monks have less patience. So she's left me in a big, empty house with nothing but my own thoughts."

Don't get your hopes up. My dad is too set in his traditional ways to change.

"And?"

"And"—Dad tousles his perfect part. He only does that on a boat when he's deciding how fast to tack—"you were right. I didn't know my dad. He died when I was five, so what do I know about being a good one? And that's all I ever wanted to be."

Don't trust this. No matter how you want to.

Because I remember the apathy on his face when he told me to leave. He withdrew all the money from my account, told my mom not to speak with me, and pointed to the door.

I walked out with twenty-two dollars in my wallet, a duffel bag of clothes, my toothbrush, and a heart so stunned it didn't feel anything for months.

And when it did, all that crushed me were waves of disappointment.

"So your grandma raised me right," he says, "all on her own. But I remember all the talk, all the judgment and sneers when she never remarried though she had courters. A society widow back then remarried, and the looks we'd get in church and down at the club? I sensed them over the years. Then my football buddies gave me hell because my mom spent *a lot of time* with her best friend, Ms. LeeRay, and no men. Do you remember her?"

"Barely." Ms. LeeRay died when I was a boy. All I remember is she was always with my grandma and giving me Junior Mints and that my grandma wasn't the same after she died.

"I knew who she really was to your grandma," he says, "and I loved Ms. LeeRay too. And you can act all proud as you want nowadays, but back then, it was unheard of. A scandal at the least and dangerous at the most."

"Times have changed, Dad."

"Yes. But some things may never." For the first time in years, Dad looks me in the eye and I see the man I used to worship. "That's why I got so angry, Son, because I was afraid. What you did at The Citadel? Hell, at many places. You could get hurt. Or killed."

"You realize if I'd been caught with a girl, I'd get high-fives? She'd get shamed, but I'd get notches on my belt. But because I fell in love with a man, a good man, my whole life got destroyed. And you were part of that destruction."

"I was afraid for you. And people act out when they're afraid."

"Admit it, though." The rain starts again. It's a mist I'm thankful for because I'm fighting back tears to say it. "You were ashamed of me too. I saw it in your eyes."

There are many emotions that pass over a person's face. Shame is not one you forget when it's cast your way.

Years can pass, but it's powerful and it creeps up on you. The fight is not letting it pass across your face in the mirror. To not let someone else's problem become yours.

A lump swallows down his throat. He looks away at the water and I'll wait an eternity to hear him at least say it.

"What I figured out this month. Hell, all these years without you was that I was ashamed of *myself*." That shocks me. "I should've been stronger for you. I should've stood up for you."

It starts to fracture. The ice around my heart for him. It starts to fall off in chunks into the ocean that's separated us for too long.

Charlie was right; this hurt me more than I could admit. My parents rejecting me, after so many years of love; it shredded my soul and I wasn't the same.

I settled for distractions. For easy companions. For partners for a night or maybe a few weeks. But no one got that close again. No one got to hold me or try to heal the tattered pieces of me inside.

We don't need our parents' approval to live our lives. But their love sure is nice to have if you can.

"I'm sorry, Son." He faces me and the words that free me the most fall from his lips. "I love you... and I'm sorry."

It's not fast. It's not dramatic. He stands up and trods down the wet steps. I walk across sopping grass to meet him halfway and it's natural, the way our arms wrap around each other.

I bite it back. Emotions flood me and I just squeeze my dad once more.

"So does this mean you're gonna get your wife back too?"

Dad pulls back from our embrace and grins. "I told you a man does for his family. That means he eats crow for them too."

"So when I show up at the Yacht Club with Cade Bryant, you're proud." I keep my grip on his shoulder. "What if I show up with a man instead? What happens then?"

Dad pulls in a deep breath. "I get used to it."

"I deserve more than that. So does the person I love."

"I'm human. I can change but it ain't overnight. I love you, and I'll get used to it. Just be patient with me." He grins. "I'll welcome a man. But that Cade Bryant? She's a hard diamond. You'd be a fool to give her up."

I have to ask. I have to seize this moment because I'd rather confront it now in private than with dozens of witnesses. "What if I show up with a Cade *and* a man?"

Dad cocks his eyebrow.

I can see the struggle in his eyes. Like I'm asking him to change from stripes to spots to stars... in seconds.

"Then I gotta give you a toast," he says. "Because I don't know where the hell you inherited the stamina for all that."

The laugh is fast. It erupts from my chest and I pull him in for another hug.

At least he's honest.

At least he's here.

At least he's trying.

I DON'T GIVE him much time to backtrack. My dad said he'd try. Like "getting used to it" was a hit to first base and he promised me a home run if I came to play.

So I do.

Like the World Series.

I accepted his invitation to an after-regatta party at my parents' estate this weekend.

When we stepped onto the patio brimming with guests, Cade knew how to dress the part. Her demure gingham sundress is preppy, it's proper. Redix impressed me. Only he could wear seersucker pants and make them look like he didn't leave his perfect balls at the door. Because that's what most men look like in preppy fashion. Like they got money but no balls.

Cade flatly refused to let us wear bowties though. "They're lady-boner killers," she warned, so we both opted for crisp, white linen button-downs.

Jaws dropped at the sight of us entering the party. "Just a small one," my mom had said. A few hundred people under a big event tent in the back yard with dozens more spilling onto their long dock out to the river.

I knew heads would turn for Redix Dean.

He's a global celebrity, a local legend, and a visual orgasm wearing flip-flops.

But then he stayed by my side the whole time. We didn't hold hands but our shoulders brushed. Our smiles were wide for each other. His whisper in my ear was often with his sexy taunts like, "You make khakis look way too hot."

It's obvious to everyone we're very close.

And then there's Cade.

People knew her too. From her modeling. From the famous ad she did with Redix and all the paparazzi photos since. And she's in the local news some.

When she holds my hand with pride, her smile captivates, and everyone turns her way. You can't hide her statuesque beauty under any dress. And you can't miss how she's not intimidated. Not even by the South's most judgmental characters.

For two hours, we worked the crowd. We had lots of admirers and Dad made the introductions.

When he did, he didn't lie. I *am* friends with Cade and Redix. I *do* fish with her, and I *did* sell him his boat.

But Dad knows the three of us are much more and it starts to ease into his shoulders. Over the hours, he's wearing "used to it" pretty well.

So I meet him halfway.

I'm all smiles, handshakes, and chats, but I don't shove my unconventional relationship down the throats of my dad's closest friends.

Not yet.

I don't hold Redix's hand or kiss him too. Though I want to. And the affection between Cade and Redix is minimal. Mostly for this show, but also you can sense they still have shit to work out.

Mom doesn't need any time. She adores Cade and swoons for Redix.

We finally get a break from the crowd by hiding in the kitchen. Chatting with my mom who's fussing over deviled eggs the catering staff is taking out to the guests, Cade asks her, "So what was Silas like as a kid?"

"A blond water rat." She winks my way. "I could always find him down by the river."

"Did you grow up in this house?" Redix looks around at all the crown molding and my mom's penchant for anything regal and yellow.

"Yeah." I sip my iced tea and wonder how much has changed since I left. Nothing probably. But what about...

"Your room's still the same." Mom reads my mind. "I kept it waiting for you." She swishes over to me, giving me a peck. "Give them the grand tour. I've got guests to tend to."

It's almost embarrassing the opulent rooms I stroll Cade and Redix through. Room after room of yellow, coral, and green and everything pineapples and palm trees. All formal. All colorful. All very southern.

I save my bedroom upstairs for last. It's at the end of the owner's hallway and I hesitate to open it.

It's like stepping back into innocence before all the pain.

"Hey"—Cade caresses my shoulder—"let's go forward, remember?"

I turn to her, giving her a kiss, and taking my own advice. Bedrooms may not change. But people do.

I open the door and even the smell is the same. Clean linens. Lemon polished furniture. A waft of leather and boy is still in the room.

"Dude"—Redix picks up a framed photo of me playing lacrosse in high school—"I swear this could be me."

"Yeah, rub it in." Cade noses around my old desk. "Y'all both were pussy magnets in high school."

"Only for yours." Redix cocks an eyebrow while I shrug, guilty.

"What can I say?" I push open the white door to the ensuite bathroom. I used to love the giant tub in here. "I got around some."

They follow me in.

"You were twelve-years-old with a spa bathroom?" Cade marvels at all the white marble and gold fixtures.

"I just liked the tub. I could practically swim in it."

Redix leans against the double-sink vanity. His scrutiny is deep. "Did you ever get lonely? Like all this money but still, you had no one who knew the real you?"

"Yeah. Deep down I always felt like I didn't belong. For the longest time, I couldn't say why. I was just too busy being what my parents wanted."

"What freed you?"

How Redix sees my pain in a matter of seconds, I'm drawn to him. How Cade makes me stronger. They feel like the sun and I'm being pulled into their explosive orbit.

"I met Alec and pieces fell into place. I felt lucky to be with him and scared at the same time. I wasn't scared of *loving* him. I just knew I couldn't have this world and be with him also."

"Do you still feel that way?" Cade's voice hums with concern. "Like you can't be who are and have this too?"

I look over her shoulder to the large window overlooking the lawn and river. Dots of people mill about in pastels outside. Music wafts up to this second level. That's as close as I'll allow that world to affect me.

"Fuck 'em," I answer. "This is my home and family. The one my grandma worked hard for. If they got a problem with me, it's exactly that—their damn problem. Not mine."

"Just promise me." Cade wraps her hand around my waist. "If *we* ever become a problem, we talk about it."

"Yeah." Leaning back on the counter, Redix crosses his arms. "No secrets. We talk before things become a problem."

That was meant for Cade as much as me. His eyes firing into hers confirms it.

"For now." She reaches, pulling me by my neck to her lips. "We very much belong together."

It's so easy kissing her. Tasting the lemon on her lips from the pie she ate downstairs, she stirs my appetite. Gently biting down her neck while I cup her breasts, she's been teasing me with her incredible cleavage in this dress.

Yes, I belong.

I belong with them.

I turn and Redix lifts off the counter and goes next. Taking a long kiss from her before he equally shares mine, he smells like his cologne and the sun we got outside. I brush against him and the seersucker he's wearing can't contain his growing appetite for this too.

"Right here," I tell them. "I want us right here together. Where I was lonely for so long, but I'm not anymore."

In quick strides, I close and lock the bathroom door.

It's barely a minute before we're all undressed. Cade wears only a coy, sultry smile. Our clothes drape over the dry edge of the tub while she turns to sit atop the countertop of the bathroom vanity.

"I could watch you two forever," she says, spreading her legs. She fingers herself, lightly circling over the pink nub of her clit.

"You wanna watch?" Redix's deep voice likes her tease. He presses behind me and I moan as he starts stroking my cock getting hard at the sight of Cade.

We're presented with so many choices again, and we still owe Cade her night, but it's like we all know. This one's for me. This is my coming home party.

Cade's getting so ready for our fuck. The peaks of her nipples beckon my lips to them because holy hell, the woman is a fantasy in flesh.

So is Redix behind me. His grip on my shaft gives expert pumps and twists. His chest presses to my back while his hips deliver slight thrusts. Like from his position it's instinctive. There's no thought for him, only an urge to fuck as he wedges his hard cock between my ass cheeks.

"Fuck me," I tell him. "Fuck me while we fuck her together."

The steam of his breath over my ear is as hot as the look in Cade's eyes. Her fingers dip inside before she pulls them out and offers them to my lips to suck. They're glistening and taste like her tangy sugar.

"Are you sure?" Redix asks while I lick her fingers clean.

I don't answer him. Easing from between their seductive bookends, I grab my pants from the tub. There're two condoms in my wallet.

Don't judge.

I usually carry five.

Without a word, I hope it's still in this bottom drawer, and yes, it is. The same jar of Vaseline.

"Just use a little," I tell him while I tear the condom open with my teeth. It turns me on, rolling it down his hard length before I take a small swipe of Vaseline and coat his sheathed cock. "It's not ideal, but it's all I got in here."

His eyes are transfixed. "I'm not complaining." He slightly thrusts into my fist prepping his huge cock for this. "I've never done this. I don't want to hurt you."

"Just go slow," Cade soothes, scooting to the edge of the countertop. She's at the perfect height for me while I wrap my cock too.

She's so wet for this, I can tell, but I tease her. I lick her nipples, sucking them to pert, wet tips for me to play with while I say, "He starts and you get to watch."

I brace my hands on either side of her thighs and sway my back to take Redix in. Like he can intuit what I need, how to get me ready, he uses his fingers, teasing then entering me while he strokes me again.

"It's gonna feel so damn good fucking you," he says and that alone stammers my breath with Cade's perfect breasts in my face, taunting my tongue to keep licking them.

Wedging his tip, pushing it to my entrance, his husky voice urges again over my ear. "Tell me I can do this. That you want this."

And I know why he has to be sure. That'd he'd never do it any other way. And fuck, it could break my heart if I wasn't so damn hard for him and desperate for Cade.

"Yes, I want you to fuck me," I tell him before pulling Cade into a kiss. I want her lips. I want her breath. I want her with us while he does this with me.

"You're so tight," he almost sighs and it's slow, it's exquisite. It's how many minutes, I don't know, but the time he takes with the strokes he gives makes me demand more. I have to growl back coming just feeling his burning entrance, at his mass inside, taking more than my breath away. He's pushed into everywhere, my body and heart. Just like her.

"You can move," I tell him when he's finally inside and holding still for permission. "You can fuck me."

His pecs heave pressed to my back while he lets go of my cock and grabs my hips, and my breath is a struggle with his thrusts.

"Your ass feels so good," he groans in my ear and my muscles are liquid lead. Pressure dominates my senses and it's him inside me and exactly what I crave.

"Fuck me, Redix," I tell him before I nip Cade's lip and really feel his mass move everything inside me. Goddamn, I forgot how good this feels. It makes my eyes roll back, urging him on, "Yes, fuck my ass."

"You're both so beautiful," Cade sighs, looking down at how hard I am for his fuck. How I've needed this. How my jutting cock bounces with Redix's moans and thrusts. "Damn, this is hot." Cade reaches down, her nipple near my lips and hand stroking me tight.

"Fuck, hang on." I almost blow right there. My brain

blitzing, not believing this pleasure. This sight. Damn, it's paradise.

Redix holds still. I grab breaths until I have control again. Because I want more than this. I want who I am, completely.

I want both of them.

"You're with us," I tell her and Redix moves with me. Like he's glued to my back, he slightly steps forward with me and bends his legs with mine and we find the rhythm while Cade guides my cock into her ready pussy.

"Oh Goddamn," I groan because I don't know how long I can last like this. Her tight heat. His blinding presence. They both squeeze the air from my lungs and it feels so natural between them, trapping me in ecstasy that robs my reality except for this truth.

How the three of us meld, filling spaces that have ached for so long. That felt a void or a pain and finally to have this together; it's almost too much. I almost fear I can't do this. If I let go, I'll fall so deep into their love. And it's a raging one. But I try.

I kiss her, then Redix leans over my shoulder, kissing her too. Each touch of her lips fills me with awe, my mouth wanting more. I grab her hips and thrust into her pussy, finding our rhythm, driving into her while he grabs my hips, moving into me the same. Oh fuck, we're three mouths moaning with pleasure, three bodies pulled into a wild surge of pleasure, and three hearts that trust this.

"Fuck, this feels incredible," Redix swears into my shoulder. "Your tight ass is taking my cock and I can hear yours smacking into her sweet pussy. My God, I could fuck y'all forever."

And I could too.

But Cade is shaking, her eyes not looking up from how

our bodies align. She's close. I lick my fingers and circle her clit. "You like this, don't you, Cade? How we're both fucking into you."

"Yes," she sighs and she's there.

"Redix is fucking my ass with his thick cock and I'm fucking your tight pussy and you're gonna come, aren't you?"

Muffling her screams and holding still the thrash of her body to keep ours aligned, she shakes so hard. We can hear the partygoers on the lawn outside while her eyes roll back with a primal groan that sends Redix into a fast pump.

He's watching her too. Like her orgasm unleashes him every time and he's thrusting fast and "Fuck yes," I encourage him. "Fuck us both," I demand because he is and it's making me come and that sends Cade into another spasm like her first one never stopped.

Her head rests on my shoulder while she bites into my flesh with a deep moan and Redix takes my other shoulder the same way. His shaft pulses so violently, his grunts as deep as his cock is inside me and my knees get weak. I brace myself. I have to hang on to Cade while I come harder than I knew possible. It erases my brain. It yanks me down into the three of us together and drops me so deep into all of us.

It's powerful. It's goddamn amazing. I don't know how people survive this.

33

My Enemy by CHVRCHES

Two things I never thought I'd ever wear—seersucker pants and a smile so content because I was just with a man too.

And for me, it could never be just *any* man.

Only him.

Silas is the only man I've ever felt this pull toward. To kiss him. To taste him. To be inside him. And he's the only one I can watch even touch Cade and have it warm my heart instead of turning me into a raging fury.

All I've known is feeling protective over her. With good reason.

Yes, she can protect herself now, but I trust no one else with her heart.

Hell, truth is, Silas is safer for her. I've broken her heart so many times while all he does is cherish it.

Just watching the two of them, holding hands and sipping tea while we return to the party. I could feel jealous. I could feel defeated. I could bow out and resign myself to a life of misery and let only Silas love her.

But that's impossible.

I watch Cade smiling with guests. Her post-fuck glow makes her a beacon like subconsciously people can tell and it attracts them to her.

But only Silas and I see it true.

We love her.

And what we just did in his bathroom is more than true for me. It's more than sex. It's more than fucking a man for the first time. A man who was fucking the only woman I'll ever love at the same time.

It was a surrender. It was a letting go of binds that have held me down for so long.

Each time I'm with Silas, I think I'm free, only to kiss him again or feel his touch and then I feel another piece of my pain break away.

And Cade is my anchor.

Without her, I'd be too scared to do this with him. It's not right if she's not there. Nothing's right if she's not in my life.

And Silas? I didn't know a heart could expand like this. I didn't know it could morph into shapes that allow for more love.

Yes, I'm fucking glowing too. I radiate with a peace I've

never known and the afternoon sun over the river ain't got nothing on me.

I'm standing with the two people I need the most as we make our last mingle through the crowd, working our way back toward Silas's family estate.

This place makes a mansion look like a shack. I've seen palatial homes in LA. Hell, all over the world. But here, like many places in the South, it's rooted in a horrible history that only adds to the gravity of the place.

Honestly, I don't feel comfortable here, but I do with Silas. And with Cade by our side, I can suck it up.

"My, my"—a voice slithers over my shoulder—"ain't I just shittin' in high cotton to find you two here."

It's sudden. It's a trigger. It fires inside me at the sound of his evil and Cade whips around, confronting it before me.

"Senator Evans." I turn to watch her eyes go dead while her voice stays sweet. "Mrs. Evans. How lovely to see you both."

I thought I had my bearings.

I thought I was over this.

Her greeting turns Silas from his conversation to join us. They both square their shoulders at Gentry while I sip my tea and stare at the horizon.

I was wrong.

I'm not afraid of Gentry. I could pound the man's skull into chunks on the pavement.

I don't fear him. I fear the memories.

Those I can't kill.

"Mr. Van de May." Gentry gives his full attention to Silas. *What a dick.* He knows where power resides. "Thank you for inviting us to this lovely gathering. My crew is enjoying themselves."

"I won't take the credit." Silas stands beside me, his arm brushing mine while he faces my opposition. "I didn't invite you. *All* the racers and their crews are here."

"Indeed, let me introduce you to some of mine..."

And Gentry drones on with names.

He won't miss this opportunity. To be seen with the Van de May heir? To act like he has Silas's full support, it's a deft and dick political move and I'm seething inside while I feel Cade reach for my hand.

She stands on the other side of me, closer to Gentry's wife and Cade's rage is palpable. I know when it's itching through her veins. She can feel the twitch of my hand too, the way it sweats, and that's all it takes.

"Gentlemen." She drips her voice like honey. "Just how do y'all have the fine pleasure of knowing our state Senator because Gentry and I go *way* back. He's got quite the dark past you know."

Don't do it, Cade. Just walk away.

She promised me she'd follow the rules this time. That she used the law.

"That was just a little mischief among kids." Gentry laughs and his cronies chuckle with him.

I don't need to know the dickhead crowd he must run in. Do they all find humor in an assault?

"Mischief is a lie, Senator." Cade squeezes my hand, stepping toward Gentry's taunt.

Fuck, why? Why can't we ever escape this?

"You sure do keep mischievous company," she says. "Criminal in fact." Because she won't let it. Cade won't stop fighting. "I bet all these fine, traditional southern men would be well served to know the company *you* keep. On record."

I don't want it this way. I need to move on.

I don't want to be tied to Gentry like a prison sentence. I fought too hard to free myself. To find the good in all the bad we survived.

Why is Cade so obsessed? Why can't she leave it alone?

"Mere speculation." Gentry sounds delighted. Like this is a sport for him too. "Men in our positions get targeted all the time. It's par for the powerful course."

"Your position?" Cade's pulling the trigger. Silas is a witness. Gentry's wife, I can smell her perfume, she's not peeping a word.

And I know I look odd, standing like a stone, staring at the horizon, but fuck *you* world, I've fought enough.

"Your position, Senator"—*but Cade will never stop*—" is that you are cousins, golf buddies and former business associates with a man wanted in three states for rape. Derek Baucom. There's a warrant for his arrest and he's been spotted in *your* district."

Cade keeps firing. "Your position, Senator, is that you have a close association with a known drug felon we went to high school with. Taylor John. He's been in trouble with the Sheriff's office so much so his recent disappearance from *your* district is odd."

Damn, she's ruthless.

TJ's dead because of *her*. But she'll implicate Gentry just to take him down. And the seethe in her voice? No one can deny the truth in it.

"How do those scandals score on *your* political course, Senator?"

She's too damn smart.

And that peace I felt, for just a few minutes? It's like the perfect week Cade and I shared. It was my dream. It was all I wanted.

And Cade just ruined it again with her vendetta against Gentry.

"Perhaps, Senator." She empties her gun. "Your friends should know the true company you keep. Not all of them can afford such associations with known criminal *mischief*."

Throats clear at the awkwardness she just blasted into the air like a July Fourth fireworks show. Eyes dart. Feet shuffle. Distance grows between Gentry and his "friends".

No, they can't afford to be associated with *that*.

"Well, Ms. Bryant." Gentry finally seeps a reply. "You know well about mischief too. Just ask your friend, Mr. Dean. He's had not a word to say, but he doesn't need to. We've all seen his videos. We've seen the recent news. We all know about *his* scandals."

"Hold him down." My memory flashes. I can't stop it. *"Hold the pretty boy still." It's Gentry's voice. It's Derek pinning my wrists. "This is gonna feel real good." Gentry's talking by my feet, grabbing my ankles. Sand's in my mouth. I'm choking on it and a pain I've never known. "Yeah, TJ. Make it look good." Gentry's voice is a scab on my psyche. Picking it open while the feeling of the wet, hot drips of my blood across the flesh of my ass seeps back into my memory. "I'm gonna want a picture of this." The delight in Gentry's voice. The sneers on Derek's face. The grunts from TJ and Gentry's laughter.*

Gentry laughed.

He laughs.

"Nice deflection, Senator," Cade fires back, "but your scandals are illegal"... but I'm gone...

There's an open bar at this party.

I mapped it the second I walked in. I've been drinking iced tea all day but I can smell the beer they're pouring.

It lures me over.

Without a word, I don't even hear the rest of the fight. I walk away from it.

Voices are muffled. Sights tunnel. All feeling goes except for this driving urge. Steps take me toward my escape and away from those memories. In seconds, six feet stand between me and the edge of the bar.

The edge of my death.

That's how it works. Addiction picks up where it last left off. For me, I was two breaths away from dying before Cade saved me.

But now, it feels like she's pushing me there. Pushing me into one more breath left before I have to do this.

The bartender's an older man. His hands fly over bottles, flipping glasses over and pouring more escapes into a cup. The thought drops from the heavens like I pray every day for it to.

My dad would be his age.

I haven't seen him since I was five. He could be dead. He could be on a barstool. It's one or the other.

The bartender lifts his eyes and sees me staring. It's not my fame he's responding to. He doesn't know my face, he knows the question in my eyes. He stands up straight and stops his commotion to confront mine inside.

What do I want?

No other person. No other thought. No other reason I do this but for me.

No.

The pull of my heart away from this is more powerful. With every step I take away from that temptation, I move faster, my feet sure of the direction I need to go.

Anywhere but here.

Minutes later they find me. Leaning against the car I

bought Cade, I wait because it's all I can do. I'm not going back.

Silas and Cade step out the front door of his house and don't take their concerned eyes off me.

I'm not fine. I'm not drinking. And I'm furious with Cade.

What else is new?

"Are you okay?" she asks once she's feet away.

"Don't ask like you care," I answer, climbing into the back seat because I can't look at her.

Silas takes the driver's seat while she jumps into the passenger side and it's a stone silence over the three of us for the first of the two-hour drive back to Hilton Head.

"I didn't have a choice." Her voice finally cracks the quiet.

And me.

"Pull over," I bark.

Silas slows off the edge of the Lowcountry highway. He finds an unmarked sandy road, probably someone's driveway, and parks us there.

I jump out. Crickets scream around me while the noise in my head is worse.

Cade jumps out too. "Are you gonna talk to me?"

"I have to piss." I drop my fly and seek this mindless task because all else leads to ruin.

"Then piss and talk." She's by my side and doesn't flinch at my stream. It flows like the rage in my veins. "I didn't do anything wrong."

"That's just it though." I shake the dew off and adjust myself. I won't look at her. The storm blowing in overhead is far calmer. "You *did* something, didn't you? You always gotta do *something*."

"What are we gonna do? Let him get away with what he did to us? To other women? Let him keep Cam prisoner somewhere? Let him keep Pamela forever? Because he's got her—"

"And how the fuck does that bring her back?" I glare her way. "Admit it. You lose your temper, you gotta get your revenge, and you forget tactics. You piss Gentry off too much and Pamela will disappear for good. Wherever she is, she'll be joining TJ wherever you dumped him if you keep this up."

"Don't tell me how to do my job. Do I tell you how to act?" She steps my way and we know this fight. It keeps playing in our lives and it won't stop. "If you push a man like Gentry like I just did, he's gonna react. He's gonna make a move and I'll be ready for it."

"Decide. Decide now, because every time you push him, you push me too! This is how it was with TJ, and now it's Gentry. Last time, you picked TJ. When are you gonna pick me? When is our love more important?"

Silas steps out of the car. I see him in my periphery and God he's perfect because he knows to let us fight this out.

He leans against the car. Not entertained. He's concerned.

"That isn't a choice I have," Cade shouts back. "You or Gentry? No, it's been you *and* Gentry for over ten years. Face it. We can't run from him anymore."

"Face it? Fuck you! I *remember* it. Every time you poke that snake a new memory comes up. And they make me want to drink. But thank God, I'm stronger now, I can fight it off, but I'm tired, Cade. I'm fucking tired."

Her expression softens. "What do you remember?"

"I don't wanna talk about it."

"Try again."

My eyes slide shut with my inhale.

Dammit, she's right.

The secrets eat my soul away.

"I remember Gentry laughing and holding down my ankles. I remember sand in my mouth. I was choking on it. Whatever they did to me? It hurt so much I sucked in a mouthful and I'd thought I'd die like that. With Derek watching. With TJ doing the damage and Gentry laughing about it."

It burns in my throat. The words. The truth. "And I wanted to die. Of humiliation. Of pain. Of anger I couldn't act on. That's what I remembered today because you *had* to talk to him."

She rushes me, crying and wrapping her arms around my neck.

I don't hold her back. "When, Cade? When will you let this go? When can we finally be happy?"

"Life isn't always happy."

"No shit." I pull back from her arms. "I look at my ass in the mirror every day and I'm not fucking happy. But I don't go around making it worse." I point to Silas. "I wanna be like him. Like you. I wanna feel normal and free and able to move on, but you won't let us."

"I have to stop him. I have to catch Derek. I have to find Cam and Pamela too. Can't you understand that? It's my job."

The violet pools of her eyes. I've been swimming in them for years. I know their storms and their placid days. I know when she's bright and when darkness takes her over.

And I know when she's lying.

"But it's more than your job, isn't it? You said Silas helped you move on. That you feel free now. But you're lying. To him. To me. To yourself. Those three men. That night. It still controls you. And it does me too."

Tears stream down her cheeks.

"We keep doing this, Cade. We keep coming back to this same fight." A bright flash cracks the sky before thunder booms in the distance. "And it's gonna be the death of us."

She can stop that truth as much as she can the coming storm.

"Are you sure the cameras aren't working?"

That's the third time I've asked her. It feels weird. Not wrong, just a violation of my instinct because I don't trust her husband. I fear he's watching us.

"Yes," Stacey assures me. "Girl, I don't want those cameras catching what I've been doing. The renovation crew had to disconnect them for some electrical upgrades. Their crew chief made sure of it." She grins my way. "Sure of it *for me*."

"The crew chief?"

Every day I'm more impressed with this woman.

On the outside, Stacey looks like a blonde, proper, and

preppy southern Senator's wife. Like one who should have no sympathy for the less fortunate while she bestows tons of damning judgment on all who are different.

But no.

That's not Stacey Evans.

She's a conservative Senator's wife on a wild rampage. She's fucking every man she wants while she fucks up Gentry's life too. She doesn't share his cruel, narrow-minded politics or his wicked ways.

I'm gonna build a shrine to her.

Because though she doesn't talk about it much, I know Gentry's abusive with her. And she's finding different ways to get her power back.

"Yes, the crew chief." She leads me through her house, pushing past the plastic tarps concealing the construction zone that's now her kitchen. "And a couple of his crew."

My steps halt over a pile of sawdust and I'm gonna choke on the coffee from the travel cup I'm drinking from.

"The crew chief and *two* of his crew? Dayum, tell me more."

It actually tingles my pussy. The thought of it. Three men. I still haven't had my night with my two—Silas and Redix. The kind of night *I really* want.

Because Redix is pissed at me again and that's not how Silas wants to be in the middle of us.

It's Sunday. I've spent this past week alone and Stacey's sexy crew isn't working. Apparently, Gentry's away on one of his criminal golf tours, and little does he know the FBI is watching him. And Stacey Evans, his sweet devoted wife, is pointing the way to him.

We stand in a mess of a kitchen demolished while Stacey and I have the house to ourselves and she dishes while she sips the latte I brought her.

"It's incredible." The smile on her face has no shame. "Ford is the crew chief. He's so fucking hot. He's forty with this incredible body and he's in charge of everyone. Including me."

"In charge?" That raises my eyebrow. "Be careful. That's not sexy. That's abuse."

"Not like that, trust me." She sits on a new cabinet still in its box. "He's alpha as hell with his crew—and when we all fuck—but he wants to help me. Help me with my dad and the shit pile I'm in. He's raging over Gentry's control but I told him he can't do anything. Not yet."

"You told him about my investigation?"

Please don't tell me she got fucked so well and hard that she divulged that secret in a screaming orgasm.

"No, I promise. Trust me, I know when to keep my mouth shut." She smirks. "Or full of something else instead of the truth."

I laugh, relieved. "Three of them? That is a mouthful."

"Girl, don't knock it till you tried it. Because those three —Ford, Luke, and Mateo—I swear they're gonna be my salvation from this awful marriage."

"Sounds like they got you praising 'Oh my God' every day they're here."

"Uh-huh. That's why this renovation is taking so long. I make sure of it."

I love this woman.

Who knew I'd find such a close friend in someone married to my worst enemy?

But it does feel weird standing in Gentry's house. Even though he's not here, I can feel his evil in the air.

"What about you?" Stacey can read my tension. "Something's wrong, I can tell."

"The problem is something's *always* wrong."

I make a big box my seat too. I'll get dust on my jeans but I don't give a shit.

"I get a week of everything perfect, or a day of it, and shit goes sideways and it's all wrong because Redix is mad at me again."

She puckers her pretty lips, considering my conundrum. She knows almost everything (except for the truth about TJ) and she's equally torn.

"What happened to the break you were taking from them?" She challenges me. "You spent two months alone and then you're back with him *and* Silas. Is that what you want?"

"It took me two months to get my head together about who I love. I love 'em both. And Silas and Redix are good for each other. They have their own bond and I love it. I support it. Because Silas and me? We'll always be close. I feel secure in that. Whatever the hell we call it."

"But *you and Redix?*"

Her tone pushes that question front and center.

"But me and Redix."

It's the real question. One I've been asking myself for months.

I never used to question us. Not from the day we met at nine years old and I gave Redix a candy cane and my heart. I knew we were meant to be together. So did he.

That's the heartbreak of it.

Those three men. That night. The ten years since. The crimes they're still committing. The people they keep hurting.

Everything keeps me and Redix apart.

Everything makes me question us when all I want is one sure answer how we can make it work.

"I can see it," I tell Stacey. "I can see my life with Redix.

Years from now, we're married. We have kids and a house on a beach and simple things like pizza nights and coffee in bed. And somehow I know Silas is with us too and it's easy. It works and we don't fight anymore. We're whole."

Tears bite at my eyes. They burn at the vision in my heart, the dream that my soul knows is right… but it just won't happen in my life.

"We're finally healed and happy," I share through the few that fall. "But I can't see how we get there. It's like something's gotta give. Because we're so stuck in this. And if we don't get out, that dream will die."

And when I think of that. Of a life without loving Redix every day. Of not being by his side. I can live it… but it will ache with a painful void I know too well.

Stacey gets up and sits beside me, giving me the hug I need.

"Can I sound corny?" she asks.

"Please do." I'll take any answer.

"I believe in love. Even when if I don't have it yet. I still believe if you love someone it's not about needing to be right while the other is wrong. It's about accepting each other." She squeezes a little tighter. "And accepting ourselves."

Maybe I need to accept that Redix will never condone what I did with TJ. That I don't need his approval. I don't need it to end Gentry and Derek.

More like *how* I have to end them.

Redix doesn't see that I don't have a choice. Fate makes decisions for you sometimes.

"What about you?" I nudge Stacey. "Are you gonna keep accepting Gentry's abuse?"

Because it is abuse. Emotional. Verbal. Financial. That's pain too even though he hasn't laid a hand on her. Yet.

"I promise I'm getting out." She stands up, gesturing to

the kitchen in a mess. "I'm remodeling this house so we get top dollar for it. I'm divorcing him, and we're selling this, and I'll take my half of all I can get. This house too."

She kicks an open moving box. "And all his shit? Every room I remodel, I go through it." She kicks it again. "Junk he leaves in drawers. Bank statements he hides in A/C vents. I'm going through it all to get what's mine too."

I get up and peer into the box. It's full of pens, rubber bands, takeout menus; the stuff you cram in a kitchen drawer.

But then I notice it.

An old photo under a Thai takeout menu.

"What's this?" I pick it up.

"That's Gentry's old sailboat. His Dad left it to him. He's been trying to refurbish it for years but he gets too busy breaking the law and lives."

Her sarcasm hits me along with this picture.

It's of Gentry as a boy. He's standing with his dad on the bow of a Bayfield sailboat with a red boot stripe.

I had no idea he owned this boat. I know all his others. All his cars. All his condos. Everything about him that's public or on property records.

But not this boat.

"Where does he keep this?"

"I don't know." Stacey shrugs. "A couple of years ago he said something about getting the hull gel-coated. Haven't heard him mention it since."

I set the picture down on the box and grab my phone in my back pocket to snap a copy of it.

Because this is it. This is where he's hiding Derek. I know it.

Now we just gotta find it.

35

"Y'ALL JUST NEED TO TALK."

Silas hands me a wrench while I wedge my shoulders under my kitchen sink.

I know what's clogging this damn thing. Nicolas keeps dumping the oatmeal he hates down the sink. Renie makes him eat it. And he washes down the guilty evidence that he won't.

"Think I'm beginning to realize talking doesn't fix everything." I can't see Silas but I answer him.

And I can feel him.

His shin rubs against mine and every part of me feels at ease with him.

309

I wrench the pipe open while Silas jabs, "Spoken like a stubborn man who thinks fighting is talking."

It makes me grin. The shit he gives me about everything.

Mostly, he's joking. But when it comes to Cade, he ain't fooling around. He's fighting for us to work this out.

I don't answer him, proving his point while I crawl back out before pulling the drainpipe open.

"Why don't you hire someone for shit like this?" He's still on me and looking fucking hot doing it in board shorts and nothing else.

"Like you don't like fixing everything with your hands too."

I gotta see it. The guilty smile that lifts his full lips when I glance up at him from my knees.

"You're a hot, rich celebrity," he says. "You should pay someone for this so we can focus on me fixing *other* things with my hands around here."

Damn, I could rip his shorts down. I could take him in my mouth and hear his moans and *that* would fix me up just fine for a while.

And his emerging hard-on agrees.

But we're not alone. Any minute someone can walk into the kitchen.

I love having my family here, but at times it sucks. Like literally because right now, I wanna suck his cock so bad.

We both know it, so I turn back to my task.

"You can't fix some shit with me and Cade." I yank and there's the evidence gooped up in the drainpipe. "Trust me. We keep trying but it ain't working."

I knock the nasty goop out into a bucket before I hand Silas the pipe. Not the pipe I wish was in his hands but he goes down the hall to wash it out in a bathroom sink.

I watch his wide back, his tan muscles tapering to his narrow waist. And I don't miss his hard, round ass in those navy board shorts either.

And suddenly, I miss Cade.

This doesn't feel right without her. She should be with us. But we got in that fight on the side of the road and haven't spoken in a week. Like we both need to go to our corners and sit a round out.

It puts Silas in a bad spot. He sees her. He sees me. But every time I see Cade, I want to punch a wall because we're stuck in this fight.

I'm exhausted. She's stubborn. And we're fucked.

More like not fucking or doing anything because what can we do?

Talking won't solve that she'll do whatever it takes to take down Gentry. Legal or not.

Talking doesn't solve that Derek's out there somewhere. And the stalk of him threatens the safety of my entire family.

Talking doesn't solve that I'll always love Cade. But I worry.

I always thought *I* was the one that night ruined. And yes, it did its damage to me. And I'm healing.

But Cade won't admit it. Maybe she doesn't want to commit murder over it anymore, but it still controls her. She's obsessed. She's stuck in our past when I just need to move on from it.

"Hey." Renie appears in the kitchen, making me jump. "We're going to the movies and maybe some nighttime putt-putt. I gotta get him outta here."

Nicolas bounces like a puppy behind her. My mom tries holding down his shoulder and Scarlett, their bodyguard, stands behind them, very used to this.

"Alright." I trust Scarlett. Nothing happens on her watch. "Y'all have fun."

They pile out the front door while Silas comes back down the hall, cleared pipe in hand.

"You're still on your knees." His eyebrows dance.

"And we're finally alone," I answer him.

The sink can wait. I can't.

I can't look at him, and that body, and that big heart shining through that sexy smile on his face and not have this. Something I never thought I'd crave but I do now. So much.

The white string holding his shorts up unties too quickly before I drag them down to his ankles. His shorts fall as fast as his cock rises for me.

It's jutting out. Proud and ready for my lips as I lick them before dragging them down his thick shaft. All my troubles disappear with him. While his warm cock fills my mouth, I wish Cade were here. Kneeling beside me and sucking him off too. But she's not. And I want this too much. I need him too much. No matter how mad we are at each other, I know she blesses my love for Silas too.

He grabs my hair and his moans turn me on. I'm dripping in my jeans. I lock my eyes on his. "You look so hot with my cock in your mouth, Redix Dean," he growls and I can taste him on my tongue and moan at my name over his lips praising mine. My fist and mouth start their merciless pump and he thrusts right back. "Fuck yes, like that." He grips my hair harder.

Part of me wants him like this. On my knees while he comes in my throat, but another part of me wants much more of him.

I pull my mouth off his cock and stand up. I grab the

back of his neck and reply, "Your cock will look so hot in my ass too."

"Fuck." He slams his eyes close. "Don't tease me."

"I'm not."

"But…"

I know what he's thinking. I know what he worries about. And I love him even more for it.

"I want it," I swear it to his eyes and it feels right. "I want this with you."

"Without her here?" He worries about that too. Like we're moving on without Cade. Like I'm choosing him over her.

Never.

"She's here," I tell him. "She's in my heart. Yours too. We'll figure it out, I promise."

That's what my soul believes. It's just my head, my logic can't see how me and Cade will work. But when I'm with Silas, my heart feels it—we *can* work. Somehow.

We take a shower together. Standing in the massive marble-encased steamy room, our wet bodies grind into each other while our kisses get more aggressive.

What is this I feel for him? It's love. It's lust. It doesn't feel wrong but acting like I own him, like he's all mine doesn't feel right either.

You can't own this man. You can't claim him as yours. His wet hair slicked back. His perfect body with skin that feels like hard, wet satin. His hands that are so fucking strong. Yes, he can fix anyone. Even me.

When he grabs my cock and rubs it against his with our undersides touching in his tight grasp jerking us both off, I'm going to lose my mind. And all my troubles. "Oh fuck," I moan, wrapping my hand over his and helping him.

"You sure you want me to fuck you?" He presses his

forehead to mine and other than Cade, I've never felt this demand, this desperate for anyone else.

"Yes," I answer, crashing my mouth against his again. His lips are so full like Cade's, but his tongue invades my mouth. His aggression isn't like hers and I want more.

The sensitive friction of our cocks rubbing together drives me crazy and I have one thought. "Fuck me, Silas." I pant against his lips. "I'm gonna come just saying it." The surge is sudden. "Fuck my ass."

And I do. Spilling over his fist, glossing down our cocks, I groan and come so hard and I know I'll get hard again in minutes. His breath shakes, and his eyes take in the sight. Tightening his grip even more, his body follows mine, releasing spurts of his cum over our cocks too.

"Fuck," he grunts and it's so hot. His sounds and huffing ribs satisfy me as he leans back against the tile wall. "I'm gonna need a few minutes before I can."

"We got time."

Minutes later, I lock my bedroom door just in case. I close my curtains to the dusk outside and we crawl into my bed together.

Everything's ready for this. Lube and condoms are on my nightstand. Our bodies are fresh from a shower. There's nothing but trust here except there's one thing missing.

That one beautiful, maddening, sexy, and smart part of us that's not here.

"I wish she could see this." Silas kneels between my legs spread for him. He's hard as hell at the sight of it and so am I.

But I feel it too. She's missing.

It's a feeling I've suffered for so many years.

When Cade isn't by my side and sharing my life, the

void hurts. It's everything wrong and only she makes it right.

As much as Silas soothes me and satisfies me in ways I didn't know I needed, I need Cade too.

I know she's the one for me.

"Get your phone," I tell him.

We won't do this without her. He calls her, putting her on a video chat.

"Hey," she answers him and I can hear it in one word from her voice. She misses us too.

"We want you here for this." Silas turns the phone screen so she can see our bodies, our hard cocks, how we're aligned to fuck. "He wants me to fuck him." Those words make my cock leak. "And he wants you here too."

The look on her face. Even on a phone screen. I know her too well. She's not jealous. She's not angry. She's not even shocked.

"Y'all are beautiful," she sighs and I can tell she's in her bed too. "Let me just watch."

"I want you here," I confess from every part of me. "I want you with me. With us."

I stroke my cock, trying to tempt her. Because we can wait the twenty minutes it'll take her to get here. Hell, I've waited this long to ever want a man to fuck me. What're a few more minutes?

"I am *with you*." She lifts the phone up so I can see her hand pull off her silky pajama shorts exposing her beautiful bare pussy. "I'm right there with you both and you need this. Just the two of you. You should share this."

And she speaks a truth in my heart I just now realize. Like she's known it all along and now I do too.

I *do* need this. I need Silas to take me like I want. Like I ask him to. Like I give consent for, and not any other way like I fear I've survived.

I need this more than ever.

"You sure?" Silas turns the screen to his hand stroking his cock too. Like that'll change her mind.

"Yes," she says and I take the phone from him. The sight of her fingering herself to this fills me with a sudden desire, sudden ease to really let go. I let her watch while Silas leans over me, taking my mouth in a deep kiss while our hard cocks rub together again and mine jumps against his, begging for more.

She watches while he kneels back up and rolls a condom on. While he covers his fingers in lube and I bend my knees back. When his fingers penetrate my ass, playing and toying with me and prepping me for his fuck, I can't help my moans. The thrust of my hips and the urge in my cock wants so much more.

"Fuck me," I groan, my command, my permission demanding more of him and he delivers. Removing his fingers, he wedges his thick tip into me and I remind myself to exhale to take him.

"Go slow." Cade's voice fills the air. And it's hot because that's what she told me when I fucked Silas. Because she cares and she wants this too for me.

Silas does go slow. "You want this?" He almost whispers. "You want my cock in your ass?"

"Yes." The pressure is insane. The penetration almost burns and I gasp through it and love it. "Give me more."

I hand the phone to Silas so Cade can see.

"Watch him fuck me," I tell her and it makes us all moan. I can hear her on the other end, fingering herself and I know she'll come like we will.

Silas holds the phone in one hand and my cock in his

other. His hips and fist slowly match their tempo and it rolls my eyes back.

"Does it feel good?" Cade's voice asks from the phone, all the way to my heart. Like she's right beside me and knows this is the way.

"Yes," I answer her. "So—fucking—good."

I never thought I'd need this. I never imagined consenting to this. But I do. So damn much. It's building, flooding me with a hot, horny urge to do this all the time. To fuck and be fucked with no restraint. No shame or fear. My God, I want this.

And wanting this. Wanting him to fuck me. Asking him to. It's the liberation my soul needed.

"Yes," I hiss again as he drives in deeper, making my thighs shake. "Yes, Silas. Fuck my ass." It groans from someplace so deep inside me. "Fuck, you make it feel so good."

The sensation, it's new and it's maddening and it satisfies while he pulls out only to plunge back in with the sexiest damn grunts. He's loving this too. He's watching this. How hard my cock is for it, how I'm leaking for it and it makes him like an animal, rutting and fucking my ass and we're starving for more.

"Oh God," I hear Cade groan and I can imagine what she can see and it only makes me want more.

"*Harder*," I tell him. "Fuck me harder."

The look in Silas's eyes. It's dark. It's hot. It's taking over and his jaw clenches as his thrusts become brutal and just what I want. "Goddamn, your ass feels so good," he swears with another thrust. "So fucking tight." Another thrust. "Your cock's so hard for my fuck too."

I'm not going to last. Not with my first time like this. Not with how good this feels. His hard cock's slamming the air from my lungs. His fist is strangling my cock and drops land on my abs and I'm so close.

"I'm gonna come." I want them to hear it. To see it. "I'm gonna come with your cock fucking my ass and then you're gonna fuck Cade's ass while I fuck her too."

And that does it. That ends her with a groan so loud from the phone it fills the room and grabs my throat. The sound of her coming, it's imprinted on my sex, on my desire and it does it every time. I come squirting wet streams across my abs while I grunt, my fucking legs and lips shaking so hard I can't control it.

"Fuck!" It ends Silas too. He pulls out of me so fast it almost hurts but the sight, I'll never forget it. How he yanks the condom off and squeezes his cock making ropes of his cum mix with mine while his whole hot body shakes. "Redix," is all he says before he kisses me again.

"I love you" fills the air through our kiss and she's saying it to both of us.

"We love you too." Silas turns his face toward the phone still in his hand. We recover our panting breath, his cheek resting by mine while we see her on the screen. Silas murmurs, "And he's sorry."

"No, I'm not." I almost laugh at how he's forcing this on us. "She *knows* I'm still mad as hell."

Cade laughs too.

Because it's true. We love each other so much we can *feel* every emotion, all the easy ones, the hot ones, the really fucked up ones too. We can admit to them.

The question is, can we live with them? Can we survive them?

"Well then, y'all stay mad as hell." Silas flops beside me, holding the phone up so she can see us both. "Because mad sex is hot sex."

"We'll see," Cade replies and she's not smiling now. She's not convinced either.

"Y'all work this out," I say. "I'm gonna go clean up."

I grab the condom and gotta find my sea legs again. My body's not used to this sensation—freshly fucked. But I like it.

Wetting a washcloth in the bathroom, I like the sight on my abs too, watching them flex under my cum mixed with Silas's. I'm gonna want a picture of this one day soon. But for now, I'm thirsty as hell.

Night has fallen over the house. Silas is still talking to Cade on the phone, something about where old sailboats are moored on this island while I throw on a pair of shorts and wander out into the living room.

It's one with a vaulted ceiling and a magnificent view of the ocean outside. The wall of windows and sliding glass doors let me appreciate the sight while the house is quiet. Renie, Nicolas, my mom, and Scarlet aren't back yet.

I'm proud of them knowing Silas is here for the night. That's he's a part of my life too. I'm not hiding it from them. And they don't judge. They like him too. Hell, everyone likes Silas.

That thought makes me grin until I catch a sight that pisses me off.

Who the fuck left the door open?

I notice it. One of the sliding glass doors to the pool outside isn't shut all the way. A few inches are ajar and this should be locked.

Keith, my night guard, is walking his usual perimeter of the house and should've caught this.

Dammit, we've been dealing with this for so long people are getting lazy. Too comfortable.

I know who left it open. Nicolas.

He thinks we live in a barn and I have enough money to air condition the entire beach outside too.

If he wasn't so cute and if I didn't love him so much, he'd get in trouble.

Locking it closed, I glance outside. The ocean is calm. The palms sway to a light breeze. And Silas laughing about something with Cade on the phone fills my home. And heart.

I turn toward the kitchen to grab us a couple of waters and some snacks. Because he's gonna need some sustenance.

Because he's fucking me again tonight.

36

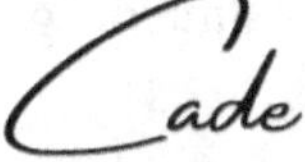

Body Say by Demi Lovato

I'M ACTUALLY SHAKING.

They're overwhelming me and my nervous system can only take so much.

It started with tulips sent special delivery to my door this morning, along with a big gift box. Inside was a crimson Alexander Wang mini dress that had Redix written all over it. The man knows fashion.

The tulips were Redix too, but the note was all Silas. And I know... he's the one who initiated their scheme.

LET'S GO FORWARD.
IT'S YOUR TURN TONIGHT.
NO FIGHTS. ONLY FUCKS.
WE'LL PICK YOU UP AT 7.

What woman wouldn't wet her panties to that? The two people she lusts for the most are orchestrating a night for her pleasure.

Yes, it's every woman's fantasy but when it's presented to you, it's also terrifying. It's too good to be real so you fear it's not.

They show up, side by side at my door, and go ahead and rip my lungs out because I couldn't breathe.

"Damn, we're lucky," was the first thing out of Silas's mouth while Redix just smiled, agreeing with Silas and his choice of my fashion.

Mix luck with lust and love and sprinkle it with a little fear. That's how I feel in this dress with a dangerously short hem. The lingerie they sent too is silk perfection against my anxious skin. My favorite Louboutins are on and my hair and makeup are done. I mixed my perfumes, dabbing both BOUND and FREE on my pulse points.

I thought that'd prepare me for this.

I thought wrong.

They're dressed in tailored black suits with white shirts. Redix's hair hangs past his shoulders while Silas has his up in a knot. Other than that difference, they're clearly a pair. And when we walk together, out to the waiting car and minutes later, into the elegant restaurant, it's clear to all eyes on us—we *are* a threesome.

Three bodies and three hearts and three minds that don't give a shit about the stares we get. The whispers. The eyes glued to us or the couple of phones that rise to our entrance.

I hold their hands while we're led to our table.

Redix planned this too. This is Luca's resort. This is his five-star restaurant. He's one of Redix's closest friends and clearly helping him roll the red carpet out for this night.

"Is Luca here tonight?" I ask as Redix pulls the chair out for me.

"He's home with Gia, but sends his best," he replies as a bottle of Taittinger's Champagne is presented to us as we take our seats.

"I don't want to drink—"

"I'm fine." Redix kisses my cheek. "Y'all enjoy the bottle. I'll enjoy my seltzer."

And that's his olive branch to me for the night.

Yes, we've been fighting. Maybe we will for a long time. There's tension between us. A question we can't answer and a divide that doesn't feel right.

It worries me. Terrifies me actually because it won't go away. Since the whole TJ thing, this space between us feels like a disease our love can't cure.

It's in my bones. It makes me ache. It hurts him too and we don't know what to do.

Silas feels like a remedy. His love soothes and gives us strength. I just hope we do the same for him.

It looks like it. He's watching our brief reconciliation with glee. He sits down on my other side and rests his hand on my bare leg.

"Let's not get too full." He orders a couple of selections from the menu before dismissing the waiter with a smile. "We have sweeter things to eat tonight."

Silas drops that tease with a grin and I only have one appetite and it ain't for anything served on a plate.

"How long has this been in the plans?" I ask before sipping champagne.

The two guilty sinners exchange a look.

"He made plans a few weeks ago," Silas informs me. "But y'all keep fighting."

"We're not fighting tonight." Redix leans over, gently kissing my cheek before his whisper tickles my ear. "We're fucking the hell out of you instead. Just like you want."

And why we wait for the French appetizers that somehow Silas knew what the hell they were and how delicious they'd be. Or why we start laughing about the over-the-top plans Redix is making for Nicolas's birthday party this week, I don't know.

We're having fun. I'm being spoiled. But I have no patience. I want this. I fear this. And it needs to happen now.

Like Redix can read the impatience written across my horny body, three small dessert plates are presented to us. Lemon sorbet.

"Send these up to my room instead, please." Redix makes the request and the entire staff reacts.

He wants to share that memory, our first kiss over sweet lemon with Silas. So do I. I'm a rush of emotions and I don't know what to hang on to. The staff leaves to fulfill Redix's wish while I look at him and then Silas.

"I want this. I want you both," I tell them. "But I'm terrified of it too."

"I've been scared as shit this whole time," Silas confesses. "From the moment you two walked into my place together."

"Why?" I thought Silas was the fearless one.

"Because it's powerful with you two—the love. I know

when y'all fight, you think it's gone, but it's not. It's even stronger then. Because at least you're fighting for it."

That leaves me speechless. Redix too.

Because Silas is right.

Fighting doesn't have to mean a relationship is over. It can mean you care so much for it that you'll defend it, you'll protect it, you'll do anything to keep it alive.

And yes.

That's the history between me and Redix.

It's carved into his skin and our hearts.

"Somebody told me something very wise," Redix says, touching my cheek before turning to Silas. "She said we can be afraid together."

I bite my lip at that memory. That moment before Redix finally told me what he'd been hiding from me for so long. His scar. His story. His pain and why he'd been afraid to tell me.

It almost snatches me down a river of tears because I love these men so much and sometimes I think fate is a shithead for the hell it throws our way.

And sometimes, like tonight, I think it blessed us because at least we're in this together.

I hold their hands proudly. We walk out of the restaurant with all eyes on us. Some judging. Some admiring. Most drooling at the sight of Redix and Silas. And suddenly fear jumps in the back seat because once I focus on what's next, desire's driving now.

I love them. I trust them. And hell yes, I want them. For one night, I won't fear it.

We make a fast trip to the suite Redix reserved. It's five-star luxury with a view of the river and I don't care. All I see are these two men, a sumptuous king-sized bed, and the luggage they've already packed and delivered to the room.

"You have us for two days. No interruptions." Silas pulls me to him, kissing me while the heavens part and all the angels sing...

Hallelujah! Praise the Pussy Goddess! I get to fuck these men for two whole days.

Redix kisses the nape of my neck while he slowly unzips my dress. The teeth of the zipper open and so do I. Air rushes my exposed back where his fingertips linger down my spine before tracing back up to the straps of my crimson dress.

He hesitates with his body pressing against my back, with every part of him hard while his husky whisper asks, "Will you choose us, Cade?"

"Yes," I answer through Silas's lips indulging my mouth, his hands skimming my hips while Redix gently bites down my neck making me moan at him dropping my dress to the floor.

They tease me. They touch me. I'm standing in the black lace bra and panties they bought for me and all my thoughts, fears, and emotions rage like a storm inside me.

For minutes my mind torments with questions without answers. But their mouths, their hands, with Redix behind me and Silas dropping to his knees before me... nothing's as strong as my body's desire for them and it takes over.

Redix turns my chin for his kiss, the one that reaches in and cradles my soul. I whimper at our truth, tears springing up to feel his love swirling with hate. But we can still do this. Our love is stronger.

Silas kisses my lips, his tongue greeting my tender clit and I groan into Redix's mouth at Silas's lavish attention. He's everything good and I cherish him.

But I worry, can this last with Silas too?

Redix teases my nipples. The lace of my bra is pulled

down, exposing my breasts still dripping from Silas's tongue and he knows just how to play with me.

"We're gonna get you so wet, Cade." He nips my ear. Silas pulls my panties all the way off. "We're gonna make you come so many times your pussy will be dripping for our hard fuck."

My knees buckle at his taunt. His promise.

Redix feels my wobble and pulls me to sit down on the chair behind him. I surrender on his lap, my back to his chest with my legs draping over his thighs while Silas follows.

"Look at you, sugar lips." Silas grins on his knees with his mouth steaming over my flesh. "We're gonna take turns fucking this sweet pussy. We'll have you begging for our cocks for days."

I groan my permission and need, grinding on Silas's mouth once his warm lips are back to sucking my clit. Leaning into Redix, I let go to this pure pleasure. Hands toying with my breasts. A mouth devouring my pussy. My arousal's wetting my thighs and Redix's hard dick pressing into my ass is driving me mad. It's like Silas senses it.

"Lift her up," he says.

Redix does, pulling me up to free his lap for Silas's access. Like usual, Redix is commando and Silas knows it. Unzipping his black suit pants, he makes quick work of freeing Redix's hard cock for all to enjoy.

When Silas sinks his mouth over Redix's fat tip, my moan matches the one from Redix's throat. Wedging Redix's cock between my lips, Silas teases us. Not letting Redix fuck me, he licks my clit and Redix's tip before rubbing it against my aching nub and I'm going to lose it. He's making my pussy drip as wet as his spit down Redix's engorged cock. Fuck, it's sexy and it's torture.

"Come here." I want him too much. "Silas, stand up."

He does; his chin glistening and his eyes possessed. I do the same to him. Dropping his zipper, he stands before me while I sit on Redix's lap and I want a taste.

It's so hot. They're both still in their suits with their cocks out and good God, I'm getting light-headed.

Silas wraps his hand around my head, guiding my mouth down his cock while I moan as he fills my mouth. My body shifts to Redix moving under me as he leans forward. He's next. I hold Silas at his thick base, pressing his crown to Redix's lips next, and damn, he loves it as much as I do. Sucking Silas's cock, giving him this pleasure, it turns us both on. So does my pussy still gliding over Redix's shaft.

We indulge him and each other. Taking turns plunging down his cock, there's not anything we won't do for him as his breath huffs thinner and thinner.

"Stop," Silas sighs. "This night is for you."

He pulls my hand to stand. I barely can. I just want to lie back in the lust that envelops me and he can tell.

"Over here," he guides me to the bed and Redix follows.

I flop down on it and insist, "Get undressed." Just so I can watch their strip. They make it a show for me, stopping to exchange kisses with me and with each other. I fling my bra off too and suddenly, I'm inspired.

"Come here," I summon them to the edge of the bed. I want us together, as close as I can. To where their bodies touch. To where I sit on the edge and revel in the sight of their cocks rubbing together. My hands can't get enough of them. Reaching for their hard chests, roaming down the ridges of their flexing abs, my hands wrap around the hard velvet of their cocks and my mouth goes next. One cock. Then the other. Over and over. No way I can get both in my mouth, but their taste mixes across my tongue, making me so hungry to try.

They kiss. They moan. They watch the sight too until Redix says, "Cade, this is for you, remember?"

"But I like this," I reply, fisting their cocks in each hand.

"I know you do." Redix grins. "But quit doing for us. It's your turn." A light flashes across his eyes. "And it's time for dessert."

Silas looks a bit confused while Redix is loving this. "Let's show him how I like to eat it."

The flood to my pussy is sudden, nerves lighting up while more wet rushes my sex and my mind is even more excited. I turn to kneel on the edge of the bed, resting my cheek against the white bedspread. The exposure thrills me like never before.

Redix spreads me open, pouring his words like honey down my crevice. "Look at our sweet treat."

I moan and on cue, Silas gets it now. Steps take him to the silver tray left on the table in the suite. Out of the corner of my eye, I watch him open the special container keeping the lemon sorbet cool while I feel Redix's warm lips kiss the small of my back.

"We'll make you so sweet"—Redix keeps teasing me—"before we get you so fucking dirty for us, Cade." Cold drops, an icy slush pours over my ass. Redix lets it drip down to my pussy and I'm dying for this.

"*Daaammmn,*" Silas mutters at the sight, at sharing Redix's fetish.

We'll be paying for new sheets in this suite and no one cares because holy fuck, they eat.

Redix's hot tongue circles my ass and I'm just going to die here and that's fucking fine because Silas kneels for his meal, circling his tongue around my clit and I can't move. I won't move. This feels too damn good.

"Oh fuck yes," I mutter into the sheets while the sounds of their sticky smacking mouths fill the air, tongues thrilling my holes and shaking my thighs. It's the only sweet sound I want to hear before Silas says, "I wanna eat her more."

He guides our bodies and I don't resist. Silas crawls onto the bed, turning, straddling my legs over him and putting my pussy over his face while his gorgeous cock is mine and Redix stands behind me.

And I don't know what's next until I hear Redix say with such deep delight, "Clean her up so we can get her real dirty."

"Oh my God," I mutter with Silas's dick pressed to my lips and Redix pulling my cheeks farther apart, so wide and so open for Silas and they can take me. I'll surrender only to them.

"Isn't that right, Cade?" It's Redix's voice, muffled with his tongue flicking my ass and rolling my eyes back. "You're so fucking hungry for our cocks, aren't you?"

I feel Silas groan into my pussy, his tongue dipping into my taste before his fingers start pounding into me and yes, I want more.

"Fuck me," I insist with my ass in the air. "Fuck me now."

Redix is in the perfect position to satisfy. It's a few seconds before I feel his invasion, his slow drive into my entire being while Silas won't stop with his mouth on my clit.

I can't speak. Groans grab my throat at this unbelievable pleasure. At Redix's huge cock stretching and fucking me to perfection. At Silas's mouth playing my clit like a maestro.

And then a wet finger, two of them press into my ass and I know what Redix is getting me ready for and I lose it.

"Oh fuck." I come so fast. It hits my body like a lightning strike, shaking my legs, taking my strength and cinching my sex so hard that Redix has to grab one of my hips to stay inside me.

"Fuck, Cade," he growls, hanging on to me because I'm not done. I reach for another breath before I groan and let it hit me again because his cock feels so good and Silas won't stop with my pussy either.

"Damn, y'all taste good," Silas mutters into where Redix is thrusting into me and I give them more, letting my body go. I growl with another dripping release all over Silas's mouth and Redix's cock and I'm not shy.

"Goddamn, she's ready," Redix almost sighs at the sight and sensation.

Like he's the one in charge for the night, which is fine by me, he directs our bodies. He lies down on his back beside me, guiding my weak thighs to straddle him next.

I gaze down at him, surprised by his choice. "I thought you said you were the only one to fuck my ass."

"Think again," he smiles and I know only like this. Only with Silas is this okay for him and I agree.

Silas kneels beside me, watching me slowly slide down to Redix's base. I want to start my ride, my show for them but Silas instructs me, "Stay right here." He lubes up his fingers from the bottle on the bed and says, "Let's make sure you're real damn ready."

Because I may need to reconsider. Redix already fills me to a stretch, to a pressure my body can perfectly accommodate but no more. Like it's obvious to Silas, probably because Redix has fucked him too. So Silas glides his fingers between my ass cheeks and gently grabs my neck with his other hand.

"Look at me," Silas says. And fuck, he can be so dominant sometimes. The man is mercurial and I love it when his usual cool sears to molten hot during our sex. "Look at me and tell me you can take this. That you love this."

Two of his fingers slide in my ass and fuck it's intense. But I'm so wet, I'm ready for it. "Yes," I murmur into his control. "Yes, it feels so good."

"What about this?" Silas likes this. There's a delight in his eyes as he eases a third finger in and it burns my edges.

"Uh," it escapes my lips. It's so much. But my hips roll without my control. My body answering louder and wanting this.

"Make her come like that," Redix insists. Like he wants to be sure. Like he wants to watch this too. He loves it when I'm on top and now he gets a new vision.

"Come on, Cade." Silas wants it too. "Ride his cock and come with my fingers in your ass."

It's not a command. It's happening. I tilt my hips just enough, my throat still in his tight grasp and my hands braced on Redix's steel stomach, it's the perfect position to rub my clit on his base while Silas relishes this.

I won't stop looking at him. "You *do* want our fuck, don't you, Cade?"

"Yes."

"Show me." Silas grins, his eyes still staring into mine. "Make that pussy come so hard if you want my cock fucking your tight ass too."

I buck at his command. At the look in his eyes. At the slam of his fingers invading me and Redix's cock filling me to the brim. My body relents with an orgasm shaking through me, opening me even more for this.

"Now," I tell him. I can't be more ready and yes, I'd even beg for it.

Redix pulls me down, resting my chest on his, and in this position, my body relaxes content. It's my home with my heart beating against his.

The bed shifts and Silas moves to the perfect position. His legs wrap over Redix's and our bodies line up. The heat of it. The touch of us together in this most intimate position. Complete surrender takes my heart.

"Be careful with her." The words escape Redix's lips and I lock my eyes on him, tears wanting to escape.

It doesn't matter how mad Redix gets. How much we fight. How much we feel so overwhelmed and defeated sometimes, we still have this. He still *loves* me. And it fills every part of me as he cups my cheeks and holds me there and I know it.

He doesn't look away as the pressure of Silas starts to ease inside me too. "Oh God," I sigh at the power of it.

"Tell me," Silas says, pulling my cheeks wide apart.

I know he'll be careful. I know he won't hurt me. "Yes." I start to pant. His penetration is so intense. "Yeah," I mewl. It's pressure to the tips of my ears. Tingling to my fingertips. "Yeah." But I want it. I don't want him to stop. "Yeah." It strains my ribs, constricting my breath.

Back and forth, Silas moves slowly in, pulling out gently to push back in again, a little more each time. "Keep telling me," he says. "Tell me you want this."

"Please, more," I beg Redix's eyes and Silas's cock. Redix is already seated deep inside me while Silas finds new space, slowly stretching my body for this. Like he's already done to my heart. I have room for him. Two men fill me with a love so great I can take their bodies and lust too. I want it.

"Yes, fuck my ass, Silas," I say with my eyes on Redix. A dark desire starts to shadow his eyes. "Can you feel him?" I ask Redix. "Can you feel him fucking my ass while you're fucking my pussy?" Even those words feel orgasmic from my lips.

"Yes." Redix thrusts his hips.

"Oh fuck," I gasp. I wasn't ready for that. "Let me," I suggest and they hold still.

I reach behind me, guiding Silas in at my pace while my thighs start to lift and lower on Redix's length. It's slow. It's a ride that drives them in, deeper and deeper until the pressure, the pain, it leaves my body and now it demands the pleasure.

They do too. Finding a gentle rhythm, Redix is enraptured under me, watching my face, feeling Silas's cock inside me at the same time. I know it's getting him off.

"Yes," Silas keeps moaning from behind. "Fuck, this looks so hot." He grabs the bottle of lube from the bed. "Here," he says and I feel more slick ooze pour over us, the glide of their cocks easing as my body takes their thrusts faster, my pace getting hungry.

"Oh my God," it's all pleasure beyond my wildest imagination. "Yes, fuck me," I'm telling them both and their hips work together, their cocks are pistons, one sliding out while the other slides in and my greed grows. And will it ever stop for them?

"Yes," I lift up from Redix's grasp so he can feel *and* watch, so I can arch my back and take more of Silas's fuck while Redix rolls his hips under me, his cock making my pussy clamp down for more.

My tits start bouncing to their dual fuck as Silas grabs my shoulders, pulling me down his length while Redix grabs my ass, his grip spreading me so wide for their matching thrusts now.

"Oh God." I can't find myself. I can't find any thought. "Oh, yes." I don't want to except for this. "Don't stop." Except for their fuck. "Fuck me so hard." And they do.

"*Yessss*, that's it." Silas pulls me harder, arching my back more. "Roll that sweet pussy and tight ass over our cocks." He drives me crazy talking like that. "Take us like you know you want it." And he knows it. "Come on, Cade. Keep fucking both our cocks."

I want to stay here. I want to stay on this edge. I never knew it existed and now I'm never leaving. There's nothing I won't do with them here. I've never let go like this. I've never known trust like this, pleasure like this.

Redix looks up at me in bliss, unable to speak from the pleasure but Silas won't relent. He's going to take me. "Your pussy's gonna come so hard because you fucking love this, Cade, don't you? You love getting fucked like this. You love two cocks inside you."

Yes, I do. I can't speak. I have no control. It's the biggest wave ever rising inside me and I fear its crash. My body shakes, scared and thrilled for its arrival while my eyes lock on Redix's and I'm safe.

His mouth hangs agape. His eyes are hooded. He's losing it too watching and feeling this.

"Come on." Silas urges me through clenched teeth. "Fucking come with my cock in your tight ass and his in your wet pussy." And he smacks my ass to make me snap. "Come on our cocks."

"Oh, God!" I convulse. I explode. No sight. No sound. It's an annihilating pleasure detonating my body stretched to an expanse it almost can't take. Everything inside me shakes, clenching down on the bliss of them inside me while it pulses through.

I swear it lasts forever, this perfect destruction while Redix pulls me down, holding me through it. With one more thrust inside, my shaking body ends Silas with deep, loud grunts, his hips shuddering against my backside, his grip so tight on my shoulders.

My breath heaves. I start to come back when Redix lifts my lips to his. He's not done. He didn't come yet, but he's close, I know it by *his* breath.

"Cade," Redix whispers against my lips. Silas is still hard inside me while Redix keeps pumping his hard cock, riding out the wave of my pleasure. "Cade." But the look in Redix's eyes. It's more than his orgasm. I know his heart. I know his soul. I see it in his gaze desperately searching mine. "Cade, please."

I know what he's begging. My soul begs it too. *Hang on to our dream. Don't let it die.*

His jaw tenses and his back arches. It locks his body in a seize he can't control, his cock pulsing inside my walls so full I feel him filling my body while my heart floods with it.

"I love you, too." I cry to his gaze clinging to mine. Because we've been through so much. And we want this. We need it like our next breath. Our love is so great it hurts sometimes and we just want to find the other side of our nightmare.

We just want our dream together.

37

∞

It's like watching two people crawl to shore. Like they've been through hell and almost drowned, but together they fought to survive.

And all you can do is feel happy to see they made it. Like they make you believe again in hope.

I'm still inside Cade. I'm still recovering my breath and I can feel their love. I can hear Redix softly calling her name and I can feel her orgasm leaving her in tremors while he comes pulsing against my cock. The intensity of it takes them into tears.

I'm not jealous. I'm not hurt. I'm in awe. It tightens my

throat, threatening to burn my eyes while I can literally feel them share this.

They've had this love for so long, they don't realize how amazing it is. How rare it is.

Cade starts crying in Redix's arms. He holds her there and I ease my way out to give them this moment. They need it. They've been through so much and they're tired of the fight.

I lie down on the pillow beside Redix to catch my breath. But I give them space, I try to give them this time like I'm not here.

But Cade lifts up from his hug and sees me lying here.

"I love you, too," she says, leaning her tear-stained cheeks over me before her soft kiss. "Thank you." She nuzzles her nose to mine.

"You're welcome." I mean it.

Redix turns to me. "You okay?"

"We're post-threesome fuck." I try to joke. "What else would I be?"

But we all feel it.

Something just happened. Something just shifted and it hits me so hard I have to turn my head.

I can't look at them.

"Hey." Cade climbs off Redix. "Hey, come here." She's on top of me, trying to turn my chin her way. "Silas, what's wrong?"

I can't talk. Not until all the pieces settle in my chest.

"Hey." Redix touches my shoulder. "We just gotta talk, remember? That's what you tell my thick skull all the time."

Cade lies on top of me, her limbs twisting with mine and I hold onto her body, onto her warmth. Redix slides up closer beside me and his touch calms me too.

"We all stay right here," Cade murmurs against my chest. "We keep holding you until you're ready to talk."

I huff a small laugh. If that ain't the truth. Cade's so stubborn she'll cling to me like a barnacle until I speak.

This moment was coming, I always believed it. I kept asking myself the question about Cade. Then about Redix. I kept my heart open to it and it just hit me like a wave over my back, knocking me down and pulling me under and I can't deny its power.

"I feel it now." I turn my head so I can tell them both. "I feel what I want now."

"Which is?" Redix's eyes can be so soft sometimes. Like the safest blue sky to fly in.

For all his brawn and swagger, he's got the biggest heart.

"I want what you two have."

"You *do* have us," Cade says.

"You know I love you," Redix says it for the first time to me and it's all I've felt for quite a while.

"I love you too." I smile at him. "Both of you." I squeeze Cade's hips. "But I want my own love. I want to find someone like y'all found each other and I want to start new and discover everything with them. And I want to fuss and fuck and fight and laugh and I want it all."

"Do you feel left out with us?" Cade's brows furrow. "I'm so sorry if we made you feel that way."

"No. That's not it. I love you both and I'm happy for you. I just feel... I don't know... selfish. I want my *own* love. And maybe I don't want to share it with anyone else."

"But what about us?"

Redix looks hurt like he's losing me. He's more afraid of this than Cade.

"I don't know who I'll meet, but I know I will one day.

I'll find them. And what if they're not okay with this? With us? I don't know."

Redix flinches. "So we're over?"

"No." I crane my neck for his kiss. He relents, giving me one back but he worries. "We're not over." I hum against his lips. "I just want to tell y'all now... I'm not staying forever."

"You need to be free," Cade says it like she gets it completely.

"Yes, I want to be free to find a love like you two have."

It's a long night while we talk it out more.

Cade understands. I see it in her eyes though I know she's worried because Redix is hurt.

He's not even mad about it. He goes straight to stunned silence until I start kissing him into a reaction. Until I touch his chest and start opening his mouth with all that my hands can make him feel.

"I feel like I'm losing you." He grabs the back of my neck. "When I just found you."

"You're not losing me." I grab him back. Cade's pressed to my back and encouraging this. She doesn't want him hurt either. "You're letting me go, but I promise I'll keep coming back."

"What will that look like?" Redix has been through so much. He doesn't like uncertainty.

"What do you mean?" I smile. "You only want me for the sucks and fucks?"

That makes him laugh. "I mean, hell fucking yes, those are great." I swear he stares into my soul. "Just don't take your friendship away too. You can't be with someone that fucking insecure that we all can't at least be close friends. Promise me that."

"I promise."

And I do, crawling on top of him, proving it with my

body while Cade joins me, and we both please him until he's sure.

Until I'm inside him while Cade has his hard cock in her mouth and I've never seen Redix writhe so much. I've never heard him groan so deep. It's more than the pleasure we're killing him with. It's a promise he's asking that we'll stay connected somehow.

And we spend the rest of the night and the next day, the three of us in bed. Or in the shower. All over that suite with room service trays sliding in and out the door, we fuck and talk and fuck again and sleep until I hope after two days, they know.

I'm always going to love them.

And yes, if I can, if we want, we can fuck too because it heals us all.

But I just wish they'd get it.

That they could see past all their hurt and pain. They have a love so great, that anyone would want it.

And I know there's someone out there waiting to find it with me too.

38

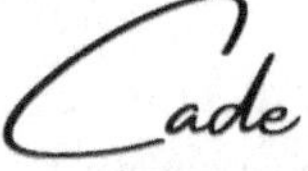

I wake up sweating, my tank top soaked and something's wrong.

Tapping my phone, it's one a.m. I'm alone in my bed, trying to recover my body and heart from our two days in the hotel suite. It was so intense. All that we felt and fucked and tried to work through.

Some of it worked.

Silas and I will always be okay. I never felt possessive over him. I want him to be happy. And maybe it's because I had more time with Silas, but Redix isn't taking it well.

Silas wanted time alone. He kissed us goodbye and left

and I could see it written across Redix's dropped shoulders; he's heartbroken.

We're not completely healed and now he feels he's lost Silas too.

I didn't want to suffocate Redix. I didn't want to run and save him. He's a grown man. He has to work this out. Silas too. We all just need some time.

But something. A nightmare? A feeling? Like that night on the beach. That horrible night when they took Redix, and I wouldn't stop searching for him.

That same eerie feeling wakes me while I throw my clothes on knowing...

Redix is in danger.

THE CONSOLE on my car glows 1:40 am when I park outside Redix's house. It's almost dark inside the house. Only its exterior lights illuminate the night. A summer storm is blowing in over the ocean, thunder rumbling nearby.

His night guard, Keith must be on the other side of the house, checking the perimeter.

I don't want to wake everyone up inside. His sister, nephew, and mom have their bedrooms on one wing of the house. Redix's owner's suite is on the other. I could go around and tap on his sliding glass door but that'll scare the shit out of him.

Fuck it. I call him.

Two rings and he picks up. "Hey." He wasn't asleep. I can tell.

"I'm outside. Can you talk?"

"Yeah, be right there."

I meet him at the front door. He swings it open wearing

pajama pants and a white T-shirt. His body is perfect but his face is wrenched with pain.

"Come on in." He steps aside.

A couple of table lamps glow in his open living room while he closes the door behind me. The ocean flashes outside under a blast of lightning, then thunder rolls while the rest of the house is quiet.

"You okay?" I worry he's been drinking.

"I'm sober if that's what you're asking."

He knows me too well. His bare feet aim toward the sofa in his living room. I follow him, watching him fall down into the cushions before he buries his head in his hands.

"We scared him away," he mutters.

"He was never going to stay." I don't sit down.

"Why would he stay?" He looks at me. "Hell, we don't even stay. We fight all the damn time."

"Let's not start one now."

I didn't come here for this. We fall into this too easily, taking our love for granted. We're tired, frustrated, and still hurting and we take it out on each other. Like we've known each other for so long, we assume we'll always survive the damage we do.

We won't.

Something has to change.

"Look, can we just..." I'm about to sit down. I'm about to put my ego down when a loud *boom* of thunder hits the air and we both turn our heads towards the windows.

"Dammit, Nicolas." Redix jumps up. "He keeps leaving the damn doors open."

The sliding glass door between his living room and pool outside is open a few inches.

Redix goes to close it but I grab his arm, the hairs on

mine standing on end. My ears strain to hear. My muscles draw up. My nerves start firing. I can sense it...

"Where's everyone?" I whisper.

"They're asleep, why?"

"Where's Keith?"

"Around here somewhere."

But I haven't seen Keith, and if he's running his usual nightly rounds, I would've seen his flashlight outside by now.

This sensation. It's what woke me up.

I reach for Redix's neck, pulling him into a kiss. He's shocked but takes it.

"Derek's in the house," I whisper in his ear like we're making out. "Don't react. Keep kissing me."

Every muscle on his body tenses against mine. We kiss again but it's not passionate. It gives me a second to think.

I snake my hands through his long hair, pulling his neck down like I'm about to devour it. "When did you last see Renie? Nicolas?"

"This afternoon. Mom too." He whispers in my ear.

I kiss his neck. "Have you heard them? Seen them?"

He kisses mine back. "I've been in my room."

That's been hours and given Derek plenty of time.

They're here. He's here. I know it.

I go back for Redix's lips, if Derek's watching, listening in, we can't blow this. "My gun and radio are in my car." I ghost his mouth with whispers. "Fight with me. Act. Follow me out there and back into this house. No matter what."

I shove him away, raising my voice. "So you think fucking's gonna solve things?"

It crosses his eyes fast. My plan. His next move. "Why not?" He raises his voice too. "You fucked him too. And we all loved it until you and your obsessions. It's your fault he left."

Is he acting?

I turn toward his front door. "Go to hell, Redix Dean. I'm not your emotional bitch."

My eyes scan. My pulse, I try calming it, but it reacts. The long hallway to the guest bedrooms on my right? It's dark. A light is on under one of the bedroom doors at the end of it.

That's where Derek is.

"Yeah, well fuck you, Cade." Redix is on my heels. This act is easy for him. But keeping calm, it's straining his voice. "You don't have the balls to admit I'm right. Go ahead, run instead of fighting for *us*. It's what you do now."

Opening the front door, *make sure you keep it unlocked*, I sneer, "I'm sick of fighting. It's all we do."

My steps eat up the distance, down his front porch while Redix follows me shouting, "Because you don't fucking listen. You're so goddamn stubborn. What are you gonna do? Jump in your car and drive away? Because you can't stand the truth?"

I do jump in my car. Grabbing my police radio on my passenger seat, I turn it on while Redix yells at my passenger window. "Come on, Cade. Grow the fuck up and talk to me. But you won't, will you? No. You always gotta..."

He keeps yelling, his shouts shaking with the thunder rolling overhead.

"This is Bryant, one forty, to dispatch." I crouch low using Redix's position between me and the house so Derek can't see if he's watching through a window. And like Redix was raised around cops too, he knows what to do too. "I need multiple units at 10 Pelican Lane. Wanted suspect Derek Baucom is inside. Possibly armed. Possible hostages.

The security guard is down. Homeowner, Redix Dean. White male. Long hair. White T-shirt is with me. I'm going back inside. Repeat. I have wanted suspect Derek Baucom. I need backup."

It rolls off my tongue while I tuck my gun into the back waistband of my jeans.

"You gonna face me, Cade?" Redix keeps shouting at my window like the asshole he can certainly act like. He's buying me time. "You gonna man up and face me?"

"Dominquez. Two ten. En route."

That's Penny. Thank God she's back from maternity leave.

"Bryant." She calls on the radio. "Advise status."

"I'm outside the home. Going back in. Suspect inside. Possibly armed."

"Bryant, wait for backup."

That's protocol.

That's not happening.

"I'll leave the front door unlocked," I answer. "Going radio silent."

I turn it off and shove it under my waistband too, pulling my T-shirt over to hide the radio and my gun. Grabbing my pocketknife from my duty belt too, I slide it into my back pocket while Redix keeps priming me with his taunts.

"You just gonna sit there, Cade? And treat me like a fucking idiot?"

"Fine!" I jump back out of my car. "You think I'm the fucking idiot. What's in your bedroom? Or on your phone?" I push past him in his driveway and storm up his front steps. "You think I don't know about all the others, Redix? How many have you fucked by now?"

"You wanna see?" He charges in behind me. "I got nothing to hide."

We stand in the foyer. Our voices raised. Our act still going but our eyes dart, looking for our next move.

"Nothing to hide?" I have an idea. "What about your family? Your mom? Does she know about him?"

That cracks his veneer. Redix can act mad at me but bring up Silas? "Yeah, she knows. I'm proud that I love him. At least we don't fight."

"Yeah? What about your sister?" I need to draw Derek out. To sound like I'm seconds from turning toward that door and raiding his hideout. "Why don't I tell her that all this time, you've been with me, you've been with him too? Whose side do you think she'll take?"

"She'll take *my* side." Redix towers over me. He's leaning in and getting into this and he turns, so I turn, following his performance. "Because he fucking listens. He asks what I need. He doesn't push me like you do. He doesn't hurt me. He only loves me back."

This is too much. This is his truth and we're not acting while that stabs my heart but my mind tries to focus.

"You love him more than me, don't you?"

The words, the passion, his truth is about to fire from his mouth but his eyes dart up, looking over my shoulder.

And it happens too fast...

Redix shoves past me, knocking me aside. He charges forward, blocking me while his huge body rushes his target.

I reach for my gun. "Redix, stop!" I can't see who he's lurching for... but it's Derek.

"Redix!"

My shout and a gunshot blasts the air. I don't scream. I hold aim while I watch his body fall forward on top of Derek.

My eyes. My sights. They track his movement. Tracking

their fight while I search for my target and where that gunshot landed.

Redix grabs Derek's wrist. The one holding the gun that just fired. He's got inches and pounds of muscle on him and he uses it, slamming his arm to the white marble floor. It knocks the gun from Derek's grasp.

Punches are thrown. Redix hooks Derek's jaw while he jabs at Redix's nose. They brawl. They're sprawled on the floor while my training takes over.

I rush for the gun. Avoiding their struggle, I grab it from the floor. Derek's not armed now. That risk is eliminated while I secure the hostages next. Redix can handle this fight, but I don't know if Derek's working alone.

Gun aimed down the hall, I approach the bedroom door. It's unlocked. I kick it open and scan the room.

Renie. Nicolas. Redix's mom, Elise. They're on the floor. Hands, feet, and mouths taped. On my right? Feet are sprawled on the ground. My back to the wall, my gun raised, I clear the room. I find Keith, their night guard, passed out on the floor. No trauma.

"It's okay." I grab the knife from my pocket. We can hear the fight, the struggle of Redix and Derek trashing the living room while I keep my gun up, covering the door with one hand and slicing through the tape over their ankles with the other. "It's okay," I tell them. Their eyes are wide. Terrified. "We gotta get you out of here."

I free their hands next. Then Renie and her mom rip the tape off their mouths.

"Grab him," I tell Renie who scoops Nicolas up in her arms. "Let's go." I keep them covered while they run toward the sliding glass door in the bedroom to the patio outside. Blue lights are flashing across the dark rainy night.

I turn my radio back on while a loud crash, a lamp

breaks in the living room and all my fear for Redix ices my veins but this is the priority. *Get his family safe.*

"This is Bryant," I call into my radio. "I'm exiting out of the back with three hostages secure. Suspect still inside. No longer armed. Homeowner is in active altercation with the suspect. Stand down."

Renie holds a scared Nicolas in her arms while she steps into the rain outside. Deputies are there, waiting for them. Redix's mom follows and they'll be okay.

I turn back toward the fight.

"Hey." Penny charges in through the open door. Two deputies follow her. "I told you to wait for backup."

"Uh-huh." She knows better. I don't follow rules because all I'm following is my instinct to protect Redix next.

Running entry formation back down the hallway, I have three deputies behind me, all with our guns held at ready.

What will I find? I don't know if I can face it.

I just gotta trust. In Redix's strength. In his fight. He can defend himself.

We turn the corner and the room is trashed. I scan it fast, my eyes landing on Redix.

The left side of his white T-shirt is drenched in blood and he's got his back to me. His hands are around Derek's neck. He's lifted him so high that Derek's feet dangle in the air as Redix's grasp chokes him against the window to the storm outside.

"Are you fucking laughing now?" It seethes through Redix's voice. He doesn't even know we're here. "Huh? Motherfucker? Wanna laugh now?"

Derek's evil face is red with rage and the breath Redix is taking from him.

I give the signal to the deputies to lower their weapons.

Penny doesn't want to. She gives me a look and I answer it, "This is his fight. Let him have it."

"Fuck you," Derek coughs. "I took everything you loved, pretty boy. You had too much."

Why Derek is so fixated on Redix, it's obvious. Tragic and disgusting. It's Redix's curse. His beauty puts most in a state of euphoria but for a few, it makes them evil with demented jealousy.

Derek's everything ugly on the inside. Violent. Insecure. Entitled and wanting to take everything he doesn't have. It doesn't matter his exterior.

So once he went after Redix and couldn't have him because my dad stopped him, he went after his sister next. And I saw the suitcase in the bedroom. He was going to take Nicolas. Not that he loved the boy. It just would've destroyed the last piece of Redix if he did.

Even through the sweat and blood pouring from him now, all Redix has ever been is beautiful. The best son, the best brother, the best uncle, and the best friend protecting us all, and few see the burden that's been for him.

But I have. I've seen the price he's paid for it too. Time and again.

"Argh!" Redix slams Derek's skull so hard against the glass. It's thick but that impact starts to splinter the perfect facade.

"Fuck you," Redix growls back, slamming Derek's head again. His big, strong hands are squeezing Derek's neck so hard, he can kill him.

And I want to let him.

My colleagues, the deputies, and Penny stand with weapons itching to do something, but they won't defy me.

Redix can do it. He can kill Derek and kill his pain too.

Derek's eyes glass over, his face so red and his body going limp. He's seconds away.

But this isn't Redix. This is rage and though Redix and I align in a perfect match in every way, this is our fatal difference.

Redix is passion and peace and everything protective. His soul has survived so much.

I'm the vengeance. I'm the one he sacrificed for so I'd be strong enough to do this for him.

"Redix, stop!"

My shout booms with a rattle of thunder, the reverberations traveling through him.

His hands drop from Derek's neck. Derek's limp body slides to the floor, unconscious.

The heave of Redix's chest, his shoulders rising and falling, he doesn't even feel that his arm's been shot. That Derek's bullet went straight through it. It's not a fatal wound but it's weeping blood down to his wrist and staining his shirt to his waist.

The deputies rush over, guns drawn while Penny cuffs an unconscious Derek. She starts calling in the medic and other deputies outside.

Chaos rains down over the house while they secure the scene. While Redix can't find his sanity and I don't even think he sees me standing before him.

He's lost in that night.

In all Derek did in the name of hurting him.

Medics take Derek out. A couple of others try talking to Redix, to address his wound but he's not responding.

"Just give him a minute," I say. "Give him some space."

The room clears. Deputies and medics stand on the edge of it while we all watch Redix on his mental edge.

"Hey." I touch his sweaty arm, the one not shot. "I'm right here. It's okay now."

His eyes, his logic, finally see me here. "No, it's not," he says. The fracture in his eyes. The pain and torment in them. I've seen this look before. It's right before he runs. "It'll never be okay what they did."

He moves so fast. Picking up the side chair beside him, he slams it into the glass window. It shatters, almost breaking to the storm outside.

And I step back. I'm not shocked. Redix slams the chair against the window again and I glance at the deputies. They're ready to intervene but I put my hand up.

"Let him," I say.

It's his house. It's his rage. It's his pain and I've never seen him like this.

Redix slams the chair, over and over until finally, the window breaks into pieces, pouring a glass avalanche over the floor. He's yelling. He's shouting. He's picking up the matching chair and going for another window. Another perfect facade he wants to ruin like they tried to do to him.

"Fuck you!" He shouts. He's never been so loud. "Fuck them!" His blood drips to the floor. Sweat pours down his face. "Fuck them!" But he won't stop.

He's in that night. The one that changed us forever and I'm right there with him. My vision blurs with the tears he's not crying while this madness takes him.

He's fought it for so long. He's run from it. Numbed it. Written about it. Talked about it.

Almost died from it.

And now... for the first time... he lets himself feel it.

Tears drip from my chin because I know his madness. I know his hell. I've felt it too. I wanted to kill too.

TJ. Derek. Gentry.

"Fuck them!" The chair crashes into the glass and his shouts are breaking my heart, clenching my teeth to his agony. "They didn't." Because he's roaring from his. He's in this pain, smashing the chair again into the glass. "Fucking break!" All his might. All his muscles. All his fury. "Me!"

It explodes to his violence. The chair lands on the patio outside over an ocean of glass and Redix crashes to his knees on the edge of his house, of his sanity.

I fall down with him. Wrapping my hands around his neck, I hang on through my sobs and he won't hold me back. He's still lost. He's still trying to come back.

"I love you," is all I can swear into his flesh. His sweaty neck smells like the blood soaking his shirt and, "I love you," is all I feel, all I can say.

The last time he was this far gone, his limp body was in my arms. He was breaths away from dying. Now, I see it in his eyes. I pull back and turn his chin. "I love you," I try to reach him again.

He blinks, gazing at me until something shifts behind his eyes, his soul forever changed.

"I get it," he mutters.

"Hey, come on." Penny startles me. Her hand lands on my shoulder and I glance to see the medics behind her. "Let them help."

His gunshot wound. They need to stop the bleeding. It's getting bad.

I let go of him and stand up. Taking steps away, I clear a path for the medics to kneel beside him, silently dressing his wound to get him ready for transport.

"They got this." Penny keeps pulling me away from him.

I resist. "I'm not leaving him." I'll ride in the ambulance with him. I'll hold his other hand in the emergency room.

I'll keep talking to him and holding him and I'll never leave his side again.

He gets it. He forgives me. He almost killed Derek and now he knows how the madness takes you. How you'll do anything for someone you love. How our love belongs to us but the hatred belongs with the ones who hurt him.

And how we can let that go now, and just go back to the love.

"I need you to come with me." Penny sounds funny. That darts my eyes her way and I see her phone, not her radio in her hand. "I got a call," she says.

Her pull, she's guiding me toward the front door, and the look in her eyes. It's scaring me.

"What's going on?" I ask her.

I don't want this answer.

"Cade, it's your mom," she says.

And I lose the next month of my life.

If I could write my ending, I'd want it to be like the one my Mama had.

Because it's always too soon. And time is never enough. And it hurts like hell to watch someone go.

But we all will.

And in typical Sheriff Gloria Bryant fashion, my Mama went out exactly how she ordered.

She even planned the goddamn menu down to the lemon cake I love and magnolia flower centerpieces I now love too.

The first week in hospice care, she was lucid. She was in no pain and in rare form.

I sat on one side of her and Dad sat on the other. We looked through picture albums and her tablet with more recent stuff.

Mama said, "We're walking memory lane together all the way to the damn end."

It was a beautiful journey. We've been blessed. I've been lucky. I'd forgotten to be thankful that even though my parents divorced before they reconciled, we still did all the holidays and birthdays together.

"Come on." I nudged Mama while we stared at a Christmas picture of us when I was sixteen. When they gave me my first cell phone as a present. "Y'all were still fucking back then, weren't you?"

"What makes you say that?" Mama giggled too much. Dad smiled, guilty as hell.

"Because look at you." I pointed at the picture. "You look way too happy over my new damn phone. And I remember it now. How y'all disappeared the hour before Santa came to visit."

"Ho, ho, ho." Mama beamed proud. "Santa did come and Ms. Claus did twice."

I was rolling. My parents were too cute. And if we weren't talking about memories, Mama wanted stories about my sex life with Redix and Silas.

"Go get a quick cup of coffee for the next two hours," she shooed my Dad away. "I gotta hear this."

Dad gave Mama a kiss on the forehead goodbye while he didn't want to stay for the details.

"All I wanna know," Dad said, "is if Silas has the same habit of going through a box of tissues like Redix used to. The ones I used to find all over my damn boat."

"Dad!" I cuddled up next to mom. "That's gross."

"Is it?" My dad's eyebrows danced. "If it's so damn gross then why'd y'all do it? All. The. Damn. Time."

"Because he might be like our *son*," Mama answered for me. "But you'd be a fool not to fuck Redix Dean. Every. Damn. Day."

Dad shuddered like that grossed him out before he left us laughing.

"Alright." Mama held my hand. Her grip was weak, cold, and comforting. "Don't spare me anything. Start with the first kiss between you three and go from there. Every smutty detail."

"Mama, I ain't giving you every smutty detail."

"You better." Her eyes sparkled until the very end. "I wanna go to heaven with a little sin on my brain. And sex is the best sin of all because it ain't really one."

It was weird at first, telling her everything. But then it was fun. And making us laugh. I've never seen my mama's eyes get so wide when I got to the parts when it was all three of our, well... parts. Of all of our bodies together.

"How did they fit?"

Mama was fascinated. Like I was sharing the results of my science experiment, not my first double-penetration with two well-hung studs.

"Well," I couldn't believe I was saying it but then again, I shared everything with my mama. "It was the *opposite* of throwing two hotdogs down a hallway."

She howled back, her frail shoulders shaking with laughter. "Oh my, Lord!" She was crying happy tears.

"Yeah, that's what I said. Many times while it felt like two giant sausages trying to thread the same tiny sewing needle."

She wouldn't stop laughing. "Then why in the Sam Hill did you do it?"

"Because what hurts at first starts to feel real good." And then I remembered it, the sensation never forgotten by my body. "And when it's Redix and Silas, and when I love and trust them… it starts to feel so damn good you don't ever want it to stop."

"Hand me a fan." Mama interrupted my story.

"Are you okay?" I reached for the church fan Penny had brought over a few days before. "Do you need me to call the nurse?"

"No." Mama barely had enough strength, but the fanning habit was too strong in her. All those years in a church in the Lowcountry swelter. "I'm fine. Wonderful actually. It's just your stories are making all my angels sing… if you know what I mean."

"Mama, this is weird."

I can't tell you how many of those moments we had. I cherish them all.

"It ain't weird. We're laughing about all the great things in life." She stopped fanning herself. "That's a helluva lot better than spending your last minutes crying over it." She squeezed my hand. "Now don't stop." She laughed. "Wait… that's what *you* said, isn't it?"

"*Yeah*, I did."

So I didn't hold back. I told her everything and she loved it like her favorite books come to life (pun intended) until the story of our last time together.

"It was powerful, actually." My head rested on the pillow next to hers. She was turned my way like I was telling the best XXX-rated bedtime stories. "The last time the three of us were together, I swear I wanted to cry. Like something came over me. At how I'm gonna miss Silas and how Redix and I can't seem to get it right."

I didn't want to burden my Mama, not then. But she

could see it along with the tears in my eyes. "Mama, I don't know what to do."

"You're not gonna know," she said. "You're gonna feel it. Not everything is tactics and training. Just let go and you'll feel the answer."

She played with my hair. I was five again and so thankful. "You know when I knew me and your dad were good again? That we were back together until the end." She stopped. "Until now."

The lump in my throat. It was a mountain holding back my sob. "When?" I barely muttered.

"When we were fussing and fighting and I started coughing. And right in the middle of telling me what a mule-headed beauty I was, your dad poured me a glass of water. Just like that. He was pissed as hell and so was I but that's love. You keep caring through the anger."

We had lots of great talks. Way too many laughs. So much so I swear we were pissing off other people on the hospital floor, but we didn't care.

Everyone visited.

When Penny came by in the first few days, she brought welcome news. They tracked the phone they found on Derek back to the location where Gentry's old sailboat was hidden on the island.

And there, they found Cam Le. Alive.

"How is she?" I was afraid to ask.

"She's gonna be okay, all things considered," Penny answered. And like my mama was still Sheriff, she debriefed us. "We found so much on Derek's phone. It's like he's been obsessed with Redix all this time. We even found chats where he posted threats and outright lies about him. It's sick."

"Is Redix okay?"

"Yeah." Penny can't help but like him now. "He doesn't care about the stuff Derek posted on him. But he created a fund for Cam. For all the victims. They'll have all the medical care, counseling, and even housing and such to get their lives back. And Silas got his family's foundation to help too. It's gonna be okay from here."

That news filled my fragile heart and I had to fight the tears biting at my eyes. "What about Pamela?"

"No clues yet." Penny hated delivering that news. "Gentry claims he had no idea Derek was using his old boat as a hideout and we found no evidence there of an alternate location. We're back at square one with Pamela."

"No, you're not." My mama sat up as tall as she could in bed. "You're gonna find her. She's gonna be okay. I promise."

Part of me wanted to believe her. Like she had the ability to give such a divine prophecy. The other part of me hated why.

Silas came by a couple of days later. He was great with my mom and took my dad to lunch a few times over the weeks to give him needed breaks. I remember that part.

But I wouldn't leave her side.

Redix came by a few times with his family. His arm was bandaged and he was back from whatever hell he disappeared into that night with Derek. Redix was so focused on my mom, and so worried about his because our moms were best friends. And Elise was not taking my Mama's passing very well.

I think that's when it started to hit me too. I barely remember Redix leaving the last time or what he said to me. I just remember his kiss on my cheek and that I was slipping away.

Days passed and with each one, Mama slipped away more into the relief they gave her from the pain.

Dad never left her side in the end either.

It was a couple of days before her last one. In one of her last lucid moments and I swear Mama looked at me like the past fourteen years hadn't happened.

Like when I was fifteen and she was waking my grumpy ass up and telling me to turn my damn snooze button off and go to school.

"Mama." I groaned into my pillow then. "Leave me alone."

"Never," she said.

"Life is lemon cake, Magnolia Cade." She said it then. She said it again one last time to me. "And you're my sweetest part."

She kissed my cheek.

And she'll never leave me alone.

I didn't recognize Cade.

Not while she stood in my storm and I trashed my house at the fury raging inside me over Derek. At all the pain he and Gentry and TJ wreaked upon our lives.

For the first time, I got it. I understood what she felt, and why she came so close to killing TJ.

If it weren't for Cade stopping me, I would've killed Derek. Just to kill his laughter in my mind. To hurt him back for hurting my sister. For all the women he hurt. To punish him for being a shitty father to the best kid in the world.

But I stopped, and finally, I saw Cade in a new light. It

wasn't perfect. It wasn't even beautiful. But it was honest. And real. And very human and just like me.

Then I didn't recognize Cade at the hospital with Mama G. Like she smiled and laughed for her mama. And she talked to me but she was drifting away.

Not even I could reach her. I could feel it on her soft cheek when I last kissed her goodbye.

Cade wasn't there.

She was lost in grief.

Silas and I hung out lots over the month. We just talked. He helped me with the repairs and window bullshit that had to be fixed on my house.

I don't regret trashing it. I needed it. I needed to break everything until the anger didn't own me anymore.

It's like anger was the one emotion for so long I didn't let myself feel. Drinking kept it away. Then when I stopped doing that, it came back.

I blamed Cade for it. All my anger, I thought it was her fault for what she did to TJ. Or almost did, but Mama G like the badass she is even in death was the ultimate one.

I guess I put all my anger on Cade because deep down, I knew she could take it. She's strong as hell. She loves me and I used the excuse about TJ because I didn't want to face who was really to blame.

Until I did.

Until he raised his gun at Cade's back and that was it. I didn't even feel the bullet through my arm. Fate wasn't an asshole that night. It did me right. That damn bullet went clean through and didn't even hit my bone. My bicep isn't thrilled about it, but it'll heal.

So will I.

Because TJ is dead. And I'm thankful for that.

And Derek Baucom's in jail and won't ever see sunlight but for one hour a day for the rest of his life.

My family is safe. And my house can be fixed.

But now I gotta fix the one thing that means the most to me.

My Candy Cade.

I still don't recognize her now.

She's dressed in black. The irony is she looks so beautiful even at a burial; it's bittersweet. Her eyes won't leave Mama G's coffin and she won't let go of her Dad's hand. He's sitting beside her, eyes glued on the same magnolia casket spray.

And I grin, for just a second, up to the hot August sky.

Magnolias.

Mama G loved them. Jeff, Cade's dad thought it'd be a great idea to name their beautiful daughter in honor of that.

And that beautiful, stunning, incredible daughter gets so damn pissed it's cute whenever you call her that name or give her those flowers.

Yep, Mama G got the last laugh.

Silas stands beside me. We were pallbearers and now we're sweating expensive BOUND cologne in the South Carolina heat.

I've cried my tears over Mama G. I couldn't help it when it upset my mama so much to see her go.

But now I'm standing strong for Cade. I'm focused only on what she needs and it's beginning to fall into place.

My skull ain't so thick anymore. And my eyes are wide open. So is my heart. I've never seen Cade like this and it's like for the first time in ten years, she needs me to save her again.

I know exactly what should happen next.

Mama G whispered it into my ear three times before she passed. And I promised her I would.

Making those plans in my head, romantic ones for later, for when the time is right, I don't notice him at first. A small crowd of dark suits and one blonde in a perfectly tailored black dress make their way to the hundreds of guests gathered in Mama G's honor.

And I can't believe his nerve.

Because he never had the balls.

He's just got pure evil.

"The fuck he will," I mutter, my steps covering ground to stop the procession of his wicked posse this way before Cade sees him. Because if she sees Senator Gentry Evans at her mama's funeral, two bodies are going in the ground today.

Silas sees it too and backs me up.

We meet them halfway across their path through the tombstones under palmetto trees and Spanish Moss.

"Turn around now, Senator," I say, "and don't make a fucking scene or I swear it will be your last."

"I told you," Stacey hisses beside him. "This is highly inappropriate and not a good idea."

Her eyes look at mine with nothing but an apology in them. I don't blame her. She can't stop Gentry's wicked ways.

I love the only one I know who can.

And she needs me right now.

"Mr. Dean." Gentry smiles too big. "As the distinguished Senator of this district, I will not disrespect the memory and service of our first woman and longest serving Sheriff in this state. I will pay my respects just like everyone else who has come to as well."

It seems like everyone who ever served under Mama G or just simply loved her is here, even Silas's parents.

But *not* this man.

"You'll turn around," I seethe, "or I'll strangle your ass back into your car and kill you there, and ain't no one stopping me. Your choice, Senator."

"Mr. Dean," he sneers. "Hollywood clout doesn't matter here on Hilton Head. You underestimate your power."

I step to him. So close I swear he still smells like that vile Abercrombie cologne he used to wear and it twists my stomach. But now, I'm inches taller, many pounds stronger, and way too mad to ever back down.

"Gentry Evans"—I grab his neck—"you haven't *felt* my power yet. But keep fucking with me and you'll feel it take your last breath."

"And I'll help him." Silas steps to my side. "And I'll make sure every political donor in the South shows you the power of never giving you another damn dollar again."

Because Gentry's so damn twisted, so evil that if violence doesn't control him, money will.

His mouth snarls. His eyes glare into mine and I'm so tempted. I could end him, squeezing his throat to death now like I almost did Derek.

But I remember.

Two women.

Two friends who still need me.

Cade.

And Pamela.

And I let go. "Leave now," I growl, "before anyone even sees you were here."

That may save him face like I give a shit. But that'll also save Cade's heart because I don't want her seeing this.

Stacey grabs Gentry's arm, yanking him back toward

the car. He wrests it away from her grip sneering, "Who the hell do you think you are?"

"We're leaving," she says. "Quietly. Or I won't be so damn silent about everything I know. You understand me?"

I see why Cade likes her. Why they became allies over that piece of shit. As they turn away, I just hope he doesn't hurt Stacey too.

"You think she'll be alright?" I mutter to Silas.

I don't put anything past Gentry, especially hurting women.

"I got her number," Silas says. "I'll check on her later."

We both return to the service, our polished shoes stepping over sandy grass. In an odd way, I'm relieved to see Cade so lost in grief and not focused on the world around her.

At least she was spared from Gentry.

For the day.

And it's a long one. Funerals in the southern heat sweat you down to your last grieving tear.

I don't know how Cade does it. How she goes through the motions, even at the party afterward Mama G wanted thrown. It reminds me of a jazz funeral meets an Irish wake. Lots of drinking. Music. Toasts. Tears and laughter.

By the end of it, I'm the only sober one.

Even Silas has a couple of drinks, enough to make him whisper in my ear, "I miss us. All three of us."

The heat of his lips on my skin firms my cock at the most inappropriate time. But Mama G supported this love. The unique one me, Silas, and Cade share.

"I miss us too." And I can tell Silas is sober enough to mean it, and to remember me saying, "But I want you to be happy. Like we got schooled today—life is short, so fill it with love."

The other person who should be here is across the room, smiling at guests while her soul is a million miles away.

"You were right," I tell Silas. "You keep telling me how special me and Cade are and you finally got through my thick skull." I reach for his hand. This whole room can see us and I'm proud. "And you're special too. And I love you. And so does she. And we'll never stop."

I kiss him. Not with the same heat, the same passion, and God-I-want-to-fuck-you-so-hard urge in my body. That'll always be here, but not today. This is love. This is our life and I don't want to live it without him either.

Silas takes my kiss before resting his forehead to mine swearing, "Because I feel this love. The one you share with Cade. I'll know it when it happens to me and I won't ever take it for granted."

"You're gonna have a helluva time beating it." I grin. "Just sayin'."

His grin back heats my veins. "I haven't found it yet, so until I do... maybe I'll visit for another sweet taste. Just sayin'."

And we leave it at that. No fucking at a funeral.

Though of all funerals, Mama G would well approve. I'm surprised it wasn't one of her dying wishes.

"Y'all go treat each other like angels," she'd probably say, "and fuck like devils too."

That thought helps me keep my shit together while I escort my crying mother out to the car. Renie will take her home. I want to turn back for Cade.

But Silas and his parents walk toward me on the sidewalk outside the event hall.

"It was nice to see you again, Mr. Dean." Silas's dad shakes my hand. "My regrets it had to be under such sad circumstances. Please bring Ms. Bryant by some other time for a visit." He slaps his other hand on Silas's shoulder. "With my son, of course."

What that invitation means to Silas, I can see it lighten his hazel eyes.

"I'd be honored, sir." I return his handshake before pecking Silas's mom's cheek. "Ms. Van de May, I hope to see you again too."

"I'll be sure of it." Silas winks my way.

I watch the three of them leave, still stunned as the logic sinks in—*Silas Van de May*.

Heir to billions. Boat mechanic to some. Hot-as-fuck man to most... and the only one I'll ever love.

I turn back to search the crowd for Cade. I want to take her home.

But I can't find her. I find her Dad, giving him another hug while he tells me, "She went home. She said she wants to be alone."

"What can I do for you?"

"Me?" he asks. "Son, I've been blessed with loving the most incredible woman for almost forty years. I'll be fine. I just wanna get back on my boat for a while."

He was always happy there. Like if he couldn't be with Mama G, his other home was the water.

I know the feeling.

But I don't like the one I have going home. The house is like nothing happened. Renie moved back into her place with Nicolas. I miss 'em like hell but she deserves to have her life back.

And though I thought my mom would never want to leave, she does.

"You need to get on with your life too," she told me the

day she left. "Quit putting it off like someone guaranteed you tomorrow."

Night rolls in. I can't sleep. I can't do anything that feels right.

I walk outside to the empty beach yards from my house. Every time I used to come out here, on any beach on this island, particularly at night... I'd think of that one.

I'll never know what really happened to me that night.

And I don't need to.

Because all I need to know is who saved me.

And I need to save her again too.

Silhouette by Active Child feat. Ellie Goulding

THE COLD TILE FLOOR RELIEVED THE STICKY HEAT ON my skin. I slid down here hours ago, by my front door and haven't moved.

I don't want to.

I just wanna lie here and let this puddle of tears grow under my cheek.

My dad needed to get back on the water and I needed to collapse. To free what I've been holding back for so long to be strong for Mama.

She said to me, "You can cry over me at first. Just

promise me you'll laugh more and annoy the hell out of people with stories of my brilliance forever."

A chuckle shakes my ribs to her words. It turns into another sob I can't stop. It convulses through me, shaking the frame of my soul and I just let it.

My hand grips the smooth tile and I hang on so I can let it all go until I don't remember anything. Until the shadows grow long across my condo from the sunset fading to night through the windows to the ocean outside.

And I fade with the light. Just letting go. Into the darkness. Thinking of her.

∾∾

"Come on."

A husky voice wakes me. Along with hands, strong ones lifting me up from the floor and into his arms.

"Come on, Candy Cade."

I smell him, vanilla and leather. I feel his hard chest under my cheek. I can wrap my hands around his neck and lace my fingers through his long hair and I don't need to open my eyes because I'm home.

"She wouldn't mind a few tears shed." Redix carries me down the hall to my bedroom. "But she'd tell you to take a shower too."

"I don't wanna," I whine into his chest.

"I'm not asking." He gently sets my feet still in heels down on my bathroom floor. "Come on. We're taking a shower and washing this day off you and then we're feeding you."

"I'm not hungry." I let him unzip my dress.

"I'm not listening." He drops it to the floor. "Now do you wanna deal with these or should I?"

He's asking about my black pantyhose. Only for a funeral would I wear them.

I look down at them, having no energy for anything while he turns the shower on. "I don't care," I answer.

"Suits me fine." He rips the back seam over my ass so fast I swear they're tissue and not silk. "Damn," he mutters, making quick work of turning my pantyhose into gossamer shreds in seconds. "That's on the menu for future nights."

"Are you getting horny right now?" I kick my heels off. I'm not offended.

"Nope," he answers, peeling off his T-shirt before dropping his jeans. His waking cock answers yes.

I swear the man has a religion against underwear.

I swear I kinda love that about him.

"Come on." He guides me under the water with him.

And it does feel good. The sweat and tears and day and grief all wash off with the soap and shampoo and conditioner he lavishes over me.

We don't use words. His care says it all. Like we could have a long conversation to confirm it, but that would be a waste of precious time.

We know where we stand.

Together again.

And when I see the fresh scar, the fresh bullet wound through his arm, it hits me too. A wave of everything he's survived, and my mama who didn't, and I start crying, my tears falling with the shower water and he just holds me tight. Wrapping his arms around me, telling me we'll be okay, I'm safest here so I cry until there's no hot water left. Until I think my tears are done for the night.

He kisses my cheek and turns off the water before handing me a towel. "Dry off and climb into bed." A white towel hangs from his waist next. "I'll go find us something to eat."

"Good luck with that."

Since Redix hasn't been around much and I've spent the past month in the hospital, there's no telling what's growing in my refrigerator.

"I don't need luck," he says, gently pushing me toward the bed. "I got delivery."

I drop the towel and climb under my sheets and it's official. I'm not leaving this bed for the next month. Hopefully, Redix can be here for most of it.

Part of me wishes Silas were here too, but for some reason that doesn't feel right. Like we gotta let him go and learn who we are again without him.

Silas has been the sweet, sexy, strong glue that held our broken edges together for so long, but that's not his purpose. He deserves better. I get what he means about finding his own love. It's not that he doesn't love me and Redix.

The three of us will always love each other.

He just wants that seed. The bloom of a new love that you find where you least expect it. The bright, brilliant one that surprises you and captivates your heart for life.

And maybe it'll be another man. Or another woman. Or another couple. Who knows with Silas.

But he's right.

The love between me and Redix is too damn powerful for *us* sometimes. Much less asking another person to navigate it too. It's like asking someone to cross the Atlantic in a canoe. Only Redix and I have the strength together for that.

And it's a strength we've earned the grueling, soul-breaking way.

"I got Thai food here in an hour." Speaking of Captain

Thinks He's In Charge, he saunters back into my bedroom. "And water and a snack for you now."

I'm hoping for Lemonheads. I'll settle for Skittles. When he presents me with a banana, I can't even.

He rolls his eyes. "I'm not fucking you with this tonight." He drops his towel and sits on the bed beside me, handing me a glass of water I reluctantly sip and then set down. "You're gonna eat it. You need your electrolytes after all that sweating."

"You saying I stink?"

"No." He breaks a piece off and holds it in front of my lips. "I'm saying it was hotter than blue blazes today and you've lost weight. Now, come on."

I turn my nose. "I don't want it."

His voice drops. "Eat it." It's almost funny.

I drop mine too. "No."

"Quit being stubborn."

"No." I bury my face in the pillow. "You're not the boss of me."

The bed shifts. He crawls over me. "Magnolia Cade Bryant, if you don't eat this damn banana I'm gonna cream your corn."

I crack my eyelids open to his silhouette over me. "Promise?" I tease. The lamp by my bed glows, making his naked, tan skin glisten above me. He's half grinning and half worried and I don't know why I'm being so obstinate.

Maybe it's because he cares so much. And we can fight and still love each other...

And I remember what Mama told me.

This is my answer. I can feel it.

"Split it with me," I tell him, trying not to be distracted by his nude body straddling mine. "You were sweating your balls off today too."

He puts a quarter piece in my mouth and then pops a piece in his, chewing while he talks, "My balls are doing just dandy, thank you."

The last half he splits, putting a piece in my mouth while he chews the rest, and these questions hurt while I swallow down the banana. They have since the night of our pretend fight that didn't feel like an act.

"Do you love him more than me?" I ask, almost afraid of the answer. "Would you rather be with him?" Not that if I lost Redix's love to Silas, I'd be angry. I could almost survive it.

"I could ask you the same thing," he says. "He made you very happy. And y'all never fought."

"Neither did you two."

"He gave me hell about stuff, but no, we didn't fight like you and me."

My heart, it's thudding. It needs to know. "So what's your answer?"

He leans forward, bracing one arm by my head while his other hand, his fingertips tickle down my cheek to my lips.

"My answer, Detective, is the same as yours." His gaze shelters mine. For twenty years, it's been my heaven. "My answer is that I love my best friend and I'm never leaving her again."

His lips near mine. My heart thuds, tears wanting to fall. "My answer," he almost whispers, "is that I love the one I share this dream with."

"What's the dream?" My lips tickle against his.

"That you marry me, please, Cade Bryant."

I can't stop them. They fall. But these aren't sad. These are sudden. And pure. "Yes."

He smiles, so true and from his soul while he confesses,

"I was gonna wait a few months but I promised Mama G I'd ask."

"She'd want it like this." My fingers thread through his strands. "She wouldn't want us to wait."

"I don't wanna wait either. Our dream starts today, Cade. Promise me."

"Our dream started the day we met."

The touch of his lips. They've never felt this soft, this real and safe and they're never leaving. They'll always be a pillow away, or at the end of my day, or kissing me by the kitchen sink.

And then his kiss turns into his deepest promise for our dream, months before we'll swear it over rings. It moves into me along with his body urging against mine.

We know this dance, this position while my thighs, my heart, my entire soul opens to him one last time because this is it. There's no going back. We know it. We feel it as his hand finds mine on his scruffy jaw and he moves it. Wedging our bodies, lining up his hard tip at my wetting entrance, he rests my palm on his left buttock.

His glute muscles flex under my grasp, the welts of his scar rising against my hand and my every next day is certain. They'll be spent loving him.

He's never done this, invited my touch of his scar, encouraging me to keep my hand here. Like we won't run from it. Or deny it. Or fear it.

It doesn't control us anymore.

Tipping my hips, rising to meet him, I want him now but he mutters down my neck, "You're not ready yet."

"Yes, I am," I sigh at his gentle bites.

"I want you wetter," he says.

And he knows exactly how to grant that wish. His long strands mop down to between my thighs and twice his generous tongue makes me come before I'm grabbing at his wide shoulders.

"Redix, now." I can't stand the urge. I have to have him. It's more than my body demanding him. It's my entire life needing to wrap around him.

He holds my hand, lacing his fingers in mine. He won't let go of it over my head while my other hand returns to his scar. To his ass flexing with his slow thrusts deep into my aching sex and we've never been this close. We've never been this open and unafraid and sure. There's no space where he's not inside me.

His lips won't leave mine, his body moving with mine; he's my answer. He moves deep inside me and this is all we are. Bodies and hearts matched. This is us. Drawing breath together. I can love others so much, but I belong with only one person.

We could fuck hard or we could fuck kinky and bad, and I know we will. For the rest of our lives we can, but not tonight.

This is about our love surviving. This is about our life going on. This is about the dream we share.

And from this night on, we'll never be apart again.

42

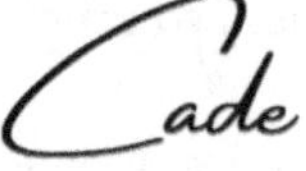

"Damn." Redix wraps around me. "Look at all the debris on the beach."

A category one hurricane came ashore the day after Mama's funeral. We knew it would and I didn't need an excuse to stay in bed with Redix for two days while Hurricane Emma barreled through.

"I've seen worse." I sip my coffee and lean back into his body as we stand on my balcony and survey the damage.

It's true. It's not that bad. Just a lot of limbs blown down from trees. At least we didn't lose lives or electricity.

"I should go check our house," he says. "We gotta lot of big trees to worry about."

"Our house?"

"Yes." He kisses my head. "*Ours*. And please finish ordering the furniture because I hate that shit. I don't know what to pick."

"You do know fashion." I turn around in his arms. "But all your taste is in your mouth when it comes to interior design."

"Hey, don't be hating on my La-Z-Boy."

"It's *not* staying in the living room."

"If you can lift it, you can put it wherever you like."

"What the hell made you order one in yellow anyway? Of all colors."

"I like it," he says. "Yellow makes me happy."

Yellow.

It lights through me. Not with a logical thought or a strong hunch. It's like a prayer I swear my mama's answering for me because she can now.

Pamela.

Yellow was her favorite color and the one she was wearing the night she went missing.

"Your boat." I pull from his embrace. "We gotta go out on your boat this morning. I'm putting my drone up. That storm knocked down lots of branches and limbs. Maybe we can finally spot something."

"We're not doing this alone." He's right on page and not wrong. "We need your dad and Silas. We got one shot to beat Gentry to wherever the hell he goes before he can cover it back up again."

It only takes a couple of hours to call my dad in from wherever he pulled his boat ashore on Tybee for the storm. Silas didn't take long to get his boat in the water and come over from Daufuskie either.

They meet us at the marina and our three vessels head

out. I have a hunch, looking at the maps Dad and I already used to eliminate some barrier islands while others are still suspect.

I was right about the storm. Limbs and logs litter the water and we all have to go slow, careful not to run over one and fuck up an engine.

We use our radios. Talking in code in case a guilty party can hear us, we act like we're looking for the bald eagles that nest around these islands.

Because there's one small island in particular. It calls to me. Records say a holding company owns it. Some company out of Delaware which makes no sense. Why would a company in a small state known for big banks own a tiny barrier island in South Carolina?

Unless someone's laundering money through accounts and into a bank account you can't trace back to an owner.

The questions fire through my mind while I send my drone up. The quadcopter buzzes through the sky while Redix has us anchored on the river. Silas and my dad navigate to other spots near the small island's shore, making sure no one arrives or leaves without their notice.

"Fuck, the signal is lagging," I mutter while I watch the camera in the remote controller in my hands.

Over the months, I've gotten good at flying this thing. But there's shit I can do about a weak signal out on the water.

"Be patient, Candy Cade." Redix doesn't annoy me. We're both on edge and his words ease my firing nerves. "Just keep looking."

I close my eyes for a second and draw an inhale, sending up a prayer to Mama. *You promised me...*

When I open my eyes again, the tree canopy below the

drone is tattered with green limbs down everywhere. The pines still stand tall but I see a clearing, a small swath of land cleared by an old water oak that fell in the storm. To its north, at the top of the crown of the fallen tree, an older magnolia still stands.

And I see it...

The rusted metal roof a rectangular structure draped with camouflage netting blown off by the storm.

"Oh my God." My hands start shaking. "Oh my God, we found her."

I don't need to enter. I don't need to set foot in there to know it.

My gun's in my backpack. My mind's already steps ahead, storming this island with my loaded 9mm, a pair of bolt cutters and a fury no man could ever survive because I *will* get my friend back.

Nine years it's almost been.

Nine years Gentry's kept her someplace and then moved her here.

I can't imagine what I'll find when I get to her, but I swear she'll be safe now.

Redix watches over my shoulder, his chest pressed to my back and he sees it too.

"It looks like an old shipping container," he says. "Fuck, this area is littered with them."

He's right and I gotta think this through.

I turn to him and while every impulse in me wants to break every rule and go in there get Pamela right now and fuck up Gentry's world for good... I won't do it.

I have a job to do, the right way. I have a dream I'm living with the man I love and breaking the rules over another evil man won't take it from us again.

"I'm calling this in," I tell him. "Hey, guys." I radio my

dad and Silas. "We found the nest. We're gonna wait for others to come see this too."

It takes an hour for me to radio the office, for multiple response units, state and federal to find their way to our coordinates. The whole time, Dad and Silas hold their position in case Gentry approaches.

But he doesn't.

His name isn't listed on this island. But if Pamela is in there, and alive, she's the only witness we need. Her and all the federal and financial crimes Gentry's been committing with his "exclusive golf tours."

And though I want to be the first one Pamela sees. So she won't be scared. So she'll know her nightmare is over. So she'll have her life and hope back, it's not safe.

I stand back while a tactical team runs advance, clearing the land for any traps or explosives that may be set for those who approach.

Thankfully, they find none.

Standing in the shade of the old magnolia tree, I wait with Redix beside me. A team enters and secures the structure and it's forever but only minutes before a big FBI agent emerges with a tiny woman wrapped in a silver emergency blanket in his arms.

Then I can't be stopped.

I rush to her.

All the times Pamela was there for me. When boys in middle school were assholes and called me "giraffe" and grabbed my breasts that barely budded at the time sneering, "You're skinnier than a boy." Or when they grabbed my crotch and laughed, "Where's your dick?" Pamela defended me.

"They just got *little* dick problems," she'd laugh and pull me down the hallway to the candy machine.

She was stronger than me back then.

And today, she's the strongest person I know.

Because she survived.

Still in the FBI Agent's arms, she's held there while her eyes squint to the sunlight and I know she can barely see but she'll know this.

"It's me." I stroke her long brown hair. Small waves of relief ripple through me that she doesn't look as bad as I feared. She looks fed. She looks pale but she doesn't look scarred or disfigured. But my heart holds strong for all I know that she's survived inside. "It's Cade. Redix too. We're here."

She can't open her eyes. The sunlight's too brutal, even in the shade. But tears fall from their corners while she says, "I knew you'd find me."

And I want to cry for her. I want to sob with relief and grief and I will many times later on.

But for now... I'm strong for her too.

ALL THE RAGE. All the fury. I don't show it except for my right hand twitching for my gun while I lead a procession of agents and officers through the front door of Senator Gentry Evans's palatial home.

His lovely wife, Stacey Evans, invites us in.

The thrill on her face matches mine because he's hosting friends for drinks this Sunday afternoon while they watch some dumbass golf tournament on the flatscreen.

For Senator Gentry Evans to get arrested in front of all his important buddies, hell yes. And you can be damn sure I'll be investigating these men too.

"This is bullshit!" Gentry's shouting toward the screen

with a beer in hand. "They need to scrap these shotgun starts."

He doesn't even see us at the threshold of his newly remodeled living room. Special glee fills me at all the fucking of other men Stacey's been doing in here.

But these men are oblivious with their backs to us and their eyes glued to a screen.

Before I say it, I send another prayer to Mama. It's like since she couldn't have justice in her life, she sure as heaven made it possible I'd get it in mine.

"Senator Gentry Evans, you are under arrest."

How those words thunder from my mouth. How they heal my soul. How Pamela and Redix and all the victims will get their justice. In public. In a trial. In a jail sentence of multiple lifetimes.

He turns my way and my smile could sell snow in a blizzard.

This is too fucking great.

I list all the crimes on the arrest warrant, making sure his friends hear each horrific one.

Gentry's so stunned. So embarrassed and knocked from his wicked pedestal, he doesn't even fight the satisfying clicks I give of the handcuffs I make sure are extra tight on his wrists.

I hope they shred his skin by the time he's in a holding cell.

I don't know what guilty party called the local news station (Redix), but they're waiting outside, getting this shot of me escorting Gentry out of his home in handcuffs.

Yeah, he's in federal custody, but the FBI agents let me have this. They know the story of Pamela, of my friend, so this one public act on her behalf, it's sweet revenge the whole nation will see.

Gentry doesn't speak a word. He's too smart. He won't indict himself any further though I don't know why he cares. There's no judge or jury he can bribe to get out of this.

I press my hand over his perfectly parted hair while I shove him hard into the backseat of a patrol car. He's wearing madras pants and a bow tie and I love this too much.

I hate those fucking pants almost as much as I do him. And I'd rather strangle him with that bow tie, but his preppy ass will get a daily beating in prison I'm sure.

He won't look at me. Staring straight ahead with his hands cuffed in front of him, I can smell his god-awful cologne as I lean into the car, my lips nearing his sweating face.

"This is for Pamela, Redix, and me." I flick his cheek. "How you like us now?" I laugh before I slam the car door behind me.

43

"I GOT THIS ONION SHIT DOWN."

I look up from the peppers I'm slicing to smile at Cade dancing around our kitchen.

"Pony" by Ginuwine is playing for old time's sake on the Bluetooth speaker and Cade's giving one helluva show for me and the empty dishwasher behind her.

"If you're gonna shake your ass in those tiny red shorts, put the damn knife down and grind it this way."

She doesn't even cry anymore when she chops onions. Hell, she hasn't cried in months.

It's been four of them since Mama G passed and since we found Pamela and we've all found the peace we deserve.

I got Pamela the best care. I found a place in Arizona where she and her mom live now. It's like a spa resort with cottages where Pamela gets all the medical care and counseling she needs.

We have a trip planned to visit her next month. Pamela looks good on our video chats in the meantime.

"Mom loves the weather here," Pamela told us on the last chat. She's starting to get a tan. "They have these really cute tiny therapy goats that we do yoga with too. They hop all over us." She even had a twinkle back in her eye. "Y'all should get one as a pet."

"Yes!" Cade was way too excited. "Let's get a tiny goat."

"Oh shit." I was outnumbered. "You two and your crazy schemes."

"The crazy scheme was you taking my mom to the Golden Globes," Pamela laughed and it felt like old times, the three of us joking together. "She won't stop talking about it."

"Good," I answered her. "Because she's going again with me this year."

I'd do anything for Pamela and her mom. So would Cade. And those details Pamela shares with a gentle smile. But she's not ready to share more and we all understand why.

Cade wants to get married at our house in Malibu. That way Pamela doesn't have to come back here and I don't blame her. I like the idea of it. Our wedding deserves a destination without the history that's here. Though we're strong enough to live with that too.

Pamela and Penny will be Cade's bridesmaids while zero guesses who'll be my best man.

"You mean you want this ass?"

Cade turns around and starts working her firm cheeks over my cock like I have pockets full of twenties.

"Woman, you better grab your ankles because I'm about to fuck one of your tight holes."

She laughs but I can play just as much as she can because damn, she's turning me on. I push the chicken in the skillet away from the heat and turn off the burner because something else is about to get cooking.

It's been like this since I got home. She's all feisty because she busted Gentry, and Derek's in jail too, and TJ's gone for good.

We're more than free.

We're happy as hell even though I had to leave for two months to film in Vancouver, so Cade's been jumping my bones every night since I got back.

I'm the luckiest man alive.

"When are you gonna tell me?" I love how she interrogates me. Turning around again, her palm glides down my length hanging heavy for her under my shorts. "What are we doing for my thirtieth birthday?"

"*Our* thirtieth birthday."

"You're older by six days, and I know you've got something planned, my sexy Sagittarius."

I taste her neck. "Are we gonna eat or are we gonna fuck?"

My hard cock in her hand ain't craving stir-fry right now.

Her lips find mine, demanding, "I want a hard answer."

"Do you interrogate all your suspects like this? Because I'd shoplift hemorrhoid cream every damn day to have my hard cock in your hand."

"I'm asking the questions." No, she's pulling my shorts down.

"I'm not answering them."

But I'm thrilled by this, and the big plans I'm making for our birthdays.

"Well then." She swishes away, leaving me and my bare boner in the kitchen. "Guess we're both not screwed."

I drop the chopping knife in my hand on the cutting board and shout, "Woman, you better run!"

Pulling my shorts back up, I chase her through the house while she squeals at my pursuit.

She beats me to our bed and flops there. "Tell me!" When she whines, it's cute. For about four minutes. "You've been whispering with Silas for weeks and I'm dying to know what it is."

"It's a big damn box of the patience you don't have." I crawl on top of her. "That's your birthday present."

"Fine." She pinches my ass. "Then what are you getting me for Christmas?"

"Double whatever you get me."

"So we're going to Hawaii for *two* weeks?"

"That's my present?"

"Surprise."

"But we just opened the store and we're slammed."

Timing the opening of my charity arts store with the holidays was a stroke of financial genius. It's also been a shit-ton of work during what's supposed to be my month and a half off before I go back to set. But it's all for a good cause and we've already raised half a million.

"I know." She tickles her fingertip over my lips. "That's why we're going after the New Year. Your artists' can handle it. Trust me."

This is going to be her first birthday, her first Christmas, her first everything without Mama G and I'm taking care of everything. Our families are coming over. We have gifts and wedding plans to make.

But our thirtieth birthdays? Mine is December eleventh and hers is the seventeenth. And yes, I've made plans with Silas.

With that reminder, I roll to my back. "I think we should wait until Saturday, until your birthday."

"What?" She jumps on top of me. "You big tease, that's three days from now."

"Yep. And I need you good and horny for it."

"But I'm horny now."

"And you smell like onions."

"Uh!" She pins my wrists over my head, almost looking offended, but her beauty gazing down at me wins all, and waiting until Saturday won't be easy. "Take that back."

God, this is the sight.

It's the one I held onto in my darkest days. When I couldn't find anything but hell, I closed my eyes and saw Cade like this. Smiling at me. Loving me. Our future sparkling in her purple eyes. And me driving her so fucking crazy she's deliriously happy.

This is what I lived for.

"Make me," I tease her.

"You said we have to wait til Saturday."

"Fucking isn't the only way to make me talk, Detective."

Her eyes narrow while her gorgeous smile grows. "Oh yeah?" She knows my spot and she goes for it. "How about this?"

When she starts tickling my armpit I'm done for. I laugh like I'm fucking five again and if she doesn't stop I swear I'll piss myself.

"Take it back." She's way too happy torturing me.

"Nope." I could flip her over. I could overcome her power but why? This is too damn fun.

"Say it." And she's way too happy.

"I love you, Candy Cade."

Because that always makes her stop and kiss me. And it always makes it better and it's so damn true.

And it will be.

Till the day I die.

44

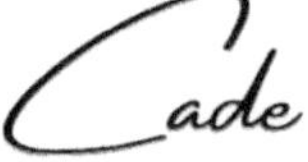

GET A CALCULATOR AND MULTIPLY "PISSED AS HELL" by a billion.

That total is less than what I feel right now.

Because it's my thirtieth birthday. And it's a Saturday. And Redix got called into an "important meeting" with the head of the studio and Daniel Pierce of all people.

So we had to cancel my birthday plans.

Whatever the hell they were.

"We'll do dinner tonight." He kissed me this morning. "And I promise I'll make it up to you soon."

"Who the fuck calls a Saturday afternoon meeting in Savannah?"

This Hollywood life on my shores is bullshit. Normal people have weekends off. Especially *my* birthday weekend.

"When the head of the studio wants to turn his fishing vacation into a meeting, you go." Redix slid his jean jacket on. "Besides, this is for Lorraine. She really wants this show."

"Fine." I really wanted to kick and scream on the bed. Instead, I threw a pillow at him. "Just go. And good luck."

I can't be mad at him. But I can punch the balls of the studio president if I ever meet him.

So now I'm staring at a holiday ham and some potatoes in my grocery cart. Apparently, I gotta cook my own birthday dinner so I grab a carrot cake for our vegetable.

The whole damn day I fume so I go for a run on the beach. That way I won't bite Redix's head off when he gets home. He texted, he's an hour away. He's super sorry and he added a line of red heart emojis.

Maybe I won't kill him. Some of my pissed-off washes down the drain with my long shower.

Then, like a cherry on my shitpie of a birthday, the doorbell rings while I'm dripping wet and wrapped in a towel.

I ignore it. It's delivery boxes.

But the motherfucker keeps ringing the bell so whoever's on the other side of this front door is about to get a new asshole.

"What the fuck?" I'm so mad I throw it open without checking.

"Ho, ho, ho," voices greet me, and light travels slower than my mood just changed.

It's Redix. It's Silas.

It's two hot men with no shirts on wearing matching

black leather pants and red Santa hats and grins that tell me they've been planning this all along.

"Damn, you look sexy when you're about to fuck someone up." Silas steps to me, crowding the front door with his lips on mine before I can utter a curse.

God, I've missed him. It's been months since he's touched me like this. Yeah, we hang out. But he hasn't been with me or Redix since our nights at the resort this past summer. And now I'm dropping my towel to the floor because it's not that cold outside and it gets even hotter when Silas cups my ass and pushes me against the foyer wall.

"Now, now." I hear Redix warn while Silas tongues my mouth, making me moan. "Rudolph, put that big, red nose away. We got plans tonight."

"What plans?" I huff into Silas's kiss.

Redix starts laughing while Silas gently bites my neck and I wrap my leg around his waist.

"You wanna get fucked right now or do you want answers?" Redix asks. "Because you can't have both."

"Who says?" I complain while Silas grinds his hard cock covered by leather into my naked pussy that's happy to get railed by the open front door.

"This horny Santa." Silas pulls away before pecking my lips. "Go look under your bed."

It's a big red box. Inside is a long, white faux fur coat. Under that is expensive crimson lingerie. I can tell by the embroidered tulle and gold hardware this is the finest lace and bondage detailing with straps from the bra that lead to a collar with a gold ring. The suspenders and thong that match are equally ornate.

"You know what shoes to wear." Redix leans in the

doorway while Silas sits on the bed, hoping to watch me change.

I already know where we're going. "Gimme fifteen minutes." I disappear into the bathroom because my pussy is already there.

The two hours it takes the chauffeur to drive us to Charleston goes by quickly. I know there'll be no fucking in the limo so I focus on the French pastry box Silas opens. It's full of savory treats we devour to satisfy our appetites until we arrive.

"Did you really meet with Daniel Pierce today?" I ask Redix while I swipe a croissant crumb off his pillow lips and devour it myself.

"Yep," he answers. "We just got a green light on a series together." He nips my ear. "But I'd never cancel your birthday plans for a meeting. I value my balls too much."

"Me too," Silas adds, saving the best for last, opening a small box with lemon lavender macarons inside. He holds one over my lips and teases, "Open up."

My mouth and thighs comply.

While Silas feeds me a yummy dessert, Redix glides his hand up my naked leg, his fingertips playing with the edges of my lace that's already soaked.

"Tell us what you want tonight," Redix insists. "It's your dirty thirty. Everything's on the table."

"It's your dirty thirty too but how are *you* gonna do this?" Silas and I fucking at the club is safe. But Redix is known to millions and that's a big risk. "You'll get spotted, even if it's a private club."

"Not tonight," Silas answers. "It's just us, some trusted friends, and guests hand-selected by Mistress Faye. Everyone's signing NDAs."

"Friends?"

"Stacey and her guests. Scarlett. Penny and her husband couldn't make it," Redix answers. "Penny was bummed but they have in-laws in town. But Stacey and Scarlett? You'd think it was their birthdays too. Who doesn't want one safe night at a sex club?"

Stacey and Scarlett? That doesn't freak me out. Hell, Stacey Evans is a young cougar unleashed. And Scarlett? I'd like to see her break loose. She's so sweet and gorgeous and deserves it.

"I even talked Luca into coming," Redix says. "He hasn't been with a woman since his wife died and that was almost four years ago."

"Four years? And you think a sex club is the best place for him to start?"

"Yeah," he and Silas answer in unison.

I can't be too worried about other people's sex lives. I'm too excited about my own.

"What about you?" I play with Silas's hair. "It's been over four months since you were with us. What have you been up to?"

It's not jealousy. I truly want him to be okay.

"I've been up to no one," he says. "Been taking some time to myself."

"Sure have been spending lots of time at my art gallery." Redix jumps in. "Wouldn't have anything to do with a gorgeous blonde artist in residence would it?"

Redix has several artists he's sponsoring. They moved to the island and give demonstrations in his shop where they feature their unique talents.

Come to think of it, Silas *does* spend a lot of time there.

"I might've invited a few artists to come tonight." Silas grins back. He doesn't know guilt.

"What?" Redix sits up. "Dude, they *work* for me. They

can't come to a sex club where I'll be fucking. I'm their boss."

"So?" Silas replies.

"So, that's inappropriate if not illegal." Redix yanks his hand through his strands. "This is a hashtag me too situation."

I sit back and love this—these two finally having a little fight.

"No, it's not," Silas replies. "*I* invited them. They're *my* guests and they don't *have* to come. And the whole world has seen you fuck. Several times."

"Help me out here." Redix looks at me. "Am I fucked?"

"You're gonna be." I tickle my fingertips down his bare chest. "By me and him. And y'all are so cute in this first fight." I look at Silas. "You must be into one of them to get him pissed off like this."

"Maybe." Silas won't stop smiling. "Or maybe I want everyone to see who I love, and how I love, and if they can accept me after that, then great."

"See." I look back at Redix. "He did it for you. For us. Now kiss and make up."

Silas leans across me, way too eager to comply. Redix leans in for his kiss and my view from the middle warms my heart and wets my sex.

"And by the way." Redix lifts my chin to his lips next as the limo parks outside of the nondescript brick building. "I hired a photographer." His lips dust over mine. "So I'll always be able to remember my very dirty thirty with my future wife."

I'm almost naked under this faux fur coat but I don't feel the mild winter air. I'm too hot for this as Silas pulls the door open for me and Redix holds my hand as we walk in.

The night is incredible. Our small group of friends and

a larger group of trusted club members are here and who gives a hell? Everyone wears states of dress in whatever rocks their socks and I'm standing with two stars of the show tonight.

Stacey and her three guys? Holy fuck, that's a story right there.

"How are you?" I kiss her cheek but still worry. We talk like we're at the coffee shop and not holding martinis at a sex club. "Your life's been turned upside down since Gentry's arrest."

"*Please*. The paperwork isn't even a pain in the ass," she replies. "As long as he's gone for good, all thanks to you, I do not dare complain."

"Yeah, I see who's been buttering your biscuit,"—I raise my glass to her—"all three of them. I wouldn't be complaining either."

"You're one to talk." She laughs. "Fucking those two men." She points to Silas and Redix talking with Luca but smiling our way. "That's gotta be hotter than three rabbits fucking in a wool sock on an August day."

I give her a hug, laughing and not giving a damn I'm in fuck-me lingerie and she's wearing a Lily Pulitzer dress with pearls like a proper tease. Because I know she's not wearing panties under that short hem.

"Besides." She squeezes me back. "It's your birthday and we're gonna watch you enjoy it."

"You're gonna watch?"

"No offense, but hell yes I'm watching Redix Dean fuck." She points to the stage at the top of the room. That's when I first notice the bed draped in black sheets in the middle of it. "And with Silas looking like his twin, girl, if you need help, I got your back. It's the least I can do."

"Thank you for the offer. But I'm happy to get used to this. I'm marrying one of them in May."

"And I'll be cheering that on too."

When she walks away, wishing me best, her group of men look eager for her arrival. They're sprawled over the purple sofa I recognize and how Stacey and those three men make sense to me; they just do.

"I can't believe I'm here." A voice sounds over my shoulder and I turn to give her a hug next. "But I'm glad Redix invited me. I need this."

I've never seen Scarlett look this hot. I mean, she's stunning even when she's not trying. But tonight her long, russet waves hang free while her hips are bound in a tight, black pencil skirt and her breasts look incredible in a matching bustier.

"It's not weird is it?" I sip my drink, searching her green eyes. "I mean, you worked for Redix and all. Feel free to bail if it is."

"Hell no." She almost punches my arm. "You can't shock me." She pauses and all she's seen of my life and Redix's almost death flashes across her eyes. "I'm happy for you both. You deserve some fun after what you've been through."

I adore her. I don't know all of Scarlett's story, but I know some of it's dark. The stunning sleeve of tattoos on her right arm hints at it. Crosses and flames and flowers and skulls.

She swirls her bourbon. The club made an exception tonight for this private event. Drinks are being poured in moderation and there's a big lemon birthday cake I see someone trying to hide on a table in the corner.

"And I wanna know who Redix's friend is." Scarlett

nods toward Luca. "He looks like a Greek God, but bigger and meaner with a dark tan."

I could tell her who he is. That he's Luca Mercier, a billionaire and one of the world's most eligible widowers and single dads. A man who's as hot and as powerful as the sun.

But that'd only warn Scarlett away. That's the opposite of what she'd go for.

"He's just a friend Redix plays golf with. He's super sweet and super European. Let me introduce you."

I don't give her a chance to change her mind. Grabbing her hand, I pull her toward the guys talking and I make the brief introductions.

Tonight, Scarlett isn't a former MMA fighter or a vigilant bodyguard.

Nope, she's my ravishing friend who needs to get laid. And she's got a big heart and somehow I know if Luca actually does this, Scarlett would never break his heart either.

They hit it off over sly smiles and curious eyes while I drag my men away.

It's time to start this show.

45

∞

DAMN, I'M NERVOUS.

Not because I'm on a stage and about to fuck Cade and Redix for a room full of people to watch. That turns me on. Or because there's a photographer about to take pictures and video too. That's hot as hell.

My hands sweat because I haven't been with either of them in months. I've missed them. And I know I'm about to feel again the power of them together and I have to be ready for it.

Yeah, I'll always be best friends with Redix.

I'll do any house project with him or just throw a football on the beach with him. No one's taking that from me.

Redix means too much. He makes me want to push myself, to be brave enough to love with everything I have, even if it wrecks me.

That's how he loves Cade so I've kept a distance from them.

They need each other. They need to be together. I think they finally get what I've seen all along.

When I see how Redix loves Cade, how she loves him back, it's like you can feel how love is worth it, what it's supposed to be like. Why people risk everything for it and swear it until their death.

That's the two of them together.

And they've inspired me to try to love like that too.

In our months apart, when all I did with Cade was hang out, go fishing, or sleep on a lounge chair beside her with books in hand while we dozed off under an umbrella together, I felt lucky.

How I finally got to love a woman like her and I don't think she'll ever know what that means to me.

For so long I had this hole in my heart that grew as I did around my love for Charlie Ravenel. But I could never have her. And I ached over Charlie for so long. Every day I felt like something was missing.

Then I met Cade.

And she's not Charlie and that's exactly how it was meant to be.

Cade's her own incredible woman. One I've never seen be so strong when she fights for someone she loves, or so lost in grief for losing the same.

Watching her and Redix at her mom's funeral and over the months that followed, I realized having them in my life is a gift I won't forsake.

Their love makes me know that's what I'm living for. To love someone like *that*.

So whoever's going to love me next needs to accept them.

I think that person's in the crowd tonight. I invited a group of people just so this one special person can see the real me.

Because I'll never hide who I am. Or who I love. No one's gonna define me, shame me or make me label it.

Fuck labels. They don't love. People do.

Amazing people like Cade and Redix and I'm excited about their wedding. It's like I can see their dream and I believe in it too.

The three of us stand together on the stage and Cade kisses me first because we've all missed this. In her long fur coat with that sinful body bound tight in red lingerie, I want to open every part of her again tonight... starting with her incredible lips. She tastes like a lemon drop martini and my tongue finds hers again and we moan at the reunion.

After a minute, Redix's lips join our kiss and it's a dance of parting lips and caressing tongues and breaths grabbed before we go back in for more, sharing much more than sex together.

They made my life whole again.

I have my family back. I have my mom laughing with me over brunch every Sunday. I have my dad taking my advice on how fast to tack when we sail. I have them asking when Cade and Redix will be joining me again.

My parents not only accept me. They love the love I have in my life.

And so do I.

I slide Cade's coat off her bare shoulders and I'm not

giving her up. Redix lays it down, fur side up on the bed and we'll always have this together.

I kneel first, dropping to where Cade's pussy hovers in front of my hungry mouth. I bury my nose in her sweet musk. It soaks her lace and I lick the delicate fabric, getting a small taste of her which only makes me crave more.

Redix watches while I pull her thong down to her thighs and leave it there. She loves this. Standing in front of the crowd, I gaze up at her looking down too. Her perfect nipples are exposed by the lace bra Redix has pulled down peak hard for all to see. For Redix to lick while my tongue takes its first grateful swipe through her lust.

Fuck, she tastes good. And damn, I've missed it when she moans like that. I tease her, parting her lips with my fingers but not letting her thighs open any wider than her thong will allow. This tease only wets her more.

"I've got a surprise for the birthday girl." I hear Redix's husky voice taunt while I take more licks of Cade and he reaches for something hidden under the covers.

I know what it is. I got so damn hard buying it and putting it there for tonight. I don't know if Cade will go for this, but if she does... *daaammmn*.

Redix kneels beside me. I make room for him while I know we look like XXX-rated stripper elves with our Santa hats and black leather pants on. And the shameless humor of it only makes me harder.

"Candy Cade,"—Redix looks up at her—"let's show them how sweet you are for us."

He pulls out his surprise—a jumbo candy cane stick.

Her smile answers before she does. "You can taste birthday boy, but not too much. I want my pussy burning for cocks, not peppermint."

Redix has such a kink for this. Months back at the hotel

suite, he showed me a whole new way to enjoy the cream from eclairs and I'll never look at them the same.

He licks the cane wet, the first few inches of it and I swear the devilish grin on his face is what makes box offices come hard for him every time he's on the screen.

"Taste her too," he tells me while he spreads her folds for his candy and my kiss.

I flick her clit while Redix teases her pussy with the candy and "Oh fuck" moans loud from Cade while someone in the crowd whistles. That only drives Redix on. He pulls the candy out, licking her arousal off, offering me a lick too and it tastes like her cum, his mouth, and mint, and damn, it's delicious.

Over and over we tease her with the candy and our tongues until her thighs shake. Until her moans won't stop and I worry she'll either fall over in an orgasm or burn from one.

Redix sees it too. He takes the candy out and tosses it aside. I pull her thong all the way off and sling her leg over my shoulder. She braces against me while I lick all the sticky mint off her sex. Redix kneels behind her and spreads her cheeks for more and she's going soon. With my tongue fucking her pussy and Redix teasing her ass she shakes over me so hard, throwing the hat off of my head before she grabs a fistful of my hair. "Oh God!" she screams so loud while someone in the crowd shouts, "Hell yes, girl," and Cade jolts. She comes so hard we have to hold her up.

Shaking over my face and soaking my chin, goddamn she's sweet and I don't know what's next. But Redix takes charge.

He lifts her up by the waist and tosses her on the bed and she smiles because she loves it.

"Spread your legs for my fuck, birthday girl," he tells

her and it's obviosly his birthday too. Unzipping his leather pants, he frees his cock, making my mouth water. "And open your dirty mouth for his thick cock," he taunts her and I'm here for that too.

I kneel by her lips and unzip my pants and Cade's tongue is waiting for me. She darts the tip of it out for my drops the second my hard cock hovers over her waiting mouth.

"Suck his cock, birthday girl," Redix keeps taunting her while he starts fucking her, holding her thighs open for his thrusts, and goddamn, they're hot like this. Cade groans with his fuck and my cock in her mouth. "Such a dirty birthday girl, aren't you?" He's gonna make her come so fast. I can tell by her breath gasping over my hard tip, her spit dripping from my shaft.

This is so fucking incredible, and then I see the photographer, some badass chick in leather taking these shots of us before I gaze into the crowd. Most are watching us. A few are fucking and the one I'm curious about has eyes locked on me.

That only makes me groan with Cade sucking my cock, pulling me closer to my edge. "Show them," I tell Cade. "Show everyone watching how we both fuck you and you love it. How you beg for our cocks to fuck every tight, wet hole you have."

That ends her. Cade's back bows while her throat moans with my cock filling it and damn I could blow right here at her coming so hard, but I growl it back.

"Come here." Redix is watching me. He knows when I'm close. "I want to suck your fucking cock too."

I stand up on the bed beside him. He cranes his neck to start sucking my cock with Cade's red lipstick and spit still on it and shit, I've gotta control it. Because I want this to last. I want to keep looking down and watching his cock disappear into her gorgeous, full pussy with his ruthless thrusts while he wraps his lips around my cock like it's his last meal.

Cade starts moaning at the sight of Redix sucking me off and Redix joins her. I slide his hat off so I can grab a fistful of his hair and that rolls his eyes back. His soft gags and expert mouth know just how to milk me. And he's gonna come too, I can tell by his tensing pecs, by his thrusts seeking something deep inside Cade.

She's rubbing her clit and is right there with us. "Yes," she says to me. "Come down his throat." Redix moans, agreeing, his vibrations thrilling my cock. "You look so beautiful with his big cock in your mouth." She's not teasing Redix, it's true. And I glance up into the crowd and find the one pair of eyes that need to see this.

That I love this man. And I love this woman. And I can love them too.

"You wanna drink my cum?" My thighs shake. I know he won't answer. I know he does. I know this will take him too. "I'm gonna come so damn hard for you, Redix."

And he goes first. His gorgeous body seizes with his deep groan, filling Cade with half his cock pulsing inside her. I can see it and that pulls me too. "Fuck!" I shout while I fill his mouth. "Fuck," I say it for all to hear while my body heaves again, another spurt filling his mouth, my cum dripping from his chin. That's all Cade needs. She's writhing again with her own orgasm and the night isn't over.

We lie on the bed cuddling together while we recover and get ready for another round. Redix drinks a seltzer while Cade eats lemon cake and I sip a Blantons. When she props up on her elbows, she gazes out at the crowd.

"I would've thought Stacey and her men would be going at it."

I glance over at the group on the sofa. "By the looks of that crew"—I'm impressed—"she's pacing herself."

"She deserves it. She's been so lonely for so long." Cade grins before she whispers, "But look." I follow her stare and Redix does too. "Scarlett and Luca are going at it."

"Good for him," Redix says and I agree.

Because Scarlett is hot as hell. I've noticed her but keep a respectful distance because she intimidates me, I'm man enough to admit it.

But right now, she doesn't look like she'll rip your balls off and fry 'em up in a pan.

No, she's riding Luca with her skirt to her waist and he's got a fistful of her dark red hair that's a lure for anyone's hard grasp. They're fucking on that chair like they're animals that need to mate to save the world.

"Four years, he's waited," Redix mutters.

"I can't imagine," I answer before wetting my whistle with whiskey.

"I can." Redix huffs. "All the years I waited for Cade. To get my shit together."

She leans toward him for a kiss. "And it was worth it."

"*You* were worth everything," he answers before pulling her into a deep one.

"There y'all go again." I interrupt them. "Looking so damn in love that I love it too."

Cade turns to me. "You gonna fess up and tell us who this person is because I saw you clocking someone while you were getting your cock well sucked by us."

"Nope." I won't look into the crowd because that'll give it away. "If they have a problem with this, then they're not the one."

"Hey." Redix reaches over her and tucks a strand of my hair back. I love it when he does that. "Don't lose a love over us. We don't have to fuck to be together. I just want you in our life always."

I wink. "You just want my handyman skills."

"I *do* like your hands." He grins. "And you look damn hot sweating while you swing that big hammer."

"Speaking of a big hammer." Cade lingers her touch down my abs. When it reaches my cock, it twitches back to life. "It's your turn."

And I don't need an engraved invitation.

"On your knees, birthday girl," I demand because this is my favorite way with her. Like the first time I fucked her and felt the power of her sex, of our sex.

Cade's amazing. It's like Redix shows me how to love and she shows me how to live. Both do it with no fear.

She's quick to obey and my cock is quick to ready at her beauty. Rolling on a condom, I watch Redix choose his place in front of her mouth.

Why she trusts us. Why she lets go and lets us take her, it's like she said. I cool her fire, and that fire is Redix. She needs us both. And we need her.

I kneel behind her and pull her back to my chest. Redix stands before us while I slowly seat deep in Cade's pussy and damn, the return of her heat makes me bite her shoulder. She feels so good I almost forgot how much.

Our bodies know this performance. People gather for it and it's a stunning sight, I know. I've watched it in a mirror. My hand finds where my cock is sliding in and out of her welcome pussy and I gently scissor her clit. My other hand toys with her nipple while she groans with Redix's cock in her mouth.

"That's it." He guides her head to where she's softly

gagging on him. "All this cock is for you." He pulls her off and lifts her chin so she's gazing up at him. I am too. He's like a statue built by the gods for sex, and that I look so much like him puffs my ego, I gotta confess.

"You're gonna suck my cock deep and fuck Silas's cock hard until we make that sweet pussy come, aren't you?" Once she nods, he guides her mouth back to sucking him and she goes to town. I can feel her clit stiffen between my fingers, her sex swelling for my cock and she's loving this.

"That's my dirty birthday girl." His taunts return. "Show them how you love getting railed by two hard cocks all night."

He has her shaking. I'm tempted too. I lean forward and Cade shares his cock with me. "Fuck yes, you two." Redix gazes down at us like he's obsessed with this, but this next one's for Cade and I know what to do for her.

I grab her throat, strumming her clit with my other hand while I don't whisper in her ear. I want everyone to hear. "You're gonna let this pussy come with my cock fucking it and his cock in your mouth, aren't you?" I take her harder, hands and cock while I growl, "Come on, Cade, you're so fucking dirty, aren't you? You're my cute little cock slut."

She bucks. She convulses in my grasp and I let go of her throat while she gasps for air. I have to grab her hips because she's coming so hard she's pushing me out but I fight to stay in her. "Yes!" she shouts once Redix leaves her mouth. We leave her gasping, "Oh my, God." I feel her arousal drip to my balls while she's still shaking. I've never felt her so wet while she says, "Redix, I know you want him too."

That's their love again. They share everything, including my love and I want it this way.

Her body still quivers but she maneuvers us around.

We have more condoms and lube for this and I ready myself. Kneeling between Redix's spread thighs once he lies on his back, Cade kisses him while I slowly take my time penetrating him. Because this is us. We have this trust. We have this connection.

Cade strokes him while she sucks his hard length too and he groans for more. "Fuck me, Silas." His husky voice drives me insane. "Cade, don't stop," he insists and that drives me deeper. "Yes." His trust, his vulnerability, it looks so beautiful across his massive strong body. The lust in his eyes possesses me. "Fuck my ass," he demands and I'd do anything for him, for both of them.

It's not my birthday but this is my gift too. I watch this stunning sight before I turn to look at the crowd.

There are those eyes again, hiding in the corner and watching me fuck Redix while he's in Cade's mouth and yes, I can't be without them.

They'll get married. They'll live their lives and have a slew of kids and I'll be there for it. Happy for them, I know it. The question is... will it just be me?

"Cade." Redix always says her name like he's drowning and she's his rescue. "Cade." Because she is. He calls her again and she knows his mind, his soul, and his heart.

She straddles him and I make room for their love because I cherish it. Leaning back and moving his thighs so she can fuck him too, God this is my heaven. It feels like it too.

I press my lips to her back. I feel his hands reach for mine and I hold onto him. "I love you." I don't know who says it. Maybe all of us... because we feel it.

We're not afraid of it. This power pulls us together. This connection saved us all. This pleasure rewards us and we won't apologize for it after the hell we've survived.

I don't know why fate brought them to me and I don't need to.

Because with her.

With him.

It's love.

EPILOGUE

Infinity by Jaymes Young

∞

Over a year later

"She's gonna eat it," I warn Redix. "Watch. She's just like her Daddy."

"No, she won't." He bounces Glory on his knee. "She's just gonna—"

And there she goes. She grabs a fistful of the homemade playdough I made and it's in her mouth.

"See," I laugh. "She can't resist. Just like you."

Redix laughs too while he gently scoops it out of her

mouth. "Baby girl, why you gotta keep proving your Mama right all the time?"

But she's too cute to ever get upset with.

Glory Bryant Dean is six months old and the perfect mix of us. She's got wisps of my dark hair and his full lips and bright eyes.

And she's got her Daddy wrapped around her little finger.

I'm a big softie for her too.

Being pregnant with her at our wedding only made it more special. Like we were finally blessed. Like our prayers were being answered so we named her after her grandma who's watching over us.

"Be careful," I warn him again. "If you get red play-dough on those pants it's gonna look real interesting in the wedding photos."

"Shit," Redix huffs before he gobbles Glory's cheeks, making her laugh. "My playdough pants are gonna be the last thing people focus on at Silas Van de May's wedding of the century."

"Ummm"—I whirl the lint roller over my lavender dress—"you forget who *you* are."

"Cade Bryant's husband?"

"You're cute." I wedge my foot into my heel, then the next one. "And you're Redix Dean who's about to star in another big series with Daniel Pierce, so I hate to tell ya, but they'll be watching you today too. So please don't fuck up your seersucker pants."

"He's the only man I'll wear these for."

"You look great." Redix could make a lawn bag look like high fashion. "But what about me in this tight dress? I got all these post-pregnancy curves and I love 'em but for a wedding? I don't know. Is it too much?"

"Hell no." He pushes away the playdough and feeds Glory a piece of banana. "You're rocking those tits and ass."

Yes, I'm loving my new curves but this is a big day for me too. "I'm nervous about meeting Charlie Ravenel today. She'll be at the wedding and I know she wants an answer."

"She's recruiting you hard, but it's your call. I support you working here for the Sheriff's office, or for her, or I can just keep you knocked up all the time."

"That won't stop me."

I smooth my dress down. Half not listening because I don't know what I want. I love my job. But I could do some good work with Charlie's security company. And the flexibility would be nice because I *do* want to be knocked up. At least twice more if we can.

"Hey." Redix's husky voice could lift me from anywhere.

I flick my eyes up and he looks so handsome. The sun shines behind him through the window. He's sitting at our kitchen table with our baby daughter in his arms and I swear he glows in a white linen shirt with his hair down.

"You look beautiful, Candy Cade." He gets up, holding Glory like she's attached to him. Might as well be and I love it. "We're all lucky to have you."

He pulls my hand, leading me out of the kitchen. "Come here. I got you a little something for today."

"I'm not the one getting married. Silas gets all the gifts."

Why is he guiding us to our bedroom? It's not like we can fuck with Glory awake. Babies are precious sex-life stealers.

"Oh, we gave Silas a gift, alright." Redix talks over his shoulder. "His bachelor party was epic."

"Any party at that sex club is epic."

My stomach suddenly flitters with butterflies remembering it. Damn, Silas needs to get married again or something because we all enjoyed that night... and then some.

And who Silas is marrying? I never would've guessed it but when I see them together, they're perfect. The love in his eyes, I think it equally surprises him and that's what's going to make today so special.

I better pack some tissues in my clutch.

"Well this"—Redix opens the top drawer of his dresser—"is just between us."

He hands me a box wrapped in white paper with a purple ribbon. And I know this is gonna mess up my makeup because *his* gifts are epic. And they always melt my heart.

"What did you get? I'm running out of fingers for tattoos and rings."

We tattooed matching infinity symbols on our wedding fingers. I thought it was beautiful and sacred, but then Redix gave me a rare violet diamond wedding ring and that can't be topped.

"Please just sit on the bed and open it, Detective." He and Glory sit beside me. "Not every conversation has to be an interrogation."

"That's *not* who you married."

I almost laugh because this tiger has changed her stripes enough. Me not asking questions though? That's not happening.

But when I pull the purple ribbon off and rip the paper to open the box, it silences me. There are no questions, only sweet tears. For a moment, I can't believe my eyes, my breath stolen by the shock of it too.

"Where did you find this?"

Redix kisses my cheek, strands of his long hair tickling it

too. "When we were cleaning out of some of Mama G's stuff. I had it stitched back up."

It's my red Hello Kitty purse. The one I wore the day I met Redix. The one that hid my stash of candy that I shared with him.

Along with my heart.

His lips return to my cheek. The one with tears spilling down it. "Maybe Glory can use it one day," he says and I love that idea. My Mama gave me this purse. "Look inside."

My hands are shaking. Why this is hitting me so hard, in the sweetest way, I don't know.

Maybe it's because Redix never stops loving me. He always wants to make me smile. Maybe it's because I cherish the day we met, and every one since, even the darkest ones because now we appreciate the light we share even more.

Or maybe it's because my mama gave me this purse and though she'd go on about me brushing my teeth and not getting cavities, my dad would sneak me candy to hide in it. Yep. Rule maker and rule breaker; they were the perfect pair.

"Maybe Glory will wear this purse and meet her best friend too," I say, turning to Redix because it's impossible for me to love him more, but I know ten years down the road, I will. And forty years from now? Well, I know how big my heart can grow.

It already loves him, our daughter, our families, and our friends. And one incredible man who's about to marry an incredible person.

Love is beautiful that way.

If you let it, it won't stop growing.

I see the gift box inside the purse. It's a necklace box

and I worry, whatever this is, I never take off the infinity necklace he gave me a couple of years ago.

When I open it, all my worry vanishes. "Oh my God." Only awe and love and tears flow. "How did you get this back?"

It's the original infinity necklace he gave me when we were eighteen. When he first proposed to me on the beach.

It got taken the night our nightmare began.

"I asked Penny to get it out of evidence for me. I knew Derek had it. And like hell if I wasn't gonna get it back one day." He lifts my chin and I search his eyes. There's so much love in them while Glory wriggles in his lap.

Redix Dean can give me all the gifts he wants and I'll cherish them all. But his love, the one that gave us our daughter and our dream, it's my new deal with God.

This is what I fight for now.

"I got you back too," he whispers against my lips, "and I'm never letting you go again."

And I kiss him. And I never thought I'd see this necklace again. For so many years, I feared they'd stolen it along with our lives and our dreams too.

But they could never take our love.

And now...

We have it all back.

THANK YOU

Thank you for reading *With Him*.
I hope you loved Cade, Silas, and Redix as much as I do.
Parts of this story are very personal to me so I'm honored to
share this book with you.

If you please, your reviews, posts, and shares are such gifts.
My readers mean the world to me,
so stay tuned for what's next.

Who is our hot, beloved Silas marrying?
His steamy standalone story is next.
ALL FOR HIM

Want more about Stacey and the men who love her?
Take out your fan for this one. Coming soon.
A SENATOR'S WIFE

What happens after Luca and Scarlet's wild one night?
Everything that's not supposed to. On your TBR soon.
CAN'T LOVE HIM

When Redix Dean and Daniel Pierce unite?
Bombs drop for Charlie and Cade.
This one will destroy.
HER RULES

Ready for more steam and suspense now?
Meet Charlie Ravenel & Daniel Pierce.
Their inferno love and story will take you to the very edge.
She's the most badass heroine
and he's the alpha who takes her, body and soul.

Get the COME FOR ME series free with your Kindle
Unlimited subscription.

The Come for Me series by
KELLY FINLEY
KELLY FINLEY
HUNT HER
Come for Me
Book Two
KELLY FINLEY
PIERCE HER
Come for Me
Book One
KELLY FINLEY
CHASE HER
Come for Me
Book Three

ACKNOWLEDGMENTS

My husband and best friend: You're my biggest fan and my greatest love. Please keep cooking for me while I write. I promise I'll always thank you.

My family: Thank you for understanding all the times I close my office door. And thanks for not reading the steamy pages. I love you all.

My friends: I can't do this without your laughter. Writing is a happy but lonely world, so when I emerge, your smiles renew me.

The KLS Team: Thank you Kat at Kat's Literary Services for your support and edits. I can't do it without ya. Deborah, your corrections and messages mean the world to me. I'm so thankful for this team.

My Cover Crew: Caroline Johnson, your covers always make us swoon. David Bodas, you're more than my favorite cover model. You're a dear friend who believed in my dream. I'll always support yours too. Big thanks to Rafa G for his gorgeous photos of David. It's beautiful work.

My Beta Team: Deborah, Jennifer, and Marsha. Y'all keep crushing it. Your comments make me giggle, edit and work harder. I love them and you. And get ready for more.

My Review & Street Team: You always have my back (more like my covers) and I'm so damn thankful. I cherish your posts, reviews, and support. Big shout out to the

Banana Book Club. Our IG chats light up my day. I truly can't do it without you all.

#Bookstagram & #BookTok Followers: It's true. There is a community and a world of friends online. I'm overwhelmed by the amazing people I've met and now adore. Every day, you make me smile. Thanks for your comments and support. And keep 'em coming.

Author Friends & Mentors: You inspire me. You school me. You help me and keep me going when it ain't easy. Thanks for the Zooms, emails, and coffee chats. You keep me strong.

Best for last - READERS: Thank you for taking a chance on my story, for giving your time to share this with me. You take my story into your heart for a short time and I'm humbled. When I get your messages, posts, and emails, they are the greatest gifts. And I promise to keep giving you more. Huge hugs.

FinleyFans - For advance and exclusive reads and more: Join me on PATREON - where I share all my reads in advance, and even more filthy fiction with fierce heroines and laughs too.

https://www.patreon.com/kellyfinleyauthor

ABOUT THE AUTHOR

Kelly Finley hates writing bios but appreciates that you made it this far. So here you go…

She lives in the Carolinas with her sexy husband and cherished family. A rebel with many causes, she fancies black leather, dirty jokes, big hearts, and smart mouths.

Thrilled by a flipped gender script and ticked off by women portrayed as weak, she noticed how many steamy, sexy heroines were missing, particularly from romance pages.

Her friends shared the same frustration and told her to practice what she has taught for over twenty years—women who kick ass.

Dedicated to writing books featuring characters we champion and love—ones with shameless heat, brave hearts, and whip-smart minds—she's most likely at her keyboard putting the next story on the page for you right now.